PRINCE OF THE
CORAL THRONE

Also by JM Lee

The Londinium Saga

Curse of the Blood Queen
Prince of the Coral Throne
Coven of the Hunted

Books 3-5 coming soon

Short Stories

Countdown
Featured in "Dark & Stormy: Sixteen Tempest-Tossed Tales"

Rite of Passage
Featured in "Shadows & Mist: Twelve Terrifying Tales"

Mabel
Featured in "Steam & Steel: Thirteen Riveting Tales"

Discontinued:
The Novus Proprius Chronicles

When October Ends
Chasing
Novus Orsa
The Complete Trilogy

www.jmlee.info

BOOK 2
of The LONDINIUM SAGA

PRINCE OF THE CORAL THRONE

JM LEE

Cover design by GetCovers

Paperback ISBN: 979-8-9917822-2-7

For more information about JM Lee, visit: www.jmlee.info

Content Warning

——•(((● ● ●)) •——

A note from the author,

While I understand not all readers enjoy content warning pages, I felt it necessary to offer a few words of caution. This book is suitable for anyone 18+. If you are a sensitive reader, please be aware that this book contains:

- Mature language
- Blood, gore, and violence
- Near drownings
- An injured animal (but I promise, Cricket is still fine!)
- Implied sexual content
- Death of a child
- Themes of manipulation, gaslighting, and domestic abuse

If you are particularly sensitive to the last point, please consider skipping the prologue.

Please read responsibly! Your mental health matters!

For more information, visit my website:

www.jmlee.info

DEDICATION

·······)ᐞᐞᐞ●ᑕᑕ(·······

to anyone whose downward spirals
are paved with good intentions.

and to those who wish
they could go to a ball with a dagger
strapped to their thigh.

Prologue

KANE
FOX MANOR - 1869

Groggy eyes peered through the windows of Fox Manor's sunroom, Kane's hazels admiring the glittering stars hanging high just across the lake. A rich, full moon lay nestled between the constellations, the perfect crisp evening to follow a peppery summer day. Running his fingers through long dark waves, a few stray strands clung to the back of his neck as a gentle breeze blew through the open door.

Across from him, Wesley sat with gangly limbs and messy hair. Soft stubble lined his chin while mossy eyes raked over a chess board. As per their usual games, the siren had made move after move that left the young teen backed into a corner and unable to win. Nonetheless, he seemed to have an affinity for failure, begging for round after round.

"One of these days, I'm going to beat you," Wesley grumbled, realizing the game was once again lost.

"I think I'm ready to call it a night, Wes. I'm exhausted from training today." Kane yawned, arms outstretched behind him.

"Oh come on! One more? I'm sure I can win this time!" The boy's words matched his eyes, pleading as they always did.

"No," he chuckled. "You have your whole life to try and beat me. I'm done for the night!"

Wesley groaned, slouching back in his chair. "Fine. You can admit that you just don't want me to win." He hid a coy smile, trying to tempt the siren.

Just as Kane opened his mouth in response, the familiar *'whoosh'* of the Fox family's portal caught their attention. At the back of the manor, they'd almost missed the noise entirely.

"Didn't Winnie say she was going out tonight?"

Her brother offered a quiet nod, his brows scrunched in concern and scooching to the edge of his seat. "She was planning on meeting up with Samuel. From our very brief talks, she said she was ending their courtship. She doesn't tell me much, but it didn't seem to be working out. Guess he's not such an honorable gentleman after all…"

Worry simmered in Kane's chest, though he tried not to let the boy notice. "She hasn't mentioned anything to me. I wish she'd talk to me, but she's been so distant. We should probably check on her. She's getting back awfully late, especially unchaperoned."

"I'm sure she kicked his ass, and is ready to tell us her victory tale," Wesley joked, offering a quick shrug before sneaking toward the front door.

As always, he feels the need to try and scare his sister, Kane thought, watching the boy hiding behind a panel and ready to jump out. They listened for Winnie's careful steps. Quiet hands opened and closed the door to avoid detection before attempting to tiptoe up the stairs.

Her little brother jumped out at once, standing between Winnie and the front door. Almost falling back, she clutched her chest in surprise and attempted to muffle a scream.

"You'll wake the whole house, you idiot!" Swatting at him, she turned her back to them.

"Mum and Dad are at the bar in town. Don't worry," Wesley teased.

Kane tried to examine her, though shadows lay across her face. All he could see were the puffiness of crying eyes, red from sorrow he wasn't aware of yet. Her shoulders slouched forward as if trying to hide, actively working to avoid his prying gaze.

"Are you okay?" he asked gently, stepping to her side and grabbing ahold of her arm with care. *If only I could get a better view...*

"I'm fine, I just want to go to bed," Winnie insisted, pushing past him and toward the stairs.

"Not so fast, Win. Tell us what happened," Wesley protested, grabbing ahold of her wrist.

Ripping her arms from their grasps, she once again tried to barrel her way up the stairs. It was then that he felt it. A strange tingle in his bones. A sort of knowing that something was off, and every second she refused to look at him, his heart broke a little more.

"I said I'm fine! Let me get some sleep, please."

Gently, Kane grasped both shoulders and turned her toward the light. As he did, his heart nearly sank to his stomach. Along her angled cheekbone, a fresh purpling bruise was welted and angry, his mind falling into a tailspin as anger crept up his spine.

"What the hell happened?" Gingerly, his fingers brushed her cheek. Every wince ensured that his sorrow and heartache were replaced by simmering anger.

"Nothing. Stay out of it!" Attempting to push past him again, Winnie sniffled. Her eyes glistened, lips quivering and her body looking as though it could cave in on itself.

"Sunroom. Now! Or I'll go to London to get Mum and Dad myself!" Wesley's insistence seemed to talk some sense into her before she groaned and obliged.

"Since when do you boss me around?" she hissed, heavy steps trodding toward the sunroom.

Once seated, a steaming pot of chamomile and lemon tea appeared on the table. Quietly, she poured herself a cup before offering some to the others. Every time Kane tried to connect with her gaze, it would dart away like a rabbit on the run from a hunter.

"Did you run into thugs on the street or something?" Kane asked, hoping that it hadn't been something or someone worse.

"Wes, why did you have the house add lemon? You know I prefer honey," she stalled, moving her spoon around in the cup.

"Winnie, stop avoiding the question! Tell us what happened!" Kane grabbed her teacup, placing it on the table in front of her.

Startled, she examined him carefully, yet still refused to answer.

"Was it that boy? Samuel?" He continued to press, deep down wondering if the question was already answered by the bruises lining her angelic skin.

"No," she muttered, though a shudder overtook her, looking away again.

"Just tell us what happened, Win. Maybe we can help," Wesley pleaded, offering her hand a gentle squeeze of reassurance.

"There's nothing either of you can do to fix it. No use dwelling on something that doesn't matter now." She stood, ready to go back to her room again.

Kane snagged her wrist once more before guiding her gently to have a seat. "You're not leaving here until you tell us what happened. Let us make this right." Deep down, his temper only seethed. *I know it was him. I knew there was a reason I didn't like him when we first met. I don't trust that slimy little bastard as far as I can throw him,* he thought.

"There's nothing for you to make right. Besides, you two don't have to know everything that's going on in my life! Stay out of it!"

With a heavy sigh, Wesley pulled Kane aside. Just out of her earshot, the two whispered.

"I don't think she's going to open up. Maybe it's too soon?" the siren asked, examining his friend whose anxious fingers twirled a few long strands of dark curls around and around.

"We could always... try other ways to find out the truth," her brother suggested, his face turning to a tight frown.

"You don't think that's a bit of an invasion?"

Wesley shook his head. "I have a bad feeling about this. I think something really awful happened. I can always make her...forget."

"Winnie will never forgive us for invading her privacy like that," he reminded.

"Would you rather let her go through this alone?"

Kane's head dropped heavy, sudden guilt weighing him down before they'd even used their various skills to extract the truth from her. At last, he took a seat across from Winnie. Grasping her hands firmly, he held them before her as though the two would sit down to pray.

"You know I care about you, right?"

She nodded, still sitting in silence.

"I'm sorry to do this, but it's the only way. Just trust me, okay?"

Her face turned to a scowl, at once realizing what he was about to do. Attempting to pull away from Kane's grasp, she was suddenly overcome by his siren song. The melodies encompassed her in an instant, soft and mesmerizing as he pushed through the barriers of her mind and into her subconscious. Their eyes glazed over as he searched for answers.

Though Winnie's mind was a heavily guarded fortress, Kane trudged through them regardless. *One day, I'll have to train her how to withstand a siren song,* he thought, watching hazy images appear around him. Bits and pieces of their friendship appeared first, though he ignored them in search of information on Samuel.

He waded past moments from her childhood, then through memories leading up to their most recent swim in the lake. At last, Kane found the object of his search. He paused, waiting to see if that memory was the one he was after.

An image cleared, Winnie and Samuel just before him. Sharing a few passionate kisses, both of their hands explored the other. A soft whimper escaped her lips, triggering pangs of surprise disgust deep in Kane's chest. *I can't watch this,* he seethed, ready to turn away and find a new memory. But then, her lover grabbed hold of her wrists with bruising force. Her attention sharpened and fear washed over her body as she tried to back away.

Foul words slithered from his mouth as she tried to create space between them. *"What we're doing is wrong. We shouldn't behave in such an ungodly manner. You should be ashamed of yourself!"*

The sentiment alone was enough reason for Kane to continue his festering hatred. Regardless, he waded through more memories of their time together. Countless dates and afternoons spent strolling along the Thames River popped up, though he wasn't concerned with those. A nagging snapshot of Samuel dressed as a proper gentleman carrying flowers and a box of jewelry caught his attention next. He entered with caution, wondering: *Will she ever forgive me for this invasion of privacy?*

The young man handed over the gifts before offering her a small head bow. *"I'm sorry for the way I acted the other day. You'll forgive me, won't you?"* Disingenuous eyes raked over her like she was a prize to be won.

She stalled, unsure what to say. But at last, a shy smiling nod accepted the half-hearted apology and they moved on.

After some more searching, Kane came across that evening's events. Recognizing the lilac dress and pinned up hair, he noted the surrounding areas. Not far from the family's portal to London, just a block away from the Library and pub he and his brother often visited with the Fox siblings.

Samuel stood in front of Winnie. With her shields up, it was almost as though she were blocking out the memories herself. Unwilling to relive them, much less share them with her best friend. But he pushed harder, trying to see what happened. His siren song only intensified, focus lasered in on that one moment.

"I don't think I can do this anymore, Sam. You and I both know we're not happy," she explained, holding out a hand toward

him in comfort.

But it didn't take long for the young man's eyes to darken with rage, dusty brown hair falling into his face. A vision she didn't recognize as he prowled toward her.

"I've spent the last year courting you! And now you tell me that was all a waste of time? I should've known you were a whore!" Samuel spewed.

Winnie took a step back. Kane felt the betrayal stir in her chest like a storm, her hand pressed to her mouth in shock. *"A whore? You're the one who..."*

"Who what? You threw yourself at me like some fucking harlot! The second you allowed me to put my hands on you, I should've known you weren't worth more than a one-time shag."

Kane could feel the knot in her throat as tears pricked the backs of her eyes.

"Please, Samuel! You have to understand! I just want what's best for both of us."

Once again, she attempted to step toward him. Tried placing her hands along his forearm to soothe the burn of rejection. But before her fingers could ever make contact, he jerked his hand. As if by accident, it landed across her face. Stinging hornets sat beneath her skin. As the siren's connection to her continued, he could feel it on his own cheek in solidarity.

"You...hit me," she'd whispered in utter shock and disbelief, stepping away.

Why didn't she kick his sorry ass? Kane wondered, his own simmering rage building the more he watched.

"How dare you lay a hand on me!" she cried, taking another step back before turning toward the portal.

"Where do you think you're going, bitch? Get back here!" The words gushed from his mouth as though he had no control of his temper, abrasive arms wrapping around Winnie's shoulders.

Then the memory went blank.

Kane pushed a little harder, knowing any further and he'd begin diving into darker territory. But alas, the memories were unavailable. Even Winnie's own mind seemed to block them out, unwilling to relive that moment. Unable to accept what happened. Unless she was willing to access them, even Kane would never truly find out what happened. But his mind could only imagine, knowing very well how cruel men could be.

Retreating from her mind, Kane stopped his siren song. A gentle hand caressed her other cheek, careful to avoid the purple bruises that lined her delicate skin. "I'm sorry you had to go through that. I pray you'll forgive me," he whispered, hoping Wesley couldn't hear him.

"And? What happened?"

"Don't worry about it, Wes. Make sure she doesn't remember this night. I have some business to take care of." At once, his wings expanded behind his back, amber eyes glowing in rage as he headed toward the portal.

"The whole night? Or just now?" Wesley called out, though he was already out of the door. Too angry to answer or think straight, he continued his crusade toward London.

"Brother?" The slurred word echoed behind him, Thoren on the roof for reasons only the Gods would know.

Kane ignored him.

"Where are you going?"

He thought about explaining everything. *Thoren might still be mad at her because she chose Samuel in the first place, but he'd want to help.* He stopped walking and took a moment to contemplate. *No...This is my fight,* Kane decided as the anger in the pit of his stomach fueled him forward. A small gasp escaped his little brother, the light of a glowing fire suddenly appearing on the roof of Fox Manor. Yet still, he continued to trek forward.

Just before him, the familiar tree branch portal glowed in welcome. Stepping through, his feet landed on the other side and met the cobblestone of London's streets. This late at night, there thankfully weren't too many patrons wandering about to witness Kane in his angelic form.

Glancing around, he spotted the pub they typically visited. *What are the chances she took him there on one of their dates?* The words swirled through his mind as he peered through the window. The brute sat amongst other young lads, sharing a few pints. They cackled and hissed their tales as though Samuel hadn't just broken the first rules of chivalry.

Kane knocked on the window, the group of young men turning to inspect the source of the noise. The darkness masked Kane's true form, only his amber eyes glittering in the night. Only a moment passed before they dismissed the sound, turning back to their conversation.

Unwilling to leave without a private audience, the siren marched toward the door. An icy rage swirled like storm clouds inside, growing more intense with every laugh and joke the boys told.

The door swung open in a fury, Kane's voice bellowing through the establishment. "Samuel! Get your ass out here. Now!"

The entire pub silenced themselves, adults and bar owners turning toward the booming voice that interrupted their chatter. Samuel's friends looked at him in worry, though he dismissed them with a cocky smirk. The act alone only added to Kane's tempest rage.

"It's alright, boys. I'll be back in a few. Get me another pint, will ya?" Carefree, he sauntered toward the exit. "Can I help you?"

Kane snagged his shirt and cravat, pulling him into the streets. "You're coming with me," he hissed, carrying them both into the sky.

A boyish scream escaped Samuel, a scared gaze fixed to the ground below. "What the fuck? Put me down!"

"You're going to pay for what you did to Winnie, you bloody

bastard. And trust me when I say, you're going to wish you were dead when I'm done with you."

1

WINIFRED
BETHNAL GREEN - 1871

Walking through the streets of Bethnal Green, the coldest of late Novembers winds nipped at Winnie's face. Pulling a winter coat tightly around her, the hem of a casual black gown brushed along the cobblestone, the heels of her laced up booties clacking.

On her arm, Kane walked with an equally thick winter coat, a gleaming smile on his face as he guided her toward Butch's old familiar pub she'd missed since Wesley's funeral. Shuffling sounds and childlike giggles escaped her two friends as they followed close behind.

"I don't see why they need to join us. It's not like we haven't been unchaperoned before," she mumbled, leaning in toward the warmth of Kane's body.

"Thoren and Ez wanted to get out of the house. Plus, we said we would do this the right way. And that means I promised your father I'd be an absolute gentleman, following all of the customary rules of courting a proper lady such as yourself." The siren's eyes darted toward her lips as they often did before returning to the short evening gander ahead.

"Is it customary to take a *proper lady* to the slums for a date?" she sneered as he opened the door for her.

His lips pursed, cheeks reddening as he waited for his brother and Ezra to file in behind them. Across the pub, Butch's eyes lit up in excitement at the sight of the young medium.

"Miss Winifred! I was beginnin' to wonder if you'd joined the spirits! How are ya?" The elderly man rushed to clear a nearby table for his four new guests, wiping down a small spill and adjusting the candle that sat along the mahogany.

The bar looked the same as it always had, yet somehow Winnie couldn't help but feel the difference in the atmosphere. Fewer and fewer patrons were sitting about. Those that did, admired the wreaths of evergreen and pine cones that lined the walls, a few cozied up in front of the fire. Next to the bar, Winnie noticed Butch's deceased wife as always, hovering and forever lurking.

"I've missed seeing your lovely mug," Ezra chimed in, attempting to take a seat with Kane and Winnie.

To his right, Thoren snagged his arm, dragging him to have a seat at the bar. "We're chaperones, not guests on their date. Let them be!"

Butch examined the situation in amused curiosity. "Chaperones, eh?" His eyebrows raised playfully, inspecting her date with the same tenacity that she'd expect from her own father.

"This is Mr. Kane Falke, an old childhood friend," Winnie introduced.

The two shook hands before Butch offered to bring over the evening's special: roast chicken with vegetables. "Or I can bring over the usual soup, if you'd like."

Before Winnie could answer, Kane added, "We'll take two of the evening's special. Thank you, Sir."

The gentleman nodded, stepping away to prepare their meal.

"This place used to be packed with folks. It takes a lot to shut down a pub like this, yet somehow Boudicca managed to make everyone afraid," Winnie muttered, eyes rested on the candle before her.

Kane placed his hand on hers, stroking gently to draw her attention to him. "It'll take some time. It's only been a month since the attacks stopped. Eventually this place will be back to normal."

"Here ya go," Butch muttered, groaning as he clutched an aching back. "When do I get to talk to my wife again? I swear the damn banshee's been throwin' plates lately."

Winnie glanced back to where the woman's essence floated, a wicked grin across her ghostly face. "I'll try to stop by soon so we can get to the bottom of this. But I suspect you're right. She's laughing maniacally at you right now."

"Even in death, she's determined to drive me crazy," the bartender grumbled before tending to his other patrons.

"You and Ez must have visited here often. Before…" Kane's words came to an abrupt halt, as if his own mind snagged on the constant reminder of the nightmare that had been their lives since September.

Winnie could only nod. "Butch was the first person to show me any kindness here in Bethnal Green. Aside from Ezra, of course. When I told him the bar was haunted, he knew right away it was his wife. We traded seances for meals, and then it just became a habit. Truthfully, I miss coming here. Everything feels so out of place now."

"Give it time," he reminded. Pointing down at her tattooed arm, he asked, "And the queen? I'd assumed that would've gone away once her spirit was banished."

With a heavy sigh, she contemplated her next words. Unsure how much she wanted to worry him, she offered him a quaint smile. "All is well." The words stung on the way out, ripping at her insides with every lie she told.

"Let's just focus on tonight, shall we? With everything going on with Melinda, I feel like you and I haven't had a moment alone together." Kane cut into his chicken, alternating between vegetables and meat.

Winnie thought back to the past month. Whether they were helping rid Chicago of its hellhound problem, or working to rebuild the wards around the estate, there was always something to do. He sometimes disappeared as well, usually returning smelling of smoke and grease. The smell brought back memories of Ezra returning from his work at the factories.

Either way, there was always some crisis to manage. Even just being there for Ezra as he mentally recovered from his first battle seemed like a constant struggle. Very little time remained for them to finally go out like they'd planned before Samhain.

"We're here now," she said, peering over the lip of her cup.

Winnie and Kane enjoyed their meal, discussing the book they'd picked to read together. Since Wesley's funeral, she'd tried desperately to escape reality, and books were always her way of doing so. It surprised her to see him pick up the same one not long after, ready to read together and discuss. Now, as they finished their meal and cider, he handed her a small box.

"What's this?" Winnie crooned, moving aside her empty plate.

"Just something small. I know we all got you the dagger for your birthday, but I wanted to get you something that's just from me." He seemed to shuffle around nervously in his seat.

Seeing his nerves brewing, she thought, *Maybe I should take my time to torture him that much more.*

Nervous fingers ripped at the decorative paper, glancing at him with suspicion. As she opened the lid to the small box, her eyes glued to a dainty moonstone ring inside. Winnie's heart nearly jumped out of her chest, setting the shimmering *thing* aside with a shake of her head.

"Um, Kane? What is this?"

His brows furrowed, analyzing her reaction as she pushed the box toward him. At last he seemed to realize what she was thinking, nearly choking on his drink in a hurry to answer.

"Oh no! You must think," Kane stuttered, struggling to form words. He snatched the box from her before continuing. "Oh, um, no! That's not what that is. Too soon, I know! This is our first official date. I promise, it's just a gift!"

From the other side of the pub, their friends sat leaning against the bar cackling. "I told you she'd take it the wrong way," his brother called, though he ignored Thoren with a dismissive wave.

She let out a deep sigh, only just realizing she'd been holding her breath. "You scared me for a moment." Tentatively she reached for the box, offering his hand a reassuring stroke before finally examining the dainty little ring.

"I saw it at the market the other day. Thought it looked like something you'd wear. Your mum is always talking about the moon. It reminded me of your family," he explained, words still flustered and face red from embarrassment.

Winnie took the ring out and slipped it on her middle finger. Her gaze dropped heavy with sadness at the mention of that word. *'Family.'* No longer one of four, but three. Uneven. Missing a vital part to be complete. *For now...* she reminded herself.

In the weeks since her decision, she hadn't told anyone. Hadn't been *allowed* to tell anyone. Anytime she so much as thought about confiding in her friends, the Elements sent radiating shocks of stinging electricity through her body until she dropped the issue.

Her mother's words still echoed in her mind. *"I hope this was worth the life of my son."* Milicent hadn't mentioned any of it since the funeral.

I wouldn't even know where to begin if I wanted to bring it up, Winnie soon realized. Too afraid they'd be furious, knowing the decision she'd made. She wasn't sure which was worse: knowing she swapped her brother for some creature, or knowing that she entertained the idea of allowing him to remain dead. *Or even worse than that – I contemplated letting all of London burn for him.*

Lost in thought, the touch of Kane's hand pulled her from her grief-filled trance. "Looks like a perfect fit." He offered her a warm smile, his thumb brushing softly against her skin. The act alone was enough to send her into a tailspin.

The nights leading up to Samhain were like a dream come true; puzzle pieces slowly working their way back together. But after the battle, those same pieces had been lost and scattered. Desperately, she tried to find them again – to put herself back together to be the woman she was before. And yet, she always felt just a little bit broken.

Kane's hazels examined her carefully. That familiar, comforting smile waiting patiently for her to resurface. Examining every movement she made with such care, making her wonder how on earth she'd come to deserve such affection.

"Everything alright? Was the gift too much?"

"No," she rushed, shaking her head. "It's perfect. I just can't believe we finally made it…here. Where we are now."

With a thoughtful nod, he added, "I have another stop for us tonight."

Excitement sent butterflies fluttering in her stomach as they brought their plates to the bar. Kane offered Butch a few coins in exchange for the meal before leaning in and whispering something to his brother. As the two spoke, Ezra poked his head around with a worried look on his face.

"Butch, here, was just telling me about some grave robbings throughout London and the countryside."

"It's nothing they need to worry about now," Thoren insisted, nudging his love with an elbow. "Let them enjoy their date for at least one night, won't you?"

"We'll catch up later." Kane hooked his arm in Winnie's, leading her toward the door.

"Aren't they coming with us?" she asked, glancing back to see Thoren offer her a quick wink before exiting the pub.

"They don't need to follow us everywhere we go." A coy smile fell across his face as the freezing winds of London's streets once again greeted them.

"Where are you taking me?" A nervous giggle escaped her as she glanced back at the alleyway leading to the portal home. Truthfully, she'd been much more of a homebody these days, desperately wanting to hide whenever possible.

"It's a surprise. Just trust me, okay?" he mused, leading her farther down the street.

The wind nipped at her skin, cold shivers running down her spine. Rubbing her hands together, a small warming flame nestled itself in her palm.

"What are you doing?" he scolded, swatting to extinguish it. "Someone might see!"

Rolling her eyes, she laughed softly. "Don't you want to be warmed too?"

"I suppose if you're going to be reckless, I may as well benefit a little." Kane chuckled nervously, though his eyes told a different story. Still, he pulled her in close to warm his hands with her magic.

With linked arms, they approached one of the nearby makeshift theaters. Jutting his chin toward the entrance, she noted that the outside was entirely dark. Not a single soul was around to indicate the place was even open. Winnie hesitated, an anxious mind causing doubt.

"Don't you trust me?" Another cheeky smile lay across his face, lacing his fingers between hers and pulling her toward the building.

That sounds familiar... Where have I heard that before? Winnie wondered. "No one's here, Kane!"

He ignored her protests, offering the back of her hand a soft kiss as devious eyes beckoned her forward.

"I may have bribed the owners to let us use this place for the night."

"Is this the moment when I find out you're actually a

murderer?" Though she joked, she could feel her heart sitting in her throat thanks to jumbled nerves.

"Just *trust* me." He repeated, something familiar about that sentence.

A strange tingling sensation spread through her mind, a nagging itch of reminder triggered by those words. "You've said that before…" Rubbing her head, spots clouded her vision and the world began to spin.

"Are…you okay?" He placed a hand on her shoulder, crouching down to meet her gaze.

Attempting to look at him, her hazy vision blocked out nearly everything nearby. As though she were up in the sky, a strange weightlessness overtook her before a nonsense of images flashed behind her closed eyes.

Samuel's prideful scowl. Later on, Wesley in front of her with Kane at his side. Their faces – she remembered the way they looked at not just each other, but her. Worry laced every inch of them, brows knit together and asking her muffled questions. A red hot sting along her cheek, eyes raw from crying.

In her mind, she heard the siren's words before anger pelted him like a grenade. *"Just trust me, okay?"* Then…rage. Kane's wings flaring behind him before storming away.

Something about these images seemed to bite at her, as though she weren't meant to remember them. The last thing she saw was Wesley's careful hand, reaching out and touching her forehead. And then it all went blank.

Winnie's name rang through her mind, repeated over and over again as firm hands grasped either side of her shoulders. Kane's voice ripped her back to reality.

"What's happening?"

"Did you have a vision? Your eyes were completely blank like your mother's." His hands were placed on either shoulder, bracing her up to keep her from falling. Truthfully if he hadn't been there for support, she'd likely toppled over completely.

"I saw something…strange."

"Do you need a minute?"

"Wesley did something to me… made me forget," she mumbled, the slurred words coming out as though she were drunk.

"Wes? What are you talking about?" Kane's head cocked to the side, examining her before placing the back of his hand on her forehead. "You don't look well. Should we get you home? We can end the night here, if you'd like."

She shook her head, senses calming down at last. "I just need a minute."

Kane pulled Winnie into an embrace, cradling the back of her head against his chest. Counting the beats of his heart, their collective breath slowed and her world stopped spinning. Memorizing the feeling of his hands braced around her, steady and protective, she slowly regained her wits.

Wesley did something to me. I know it. This is just like when we were kids and he altered my memories. I'll get down to the bottom of this, and then none of them can lie to me, she thought as she pulled away.

"I'm fine, I promise. Don't let me ruin our evening."

Grabbing the base of her chin, Kane pulled her attention up. Before either said a word, she lifted herself onto her tip toes and planted a careful kiss along his lips. She felt them curl into a smile beneath her own before he once again laced his hands with hers, and led her into the ramshackle rooms.

As they entered, the overwhelming confusion melted away, replaced by pure delight. She scanned the room, trying to count the hundreds of lit candles surrounding a piano nestled amidst the flickering flame. The familiar wave of Aelius's warmth greeted her as she stood mesmerized by the soft shadows dancing along the walls and ceiling.

"What's this?" She gasped, her hand moving to cover her

mouth in surprise. "Did you learn to play our song?"

He scoffed. "I wish. But it turns out you can hire others to play music for you."

She paused, allowing Kane to pull her into a tight embrace.

"Only you know how to make the slums a romantic place," she chuckled, realizing how intimate it felt. Theaters like this were normally a place of bets and wagers, or fights and violence. Somehow he'd taken a ragweed and turned it into a rose.

Behind them, a raven haired woman entered. Her clothes were finer than Winnie expected. A gown of navy blue hugged her curves, a fur collar pulled around her neck to fight off the biting cold. *I bet she didn't expect to be playing in the slums of Bethnal Green judging by that outfit,* Winnie thought laughingly.

The pianist offered both a greeting nod, though she said nothing before sitting down behind the keys. Delicate fingers danced along the ivory, a familiar melody welcoming the young courting couple.

From their embrace, Kane pulled her into a soft, swaying dance. That same feeling of ease settled in her chest, thinking of his first few nights back. She remembered the way he'd held her after they'd enjoyed drinks in the family bar. Thought of the small details she'd noticed, braced in his arms and listening to their song before realizing their friendship could be more than just that.

Now, surrounded by twinkling candlelight, she counted the details of his face. Etched his smile into her brain so she'd never forget the way those lips curved and beckoned her to kiss them. Tried memorizing every aspect of the moment, wondering and worrying things would fall apart again.

She met his gaze with a soft smile. "This is beautiful. Thank you."

"Is everything...alright?" Kane seemed to examine her carefully, analyzing every facial expression she made.

"Of course," Winnie lied. "I think I'm just tired. Going back and forth between Chicago and London is taking a lot out of me."

"No, I meant, is everything alright with…us?" His face lowered as though he almost couldn't bear a possible negative response.

Winnie paused, searching for the right words. Her perceived helplessness over the last month was a reminder that she was most certainly not alright, but telling her friends why wasn't an option. Time was running out. She'd be sent on the first mission soon. And yet there wasn't a soul to confide in.

"I just miss my brother," she mumbled, tears biting at the backs of her eyelids.

"I hope you know how much you mean to me. I meant every word I said after…" There didn't seem to be an end to his sentence.

When words failed, there was only one thing she was certain of that would fix the solemn silence between them. Cupping the side of his face, she ran her fingers through those dark waves, then along the stubble of his cheek. Beckoning him closer, she waited for her lips to graze his own.

At first, it was delicate. As though he treasured those precious seconds. But as the kiss continued and their bodies collided, a burning need only stirred inside her. Helplessly, she pulled him closer as if his warmth, his body, was needed to survive. Her tattooed arm glimmered amongst the candlelight, a living flame in her soul reawakening with every second his skin touched hers.

Kane's strong arms lifted her, both momentarily forgetting they were not alone. A sour key played across the room, the pianist pulling them from their arguably immodest frenzy, considering they were still in public. Gently, he set her back down and glanced at the glowing marks on her arm.

"Easy now, love. We have enough flames in this room. The last thing we need is for you to burn Bethnal Green to the ground," he purred, trailing a line of kisses down her neck.

She barely heard a word he said, focused only on his soft lips and unsure if she'd ever get enough of them. Not until they explored every inch of her body would she feel satisfied.

"So much for being a gentleman." Her hands rested on his chest, wondering if she could get away with some teasing. *Better not while that poor pianist is here*, she decided.

Kane silenced her with yet another kiss, pulling their bodies together to continue dancing for the remainder of the songs. Allowing the soft tunes to reverberate through her, Winnie closed her eyes and released another heavy sigh. Sharing a moment of much needed peace, the sound of a shot fired just outside sent them on high alert.

"Shit! Ez!" Her gaze darted toward the door before landing back on her date.

"Go check on him! I'll take care of this," Kane urged, knowing what she needed to do.

Winnie sprinted outside, her own pistol withdrawn and ready to fire. As she entered the streets of Bethnal Green, a crowd dispersed. *Another robbery gone wrong*, she thought, seeing a group chasing after a man on the run. Pounding feet raced back toward the pub.

When she didn't see Thoren and Ezra through the window, she bolted across the street. Barging into their flat, she saw him immediately. Hunched in the corner, arms over his head and rocking. Thoren seated next to him, hand on his back and shushing him softly as the siren tried to calm her friend's nerves.

This is the third one this week, she thought. Living in the slums didn't seem so easy anymore. Gunfire had never bothered her friend before. But ever since Samhain, he couldn't seem to handle the pang of bullets or cries of victims as they rattled the streets of London.

Crouching down to meet Ezra's view, she noticed Thoren humming soft, calming tunes. "Are you using magic?"

The siren nodded, continuing the lullabies Winnie faintly remembered from the Falke brothers' mother.

"Ez, look at me." Her words were hushed, pulling his face toward her. "Breathe with me. Inhale, one, two, three, four. Hold… Breathe out, two, three, four. As many times as it takes." It was the same process they'd repeated over and over again the last month since the battle.

"I…saw him again," he tried to say, though the words seemed to falter, barely audible between trembling breaths.

Quickly she glanced around. "I don't see anything. Is it the same one? The one you…"

A hurried hand covered her mouth. "Sh! Don't…say it! He was just here. He might come back!"

"There's no one here," she tried to say again, though her friend just retreated into his own body once more, hands pulled over his head.

"That's what I keep telling him," Thoren whispered, pulling her to stand near the door. "I don't know what to do. Every time we hear a gunshot, he loses it. He can't stay here."

Ezra continued to rock in place, repeating his words over and over again. "He was just here. He's always here. Always watching. Always calling me a…"

"We should take him back to the manor. I know he said he didn't want to stay at the house after the battle, but at least he won't hear any gunshots," Winnie suggested.

Thoren nodded carefully as Kane rushed in wildly. "Is he alright?" He ran to her side, checking her over as if worried she was hurt rather than Ezra.

"No," she whimpered, holding back tears. "This is all my fault. The fight only happened because of me. I'm the reason my best friend is in pieces!"

Thoren braced his arm around Ezra before offering his temple a careful kiss. "Let's get you somewhere quiet for the night," he whispered softly.

"I saw him… Those eyes. They haunt me."

"I know, moró mou. Let's get back to the manor." Thoren's words trailed off as they exited the flat.

Kane and Winnie waited back for a moment, saying nothing. At last, they wandered toward the portal as well, trying to maintain some distance.

"I wish I knew what he was seeing," she mumbled.

Approaching the portal her family had struggled to recreate only a few weeks before, Thoren and Ezra stepped through first. Winnie and Kane followed shortly after, the small zaps from the imperfect magic snagging on their skin as they entered the estate's grounds. The light on the front porch gleamed in welcome as it always did, the door swinging open as if to say 'hello.'

Before she could retire to her room, Kane stopped her. "Care to join me for a drink before we go to bed? Clear both our heads a little?"

Setting her worry aside, she nodded and accepted his hand once more. As they entered the family's bar, thoughts of panic still raced through her. It was nothing an hour or two in front of the fire couldn't fix, trying desperately to forget the haunting cries of her best friend.

2

KANE
FOX MANOR - 1871

Several weeks of planning, and only a little bit of begging, before she finally agreed to go out on their first official date. Weeks of working late shifts at a grimy London factory, saving money in hopes that the night would be perfect. Spending every last penny on bribing the theater owner to allow a private event. Only for it to be interrupted by the usual transgressions of Bethnal Green.

When she asked if he was disappointed, he carefully smiled and told her *'no,'* but it was a partial lie. Deep down, it only mattered that she enjoyed herself, crafting a memorable night. But it certainly stung to know that weeks of planning and saving were ruined by a few fools in the slums, desperate for some cash.

He thought back to the poor pianist, who'd looked at him with such betrayal. As though she thought he'd lured her there to kill her, despite his promise that he simply needed help with a romantic gesture. *Nothing seems to be going my way these days,* he thought before setting his regrets aside and focusing on the beauty in front of him.

Walking toward their respective rooms, Winnie's laughs echoed through him. A savory reminder that no matter what, the night could never truly be ruined so long as they were together.

"It's nice to see you smile again." Planting a delicate kiss along her cheek, he stalled outside her bedroom door. "I've tried to give you space these last few weeks. I hope you know I'm still here for you whenever you need me."

Gently, Winnie pulled him in for another embrace. "I don't need as much space as you think I do."

Kane savored the small act of connection, propping his chin on the top of her head. Breathing in the familiar smell of her lavender soaps and floral perfume, he couldn't help but run his fingers through her soft curls.

"Big day tomorrow. We should probably get some sleep." Though he didn't want to leave, he offered a careful goodnight kiss before backing away. *Be a gentleman,* he reminded himself, wondering if her father was somewhere spying to be sure.

She paused, eyes darting between him and the door. *I think someone isn't ready to say farewell just yet,* he thought deviously.

"Do you want to come inside for a few minutes? We can continue discussing whether Reade's new book is suitable for a *'proper lady'* such as myself."

Kane's cheeks flushed, glancing down the hall at the grandfather clock. He nodded, filing in behind her. Winnie snapped her fingers, igniting the flames within the fireplace across the room. The dark swirling lines of her arm glittered like heated coals beneath her skin, a playful smile sitting across her lips. They took a seat before the hearth, though only a few minutes passed before their conversation on books came to a halt.

Looking up, he realized her attention was no longer plastered to the pages or the fire, but instead on him. His lips. The realization sent coursing electricity through every inch of his body, noting every movement she made to bring them closer together.

The same drive that led him to lift her into the air in the theater now begged to touch her. Except this time, no one else was around to keep them in check. The promise he'd made to her father swirled around in his mind, only to dissipate as she planted herself firmly in his lap.

Wrapping her hands around his neck, Winnie carefully grazed his lips with her own. Slow, as if testing the waters, she pulled away and awaited his response. Kane grasped her waist, the other pulling her hair to the side to expose her neck to tender kisses that cascaded down like rain. While he worked his way across her skin, his name slipped off her tongue.

"I'm sorry...I've been...so distant. I," she stuttered as more sensual kisses moved across her collarbone, and up the back of her ear.

When her words ceased, he planted another kiss along her temple. "Yes, love?"

"I..." Pulling away for a moment, he could see the gears in her head turning as though she needed to choose her words wisely. "I have to tell you something..."

Kane ceased his kisses, curiosity peaked. "What is it?" *This seems like odd timing,* he thought.

Opening her mouth to speak, she was silenced by an unseen force. Clutching her head, she slouched forward with a groan.

"Winnie! Are you okay? What's happening?" Panic coursed through him, grabbing the sides of her face to inspect her more carefully.

Silence fell and her muffled cry stopped. When her body finally stopped shivering, she refused to look at him. "I..." Once again, the words didn't seem to form. "I shouldn't have said anything."

"What the hell was that?" Though she'd scooted away, he made it a point to pull her closer again. A nagging worry stirred deep in his chest, awaiting answers. "What secrets are you keeping from me? Just tell me, please. I didn't think we'd ever do that to one another."

Though she'd been avoiding his gaze before, her attention snapped to those words. "Like you're one to talk! You have been keeping secrets from me for two years! My mother loved you and your brother like sons, and yet no one will tell me what you did to get yourselves banished from the estate!" Her face turned to a scowl, the swirls of her arm lighting in fury.

"I don't know how many more times we can have this conversation. What I did was awful. And I know you'll never forgive me for it."

"We've *all* done terrible things. None of us can claim innocence. Just tell me what you did and I promise, I won't think any differently of you. I...I love you, Kane." Hurt seemed to sting the backs of her eyes.

That's the first time she's said that... But, can I tell her? Confess that I invaded her privacy? Did something terrible with the information I uncovered... Thoughts raced through his mind, unable to look at her.

"Say something, please! You can't be upset with me when you, yourself, can't even open up." She kneeled before him, grasping both sides of his face.

"Let's say I finally spit it out, despite my better judgement. Would you finally tell me what's going on? It's obvious something's been bothering you. You're been strange ever since you came back from Wesley's funeral with that giant book."

He waited patiently for a response.

"I want to, but...I can't. I'm not *allowed* to."

An obstinate huff of laughter escaped him by accident before he said, "If you can have your secrets, then so can I."

"Fine," she hissed, standing up and turning toward the fire.

Grabbing her wrist, he turned her back to face him. Kneeling, he wrapped his arms around her hips, staring up at his raven-haired beauty. "Stubborn as usual," he tsked.

"I physically cannot tell you. There's more going on than you realize, and until I'm allowed to say anything, you just have to accept that."

Planting a kiss on the top of her hand, Kane trailed more up her forearms. Curious fingers ran along the laces of her corset, savoring the way her cheeks flushed and her body squirmed with need. "What have you gotten yourself into, Ms. Fox? And why are you unable to tell me?" The words purred from his mouth, eyes darkening when he noticed her tattoo heat once more.

A long sigh escaped her, grabbing ahold of his chin and forcing him to stop his teasing trail. "Does fighting get you off, or something? Let's forget I even brought this up. Maybe just pretend for tonight? I feel like our first official date has been a disaster." Running her finger along his lips, she moved as close as she could until they were almost touching. "Please?"

Still staring up at her from his knees, he cocked his head to the side in contemplation. At last, he mumbled, "Disaster or not, I wouldn't have it any other way."

She sighed, leaning in for another kiss before he interrupted her.

"However, I am going to leave you now."

"Why?" she protested. "You keep doing this! You keep leaving whenever I want you to stay! Why is that?"

"Until you tell me what's going on, I will keep my promise to your father and remain a gentleman." A coy smile formed, remembering this same antsy need the first time they'd kissed.

"You are such a tease, Kane Falke! One day, when you're ready, I may just have to return the favor. Even begging on your knees won't be enough for me, then."

Her words were smooth as honey, watching his every move as he stood towering before her. Resting one hand on his chest, she let the other fall to explore lower and lower until any sort of rational thought disappeared from his mind. *I need to leave. Now, before she continues to...*

"Goodnight, Winifred." His words came out a playful growl, grabbing her hands and holding them in front of her to confine her merciless teasing.

"Goodnight, Pigeon."

"I hated it when Horace called me that. Hearing that name from your tongue is even worse," he insisted, offering the top of her hand a gentlemanly kiss in preparation for his departure.

"Annoying when someone doesn't call you by your proper name, isn't it?"

Stalking toward her armoire, Winnie removed bits of jewelry and allowed her hair to fall freely past her shoulders. Their eyes connected through the reflection of the mirror, her coy smile beckoning him to stay.

"I thought you were leaving?" she asked, slowly unlacing her corset. Moving her dress aside, her shoulders exposed, he caught himself before he could do something that would negate any sort of promise he'd made to her father.

"See you in the morning, love."

A frustrated huff escaped her, merely watching as he exited for good.

The next day, Kane woke up early. The entire manor still slumbered, unaware that the siren was up and anxious. Sleeping these last few weeks had proven to be quite a challenge. Worry laced almost all the dreams he had. Nightmarish images flooded every sleeping second. Whether it be reminders of his lost parents, the banishment two years ago, or the terror of Samhain, it all reminded him how much he'd been through.

He often recalled the feeling of Winnie slipping out of his arms after the funeral. The strange emptiness he'd felt when she vanished. Only for her to turn up several yards away with that mark on her hand. *At least it looks to be from the Elements. I pray it's not from something nastier, taking advantage of her grief,* he thought.

Carefully, he stalked down the hallway. Knocked on her door

ever so softly before entering with feline grace. He needed answers. Knowing she was keeping secrets from him, he couldn't help himself.

Laying soundly in bed, Winnie's face was buried in a pillow. Her hair fell wildly around her, soft snores escaping the lips he so desperately craved. *She looks a bit like a baby raccoon,* he thought, though he loved her for it still. *I should have some time before she wakes. Where is that damn thing?*

His thoughts raced as he looked for the leather bound book she'd held after the funeral. As he searched, checking stack after stack, he thought to himself: *How have I never realized how messy she is?* At last, he saw it. Moving a few books that lay atop the familiar leather binding, he recognized the twin mark on the cover that matched the brand on the inside of her palm.

Reaching for it, the edges seemed to twitch as though energy was bursting inside its covers. Ever so slightly, the book retreated from his touch. He lunged toward it, attempting to grasp the wily thing. He tried again and again, desperately hoping he wouldn't wake her. With one final dive, his hand finally made contact with the cover.

Before he could secure his grip on the object, a sharp tug pulled it across the room. Startled, Kane turned to see Winnie sitting upright and floating in bed. Her eyes were a blank canvas, just as they had been the night before. An outstretched, branded hand grasped the spine carefully, the room heating to molten lava.

"Do not touch what isn't yours, siren!" Several unrecognizable voices layered overtop one another, booming through the room in anger.

"I – I'm sorry," he whispered, holding his hands up in a sign of submission.

Her body fell back suddenly, still clutching the book in hand. Racing to her side as she muttered incoherently, he eased her awake. Softly calling her name, he brushed the hair out of her face with care.

"What are you doing here?" Winnie's arms moved to stretch, though she quickly realized what she was holding.

"What is this thing?" he asked, tapping the cover. Every time he made contact, small electric shocks shot through his fingertips.

"It's nothing." Still waking from her deep sleep, the shrill words came out an obvious lie.

"You can't keep saying it's nothing, Winnie. Any time I touch this thing, weird shit happens. I know there's something going on!"

"What do you mean?"

"I mean – if Miss Leona were here to see what just happened, she'd immediately call a priest to have you exercised!" Taking a seat at the edge of her bed, he watched as she continued to clutch the object to her chest in protective defiance.

"You were snooping through my stuff?"

The words stung more than he'd expected.

"Not snooping, no. Just..." His words trailed off before admitting, "I guess I was, wasn't I?"

Her eyes lowered. "I just need you to trust me right now. As soon as I can tell you, I will explain it all. But I need you to understand that, for now, I have to do this alone."

"Are you safe?" His question seemed to catch her off guard.

"What do you mean?"

"Whatever you're doing – are you safe? Why can't I help you? Protect you? Anything. I just want to make sure you're okay." He reached the side of her face, pulling her in forehead to forehead.

"I am. I promise, I'm safe. You don't have to worry about me. The second I'm allowed to, I will tell you *everything*. But for now, you just have to trust me. I know how hard that is, but please."

"Fine. But only because I love you. I know you can take care of yourself, but I need you to know I have your back in case something goes wrong. I want to help." Pulling away, Kane walked toward the door.

"I promise," she whispered, though the crinkle in the corner of her eye, the way she refused to look at him directly, told him it was yet another lie.

"I'll see you downstairs?"

With a nod, she hid the book beneath her pillows and pulled the covers up around her.

—•‹ ‹ ●●● › ›•—

WINIFRED

"*Are you safe?*"

The words she hadn't expected that knocked her world off its axis. *I don't even know the answer to that question. I'm not safe. Not really. I have no clue what my mission in Marvivia is. I have no answers from the Gods. All I know is that my time is coming soon, and I have no idea what to do. And no one to talk to about it!*

But regardless of her endless worries, she'd smiled and nodded. Lied through her teeth and told him she was fine. Never had deception stung so sharply. Glancing at the clock on her nightstand, she realized how ridiculously early it was. Pulling the covers over her head, she fell back asleep into another dream-filled trance.

At first, her dreams were quite average. But they were swiftly interrupted, the images before her melting away to make room for a new space. Wherever she'd ended up felt…different. Like she was somewhere she'd never visited before. Similar to Oblivion, but not quite. It took a few moments to recognize the familiar pub before her.

This place… it didn't feel like anything she was used to. In Oblivion, there was only nothingness. Here, she seemed to be in a duplicate of the bar, though small details weren't quite right. As if someone created the room from memory rather than actually taking her there.

A few patrons sat around the establishment, though strangely none of them had any distinguishing features. As though they were mere puppets. Their foggy mouths seemed to move, but only a low hum buzzed as they all got up and left the bar in unison.

At last, a familiar face appeared. Taking a seat before her, glittering mossy eyes and messy hair appeared. A grin sat from ear to ear, welcoming her.

"Wesley?"

He nodded cheerfully. "I was wondering when you'd find your way here."

"What do you mean?"

"That doesn't matter. All that matters is that you're here now."

Soft murmurs continued to swirl around them, Winnie's skin crawling and senses on overdrive. "We're not alone, are we?"

He shook his head, but didn't bother to explain.

"Are we in Oblivion?"

"No," he responded with a chuckle. "Oblivion is between. This is after. Keep up, will you?"

She could feel the strange beings as they approached, circling around the stranger in the unknown. Never had she felt so out of place before. The only welcome she felt was from her brother sitting across from her, feeling strangely like an anchor to that odd little duplicated pub.

Wesley turned to look over his shoulder, though Winnie couldn't see anyone else with them. "Oh her? She's my sister. We won't be long."

"Who are you…" She never got to finish her question.

"It's strange over here. I'm still getting used to everything. But I wanted you to know I was okay. I figured you're probably taking all the blame as usual." Sad eyes examined her carefully, drawing her attention away from the slithering sounds around them.

A moment of surprise caught her. "You've been watching us? The family, I mean?"

He nodded with a smirk. "I try not to watch too much. Don't want to see anything *unseemly*. I accidentally peered in on you and Kane last night. If only I could burn my eyes out in the afterlife."

They both chuckled, though the humor quickly faded. *This isn't my brother. It's his spirit. He's still...dead,* she thought.

"Just know I'm always there with you in spirit. I'm content and happy. I don't blame you one bit." There was a long pause before he finally added, "Your first mission is coming up, isn't it?"

She cleared her throat, trying desperately to think of what to say. "First one, yes. Marvivia. Looks like I'll finally get to visit like we always wanted to."

"Have some fun for me, will you? Find a dolphin and enjoy yourself a little while you're there." Sad eyes glanced toward the exit.

Her mouth opened to ask more questions before she heard a sharp ringing in her ears. She turned toward the door of the pub, only to see glowing light.

"Looks like you have to go back. Catch you next time?" Wesley chuckled, waving solemnly.

Before she could say a true goodbye, her eyes shot open. Once again sitting in her bed, her mind raced wondering where she'd ended up. It clearly wasn't Oblivion, a place she'd come to know all too well. Continuing to contemplate, she dressed herself for the day before sauntering down the hall to find Ezra.

3

EZRA
FOX MANOR - 1871

Standing before a mirror, Ezra glared at himself. Grasped the scar along his neck; the handprint left behind by the vicious queen. Traced the ridges where fire had burned, noting the different color of his skin like a stamp marking him. *I killed someone,* he thought. Seeing that scar was a near constant reminder of that. *I've become a killer.*

The hair on the back of his neck stood, a strange tingling spreading from the base of his spine all the way up. *He's coming,* he panicked. *He'll be here any moment. I can always tell when he's close by.*

The air around him chilled, a huff of clouded breath escaping his lips. He squeezed his eyes shut, hoping it would make the strange vision go away. "If I don't look at you, you don't exist."

A deep chuckle echoed through the room, drawing closer and closer. Stumbling footsteps approached, the laugh growing louder with each passing second.

"You can't ignore me forever," the man seethed.

Ezra opened his eyes, knowing what he would see next. Behind him in the reflection of the mirror, the figure of the hellhound he'd murdered during the Battle of Samhain waited. A slithering hand reached around his neck, wrapping itself over the handprint scar left behind by Boudicca.

"You're. Not. Real." His lip quivered, bitter ice spreading

through his body until every ounce of warmth vanished.

"Then why are you so afraid?" A phantom breath brushed against Ezra's ear.

"What are you?"

"You should already know what I am." The man's eyes turned dark, pupils dilating as he retreated. His head snapped to the sound of a knock on the door. "Until next time, killer."

A heavy sigh escaped Ezra, shuffling toward the door. Winnie stood on the other side, patiently waiting with her arms across her chest and dark circles under her eyes.

"You look exhausted," he noted, offering her a quick hug before she wrapped her arm behind his back.

"Didn't sleep well. You?"

"If you mean to ask: have the nightmares continued? The answer would be yes. Can't seem to escape the constant torment." They began their slow trudge toward the kitchen, arm in arm. The air around them felt stale; a constant reminder that this home didn't feel like it once had. As though the house mourned alongside them.

"You have to stop being so hard on yourself, Ez. I know the first time is hard, but you didn't kill anyone. You *defended* yourself. There's a difference."

"I don't know that I'll ever see it that way." He loosened his arm from hers, accelerating his pace to reach the kitchen first.

As they walked through the archway, he noted Milicent. She stood before the oven, pushing eggs around a pan with glazed eyes. Ezra stood beside her, placing a careful hand on her back. It took a few moments before she realized someone was there, glancing sideways before rushing to hide her tears.

"Why don't I?" Gently, he took the spatula from her hand.

She nodded, not saying anything before grabbing a cup of coffee and taking a seat near the windows. Winnie took a seat next to her mother, brushing her fingers over Milicent's hand in solemn solidarity.

Focusing on the eggs, Ezra asked, "Where's everyone else?"

"I believe the brothers are out for a run. Tara was caring for Cricket last I checked," Winnie answered, her attention fixed outside.

As if on cue, the sunroom door opened and a rush of cold wind blew in from around the corner. Both Falke brothers sauntered in, huffing with beads of sweat running down their temples and along their muscled bodies. *How did I manage to land that man?* Ezra wondered, his gaze roaming every inch of Thoren's chiseled figure.

"I can read your mind when you look at me like that," his love joked, offering a lingering kiss along Ezra's lips.

Kane entered, wiping his forehead before taking a seat at the counter rather than next to Winnie. *Seems odd,* he thought. *Why won't they look at each other?*

"Everything alright?" Thoren asked, noting their distance.

"Mhm," Kane mumbled, though his lips were pulled into a tight line as he focused on a piece of bread in his hands.

"Melinda's waiting for us. We need to eat quickly," Winnie muttered, getting up from her seat and grabbing a slice for herself as well. Her eyes raked over Kane for a moment, though Ezra couldn't get a good read on what she was feeling.

"If you ladies are done runnin' around and gettin' dressed, perhaps we could go," Tara chuckled, entering from the hallway.

Cricket ran past her straight toward the stove, his nose high in the air and curiously sniffing. Ezra finished the last of the eggs and spooned them onto plates for serving. "Away with you," he teased, nudging the shuck with his bum. Dropping a small piece onto the floor, he glanced around to see if anyone would notice him feeding the strange creature.

"Tara – as insufferable as ever," his love muttered, glancing over the edge of a cup.

"Me? Insufferable? I thought you were the one everyone said

was obnoxious. And rude. And…"

Winnie cut her off. "What's wrong with you two? You're never at each other's throats *this* much."

"Your friend needs to mind her own business. I wouldn't have any trouble with her if she could simply keep her mouth shut." Thoren's eyes darkened, a hint of flames burning in his pupils as the redhead took a seat at the counter.

"There's no need to be hostile," Ezra cut in. He placed a hand along the base of Thoren's back, hoping the mere act would calm him. "As flattering and not at all embarrassing as it is to have you constantly defending my honor, I promise I can fight for myself."

"Can you? Last I checked, you've been useless since Samhain." Tara reached for a piece of bread, though Thoren swatted her hand away.

"Bread is for friends and family. You are neither of those." In an act of defiance, he broke off a piece and offered it to Cricket.

Winnie's attention sharpened onto her friend, eyes wide as she seemed to work through the awkward tension in the room. "Where is this coming from?"

"I tried to go paroling with this one a few days ago. Let's just say, it didn't go well. Do you want to tell them what happened?" Her glare pierced Ezra's skin, each word another reminder that he was never doing enough.

"I…saw the man again. I likely almost got us killed." Guilt lingered in every word as he leaned along the counter, pushing around the eggs on his plate.

"You're lucky there was only one hound. Had there been more, we might not have made it. I can't take a blubbering mess with me. I need someone I can actually count on."

Thoren's fist slammed onto the counter. "I've had enough from you." The air around them heated slowly, his rage simmering with each passing second.

"I've had enough of you, too! This is why I don't like staying here. Somehow I always have to be around *you* and your petulant feckin' attitude!" Tara stood, the stool behind her clattering to the ground.

Winnie jumped between her two friends. "Both of you, quit it! We don't have time for childish behavior. We can't afford to turn on one another right now!"

"I know I'm a liability. I'm sorry... I'm just..." The words wouldn't form, Ezra looking to the ceiling as though it held answers.

"You have to give your mind time to heal," Milicent interrupted. It was the first she'd said since he'd entered the kitchen.

He could only nod, tears welling in his eyes.

"We don't have time for you to *heal.* Remember what you told me?" Her glare landed on Kane. "This isn't a fecking vacation. That's what you told me back in October. We're always in danger. You either work your shit out, or you die!"

Anger broiled inside Ezra. *I can't take this anymore,* he thought as every inch of him heated with rage. A sudden crash, then the clatter of glass, startled the group. They turned, a small boulder settling on the floor.

"Where did this come from?" Thoren picked it up, glancing through the broken window.

"I need everyone to stop fighting. Especially around me. *About* me. All of it! I know I'm a mess. I'm working on it." Ezra dropped his fork, leaving a full plate behind and rushing toward the sunroom.

The air in here is too thick. I can't breathe, he panicked. Picking up his pace, he ran outside. Though he didn't wear a jacket, the cold air felt good. Like a reassuring hug as he settled his nerves. *I have to figure this out. I can't keep putting everyone in danger.*

Opening his eyes, he locked in on the man standing along the woodline. The hellhound he'd killed once again lingered, waiting to be spotted. Glancing down at the beast's chest, crimson spilled out as his smile widened. Mouthing the word *'killer,'* he at once vanished just as he always did. All Ezra could do was rub his head, wondering when the strange visions would cease, and his mind would finally allow him to be at peace once again.

4

MELINDA
CHICAGO - 1871

Standing just outside her room in the Chicago Orphan Asylum, Melinda waited in front of the mirror passageway the Fox family conjured only a few short weeks before. The group used it regularly to get back and forth between London and her home, always vigilant to ensure the many new residents never saw them. Or at least they tried. They'd been caught a few times, yet she was surprised by how easily it was to convince others that they hadn't seen real magic. It seemed the mind preferred logic over the truth.

They were supposed to be here an hour ago, she thought. Pacing before the mirror, she contemplated stepping through herself. Melinda hadn't been back to the manor in quite some time, too haunted by memories. Just down the hall, echoes of the older children receiving their usual studies made way to her ears. On the other end, the humming of the seamstresses and their machines whirred endlessly, trying to reclothe those impacted by Boudiccca's destruction. The entire orphanage worked to fix the aftermath of what was now called 'The Great Chicago Fire.'

Since that dreadful night, the orphanage had taken on dozens of homeless families. It'd been weeks since the building had a quiet moment, children constantly playing while families stressed, workers rebuilding the city. Thankfully, her room was often quieter on the second floor.

"Ensure no one sees them arrive," Miss Leona reminded with a scowl as she passed, a basket of clothing in hand. Her gray hair was pulled back into a tight bun as usual, a dark modest dress scraping the ground as she walked down the stairs.

Melinda nodded before glancing at a clock. *They're now extremely late,* she thought, about to reach for the glistening surface.

The last month away from Fox Manor was necessary. Though she'd missed most of the fight the night of Samhain, the sounds of the battle still haunted her. The screams of terror; the stench of death. The strange out-of-body helplessness she'd felt while Boudicca's daughters inhabited her body, taking complete control of her actions.

The image of Wesley's body laid across Ezra's lap was seared into her mind, lifeless and doll-like as the glamor around him faded. *I still wonder if the others knew of his true face.* Her hand retreated from the mirror, a group of rowdy children running past.

"Not too loud, Otto! Miss Leona is preparing lunch, and others are trying to learn! She'll want you all settled and ready to eat any moment!" Melinda's words fell on deaf ears, the children ignoring her warnings, continuing their wild chases.

The boy leading the group, Otto, was truly wild. He was one of the oldest kids at the orphanage, though still only a mere six years old, with untamed eyes and curly hair that rivaled any sort of attempt to tame it. He'd been with them for several years now, always returned for his unruly nature and the strange things he said.

He reminded Melinda a little of herself. As a child, she'd also experienced the heart wrenching feeling of being unwanted. The gift of true sight had been more like a curse to her. It seemed most people didn't want the truth. Though Otto didn't have such a gift, potential families often complained that he spoke to the shadows as though figures were hidden in their depths.

Turning toward the portal, Wesley's onyx necklace gleamed as it recognized the kindred magic just ahead. Stroking the little pendant gently, Melinda fought back tears. After his funeral, Milicent gifted it to her hoping they'd 'keep in touch,' as the woman put it. It seemed she had no plans to help rid Chicago of the problem they started.

Wesley's parents seemed like ghosts of themselves, mourning the loss of their son to the point of becoming nothing more than mere skeletons. A haunting aura of darkness followed them wherever they went, something Melinda couldn't stand to be around. *I haven't seen that kind of pain since I watched my uncle wither away,* she'd thought the day she noticed Death's lingering presence.

To her relief, the others were more than willing to help her city. Though Melinda was used to others disappointing her, she just hoped that they wouldn't let her down the way countless others had. Being abandoned wasn't something she took lightly.

Reminiscing, she couldn't help but recall the day Wesley took her to London on their secret excursion. His eyes were solemn, avoiding hers as they explored the nicer parts of the city. Gardens, small shops, coffeehouses. And yet, her favorite place at the time was still Fox Manor.

In all the ugliness and beauty she'd witnessed, the estate was the most peaceful. That quickly changed after the battle. However, what he'd told her that day stood out the most in her mind.

At the time, she'd thought his dismissive attitude about spending more time together after the fight was meant to insult. Now she wondered if he knew all along. *Perhaps he was trying to protect me by not getting too close,* she thought.

Honestly, Melinda was furious with him. Still. Unsure if she'd ever fully forgive him. *I could've fought. Should've protected him. Been by his side. And I'm just as upset with the others for not stopping him. I don't understand why Boudicca held a grudge for centuries.* Her thoughts paused for a moment. *I can't believe I wasn't strong enough to withstand his powers in the first place.*

Despite her anger, she missed him terribly. The goofy smile and his gentle nature. The way his nervous hands fiddled with the buttons on his shirt whenever he talked to her. How those same hands ran through his wild hair, trying to tame the cowlick that never ceased to go its own way. All she had now were memories and that necklace. And now she'd never know what their friendship could've turned into, had they been given more time.

Downstairs, Miss Leona's call for the children ushered them calmly toward the dining room.

"You should've known I'd get them settled," Otto snickered, leading the group downstairs.

She shook her head with a smile, tussling his hair as he sauntered by. Tapping her foot anxiously on the floor, she debated one last time if she should cross over to the estate. Mere seconds before wandering through herself, Winnie's amber eyes and glowing smile appeared through the haze of the mirror. Tara stepped in behind her, followed by Cricket, Thoren, Ezra, and lastly Kane.

"What took you so long?" Melinda protested, reaching for each to give them a welcoming hug.

"These princesses took all mornin' to get ready," Tara scoffed, pointing at the gentleman of the group.

Thoren opened his mouth to respond to her jeer, though Ezra placed a hand on his chest to stop him.

"Are you hungry? We can have some lunch before our meeting with the new mayor."

The group shook their heads before following Melinda toward the front door. Pulling on her winter coat and scarf, she led the group outside.

"Why does he want to meet with us again?" Thoren's words were laced with suspicion.

"As the hellhound attacks increase, so has the awareness of the people. More and more citizens are realizing that these beasts aren't just hungry wolves. There's only so many lies you can tell before enough of them see a hound turn to a man or woman. The mayor is now painfully aware that magic and monsters are real. I've offered our services, and he's interested in hearing what we have to say," Melinda explained.

"Tonight is his celebration, right?" Tara linked arms with her, Cricket prancing at their side.

Melinda nodded.

"I've already told her several times. We're not going," Thoren interjected with a roll of his eyes.

"Maybe you're not going, but I am! I've been cooped up in that house for too long. I need to get out a bit; explore on my own. I'm ready to kick some hellhound ass!"

"These two have been at each other's throats the last few days," Winnie mumbled, glaring at her two friends.

"Why's that?" Her gaze flickered between the siren and the redhead as they stepped outside.

"When Tara learns to keep her opinions about my love to herself, I'll gladly consider her a friend again." Thoren placed an arm over Ezra's shoulders, attention sharpening.

"I told you, I'm fine! I know I'm a bit of a mess right now. We can all see it," he countered, the aura surrounding Ezra clouded with embarrassment. Waves of muddled fog buzzed over his head, though no one but her would notice. The lingering grasp of Death lay on his shoulder too, though it didn't seem to be here to collect anyone.

Just behind them, the door to the orphanage slammed open in a fury. Miss Leona stormed out before fussing, "One of the children just told me she saw people walking through a mirror! I told you that if you're going to have this strange contraption in the Asylum, you have to be careful! If the Matron finds out I've allowed witchcraft, she'll have my head!"

"How I've missed you, Miss Leona," Kane sighed.

"You're well aware that I don't condone such sorcery here! I would do well to smash that mirror myself, and force you to take a boat!"

"You're welcome for saving you," Kane snapped, Melinda noticing a fuzzy haze of anger swirling around his head.

"By the grace of God, I'll always be grateful. However! I don't appreciate an open door right in the middle of the second floor. You have to be more careful!" The reds of Miss Leona's cheeks flared as she spoke, her chest heaving anxiously.

"I know, Miss, I'm sorry. We'll make sure no one is around next time. But we either let them come and go as they please, or you'll have to fight the hellhounds yourself," Melinda retorted.

Behind her, Kane snorted a quick chuckle. The woman huffed once more, turning to go back inside to tend to the children.

"Don't mind her. She's just a little uptight. We're eternally grateful for you all."

"It's what my brother would've wanted," Winnie added, a sad smile falling across her face.

The words threatened to sting the backs of Melinda's eyelids like enraged hornets, but she held them back with every ounce of strength left.

"Any word on where the hounds are staying?" Thoren asked, focusing the conversation.

Melinda shook her head. "There's rumors, of course. Some brave souls have tried to follow them back to their camps, but they never return. We usually find them gutted in the center of town as if they're trying to send a message."

"When I spied on them before Samhain, they were hiding out in the woods. That would be a good place to start looking," Winnie added, linking her arm with Kane's.

Melinda couldn't help but notice him retreat a little at first, though a moment of pause was all that he needed before pulling her in closer with a strained smile. For warmth or comfort, she wasn't sure. The energy between them seemed scattered, the usual glittering glow strangely fragmented.

"What of the new mayor?" the eldest Falke brother asked.

"Some are saying he's involved somehow. I don't believe it. If he were a hellhound, I'd be able to see his true face." Melinda ushered the group down the street, leading them toward the Mayor's home.

"There's *is* a ball tonight, isn't there?" Tara pestered.

With a chuckle, Melinda answered, "Yes there is."

"We're. Not. Going." Thoren's words were short, a glaring disdain aimed right for her.

"Actually," Melinda began with caution, Tara's eyes lighting up in hope. "We've been asked to go as protection for Mayor Medill."

"Yes! I told you!" Tara jumped up and down, her clapping hands riling up the shuck at her side. Though she sneered at Thoren, he rolled his eyes and ignored her entirely.

"There's rumor that hellhounds may strike tonight. Medill has his own protection force, but he wants us. When I informed him of our fight back in October, he specifically requested we be there for our...various talents." The words bit her tongue on the way out. *Never thought death and destruction could be considered a talent.*

"I think it's best if Ez and I take the streets. We can be on patrol while you're at the event. If something goes wrong, we'll come running," the siren interjected.

The group nodded, Winnie's eyes flashing to her friend in worry.

"You could stay here at the orphanage to protect the kids," she suggested.

"No, I need to help. I'll be fine." Ezra's words were equally as quick, as if trying to convince everyone, including himself.

"Given that this is a ball, we have to dress up, right?" Tara asked eagerly, standing behind Winnie and poking at her impishly with delight.

Melinda chuckled with a quick nod.

"You know I'll never say no to fancy dresses and weapons," she said at last, turning to scheme with her friends.

5

WINIFRED
CHICAGO - 1871

W innie straightened her dress, looking herself over in the mirror one last time. She hadn't dressed nicely since Samhain, too afraid to relive the memories of that night. The dazzling dress she'd worn before tearing it off, only to be covered in shimmering blood shortly after.

Pinning the last few strands of hair in place, she was careful to leave a few stray curls bouncing down her back with small onyx pins to keep the rest up neatly. The little gems would've blended into her dark hair were they not surrounded by glittering rhinestones.

Her dress was crafted of fine golden-cream silk, just enough shine to catch the eyes without drawing too much attention to herself. A layer of delicately woven, black chantilly lace adorned the top, a wide hoop skirt underneath to keep the fabric from catching on her legs.

The neckline was lower than she was used to, exposing her shoulders and collarbones where her usual onyx necklace lay with matching earrings dangling from her ears. The moonstone ring Kane had gifted adorned her middle finger as well, a reminder that he was waiting for her below.

Better hurry, she thought while straightening the layered lace bustle at the back one last time. Exiting their temporary room, she followed the sounds of giggling children playing in one of the lower level sitting rooms. Her heart swooned as Kane's booming laugh beckoned her to come downstairs, his joy evident by the sounds of it. Peeking around the corner, she watched for a moment as the siren told a few of the older children wild tales of his home back in Greece.

"What are you doing here in America when you could be on an island, lounging around?" Otto questioned, a quizzical brow raised.

"That eager to get rid of me?"

"Well no. Of course, when you leave, you're taking me with you. But I'm just saying... it sounds like heaven!" Every squeaking word only made Winnie chuckle to herself.

"It's not as peaceful as it sounds. Sometimes it's the people you surround yourself with that make a place heaven. Not so much where you're staying." Sad shoulders shrugged, his back still turned to Winnie.

A little girl, about five, sat waiting eagerly to ask her questions. "What do you do on the island?"

"Well, aside from work, I always enjoy a good day of flying," Kane explained, not very careful when choosing his words.

"Flying?" Otto once again cocked an eyebrow, inching forward. "You're not making much sense, you know."

A deep belly laugh escaped him. "Can I tell you a secret?" His words came out a mere whisper, Winnie barely able to hear from the hallway.

She contemplated for a moment, unsure if she should stop him. *The chance that the kids will believe him is unlikely,* she tried to reassure herself.

The children nodded in eager anticipation, moving in closer and closer ready to devour his secret.

"Sometimes I have wings. And I use them to fly all over the place like a bird!" Kane tried to whisper, though his enthusiasm outmatched his attempt at being quiet.

The children burst into sudden cackling laughter, scooting

away from him.

"Like a bird? That's not true!" one of the girls cried, clutching her sides in hysteria.

"What nonsense are you telling these children?" Miss Leona's sudden appearance next to Winnie startled her, jumping back before Kane could catch her snooping.

"He said he can fly!" Otto's eyes twinkled, examining the siren with pure fascination.

"Mr. Falke hasn't explained that his stories are all make-believe. Don't go getting any ideas that you can jump off the roof and suddenly know how to fly, Otto!" A small huff of frustration escaped her, smoothing her dress anxiously.

"Oh really? Make-believe you say?" Though his back was still turned, Winnie could almost hear the smirk in his voice. Before anyone could blink, Kane's shoulders shuddered and his broad, hawk-like wings expanded out behind him.

With a loud gasp, Miss Leona cried, "Heavens to Betsy! Put those away!"

The children squealed, lunging toward the siren and running their hands over the plumage with gentle curiosity.

"He's an angel!" one of the little girls cried with a squeal of joy.

"You heard it here, first! Looks like your very own God sent me just to torment you. Who knew," he teased.

"Even the devil was an angel once," she grumbled, clapping her hands furiously toward the children. "Off with you! It's time for bed!"

In what seemed like an attempt to help the woman out, Kane withdrew his wings.

"Get them back! Get them back!" Otto shouted, jumping up and down while grasping Kane's shoulders tightly.

He allowed the boy to dramatically shake him before adding, "You need to get to bed, little one. Maybe next time!"

A low grumble escaped the boy as he turned and walked up

the stairs with slouched grumpy shoulders and a pout capable of tearing out one's soul.

"Always causing trouble, aren't you?" Winnie joked, stepping through the threshold finally.

Kane turned in surprise, clutching his chest in awe just as he had the night of Samhain. "Even more radiant, everyday. How do you do it?" Grasping her hand, he offered her a gentlemanly bow before planting a soft kiss atop her hand.

Tiny butterflies fluttered in her chest as her eyes connected with his. He wore an outfit similar to Samhain, with black pants and a button down. A fitted white and gold waistcoat lay overtop. He hadn't pulled on his dress coat yet, the sleeves of his shirt pulled up to reveal the delicate ink she still admired about him despite having grown used to its appearance. *I'll need to cover my arms with gloves,* she thought, reminding herself that a proper lady would never expose inked skin.

"You clean up nicely," Winnie hummed, running her hands over his beard which he'd trimmed short for the evening. "I see you're armed and ready as well."

"And you, my love? Are you ready in case something happens?"

Noting the whereabouts of the Asylum's residents, she pulled him aside. First, she moved the fabric of her bustle to reveal a hidden pistol. Lifting the hem of her skirt next, she uncovered the gifted dagger strapped to her thigh, sheathed and read for a fight.

Kane's jaw dropped as she noted, "It's a little uncomfortable, but I'll manage." A small chuckle escaped her as he grasped her leg firmly.

Gently, he nudged her until her back was pressed firmly into the wall. Kane's eyes roamed her body, first examining the hidden weapon, then trailing up until he met her gaze once more. His hazels flashed wildly to her lips, his breath steadily increasing with every passing second. Using her leg to pull him in closer, his body pressed into her own.

Looking over his shoulder at the archway, she could almost read his mind. Leaning down, he eventually mumbled, "Gods, you tease me."

"Still determined to be a gentleman? Or are you ready to admit defeat?" she teased, heat and electricity coursing through her core as trailing kisses moved down her neck and across her chest.

Kane stalled, the gears in his head turning. *I love seeing him squirm, but I don't know how much longer I can stand this constant game,* she thought. Before her hands could explore beneath his well-fitted suit, hurried footsteps entered the room.

"Good Gods, you two! Get a room! We're practically in a feckin' church!"

Kane's head dropped to her shoulder for a moment, a deep chuckle escaping him before releasing her leg. Winnie's blushing cheeks turned toward her friend before fixing the hem of her dress.

"Your timing is impeccable, Tara. I'm pretty sure you aren't supposed to use their lord's name in vain *or* cuss in an orphanage. I think it's official – we're all going to hell," Kane said with a grumbling laugh as he straightened himself out.

"One would have to believe in their hell to attend," she noted before offering a quick shrug and walking toward a nearby mirror.

Kane turned back toward Winnie before offering her a final, delicate kiss on the cheek. On the other side of the room, Tara brushed her fingers through the curls that lay down her back as Winnie took a seat on one of the sofas.

Examining her friend, Winnie couldn't help but notice the lavishness of Tara's dress. Usually, she stuck to earth tones or reds the color of wine. This night, she'd chosen a gown of soft lilac, a surprising compliment to her fair skin and red hair. Layers of ruffles lined the skirt, synching at the back with white roses pinned in the bustle.

The corset top hung low to expose cleavage, covered with a layer of white lace along her shoulders. More white roses sat at the top of the corset, her layered necklaces sitting in the crease of her breasts. Dangling pearls hung from her ears, matching nicely with the decorative flowers.

"You look beautiful," Winnie crooned before taking Tara's hand and twirling her in a circle.

"I'm sure Kane has already told you how stunning you look as well! I'm so excited for tonight," she squealed. "Thoren and Ez have already gone up ahead. They'll be patrolling all night as planned."

"What about Cricket? And Melinda?" Winnie asked, grabbing her coat and throwing it over her shoulders to prepare for the cold winter winds.

"She's already gone up ahead of us," Kane noted as they exited.

"Cricket stayed behind at the manor. I doubt they want to add more beasts to the party. Melinda will be greeting people at the door using her magical eyesight, or whatever it is that she does, to stop anyone from entering. It'll be our job to protect the mayor inside. He has guards of his own, but the whole town knows them. They won't be suspecting us," she finished, fastening a rogue curl.

Kane glanced down at Winnie, stars glittering in his eyes as he extended his hand and offered her a gentle kiss. "Be my date?"

With a smirk, she curtsied before hooking her arm in his.

"Always."

Kane flagged down a passing carriage, the trio stepping in and huddling together to fight off the biting cold. Bumping down the road, they witnessed the aftermath of Boudicca's destruction. Winnie almost couldn't bear to look. The rubble lining the streets brought back too many guilt-ridden memories, the soul of the queen stirring in excitement within her body. Bodiless eyes glared back at her, realizing a medium was in their midst.

At last, they rounded the corner and returned to the half of the city that remained standing. Exiting the carriage, she took in the sight of a massive cathedral that reminded her a bit of the ones back home. Hundreds of stained glass windows adorned the outside, large spires reaching to the heavens.

Just outside the building, Melinda waved to them in excitement. As they got closer, Winnie couldn't help but admire the young woman in her beauty, a shy smile gracing her angled face. Natural curls were pinned to one side by a red rose, small golden earrings pinned to her ears. The front of her emerald long-sleeved gown was flat, a stacked bustle of lace and beaded edges cascading down the back. A fur collar sat atop her shoulders, helping to stave off the icy chill.

"Thank you for coming! It means so much to me," Melinda said softly as a group of finely dressed men approached. She glanced over them before nodding to the guards at the door. "We've already caught a few trying to sneak in. Hopefully, tonight will just be a fine evening where you can enjoy yourself."

"Careful, you may curse us," Kane joked, looking around nervously.

Tara hooked her arm in Winnie's, pulling her toward the entrance. As their laced booties met the stone stairs, she leaned in and whispered, "I hope I don't catch fire the moment I step through the threshold."

Winnie giggled, entering the cathedral with wide-eyed amazement in complete awe of the artwork inside. Huge vaulted ceilings were covered in all manner of colorful paintings. *Those hand-drawn images must have taken years,* she thought. Ornately carved piers lined the sides, the center open with the pews removed to make room for the event.

Mayor Medill circulated around the room, talking to various party-goers. Making eye contact from the other side, his movements were quick as he approached. The mayor was an older man, slim and tall with a thick white beard and slightly disheveled hair. Especially for a politician. *I expected him to be more put together for such a big event celebrating his election,* she thought.

Taking Kane's hand with a hearty shake, the mayor said, "Thank you so much for coming." He leaned in and whispered to the siren, "And thank you for watching my back tonight."

Kane motioned for the ladies at his side, though Medill didn't seem to understand what he was gesturing toward.

"Are these your...dates?"

"They're here to help as well," he clarified, face clouded in confusion.

Both ladies reached out first, shaking the mayor's hand before introducing themselves. His movements were careful, examining each up and down in obvious hesitation. His eyes rested on Winnie's tattooed arm peeking from beneath her gloves, looking her over as though she were no better than an inked harlot.

"I take it you're not used to women doing anything other than cooking, cleaning, and child-rearing?" Winnie grumbled.

Nervously, the mayor chuckled before excusing himself to attend the rest of the party. Winnie scoffed, eyes pinned on the mayor.

"That was rude," Tara mumbled. "Maybe we should feed him to Cricket."

"As much as we may hate this, ladies, you must remember you're not at the manor. Things are not the same in the real world," Kane warned, watching as new attendees arrived.

Both ladies shared an annoyed glance before rolling their eyes.

"Don't make excuses for him," Winnie seethed, anger and annoyance burning her insides.

Tara glanced around the room before asking, "I suppose we just entertain ourselves then?"

"Let's not get into any trouble tonight. We're here to work, not play," Kane warned again, glancing around at what could've been eligible suitors.

"That's the only reason I came," she teased with a sly smile, heading toward a beverage table.

"She doesn't learn, does she?"

"Let her have some fun. Maybe she'll actually meet someone nice for once," Winnie muttered, glancing around the room nervously.

An orchestra sat at the end of the cathedral, the music changing from slow and calming to upbeat and lively. A few of the attendees danced, moving gracefully over the church floors.

"I don't understand why you accept the mayor's chauvinistic attitude so easily," she grumbled.

"Perhaps seeing you and Tara like this, he'll think twice before assuming men are the only ones who have the ability to protect." Playfully, he nudged her before looking out at the dance floor. "Care to join me?"

"You never used to like dancing," she noted, accepting it carefully.

"I suspect I never had the right partner before." A small wink fell from his devilishly handsome face, his fingers interlaced with hers and the other hand rested on Winnie's waist.

Feeling the pulsing energy of the music, Winnie enjoyed a few quiet moments before he finally spoke again.

"I know I already asked you this, but I feel the need to ask again: Are you alright?"

"I told you I'm fine," she lied.

"You went through a lot on Samhain. We all did. Just because you don't show your pain as outwardly as some doesn't mean I don't *see* you. I can tell you're not okay."

"I'm fine, Kane. Really!"

He didn't have to say a word for her walls to crumble. His head tilted to the side, digging into her essence and leaching out the information he sought. Since they were children, he'd always been good at that.

"Okay, fine. I'm not okay. Happy?"

"I'll never enjoy seeing you suffer. I just want you to talk to me."

She paused, searching for the right words. "I can still feel Boudicca, slithering inside me like a viper. That's one of many things bothering me." With a heavy sigh of relief, she felt she could breathe again. *Thank the Gods someone finally knows,* she thought.

Kane's eyes widened in surprise. "When were you going to tell me this?"

"I didn't want to worry you. Any of you! I have a lot to… figure out." Her half-hearted response didn't seem to sit well with him, glancing away as though he couldn't bear the thought of the queen's attachment.

Opening his mouth to ask more questions, she quickly silenced him.

"And it really bothers me that you won't tell me what happened two years ago! Ever since Wesley passed, I've had these memories resurfacing. I know you two messed with my mind that night. I know he did something and that you were involved!" She shot daggers of accusation his way.

His face paled, too stunned to speak. "You're…remembering? What have you seen?"

"Tell me what you two did. You want me to feel better and open up? Then be honest!" Her tattooed hand flared in anger, the burning embers under her skin daring to be set free. Any hotter and she'd lose the glove hiding Boudicca's mark.

"That night…was the night you ended your courtship with Samuel."

"I've gathered that much," she snapped. "But somehow I don't remember anything that happened."

"We saw how distraught you were. Saw the bruise on your cheek. I assumed the worst. You didn't want to tell us, so we…"

The music stopped suddenly, like a train derailing from its tracks. The attendees looked around in shared confusion, murmured whispers and conversations stalling. A thin, icy breeze gusted in from the open door.

"Everyone stay calm." A man's voice boomed from the crowd.

Tara appeared next to Winnie, her eyes searching the room just like everyone else. At last, she leaned in and whispered, "I think I recognize that voice…"

Kane's grasp loosened around Winnie's waist as he sprinted toward the mayor, pistol drawn and ready to protect. The two ladies joined at his side, retrieving their guns from hiding.

Winnie heard the whimpers first. Before them, the crowd parted at last. Just before the exit, Melinda stood with a bloodied nose and wild look in her eyes as fury seemed to burn her from the inside. A man's forearm was wrapped around her neck, a gun pressed to her head and unwavering.

His athletic build towered over Melinda, Winnie shuddering as she noted the electric blue eyes staring at the mayor. Recognizing the barbarous scar lining his face, she held her pistol toward him ready to fire.

"Some familiar faces I see," Alaric, the hellhound's leader, crooned. "Hello again, little fawn. Was wondering when I'd see your pretty face again."

Tara's face flushed, cheeks redder than an apple as she aimed directly for him. Winnie scanned the room, desperate to see if there were more. One hand held the pistol tightly, unsure if her shot was good enough to get him between the eyes. Her other arm flared in readiness, prepared for a fiery fight.

Then, something in her awareness shifted. Seeing small spots before her, the air around Winnie thickened. For a moment, a heaviness sat on her chest and she felt she couldn't breathe. Soft whispers slithered toward her, the sounds of the Elements getting closer and closer.

It's time for your first task. Their voices were plain, as if unable to comprehend the position she was in.

Invisible buzzing bees circled her head, making her swat to push away the agonizing torment of what was to come. "I'm not ready," she mumbled, trying not to draw attention to herself. Still, the electrifying build of the jump only became more and more intense.

"Winnie? Are you okay?" Kane peered at her sideways, likely wondering who she was talking to.

As the words escaped his lips, a sudden roar broke through the crowd. A massive horde of hounds erupted into the cathedral. Snapping, frothing jaws lunged for the party-goers, the mayor's guards aiming wildly for the beasts that outnumbered them. A mad craze of fur and claws darted around the room, gunfire raining down through the party.

No one was safe.

Trying to aim for a hellhound up ahead, Winnie's shot missed. A low whir surrounded her, the jump getting closer and closer. "No, no, no! Kane?" Her vision blurred, unable to tell who was around her.

"I'm right here! What's wrong?" His words broke through the overwhelming chaos before fading away.

"They're taking me," she cried, clutching her head as the humming intensified and only it could be heard. When she closed her eyes, the picture of a stoney fortress was visible, followed by the glimmering underwater lights of Marvivia. At once, she vanished leaving nothing behind but the lingering scent of her perfume and the clattering of her fallen dagger.

6

KANE
CHICAGO - 1871

"**W**ho's taking you?" Kane bellowed, fighting off an incoming attack. Firing a shot into a nearby hellhound's skull, he turned to find that she'd vanished.

Confusion washed over him, trying to make sense of what happened. The fear in her voice when she'd called out made his stomach turn. But he didn't have time to sit and speculate. The howls alongside screams of terror ripped his attention away from where she'd just stood.

Tara's back pressed against his, her pistol firing one bullet after another. She swooped down, grabbing Winnie's dagger before returning to a fighting stance. "Where the hell did she go?" Her words were barely audible over the pangs from her gun.

"Not a clue. Let's survive this first; then we can figure it out," he rushed, at last running out of bullets. Beside him, the mayor clutched his arm with clammy hands.

"You can get me out of here, right?" Terror-filled eyes examined the siren, pawing at Kane's arm like a needy dog.

Shrugging off the mayor's grip, Kane nodded before focusing on the hounds. "Stay behind me. Don't let anything sneak up on us."

More beasts funneled into the cathedral, Alaric inching his way forward toward the duo protecting the mayor.

"Hand him over, and this all ends now. No one else has to die," their leader shouted, his hounds ripping apart the decorations and slashing wildly at nearby innocents. It didn't take long until screams turned to murmuring cries, blood pooling around mangled bodies. Those that managed to survive the first strike huddled in corners, cowering before the creatures in their midst.

"Let me go," Melinda spat.

Alaric pressed the gun harder into her temple, her teeth bared and ready for a fight. Her hands strained against an unseen force, as though magic kept her pinned in place.

Kane studied the room, plotting as quickly as he could. Taking a deep breath, he knew there was only one option that would hopefully ensure their survival. "As soon as I start to sing, I need you all to *run*."

The mayor grimaced at him, silently mouthing the word *'sing'* in confusion. *Melinda must not have told him what I am,* he thought. Tara nodded, grabbing ahold of the man's arm.

"Ready?"

Taking in a sharp breath, Kane said a silent prayer to Caelus before sending a protective barrier around the few remaining survivors. Parting his lips, soft tenor melodies embedded themselves into the hellhounds' minds, ensuring euphoric disaster. All movement stopped, chomping jowls ceasing as their eyes glazed over in a haze.

Tara and Kane pulled the mayor toward the exit, hellhounds scattered along the ground in shivering pain. Still clutching a gun to Melinda's head, Alaric didn't seem to react like the rest. Instead, he appeared to be in more of a trance than howling affliction.

Drawing her head forward, Melinda delivered a harsh blow that sent him stumbling back. It seemed to pull him from his trance early, attention locking in on those trying to escape. Inches from the door, weaving through lines of convulsing beasts, the sounds of wild gunshots made Kane stall. A final bullet released, the mayor stumbling to the ground with Melinda not far behind.

Just as Kane's feet were about to hit the stairs leading outside, he turned. Medill reached for them, face contorted in pain and hands clawing at the ground. Alaric effortlessly pulled him back inside just as surrounding beasts regained their conscious minds.

The mayor's screams echoed through the hall, Melinda's muffed cry almost completely masked as she sank to the ground. Peering down, they both realized her emerald gown was slowly turning crimson. Kane darted toward her as hounds inched closer and closer, ready to feast.

"Just go!"

"Like hell we're leaving you!" He picked her up, sprinting back toward the door with Death not far behind.

A beast managed to get a hold of her dress, dragging them back toward the masses. Kane's fingers gripped hers, suddenly finding himself in a game of tug-of-war with Melinda's life on the line.

"Caelus, a little help?" His prayers were met with a sudden burst of wind, the force pushing their attackers away allowing him to secure her in his arms.

Tara and Kane didn't waste any time, sprinting toward the Chicago Orphan Asylum. Peering down on occasion, he watched as Melinda faded in and out of consciousness.

"Hang in there, Melinda. We'll get you home," Kane panted.

Up ahead, Tara flagged down a passing carriage. Jumping inside, the siren laid Melinda down to begin his soft, healing song. Though without his full concentration, it didn't seem to work properly. No matter how hard he tried, his mind raced back to the sound of Winnie's voice, echoing through him like an alarm. Tara hung out of the window, urging the driver to go faster.

"I guess my family is cursed after all. Maybe…I'll see my uncle. And Wes…Sooner than I thought," she whispered.

"Don't you dare say that! I need you to hang on!" he ordered, scooping her up and exiting the carriage.

Barreling through the door, they were safe at last behind the wards of the building. Their sudden arrival drew out nearby residents, guests and workers alike. Still carrying Melinda, Kane raced up the stairs toward the portal.

"I'm taking her to Milicent! Warn the others," he bellowed, Tara nodding before stepping onto the porch.

From the third floor, rushed steps raced toward him. Miss Leona waited by the portal, eyes widening at the sight of Melinda unconscious in his arms.

"Is…she okay? Kane!"

"She will be, but I have to go," he yelled, pushing through the mirror toward Fox Manor for proper healing.

—◦((●●))◦—

TARA

Stepping onto the porch, Tara thought: *Warn the others.* She repeated it over and over in her mind, wondering where Thoren and Ezra could be. *Did they hear the gunshots? Do they even know we're in danger?*

A full-bodied chill ran through her, not just from the winter winds but also from the silhouette posted just across the street. Staring at her. Though the beast's face was covered by darkness, she was almost certain who it was without even having to check.

"Why don't you come on out, little fawn?"

"What do you want?" Reloading her gun, she was ready to fire.

"I just want to talk," Alaric purred, arms up over his head in submission as he stepped into the light.

His dark attire allowed him to blend into the surrounding areas, the light barely illuminating that disastrously handsome physique. The pale blue eyes, examining her carefully. A jawline that could kill, and perfectly plump lips that could talk anyone into doing his bidding. Taking in the sight of him, she couldn't help but

73

think: *If he's as evil as everyone says he is, why does he have to be so damn pretty?*

"You shot my friend. Why should I talk to you?" she spat, aiming her pistol straight for the chest.

"That's all you're mad about? Hm. My target was the mayor. I promise, I didn't mean to hit her. Is she alright?" His voice was softer than she'd expected.

"Like you give a damn!" Tara fired a warning shot at his feet, inching toward him.

He didn't flinch, as if knowing she hadn't planned on actually shooting him. "Plucky little thing, aren't you? Well if you won't talk to me, I might as well leave. I have some business to attend to."

Alaric began to saunter off into the shadows, unphased by the gun pointed at his back. She shot another warning, this time nicking his ear. *Perfect aim,* she thought with pride.

"Take one more step, and the next bullet will come out between your eyes. Or I can think of some other nasty places I can aim for instead. Say, how long can a man survive with a bullet to the..."

Alaric spun around, silencing her with a scowl. Reaching for his ear, he pulled his hand back to reveal glimmering red. "And here I thought you wouldn't shoot me," he hissed.

Only a few feet away from the beast, she demanded, "Where is Medill? Return him now!"

"He's not who you think he is," he began, closing the gap between them.

Though she was tall, he seemed to loom over her like a nightmarish prince, the necklace around her throat glowing in warning. Tara was all too aware of what this man was capable of.

"And who exactly is he? Last I checked, you're not one to judge a man," she grumbled, her heart beating thunderously in her chest.

Mere inches away, he pushed the barrel into his forehead with a sudden arrogant smile. "You won't shoot me."

"Try me," she spat, cheeks flushing before cocking the gun.

Something in his eyes stirred. She watched them trail her body, a sort of animalistic playfulness she wasn't expecting.

"You know, you look a bit like a cupcake in that dress," he mumbled, tugging on the laces along her shoulders before stealing one of the roses pinned to her skirt. A trail of cherry red sullied her lilac gown, as if marking her for his own sick amusement. "I liked you better in that alluring little costume you wore on Samhain. The antlers really did it for me."

"You have no business thinking of me at all, beast!" Pushing the barrel harder into his skin, he only seemed to respond with an even wider, wolfish grin.

"Tara?" The sound of Ezra's voice pulled her attention away from the hellhound leader.

"Until we meet again, little fawn," he crooned, putting the stem of her stolen rose between his teeth and turning to his wolf form. Before her friends could see him, the creature disappeared into the darkness

Clearing her throat, Tara's heart finally ceased its chaotic thumping. Her hands shook, cheeks flushed with anger still reeling from his snide comments.

"What are you doing out here?" Ezra called, arriving with Thoren at his side.

"We need to get to the manor. Melinda's been shot!"

"We heard gunshots, and came running. I had a feeling it was too good to be true since we didn't see anything where we were at," Thoren muttered.

Tara's friends ran ahead of her. Just as she was about to enter the orphanage, a startling howl commanded attention. Turning, she saw him. Alaric with his glittering blue eyes. The beast waiting down the street, just watching. As though he'd found his next meal.

7

WINIFRED
LOCATION UNKNOWN

If there was one thing Winnie knew for certain, it was that some sort of instinct kicked in when the threat of danger took hold. A voice in her head whispered, *"Take a deep breath."* With mere seconds to oblige, she sucked in as much oxygen as she could before landing somewhere deep, dark, and cold.

Salty water stung Winnie's eyes, a strange overbearing weight pushing her further down. A murky abyss threatened to swallow her whole, panic coursing through her when she couldn't take a deep breath in.

Paddling through the water, she tried desperately to swim toward what she hoped was the surface. The ballgown wrapped itself around her legs like a noose. Shimmering lights twinkled in the distance, but there was no way she'd make it in time. The darkness broke slightly, small rays of moonlight fluttering up above.

Slowly making her way up, the seconds that passed left like a lifetime. With screaming muscles, she pushed as hard as she could but it didn't seem to be enough. Instinct took over, struggling against the currents that threatened to take her life.

Flailing arms fought their way forward, but it was useless. *I can't move fast enough,* she thought, paddling to no avail. Keeping calm didn't seem to be an option as Death's glimmering outline appeared just out of reach.

"Elements! Why send me here just to kill me?" Winnie cried out, hoping they could hear her. Not a single sound whispered from either of the deities as though they enjoyed watching her struggle.

Off in the distance, something darted. Approaching at a speed she'd never seen before, Winnie's stomach twisted in knots as her vision spotted. *All this work just to get eaten by a shark,* she thought cynically. Some primal instinct kicked in, diving away from the creature. It was unclear which option was better: continue to the top or attempt to swim away. A muffled scream barely escaped her realizing she didn't have time to figure it out.

Reaching for weapons, the gun slipped from her hands. *Not that it would do me much good down here anyways,* she panicked. Moving aside layers and layers of fabric, she realized her dagger was no longer sheathed to her thigh. A full-bodied force slammed into Winnie, grasping her elbow firmly. It took her a moment to realize it was dragging them both toward the surface.

With burning lungs and blurry vision, she felt the sea caving in on her. The urge to inhale almost overtook her, too close to accepting Death's awaiting kiss. *Almost there,* she thought, though truthfully she didn't know if that was true.

The surrounding chill subsided, feeling weightless as the pain in her lungs turned softer with near euphoric bliss. Seconds. That's how long she had before losing consciousness. With only moments to spare, her head speared through the surface of the water, vision tunneling back as she gasped desperately for air.

Fighting the treacherous currents, Winnie finally looked at her savior. Expecting to see someone resembling Afissa, utter shock awaited as a pair of dark, coal eyes stared back at her. Unnaturally round and larger than usual, they looked her over in a sort of unexpected concern. Short stubble and gray skin peppered with dark spots covered the creature's body. Below the surface, Winnie couldn't see much of its tail, but it was clearly not one of the merfolk. *That means this creature can only be one other thing...*

"Get away from me!" Winnie wheezed, attempting to paddle away.

"Shh, calm down." A soothing, trance-inducing voice sat on the other end of the lulls.

Fighting the pacifying melodies, she continued in the opposite direction. "I've heard horror stories of your kind! I don't care to know why you saved me. I'm sure it was just to eat me!"

A sudden wave crashed, sending her right back toward the female without any luck of escaping. Her strange savior only chuckled, turning her head to the side to examine the odd little witch who'd gotten herself lost in the middle of the ocean.

"I'm not going to eat you. Despite what you may believe, most selkies don't like the taste of humans. We prefer shellfish."

Winnie eyed her sideways, still unsure what to think.

"There's no boats around for miles. I don't really understand where you came from. Can you try to calm down so I can get you to safety?" Thin lips curved into an inviting smile, revealing a set of fangs ready to tear into flesh.

With a sigh of frustration, Winnie turned back toward the selkie. "Where the hell am I?"

"Miles and miles from shore. You'd never make it swimming. Especially in that dress," she said with a smirk.

Though she hesitated to confide in the creature, she knew that her only option was to cooperate. "I need to get to Freedom's Fortress or Marvivia."

"Even with my speed, we'd never make it to the fortress. Marvivia is close by, however. How do you know of its existence? They've kept it a secret from people like you."

Winnie hesitated, unsure how to answer. At last, she deflected. "What's your name?"

"Brenna," the selkie replied, the words still purring from her mouth as smooth as silk.

There was a moment when neither woman spoke, both eyeing each other carefully. Winnie couldn't quite make up her mind. Though she didn't have much of a choice, trusting a selkie after the tales she'd heard growing up didn't seem like a wise idea.

"And you? One usually offers their own name in response." A dry laugh escaped the selkie, wading in the water before her.

"Winnie."

"I can get you to Marvivia if that's where you need to be," Brenna offered, nervous eyes looking down below the surface. "Think you can hold your breath for a while?"

"You…want to take me down there?" A nervous gulp followed.

"Don't worry, I swim fast. Their buildings have air. You'll be fine, I promise." Reaching for Winnie, she seemed to sense the continued hesitation.

Eyes widened in fear, she asked, "How do I know you'll actually take me there?"

"Guess you'll just have to trust me." With a lazy shrug, Brenna floated onto her back leisurely. "If I wanted to kill you, I would've done it already."

"Aren't the selkies and mermaids at war?" Winnie asked, thinking back to the tales Afissa told her growing up.

"We are." Sad eyes examined the wide open ocean before focusing again. "I'd offer to take you to my home, but thanks to the mermaids, I don't have one."

Sudden guilt stirred in Winnie's chest, feeling remorse for something unknown. "And you swear that you…*don't*…eat people?" *I'm almost afraid of the answer,* she thought.

"No," she grumbled, clearly growing tired of the constant distrust. "One last thing: I'm going to drop you off. I obviously can't stay."

Winnie nodded, taking a few deep breaths. She tried to look below the surface, though couldn't see anything past the fabric of her dress ballooning around her legs.

"When you get down there, ask for Oslind. *Only* speak to him. Don't mention my name to anyone else," Brenna warned.

Glancing at the selkie sideways, Winnie's mind began to wander. *How would a mermaid and a selkie know each other?*

"I know it's hard, but we have to trust each other right now. You're putting a lot of faith in me to get you down there without drowning. I'm trusting you to never utter my name near anyone other than him. Got it?"

Winnie contemplated a moment, peering around the ocean one last time. There truly was sod all around; not an island or boat. Nothing. At last she nodded. Taking Brenna's outstretched hand, the selkie offered her a delicate smile. *So human,* she thought, *one could almost mistake it for harmless.*

After one last final inhale, the selkie took off underwater. Clinging to her body, Winnie held on as tight as she could. Shutting her eyes to fight back the sting of pelting salt water, she could only pray that she'd make it to a place with air in time.

Brenna moved faster than Winnie expected. Like a bullet from a gun, the selkie moved with such swiftness it was almost enough to make her insides feel like outsides. *Not even Afissa swims this fast,* she thought as the lack of oxygen once again nipped at her lungs. Traveling toward the bottom, Winnie's chest tightened and back muscles spasmed. Her body craved air like an addict, ready to release and take that final breath.

Just as she was about to give into temptation, her body catapulted through a strange gelatinous substance that somehow didn't stick to her body. The selkie threw her like a javelin into what could only be described as a thick, shimmering wall. As Winnie opened her eyes carefully, she realized she was seated on the floor of a pub, the pearl-like doorway she'd just passed through behind her.

The entire room's walls and floors mimicked the coloring

of abalone shells. Shimmering browns, greens, and blues shone beautifully amongst glowing white lights that illuminated the bar. Seaweed and greenery decorated the place, along with seashells and the occasional large fish skeleton.

Coughing and gagging, Winnie attempted to take a deep breath. With a pounding head and seizing muscles, the fabric of her dress weighed heavily on her, feeling like a sack of bricks strapped to her legs.

It didn't take long before the members of the underwater pub surrounded her with weapons pulled and aimed at her throat. She glanced down at a shimmering blade, the handle decorated with swirling seashells and corals. If it weren't pointed at her artery, she may have stopped to admire it.

The faces staring down reminded her so much of Afissa. Though their features varied greatly, they all shared the same shimmering scales lining their angelic skin. If their hair wasn't milky white, it was deep charcoal, often matching the tone of their skin.

"Name?" One of the merfolk dug the tip of his blade into her neck.

Shivering, Winnie stuttered. Unable to form a single word, the pain coursing through her body continued to build and build. *It feels like my brain may implode,* she thought helplessly.

"You're not a mermaid. What the hell are you doing down at the bottom of the ocean?" one of the females asked, crouching down to inspect her carefully.

Winnie's eyes darted between the mermaids as they surrounded her, unsure how to answer their questions. They only peppered her with additional inquiries, more and more weapons exposing themselves the longer she stalled.

"What's your business?" another barked.

"Freedom's Fortress," she stammered, finally able to form some kind of answer.

In unison, the mermaids scoffed. A few even laughed at her.

"Headed in the wrong direction, aren't you?"

At last, Winnie's mind cleared enough to think back to Brenna's words. "I need to speak with Oslind! It's urgent!"

Of all the people that surrounded her, only one still sat at the bar cupping a drink in hand. She could see his shoulders tense at the mention of that name, slowly turning around to examine the intruder in their midst.

"What the fuck do you want with me?" His tone was harsher than she expected, quite the contrast to the selkie who'd just saved her life. The man slouched back onto the bar lazily, eyeing her with careful consideration.

"I…need your help. Can I speak to you privately?" Her voice was a mere squeak, looking around at the others nervously.

The group of mermaids backed off, lowering their weapons before a few snickered and walked toward the fair-haired man that now stalked toward her. Oslind shook his head in distaste, finishing his drink before setting the glass down on a nearby table.

"I don't help wet rats," he grumbled, standing just before her.

"Fine. If you won't speak with me, then I need to see Afissa. Tell her a member of the Fox family needs to talk to her." Attempting to get up, Oslind pushed her back down only to be tangled by the wet evening gown still pinning her with unnecessary weight.

"She's away on official business," Oslind began, eyes narrowing in on her. "How do you know my mother?"

It took her a moment to respond, suddenly seeing the uncanny resemblance. Pearly white hair tousled around his shoulders with a slight curl just as Afissa's always did. Glittering teal eyes scanned the area every so often. Though, his mother had a warmer demeanor about her.

"She knows my family," Winnie tried to explain. "If she's your mum, surely you've heard her mention the Fox family? Milicent and Ernest?"

Oslind shook his head. "I'll handle this one," he said, waving away the few mermaids that still stood with weapons ready. Dragging her to a standing position, his grip on her arm was just a little too tight.

"Have fun," one of the armed mermaids crooned before having a seat at the bar.

"You better start making some sense, or I'm throwing you into the ocean. Trust me, I'll gladly watch the nearby sharks tear your body limb from limb if I don't like your answer. Unless you'd rather take a stab at the kraken." Oslind's voice was a low grumble.

She gulped, surprised by his aggression. Of all people to be kind-hearted Afissa's son, she hadn't expected *him.* "I met your friend…"

His attention darted toward nearby merfolk, nervously shifting from one leg to the other with a sudden urgency she didn't quite understand. "Fine. But you'll have to hold your breath again."

"Please, no. I don't think I can do another swim," Winnie whined as he pulled her toward the door.

"You can't stay here! My place isn't far. It'll be quick, I promise." He waved at the bartender, then at the others. "Deep breath."

Once again, Winnie was being dragged through the water, utterly helpless. She needed to figure something out and fast. *How the hell do the Elements think I can manage this mission without any way of breathing underwater?*

Oslind's swim was much slower than Brenna's. The water didn't sting quite as much against her closed eyes, the pressure a little less agitating this time. He pushed her through another opening before falling onto a different floor. Gasping for air, the salt water burned her throat. The mermaid peered through one of the windows, pulling down the shades to ensure privacy.

"Brenna caught you, did she?" His voice was different than it had been at the bar.

"Yes," Winnie managed to choke out. Once again, her muscles

simmered violently beneath her skin. Different than Aelius's fire that coursed through her, they seemed to cramp and bubble, her head dizzy as the room spun.

"Who the fuck are you? You can't just come barreling into the bar asking for me. It makes the others suspicious. We're in the middle of a war."

Winnie tried to explain, but the words wouldn't form. She clutched her pounding head, a ringing in her ears from the suffocating pressure surrounding her.

Oslind groaned, walking to her side and placing a hand on her forehead. Within moments, Winnie's body ceased burning and a warm sense of euphoria spread over her. As he perched in front of her, she couldn't help but notice the shimmer of his dark teal eyes, deep and rich like Afissa's.

"Get changed first. Then maybe we can talk." He pointed to a door at the end of what looked like an underwater flat.

The room's walls and floors were similar to the bar, the shimmering of abalone shell offering a strange peaceful serenity. Though there wasn't much furniture, there was at least a set of sofas for lounging, as well as a bed and bathroom at the back. There was no kitchen or eating area as far as she could tell, but stacks of books and weapons were piled along the corners.

Clutching her shivering sides, she asked, "You have women's clothes here?"

"Mhm, don't ask," he mumbled, taking a seat on the sofa before picking up one of the many scattered works of literature. As she passed, he pointed at a small dresser just beside the large double bed. "Bottom drawer. All the way in the back."

Pulling out a pair of tight pants and loose men's shirt, she scowled. "Not what I had in mind when I thought of women's clothes."

"I'll get you a wetsuit tomorrow. It'll have to do for tonight." His eyes remained fixed to the book in hand, almost ignoring her as she entered the bathroom to change. After dressing quickly and wringing her hair of excess moisture, she joined him on the couch.

"Explain. Now." The words came out cold and demanding, brows scrunched in distaste.

"I'm here to help out in the war," she began, though he interrupted her.

"Our war?"

"Maybe the human one? I'm not sure. I think I need to get to Freedom's Fortress." Leaning forward, she pulled her sopping wet hair into a tight bun. Stealing a nearby blanket, she pulled it around her trembling body.

"You're miles from shore. You'll never make it there without drowning," he said with a lazy shrug. "I'm still not even sure how you knew about us in the first place."

"Our families are close. That's how I knew of Marvivia. But I think I'm meant to go back to help the humans. I'm just not sure…" She closed her eyes, thinking of the thick leather-bound book the Elements had given her. It appeared on her lap, both of them equally surprised by its sudden appearance.

"Are you a witch?" The words seemed to slither from his mouth in discomfort.

"Yes," she said at last, placing her branded hand over the emblem on the cover.

The pages turned, flipping back to the same entry she'd read previously. There was no additional information other than the date and two names: Marvivia and Freedom's Fortress. The nickname Fort Monroe received during the Civil War had only recently been added, shortly before her date with Kane. Now, she couldn't help but wonder what in the world it meant.

"Is it 1861?"

"No, it's 1837. You can call me the little mermaid," he scoffed. When she looked at him in confusion, he clarified. "Yes, it's 1861. How could it be anything else?"

"Well…"

"You must never tell anyone you're from the future," the Elements hissed, sending punishing electric shocks through her body.

Clutching her ears, she waited for the ringing to subside. Oslind only looked at her in concern, wide-eyed. *He must think I'm an absolute lunatic,* she thought.

"Still feeling the pressure from the water? There's a few other remedies we can try if needed," he offered.

"I'm fine, sorry. There's a lot I can't explain. I just…need to get to Fort Monroe," she repeated, her mind muddled and waiting for the ringing to cease.

"Once again – there's no way you're getting there. Not with my help anyways."

Turning her head to the side, Winnie thought about her strange selkie savior. "Can Brenna get me there?"

"Let's not mention her name anywhere in this city. Ever. Selkies aren't exactly welcome in Marvivia," he rushed, as if urging her to keep her voice down.

"How *does* a mermaid become friends with a selkie?" she asked playfully, realizing she was making him nervous.

"No one knows about…her." He averted his gaze. It took a moment before Winnie realized his shoulders were slouched forward, making him look sad for once.

"Women's clothes and a girl you can't tell anyone about? Are you two?"

He never let her finish her question. "No. But for her sake *and* mine, keep any knowledge of her to yourself. Got it? Or else, we'll have to revisit the whole shark thing again."

She nodded silently, trying to hide a smirk.

"Truthfully, I don't know how to help you. You don't seem to understand why you're here. Somehow you managed to get to the bottom of the ocean, but can't get back up again. Is there anything about you that makes sense?" Oslind stood, rubbing the back of his head.

"I'm sorry. This is all so confusing…"

"Why don't you get some rest? We can figure it out in the morning. The pressure from the water can really mess with your head if you're not careful," he suggested.

She nodded, grateful to have a safe place to sleep for the night. Looking around his room, she asked, "Where will I…"

"You can sleep on the couch. I'm not gentlemanly enough to give you my bed," he rushed.

Winnie chuckled before mumbling, "Fair enough."

Offering her a set of blankets and pillows, Winnie made herself comfortable. With heavy eyes, she was more ready for rest than she'd realized. Wading through treacherous waters had taken more out of her than she thought possible. Not to mention the actual jump itself.

As she lay on the small couch, her mind crawled back to Kane. Glancing at the moonstone ring wrapped around her middle finger, she couldn't help but yearn for him. *I need to figure out my purpose, and fast. So I can get back to my time, and help them escape the cathedral,* she thought.

She clung to their memories together while drifting to sleep, picturing his soft lips along her own. Wishing the couch that pushed up against her back was actually his body instead. It didn't take long before she was asleep, surrounded by hazy images of Chicago and the hellhounds.

8

KANE
FOX MANOR - 1871

Unable to pull himself from a trance, Kane sat hunched forward on one of the sofas in Fox Manor's sunroom. Across from him, Milicent and Ernest worked steadily on Melinda, pads of bloodied cotton strewn along the ground. A metallic stench and sharp sting of cleaning alcohol clung to the air, overwhelming his senses. Cricket's paws tapped just in front of the door, panting with excitement as Tara, Ezra, and Thoren barreled through.

"Deja vu?" Milicent mumbled, dabbing at the gunshot wound in the young woman's side.

Melinda lay on the cot, clutching the edges with a grimace wearing bloomers and a loose shirt. Between sharp inhales, she managed to chuckle and mumbled, "At least I'm awake this time."

"Kane's song started to work, but the bullet stopped his magic from healing you all the way. I can take care of that no problem." Ernest squinted as he reached a telekinetic hand toward the tiny bit of metal that managed to cause so much pain and destruction.

Kane focused on Thoren, only to return his gaze to the floor where it had been glued since he got back.

"What's wrong, brother? Why aren't you over there healing her?"

"I don't know, I tried. Didn't work," Kane muttered, rocking in his seat. Covering his face, the images of Winnie disappearing played on repeat in his mind.

"Want me to finish what he started?" he offered, checking on Melinda.

She shook her head. "I'll be fine. Save your magic for someone who needs it."

Thoren glanced around the room, brows furrowed in confusion. "Where's Winnie?"

"I don't know." Kane's hands muffled the sound.

"Snap out of it!" His brother grasped him by the shoulders, commanding attention. "What *do* you know? Right now you look like a blubbering idiot!"

Ezra joined them, placing a hand on his love's back before gently guiding him away. Crouching before the panicked siren, his soft features coaxed a response. "Did she get attacked by the hounds?"

"No, she just disappeared," Kane said with a heavy exhale. "One minute she said 'they' were taking her, the next she was gone." *It feels like everyone's eyes are piercing into me,* he thought.

"You're not making any sense," Ezra muttered softly, offering a surprisingly calming stroke along his back.

"I know I'm not. I don't know how to make sense of this. One minute she was there and then 'poof.' It was like she was never with us in the first place." His frustration continued to bubble up inside, every stare and glance sending speers of doubt.

"She's fine," Milicent added softly, stitching up the last bits of Melinda's wound and applying a healing ointment.

"How would you know?" Getting up from his seat, arms crossed over his chest, Kane approached Winnie's mother.

"I can't give you as much information as you likely wish, but I can tell you she's okay. I don't have all the answers, but I was asked to simply relay that message. She's being rather naive right now, bordering on stupid, but she's at least alive." Her face pinched in dismay as she explained.

"You knew something would happen, and you didn't warn

us?" His voice boomed across the room, threatening to rattle the windows as Caelus's powers swirled through his body.

Ernest stepped between the young siren and his wife, placing a daring hand between them. "Watch how you speak to my wife." His visage turned dark, a sight Kane had rarely seen since knowing the Fox family.

"You'll come to learn, my dear, that Fate has other plans. Just because I am clairvoyant, doesn't mean I'm at liberty to tell every living soul what will happen. Besides, Destiny is a tricky thing. Even if I'd said something, everything would've worked out the same way. There's no use," she huffed, patting Melinda's shoulder and helping her up.

"She doesn't even tell me everything, and I'm her damn husband," Ernest grumbled, taking a seat on one of the loveseats by the window.

"Take these," she added softly, handing Melinda some vials of healing ointment. "Apply that salve regularly, and you should feel much better by morning."

The young woman nodded in quiet thanks before moving to put on a proper shirt at last.

Kane opened his mouth, ready to put up a fight for the information he couldn't live without. Milicent held up a commanding hand mere inches from his face as if to shun him entirely.

"I'm done discussing this with you. Winnie's fine, that's all you need to know. When she's done with whatever it is she's doing, she'll come back. We must pray to the Gods that she doesn't get herself killed in the process. She knows what she's doing."

Walking toward the stairs, Ernest's sad eyes glanced between the young group of friends. He didn't say a word, only seemed to carry a cloud of sadness with him as they exited the sunroom.

Winnie told me she was safe... She lied to me. Again, Kane thought, mind once again racing.

"We need to get the mayor back," Melinda began through clenched teeth, pulling a bag over her shoulder with a wince.

"How much do you know about him?" Tara took a seat beside Ezra. She squirmed with a tight frown, trying to move the bustle of her dress aside to allow for more comfort. Tugging at the bottom of her corset, she eventually sighed and stood instead. When Melinda didn't say anything, only glancing at her in confusion, Tara continued. "What if he's not who we thought he is?"

"Why are you asking this?" Thoren raised a brow in suspicion.

"I...I'm just curious. The townspeople talk..."

"No, that's not it. We haven't spoken to anyone besides those in this room. The Tara I've come to know and loathe always says things for a reason. She doesn't just mutter words at random. *Why* are you asking?" Pacing toward her, he leaned down to make direct eye contact.

Cricket stood from his leisurely spot, only to growl at Thoren in warning.

"Loathe?" The reds of her cheeks heated in anger, fists balled at her sides.

"Ease up, Thor. There were others in Chicago that wondered about his allegiance, remember?" Ezra wedged himself between the siren and the redhead.

"Suppose next you'll tell me that I look like a cupcake, too," she muttered.

Kane's attention snagged onto her words, joining his brother's side. "Cupcake?"

"Long story..."

"No matter what, we need to find him. I made a promise that I'd protect the mayor," Melinda chimed in, one hand on the door handle and the other placed on her hip in annoyance.

"You just focus on healing," Thoren insisted, following behind her. "We – as in the rest of us – can look for him tomorrow. For now, you – as in just you – need to go home and rest. Give yourself some time to recuperate. We can't have one of our best fighters on the sidelines again."

Melinda seemed to flinch at his words, her eyes revealing a hidden truth that Kane couldn't quite put his finger on.

"Fine," was all she said before heading toward the portal.

"I'll escort her back. See you upstairs," Ezra mumbled, following after the young woman with hurried steps.

"Remember when Kane said you were insufferable? In the past I may have stood up for you, but lately I think he's right. How Winnie ever had a crush on you, I'll never understand," Tara hissed, whistling for Cricket to follow her upstairs toward her room.

Thoren rolled his eyes, glancing toward his brother. "Milicent said she's fine. Quit your worrying."

"Something doesn't feel right. I can sense that she's in danger," Kane mumbled, rubbing his temples feverishly.

"You heard what I told Melinda. Tonight, we just need rest. We can figure it out tomorrow. I trust Milicent when she says her own daughter is alright. You should too." With that, he patted Kane on the back before heading up to his own room.

Rest? Not sure how I could possibly do that when I don't even know where she is, Kane thought with a grumbling yawn. But alas, tired feet carried him to his room in hopes that perhaps he could get a little bit of shut eye before he'd inevitably wake again in a few short hours.

9

WINIFRED
MARVIVIA - 1861

Pacing impatiently with chattering teeth from the frigid cold, Winnie's mind raced back to her friends in Chicago. Afissa's son woke up before her, long gone several hours later. The only sign he'd left behind was a wetsuit, a strange sponge-like bread, and water left out on a table. She'd slept fitfully that night, waking every few hours in a panicked cold sweat, wishing to escape the strange dream she was living. Strange phantom songs appeared in her dreams, unsettled by their haunting tunes.

The bread wasn't much, but it was at least something to stave her biting hunger. As Winnie munched on it, she couldn't help but wonder why Afissa never mentioned Oslind throughout their years of knowing one another. *She never talked about her husband either,* she realized. The notion was strange given how open her 'aunt' had always been with the Fox family.

Examining the wetsuit at last, she thought it was odd that the texture and overall look was different than most. The typical uniform consisted of tight brown pants and a fitted top; often a corset for the feminine figures. It mimicked the shimmer of abalone shells, just like the walls and floors of most establishments. *They must really like teal and brown,* she thought, glancing around the room.

The suit in front of her was the opposite; darker than what she was used to. Rather than smooth and silky, the outer fabric was rough and mimicked igneous rock. A soft citrus glow radiated from under panels placed along vital organs, giving off heat the closer her hands crept. As she pulled on the skin tight outfit, a sudden warmth enveloped her body, and she was comfortable along the bottom of the sea at last.

After dressing, Winnie glanced out the window to marvel at the city. Oslind and Brenna had dragged her too quickly to even attempt opening her eyes underwater, the salt ensuring a constant sting. At least from his flat, she could see some of the submerged metropolis in all its beauty.

The merfolk's living pods were different than she'd expected. Most of the structures were made of coral on the outside, with windows and portal-like doors shimmering ivory like pearls. Though the material was hard beneath her touch, everything seemed to move and shift with the tides that pushed the city back and forth gently all day long.

Just before the largest structure in Marvivia, a gargantuan statue stood of a woman with a halo of spikes behind her head. The ever-so-recognizable trident sat in her hands as though she protected the citizens of Marvivia.

Between dwellings and establishments, the sandy floors were scattered with tiny sea creatures, coral reefs, plants, and mermaids. Children played while the adults worked, trained, or stood guard along the outskirts. The bottom of the ocean was rich with life, very few places uninhabited until the outer limits of the city gave way. Only the deep, dark ocean waited beyond. Glittering orbs of white light were scattered about, illuminating the reach of the city, driving away most of the larger creatures that occasionally sulked in the abyss.

Despite Marvivia's beauty, Winnie found herself realizing this underwater community was quite terrifying. Gigantic squid, sharks, and other predators swam through on occasion, guided away by patrols to keep the city safe. They were the kinds of monsters she'd only read about in books, hoping to never encounter the sticky tentacles or snapping jaws of oversized monstrosities.

When she was done admiring the world beyond, Winnie released a deep sigh of frustration. *I hate feeling trapped like this. I can't leave even if I wanted to,* she thought, her mind stuck on her friends back home in need. Glancing down at Kane's ring, she wondered: *Do they even know I'm gone? I don't know how all of this works…*

Taking a seat on the floor, Winnie called for the leather-bound book. Flipping through its pages for likely the hundredth time that day, she wondered if she'd missed something. An unknown language was still scribbled throughout, unwilling to reveal its secrets to her.

"Fine," she huffed out loud to the empty room. "If this can't help me, I'll call on them, myself."

Winnie closed her eyes, picturing the Elements before her. Wondering who would respond first, she thought of the nagging heat that lay dormant beneath her skin, and thought perhaps Aelius would be a good place to start. Pleading for an audience, she waited.

"I know you can hear me. You're always around," she whispered begrudgingly. When nothing happened, she shifted her focus. "Fine. If not Aelius, then Gali?"

In her mind's eye, she visualized the elements swirling around each of the deities as they had the day she'd met them face to face. A small tug sat on the other end of her prayers. Allowing her essence to float above, Winnie left her physical body behind and opened her eyes to a surrounding darkness.

"Hello?" she called out, still seeing no one. *This doesn't feel like Oblivion,* she thought curiously, wondering where the hell she'd traveled to now.

For a few moments, eerie silence waited for her. The feeling of others watching from a distance, unwilling to speak, made her skin crawl. After a short wait, Gali appeared at last. The tentacles of an octopus lay behind her this time, wrapped around her navy blue body as her seaweed hair lay across one shoulder. The same ivory eyes that looked Winnie over only a month before examined her curiously now.

"You called?" For once, the goddess didn't look stoic as a small smirk graced her lips.

"I need help…"

"You are meant to figure out these missions on your own. I cannot help you. Nor can Aelius." Her exterior turned icy, the waves encompassing her body stirring anxiously.

"If you can't help, why did you come?"

Gali paused, lowering her head with a thoughtful nod. Her seriousness broke more, though uneasy eyes peered at the darkness as though those same entities Winnie felt were still looking. Raising her hands above her head, the goddess created a dome of ice, blocking out nosey intruders.

"Why are you being so cryptic? Will you help me or not?" Though in the past, Winnie would never have dreamed of speaking to an Element in this way, she was beginning to realize forwardness worked better with them.

"There is something bigger going on that you know nothing about, Winifred. These events have been in motion for centuries. Across time and dimensions, many have schemed for longer than you can imagine. I can only do so much. They cannot think I've overstepped my bounds," Gali explained, stepping closer and lowering her voice.

"Are you talking about the other Elements?"

Gali shook her head, refusing to answer.

Across dimensions? Winnie wondered. *How many are there?* "How do I get to Freedom's Fortress from here? I have no way of traveling without being able to breathe underwater," she asked.

"I cannot say. But I will tell you to think of your past. Use the knowledge you possess of your family to guide you." A gentle hand lay rested on Winnie's shoulder as the soft words escaped the goddess.

Winnie scoffed. "That doesn't help me at all."

"You must ask the right questions."

"I heard the four of you say that I can't tell anyone I'm from the future," she began.

Gali nodded, pacing before her.

"What do I do when I'm recognized? Surely Afissa will know me when she sees me. Or will at least suspect something fishy is going on. No pun intended." Winnie crossed her arms, waiting for something useful.

"Ah, now that's something I can help with," she said with a smile, materializing a small necklace in the palm of her outstretched hand.

Winnie glanced down at the golden scallop hanging from a dangling chain. As she pulled it over her head, a wave of energy passed through her.

"When you wear this, no one will recognize you. It will help you remain undercover. Both for this time and your future. Not even your parents will know it's you."

"My parents? They aren't here," she started to say, though the goddess seemed to offer a knowing nod. Gali circled her as though she were waiting for more questions. Winnie's mind could only ramble on, thinking of everything and nothing all at once. "*Why am I here?*"

"To ensure the balance between the magic and the common worlds remains intact. You should recall our conversation from your deal." Rolling her eyes, Winnie noted the surprise amount of humanity suddenly glistening throughout the goddess.

"I don't know how my presence here can impact that balance. It doesn't make sense!" She groaned, rubbing her temples as a lingering headache formed.

"What was your biggest concern before Boudicca attacked on Samhain?" Gali folded her arms across her chest, waves sloshing around her torso.

"We were outnumbered. We only had Lycan and Afissa's people couldn't..." Her words trailed off as the pieces slowly clicked together.

Gali nodded with excitement.

"Am I here to secure an alliance with them? Surely that's not all there is to it." Winnie cocked her head to the side curiously, awaiting more clues.

"That and so much more. You'll see," she beamed.

"If I secure an alliance, wouldn't they have helped us when we asked in October?" *Trying to figure out these timelines and rules is making my head spin,* she thought.

"Your mother and father asked. But *you* are the one that will secure the alliance. *You* will do what's necessary to ensure they help your family in the future. And trust me when I say: you're going to need their army." Gali stepped away, the tidal waves of her body turning dark with worry.

Winnie's heart sank. "There's going to be another battle, isn't there?"

The Goddess said nothing, only looked away at the melting ice dome that still surrounded them.

"Please, answer me!"

"I cannot tell you anything further. Just...secure the alliance. For the sake of you, your friends, humanity. All of it... Don't be afraid to think outside the box. There are several roads you can take. Most of them lead you down a dark path. Make the decision that sits right with your heart, not your mind. Trust your instincts."

A few moments of stalled silence passed as Winnie tried to take in all of the information provided. *None of this makes any sense to me,* she thought before finally thinking of another question to ask.

"Are there others like me?"

Gali stopped for a moment, clearly trying to decide if she could answer that question. "In your universe at the moment, no. Though there may be some who could travel...with your help."

The ice dome around them dripped, small fractures in the glistening surface letting in the distant feeling of once again being watched.

"How many of us are there?"

"Your kind are few and far between, but every few hundred years a new one appears. We aren't sure what allows your body to dematerialize in order to travel. We aren't even sure where the energy comes from." Gali approached once more, placing a gentle hand along Winnie's shoulder.

"I remember you mentioned that when I made my deal. Something about being able to travel to Oblivion?" Winnie looked down at her hands, then her body. *What the hell is wrong with me that makes me able to do this?* Her thoughts continued to race as the words popped into her mind.

"There's nothing wrong with you, Winifred. Being so close to Death, your abilities are special. We suspect that may have something to do with it. Many people can see spirits, but most cannot visit the land between." Her eyes turned soft, almost motherly, as she leaned down to meet Winnie's gaze.

The mention of that dreaded word – Death – brought her back to one of the real reasons why she'd called on the goddess in the first place.

"Will Kane and the others be okay? When I go back, I'll be able to help them escape, won't I?" The words slipped from her mouth in a hurry, leaving her to wonder why she hadn't asked that in the first place.

Gali straightened herself, confusion pinching her face. She seemed to stop and think for a moment, her body once again turning icy with worry. "You do realize that, with the way you jumped, the time that passes here, passes there as well?"

The world seemed to cease its constant turning.

Winnie's heart sank again, tears burning the backs of her eyes. All she could picture was the devastation of her friends, Kane most of all, to see her just vanish midair during such a dangerous encounter.

"So what? They think I'm just…gone?" The words were a mere squeak.

The glimmer of an image appeared above Gali's watery hand. Stepping forward, Winnie peered through the surface to see Kane, Tara, and Melinda escaping the hounds and running for their lives. Melinda received treatment from her mother shortly after, Kane in the distance with his head held in his hands and rocking in a panic.

"They must think I'm dead!"

Gali shook her head before lowering the image. "Milicent has been given direction to reassure your friends that you've made it safely. And yet, he searches for you. Do not allow his siren song to tempt you into distraction." Her words of warning washed over Winnie, ingraining itself into her heart. The surrounding dome once again cracked, ready to cave at any moment. "With time, you will learn to control your powers. Then, you will be able to pick when, where, and with whom you go each time."

"The four of you said I can't tell anyone about what I'm doing. What the hell will I tell them when I get back?"

Gali said nothing, only stared at Winnie in silence.

With a grumble, she continued. "Is there a way for me to speak to Kane and the others? Explain…something. Anything! So they know I'm not dead or abandoning them?"

"I cannot say."

A sigh escaped Winnie, frustration building deep down as her arm glowed like burning embers.

"Be careful of that one as well," Gali warned, pointing toward the markings. "I know she remains tied to you. Don't let her tempt you to darkness. As easy as it may be."

Winnie nodded, trying to think of anything else she needed to ask. "Can I see Wesley? You told me that I could see him when I made my deal."

The Goddess stalled, once again thinking her answer through. "You've already seen him. In your dream the other night."

Winnie opened her mouth, ready to counter with another request, when Gali's protective dome faltered at last. Falling to pieces along the ground, the soft clatter of shards rang through her ears.

"I cannot help you. You must figure out the rest for yourself." Her voice was stern now, as though she put on a show.

Peering eyes once again prickled Winnie's skin, making her wonder who it was that watched in the void. "Thank you," she mumbled, lowering her head before feeling her soul's essence cascading down until the weight of her body returned.

With a shake of her head, Winnie attempted to clear the surrounding haze. As her body lowered from her levitating spot, the familiarity of her own realm was a welcomed sight.

Just as everything slowly returned to normal, she turned to see Oslind storming back into his underwater flat. Marching over in a fury, he pressed a blade to her throat.

10

TARA
FOX MANOR - 1871

Tightening the laces of her well-fitted corset, Tara finished dressing herself for a day of patrolling Chicago. As she fastened the buttons of her trousers and pulled on a warm coat, Cricket nudged her playfully.

"I know, I know. You need to go out," she crooned as she pinned the last of her red hair up. A heavy yawn escaped her, tired from a night filled with worry. Her anxious mind had raced back to the attack at the ball, replaying those moments over and over again. *I wish Winnie were here to talk to,* Tara thought. *She's probably the only person I could tell about the encounter with Alaric that wouldn't judge me for it.*

Exiting into the hallway, hearty laughter echoed through the manor. Memories from before Samhain surfaced in her mind, thinking back to all the fun she'd had with the Fox siblings. *There was a time when even Thoren and I got along,* she thought as she approached the kitchen.

She recalled mornings spent watching Milicent and Wesley cook breakfast, then huddled by the window with Winnie watching the animals just outside. Meanwhile, the Falke brothers were usually out causing trouble. It all tumbled back to her, a stinging burn sitting just behind her eyes. *I said I would stay with Wesley during the battle. We should've gone after Ezra together,* she scolded. *Perhaps I could've stopped this.*

Across the room, the blonde stood at the gas stove spooning spiced porridge into bowls with his love. The *siren*. Easily one of Tara's least favorite people at the moment.

"Good morning," Ezra sang before handing her a cup of coffee.

Walking past them, she opened the door for Cricket so he could run his usual morning laps. "Our best friend is missing, and you think it's wise to make breakfast as though you don't have a care in the world?"

"We still have to eat," Thoren huffed, handing her a bowl before scooping some for himself. "My love tells me that I've been too much myself lately. I'm sorry for my comment last night. I don't loathe you, Tara. *Dislike* would be a better word, but you know what I mean."

Ezra elbowed him with a scowl.

He threw his hands up in a sign of submission before adding, "Kidding!"

"Why do neither of you seem worried about Winnie disappearing?" Her question came out between mumbling bites of warm oats.

"Seriously? Did no one hear her mother last night? Milicent said she's *fine*. Until we hear otherwise, I'm going to trust that she knows best." Thoren took a seat by the window before the other two joined him.

"I suppose you're right, but I doubt your brother will feel the same. She is known to run off, afterall. If she hadn't fecked up that seance, she likely never would have called me back in the first place," she huffed, pushing her breakfast around with a spoon. "Melinda – still in Chicago I presume?"

Ezra nodded. Tara traced his line of sight to admire the family's lake, a thin layer of ice along the surface thick with morning fog. "We'll need to go back today, and start looking for the mayor. I worry she won't rest if we leave her unmonitored."

"Melinda resting is about as likely as Cricket finally realizing he's not a pet, and eating us all," Thoren teased.

She rolled her eyes, kicking him under the table.

At the back of the room, heavy footsteps startled them. Kane stood in the doorway, dark circles under his bloodshot eyes with arms braced on either side. "While you look for the mayor, I'll be looking for Winnie."

"You look like hell," his brother mumbled, pointing to his own eyes in reference.

"Couldn't sleep. I spent most of the night trying to call her back, and tearing her room apart looking for that damn book," he grumbled, taking a bowl for himself and sitting alone at the kitchen counters with hunched shoulders.

"What book are you talkin' about? The one we were all reading?" Tara asked, curiosity peaking. She thought back to their impromptu book club, though in recent days Winnie had all but replaced Tara with her new boy toy.

"No." He released a heavy sigh before continuing. "After Wes's funeral, she came back with an odd leather-bound book and a branded hand. It has to be connected to this. I can feel it." Finishing the last few spoonfuls, he stalked toward the sink to discard the dirty dish.

"She's quite capable. I'm sure she'll be alright, wherever she is," Thoren reassured, though it fell on deaf ears.

"It's not a matter of her capability. You heard Milicent. She's being naive about something; something that could get her killed. Excuse me if I'm a little worried about the woman I..." His words cut short, turning away from the group.

"You can say love. We all know it," Thoren teased, sharing a knowing glance with Ezra.

"I just want to protect her. Make sure she's okay..."

"I know," Tara began, getting up from her spot to offer his arm a gentle stroke. "She's still processing Wesley's death. We all are. Maybe this is just something she needs to do right now. We can't forget that her first instinct is to run away. Look at what happened two years ago."

Kane nodded in silence, avoiding her gaze before wandering back to his room. Silence spread in the room as she took a seat with the others again.

"I think you owe Ezra an apology," the siren said at last, ending the quiet.

"Thor, I told you it's fine! Drop it!"

Glancing at Ezra, she nodded. "No, he's right, Ez. What I said was cruel. I know what you went through that night was tough. Sometimes we all forget what that first…kill…is like. It doesn't excuse my comment. You're not a liability to the group; I hope you know that. I really didn't mean it."

The blonde's eyes fell to his hands as if unsure how to answer. "Whenever I'm alone, I see him. It's like he's haunting me. I can't explain it. Most of the time he just shows up, and then poof he's gone before I can do anything about it. Other times, he's waiting in the shadows. Taunting me. Always hovering in the corners of my vision."

"You have to release the guilt," Thoren muttered, placing his hand over his love's. "You've spent so much of your life feeling guilty for one thing or another. Let this one go. What you did saved us in that moment. That's what really matters."

"Tell that to the demon tormenting me," he scoffed before getting up from his spot to place his bowl in the sink. Thoren did the same, both exiting toward the sunroom.

"Just like that? You're going to leave me, the *woman,* with the dishes?" she yelled from the kitchen. All she could hear were snide giggles. "If someone doesn't do it, Milicent will yell at us again," she mumbled before taking a grumbling stand to clean up from breakfast.

Later that morning, Tara and the others rejoined Melinda in Chicago. The familiar sting of the transition bit her as they arrived at the Orphan Asylum, a group of children playing tag in the hallway. Their joy masked the group's sudden appearance, Miss Leona trying to settle them as they ran around. Cricket joined them shortly after, only adding to the chaos.

Otto's eyes landed on Kane, a squeal of joy nearly piercing their eardrums. "Come play, Mr. Falke!" the boy cried, jumping with excitement.

Even the worry he had for Winnie couldn't outmatch the child's enthusiasm. Tara watched as his scowl slowly drifted, a small glimmer of a smile forming across his face.

"Come on, come on, come on!" Otto continued to bounce, his pestering insistence only making Kane's frown disappear even more.

"Not today, mikri. We have some work to do. I think Miss Leona needs you to get the others settled for your lessons." He pointed to the older woman now waiting down at the end of the hallway, arms crossed over her chest.

Tara thought back to the first time Kane called the boy by that nickname. The way his face had twisted into confusion, only to brighten into a beaming grin when finding out it meant 'little one.'

"No one's ever given me a nickname before," he'd said through joyous, jumping laughter.

Now, the boy groaned in annoyance, huffing as he did what was asked. The other children filed toward the sound of the Miss's voice, Melinda appeared just outside her room, dressed and ready to go.

"You don't think you're going out, do you?" Tara asked, blocking her path as she attempted to walk toward the stairs. Cricket ran from the other end of the orphanage, only to help his owner block the attempted escape.

"Good morning," Melinda sighed, her head falling to the side

106

in annoyance.

Miss Leona called from the lower landing. "I already tried talking her out of it. It's no use," she grumbled, though the young woman just rolled her eyes.

"I'm fine! Milicent's ointments work wonders."

Tara reached out, poking at the site of her wound. Sucking in a sharp breath, Melinda winced before clutching the redhead's arm for support.

"Thought so."A commanding finger pointed back toward her room. "Go and lie down before I have one of the big ones force you to."

Ezra held his hands up. "It wouldn't be me. I've seen you fight. You're free to go as far as I'm concerned."

Melinda opened her mouth to object.

"You heard her. We don't have time for this. Back to bed." Kane stepped forward, his face serious and unwavering.

"Fine," she hissed, removing her coat and sulking back into her room.

Tara released a sigh of relief before adding, "I was expecting more of a fight if I'm honest."

"What are the odds she follows us out?" Ezra joked, though he seemed slightly serious. "Maybe one of us should stay back and keep an eye on this place."

"Do what you want. I'm leaving. The faster I help with this patrol, the sooner I can get back to looking for Winnie." Kane stalked down the stairs without so much as a goodbye.

"He sure is moody without her," Tara mumbled, the front door opening and closing below. To her side, Cricket seemed to nod in agreement, paws tapping and ready to go on an adventure.

"Why don't you stay, moró mou? We can go look for leads on the mayor and the camp," Thoren offered, leaning in to plant a quick kiss on Ezra's temple.

He nodded, heading toward the classroom where Miss Leona

107

prepared the children for their daily lessons. Thoren rushed off after his brother, Tara and Cricket walking leisurely down the stairs to begin patrolling.

Glancing down at the shuck, she couldn't help but offer a sad smile. "I'm sorry you've been so cooped up. I know you're just like me – we like being on the move, don't we?" she crooned before offering Cricket a pat on the side.

Once outside, the two of them wandered around rather aimlessly at first. *Do I ask around about the mayor? Do I look into his background?* As the questions popped up, she thought back to Alaric's words. Unsure why she was so quick to believe the hellhound, she countered his claims in her mind. *I doubt the mayor is an unseemly man. Perhaps a bit of a chauvinist, but he can't be that bad,* she tried to reassure herself.

Cold wind nipped at her skin, the lingering smell of incoming snow heavy in the air. All around her, citizens worked tirelessly to rebuild Chicago. Witnessing the rubble, she realized the cover of the previous night's darkness had done a good job hiding Boudicca's destruction. Though Winnie had told her stories of what happened, seeing it in person during the daytime was entirely different.

Their progress was slow, yet the city seemed to be coming back to life. Tragedy brought people together, ready to fix their community. Pacing the worksites, a lingering distrust made the air feel stale. With hellhounds attacking at random, tension loomed like smog. Heavy enough to suffocate on.

Suddenly, Tara was aware of someone standing behind her. Cricket's hackles raised, letting loose a growl as they both turned to inspect. Three figures stood, waiting to be noticed. In the center, a towering man hovered with a sledgehammer in hand. To his left, an amazonian woman waited with arms folded across her chest. At his right, a shorter, younger man stood with equally as daring a look on his face.

Glancing between the three strangers, she couldn't help but wonder if they were family. Aside from similar facial features, they also shared the same triskele tattoo. The three swirls stood among a dark, circular background, identical on the top of each hand. Their dark skin was peppered with freckles, a slight reddish tint to their brown dreads that hung heavy down their backs.

"Who are you?" the man in the middle demanded. His booming voice sent waves of shock through her system.

"I'm here to help," she said carefully, raising her hands in submission.

"We watched you run away last night. Didn't help our mayor, did you?" His questions continued to pester, Cricket's hair rising in response as a snapping jaw lunged at him.

"Tame your mutt," the woman hissed, reaching for her pistol.

Tara let out a soft click of her tongue, the shuck calming himself. She stepped in front of him protectively, face in a tight scowl as she made eye contact with the woman.

"Hands off the gun, now! One command, and he'll tear your face off. That's if I don't get to you first," she threatened, the group's eyes flashing to each other in amusement.

The one in the middle seemed almost impressed as he lowered his sledgehammer, bracing it along his leg.

"I bet I could take on a tiny little thing like you," the woman scoffed.

With weaponless hands, the towering woman reached toward Tara. Snagging her wrist, the redhead twisted until she was brought down to her knees. Though most would likely squeal in pain, the woman's face turned to a devious smirk.

"Don't you dare touch me *or* my dog." Her words were quiet, so only the kneeling female could hear. "Now can I go on and do my feckin' job? I'm looking for your damned mayor."

The woman stood, stepping back with a look of bewildered admiration plastered on her face. The trio glanced between one another, ready to return to work. The man holding the sledgehammer placed it on the ground beside him, not taking his eyes off of Tara as she walked away.

Watching curiously, the youngest of the three moved his hands in a language Tara didn't understand. The other two responded, though the sound of a howl tore their attention away from one another. It wasn't long before everyone nearby was alerted to an unknown presence.

11

WINIFRED MARVIVIA - 1861

Sitting cross-legged with her hands above her head, Winnie waited. The rage in Oslind's eyes spoke volumes, his chest puffing in anger. For a moment, she could only analyze his movements patiently as he scanned her body and surrounding area.

"Are you waiting for me to say something?"

He only pressed the blade further into her neck, making her wince. *Mum always told me that my tongue would get me killed one day,* she thought.

"My mother is back. She's never met anyone with the last name Fox." Oslind's gaze narrowed on her, feet shifting beneath him with unwavering focus.

Every nip of the weapon along her skin made her blood slowly boil hotter. Aelius and his magic stirred deep within, begging to be set free. As she worked to calm the embers, she finally realized: *They must not have met yet.*

"I'm not sure how to explain this but…" Before she could finish her sentence, Oslind interrupted her.

"You either start giving me some real answers, or I gut you right here and throw you out as chum for the sharks!"

With an accidental push, the blade broke flesh at last. A trickle of blood spilled from her neck, a fiery vengeance awakening. She wasn't sure which pushed her over the edge more: her own frustration, or Boudicca's quiet, slithering soul. The familiar swirls along her arm glowed in warning, ready to blow the flat to bits.

"Get that blade out of my damn face." Winnie worked hard to keep herself calm, though the words spilled through her gritted teeth.

Still, Oslind was relentless. When he wouldn't budge, Winnie grabbed the blade pressed to her throat and allowed the molten lava beneath her skin to release. Though the color was that of pearls, the texture ended up being consistent with metal. It softened and bent just as any blade would, unable to withstand her elemental gifts. Turning the tip upright, it now looked to the heavens.

A look of defeat crossed his face as he examined the end of his weapon. A sort of morbid curiosity followed his attention before tossing the blade to the ground. "No matter what I do, I can never win! Who *are* you?"

"You seem a little flustered," she noted with a tilt of her head, sly as a fox. "It's hard being stuck between two worlds, isn't it?"

With a grumble, he took a seat on the sofa and asked, "What are you talking about?" Teal eyes flashed to her, attempting to hide his worry.

Getting up from her seated position, Winnie took a seat across from him in the same spot she'd sat in the night before. Dabbing at her neck, she waited for the stinging to stop as she looked him over curiously.

"The selkies and merfolk. It's been years since you began your war. I doubt anyone would appreciate that you enjoy spending time with one of them." Though it wasn't meant to be a threat, it certainly sounded like one as the words tumbled from her mouth.

"You don't know what you're talking about," Oslind whispered, rubbing his face as though a nagging headache sat beneath his temples.

"I can recognize someone who's lying for someone they care about. You're torn between two very different groups. From my memory, your mother is a powerful leader here, making you prominent as well. Afissa is a kind woman, but I doubt she wants her son hanging out with selkies." Her eyebrows narrowed, noticing him squirm uncomfortably.

"Why are you bringing this up? What do you want in exchange for your silence?" Leaning back in his chair, he attempted to appear calm and collected. But Winnie could see the way his breaths increased in rapidity, and skin glistened with nervous sweat despite the chill in the air.

"It's hard to answer that question. Just know that I don't mean any harm; I just need your help."

A defeated huff of laughter escaped him, looking away from her in annoyance. "So you don't even know what you're doing? You expect to sit in my living room and threaten me without having a single idea what you want in exchange?"

"I just know I'm here to help. I don't know *how* yet, but that's it. I'm sure meeting Brenna first has something to do with it."

Rubbing his temples, Oslind asked, "Winnie, right?"

She nodded reluctantly. "While I'm here, you should probably call me by a different name. Perhaps Lucille – it's my middle name."

"Lucille, Winnie, whatever. I don't know how to help you if you don't know why you're here. You're making no fucking sense."

"I know – I'm sorry. I can't explain it all. But, I think my parents need to get here somehow. It feels important that they come. They can help you in your war."

He perked up a moment, sitting forward in attention. "Go on…"

"My father can make a contraption that allows humans to swim and breathe underwater. The intention was to allow them to help Marvivia in its fight," she explained cautiously.

"And where is this contraption?"

"I don't think it's been made yet," she blurted. Winnie heard the familiar ringing in her ears, though the Elements didn't fully punish her for her words. *I need to be careful what I say next,* she thought.

"Are you some kind of seer?" he mused.

Though she shook her head at first, she eventually muttered, "Yes! A seer. I have visions! That would make sense."

Oslind shook his own head in disbelief, crossing his arms while she fumbled with her words. "A witch and a seer? Seems extraordinary, really."

"My father; his name is Ernest Fox. Your people should reach out to him. Bring him here, and he can make the contraption. Then I'll be able to get to Freedom's Fortress as well!"

He seemed to contemplate for a moment. "You realize aid in the war would be life-changing for my people."

"Yes I do. I believe that's why he creates it. And in the future, should we need your help, hopefully the merfolk will help us in return."

He glanced at her sideways, caught off guard by her intentions. "There's that exchange I was waiting for. In the future you say?"

"I can't tell you much. But many years from now, there will be a war. We'll need your help to ensure we win." The ringing in her ears started back up again, louder this time.

He opened his mouth to ask more questions, though she cut him off.

"I can't explain anything more than that. I just need to know that when we call on you, Marvivia will help."

"That's not my decision to make. That would be my father's," Oslind added, getting up from his seated position to pace.

"Perhaps I can speak with him, then. Secure some sort of alliance. In exchange for my father's help," she suggested.

Oslind scoffed. "Good luck. He's not one to negotiate, but you can try."

"First, I need to get my father here to work on the breathing apparatus," she muttered. "I can send him a letter. While we wait,

I'll continue figuring out why I'm here."

"My father will need to see it before you send it out," he mumbled.

"He's that high up in leadership?" For a moment, she wracked her brain trying to remember the stories Afissa told of her family when Winnie was little.

With a cynical laugh, Oslind nodded. "Yes, I think being king would make one pretty high up, right?"

"Afissa never mentioned...so that makes you..." Her mind raced as the words tumbled from her mouth.

"A prince. Yeah, don't remind me." Pacing toward an icebox in the corner of the room, Oslind poured himself a drink before offering her one.

"It's barely past lunch time," she scoffed, refusing the glass. *He certainly doesn't act like royalty,* Winnie thought.

"Suit yourself," he mumbled before taking a slouched seat across from her again.

"So the Prince of Marvivia *really* shouldn't be in love with a selkie, then." Her eyes remained fixed on the other side of the room, avoiding his gaze.

Oslind couldn't seem to tear his attention away from her. "Don't say anything. Please." For once, he wasn't snarky or rude. Instead, desperation sat behind his voice, pleading with her.

She stalled, enjoying a few seconds of having the upper hand. "I promise, I won't."

A long sigh escaped him. "Just write the letter. I'll make sure it gets to my father for review before sending."

She nodded, conjuring up pen and paper. Focusing on the words that would hopefully save her family and friends ten years from now, she wrote as convincing a letter as possible.

For the next hour, Winnie schemed. She knew that the letter would need to be precise to convince her father to come help.

This time period was clouded in her memory, though she would be around nine and Wesley seven. In only a few short months, little Winnie would be forming her lifelong connection with Gali, finally able to wield the element she'd been dreaming of for years.

After drafting several versions, she eventually handed it to the mermaid for review. After a few read-throughs, he finally dropped it lazily into his lap with a heavy sigh.

"You make it sound like this machine is all my idea," he grumbled.

"And when it's a huge success, you'll be Marvivia's hero!" With a shrug, she took a seat beside him.

"And if it backfires, it'll be my ass on the line."

"Trust me. It *won't* backfire. You'll be the victor in the whole situation, and everyone will be grateful. Your father and mother will never be more proud," she said with a forced smile.

Glancing at the letter in his lap, she could see the gears in his head turning. At last, he got to his feet nearing the pearl doors. Oslind glanced back at her before adding, "You're coming with me."

"How…"

"We'll do what we did yesterday. I'll stop between buildings so you can catch your breath. I want you there when I give this to my father. I'm telling him you're a seer that had a vision, or something. If I offer this information alone, he'll just be suspicious."

Winnie nodded, stepping beside him.

"I brought you these," he added, handing her a pair of goggles to cover her eyes. "Some of the merfolk have sensitivity to the saltwater. Figured you'd probably be the same way."

"Wow, you did something nice for once," she sneered.

"Don't thank me yet. Due to the cold, I had to give you an old selkie uniform. If we get cornered, tell them you're with me. Shouldn't be too hard to prove you're not part seal."

Winnie nodded, looking down at the glowing panels along

her organs and extremities. "I didn't realize selkies needed warmth down here. Do you not feel the cold?"

He shook his head before adding, "When we're done, I'll show you the city. There's no use being cooped up here." The first smile she'd noticed drew across his lips, a dreamy sight indeed, pushing aside a lock of wet hair.

"I hope they don't ambush me again. You merfolk certainly seem to dislike intruders."

"That's an understatement. I would hide that shell around your neck, too. Many of my people will immediately recognize it and know you're hiding your identity." He motioned to the new trinket around her neck. Glancing at her suspiciously, he was clearly still trying to figure her out.

Tucking it away beneath her corset, she asked, "Can you still see me as I was? Or do you see a new face?"

"There's some slight difference, but overall I can tell it's you. I saw you long enough before you put it on for the magic to have no real effect on me," Oslind explained.

"Good to know, thank you."

He nodded, reaching for her hand. "Hold your breath."

Within moments, she pushed through the pearly white doors and into the frigid ocean, water whipping past her ears. At least this time, she didn't have the weight of a ballgown slowing them down.

12

KANE
CHICAGO - 1871

Kane stalked the streets of Chicago, Thoren trailing behind him at a distance. Admiring the heavy clouds in the sky, he wondered, *Is my brother waiting for me to turn around and talk to him?* Arriving amongst the rubble of Boudicca's aftermath, he felt a hand grasp his shoulder at last.

"Talk to me, brother." Thoren's voice was soft; gentler than he'd been since the weeks after Samhain.

"I'm not in the mood to talk." The words bit from Kane's mouth in anger, tugging to escape his brother's grasp.

"She'll be fine. You and I both know she can take care of herself." At last, Thoren stood before him, blocking every attempt he made to get away.

"I find your utter lack of concern infuriating! She's one of our best friends, and you don't seem to give a damn that she's just 'poof' gone!"

With a sigh, he glanced to the ground. "It's not that I don't care. You and I both know that. I just know that she's smart and capable. She can protect herself! There was a time when you understood that as well, but lately you're acting like..."

A moment of stalled silence heated the air between them.

"Like who?" When his brother didn't answer, Kane cocked his head to the side and pestered on. "Say it. Say I'm acting like him."

"As much as it may hurt to hear, you know I'm right. You're

acting like our father. We'd still have somewhat of a family if he hadn't gone mad the second we lost our mother. He charged straight at the enemy, outnumbered with no plan. And because of it, he's dead. If you're not careful, you'll end up the same way."

He scoffed. "I can't believe you…"

"Can't believe I'd be honest? Do you even know me, brother? Telling people their harsh realities is one of the many reasons you all talk negatively behind my back! Still, it doesn't change the fact that sometimes you need the truth more than the sugar-coated lies you try to sell yourself." A demanding finger jabbed into Kane's chest with every word. He could see it; the anger in Thoren's eyes as the fire within his soul stirred, slowly awakening.

"I'm allowed to be worried about her. I'm not sure she thought things through this time. What if the grief was too much, and she made a terrible decision without consulting anyone? Not even her own mother seems to fully understand what's happening. If she couldn't talk to me, then she should've at least discussed it with Milicent." Rubbing the back of his head in worry, Kane couldn't stomach looking back at his little brother.

"You can't change whatever decision she's made. All you can do is hope and pray to the Gods that she'll outsmart whatever challenges she's facing. Let's be honest – she's quite crafty." With a soft chuckle, he placed a hand on Kane's shoulder. "I'm sure she'll be just fine, but you have to be patient. You can't drag yourself into madness while you wait."

A deep exhale escaped him, offering a careful nod. "I just wish I could see her. Make sure she's okay."

"There is a way, you know," Thoren replied, crossing his arms over his chest in thoughtful consideration.

With his curiosity peaked, Kane motioned for his little brother to continue.

"You don't remember Mum's little ritual?" A brow raised on one side, curious eyes examining him. "You don't remember our parents sharing visions whenever they were separated?"

Slowly, the memories started to return. He recalled the flower petals surrounding their mother, and the sweet smell of rose scented candles. "Father wasn't magical though," he added skeptically.

"It doesn't matter; he didn't need to be. Their connection was strong enough. Our grandmother always said they were soulmates. I assumed that was the reason they could send messages back and forth." His brother's attention sharpened onto something in the distance, as if sensing trouble.

"I don't remember how to do that spell."

"I do; I can write it down for you. But only if you promise to stop acting like a sorry sap."

Finally, a smirk formed across Kane's face as he nodded once more.

"Do you think your connection to each other is strong enough, though?" Thoren's eyes widened, as if he hadn't intended the words to sting as much as they did.

"I don't appreciate what you're insinuating." Once again, Kane's arms crossed over his chest. With each passing second that his brother stalled to answer, he felt his shields rise higher and higher.

"Oh please, you're barely even a couple. You went out on your first official date only a few days ago. And you mean to tell me that you're *suddenly* soulmates?"

"I can still try," Kane shot back, anger making his own blood boil. "If you recall the healing circle, I saw something that night! She was glowing like a damn angel. It has to mean something! No one else around us looked different. I felt it then. I feel it now."

Thoren chuckled. "Ezra claims he saw me glowing that night, too. But I doubt it means anything. It was likely just showing us what our brains were too afraid to admit to our hearts. You've been pining over her for years without even realizing it. The healing ceremony just helped you figure it out sooner."

"You're wrong." Kane shook his head. For a moment, the conversation stalled. Unable to get past his brother's comments, he thought, *Perhaps a change in subject?* "What are you going to do about Ezra?"

Thoren released a heavy, grumbling sigh. "Seriously? You, too? Don't tell me you agree with Tara?"

"He can't fight. Whenever he hears the sound of a gun, he turns into a frazzled mess. We can't afford to have another person go missing or dead." Though unintentional, his words came out sharp – spearing Thoren with every syllable.

"He's dealing with the fact that he had to kill someone. Have some damn compassion, Kane! I never knew you to be so heartless, especially after what we went through. You remember how I was after our first battle!"

Thoren's words burned themselves into Kane's mind. *I suppose I haven't stopped to really think this through before bringing it up,* he admitted.

"I'm sorry, I didn't mean to call him a mess. I just know that he needs to find a way to move past it. We aren't safe here. He needs to be able to defend himself. I don't think any of us can handle losing another friend."

The apology seemed to pull Thoren from his anger as he offered a nod.

"I know you're right, I just don't know what to do. He did better yesterday when hearing the shots from the ball. There was only a slight panic before we were able to come back to the orphanage. But he keeps seeing the face of the man he killed."

"You could offer to help him with, you know..." Gesturing toward his throat, Kane continued. "He doesn't have to remember that night as vividly as he does now. Doesn't even have to feel the guilt if you don't want him to. You could block some of those more painful memories for him."

With a cynical laugh, Thoren's gaze remained fixed on his brother. "The fact that you would suggest that after what we went through in London is outrageous. You and I both know how dangerous and corrupting that kind of magic is for our kind." Thoren's face turned to a scowl, eyes narrowing in on his brother once more in disbelief.

"I'm not saying it's a good option, just know that it is one. If you won't do it, I can. I've done it before, and I still live to tell the tale," he muttered with a shrug.

"Barely. I won't let you go down that road again. How long did it take before you recovered?"

"We have to go back at some point. Back home. What will you tell Ezra when the time comes?" Kane waited, seeing the gears in his little brother's head turning.

"We don't *have to* go back..."

"Yes we do. Eventually. I'm not saying it has to be now, but at some point we both have to fix the trouble we started before coming back to Fox Manor." A small smirk formed in the corner of Kane's mouth, thinking of the small inconveniences he'd left behind that were more nuisance than harmful.

"I don't know if he'd come with me, but...I don't want to be separated from him. Ever." Pacing for a moment, Thoren kicked a rock at his feet.

"Will you tell him about Sezen?"

His attention snapped onto his brother. "Shit... I didn't even think about her."

"We both have a lot to think about, don't we, little brother?"

Pinching the bridge of his nose anxiously as though a nagging headache formed, they both alerted to the sounds of gunshots firing down the street.

"Never a dull moment," Thoren grumbled, Kane following close behind as they ran toward the lingering echoes of a fight.

13

EZRA
CHICAGO - 1871

Doodling on a loose piece of paper, the sounds of an ongoing lesson echoed through Ezra's ears. Sitting at the back of the makeshift classroom, his mind wouldn't allow him to settle. Instead, he found his fingers moving a pencil around aimlessly, dark swirling lines of terror filling the paper. When at last he couldn't stand to look at the dark rings for eyes staring back at him, he crumpled the paper up and grabbed a clean one.

Miss Leona's lesson on basic math caught his attention, taking a few notes as she explained the problems in the simplest way possible. A wide range of ages sat at small desks in the room; anywhere from children Otto's age, to older kids who sought refuge at the Chicago Orphan Asylum after the fire.

Perhaps I should actually pay attention, he thought as he carefully jotted down the numbers on the chalkboard, haphazard lines of unfamiliar writing etched into the sheet. Thoroughly sucked into the lesson, Ezra was startled by the hand that grasped his shoulder.

Rushing to cover the paper, he turned to see Melinda's shining smile greeting him. Her dark eyes peered down at the scribbles, moving his hand away to reveal his attempt at learning something so simple. *Even children can do this. Why can't I?*

"I was just…um," he stuttered, though he didn't know what to say.

"There's no shame in trying to learn," she began, patting him gently on the back. "No matter how old you are."

Ezra stood, exiting the classroom so they wouldn't disturb the children's lesson. Melinda followed him out quietly, hugging her sides with a wince from her healing wound.

"I…well, growing up. We couldn't afford for me to go to school. Every waking second was spent working or running the streets." The pinks of his cheeks heated, avoiding her piercing gaze.

"It's okay, friend. There's no need to be ashamed. Trust me, I can understand why the need for knowledge is so important. There was a time when my people weren't allowed to go to school at all. I find it admirable that you want to learn."

There was a moment where he didn't say a word, unsure how to respond. At last, she reached out and grabbed his arm gently.

"What's wrong? Your energy has been so muddled since Samhain."

"Everything," he whispered, squeezing his eyes shut hoping it would block out the constant, daytime nightmares.

"You're not alone." Her words came to a stall, once again grasping his arm and offering him a reassuring squeeze. When he finally looked back at her, she added, "I haven't been seeing things, but I did walk with Death. Somehow, I still live to tell the tale. That doesn't mean it's easy to live with."

"I want to be useful, but I don't know how to stop seeing…" His words were cut short when the sound of a familiar hiss caught his attention.

"Me?"

Startled eyes darted behind Melinda, seeing the familiar face of the haunting hellhound lingering just beyond. Again, the man's chest remained bloodied, a feline grin taunting Ezra. She glanced over her shoulder only for a loud gasp to escape her.

The entity peered toward Melinda, a strange panic settling over his ghostly face as realization set in. Only a moment passed before he vanished with a mere blink.

"Can you see him?" Hope flared in Ezra's chest, grabbing her by the shoulders.

"I don't know what I saw. I didn't see a person, but there was definitely *something* there. You've been seeing that darkness ever since Samhain?" Turning toward Ezra, a strange fear seemed to exude from her body.

He could only nod silently, unsure how to respond.

"I don't know if you're one for prayer, but I think you should consider it. Though I couldn't see what that thing was, I could certainly feel it. I've only felt evil like that one other time."

"When was that?"

"Boudicca," she whispered, as though the queen would hear her and come back for more.

A cold chill spread through Ezra's body, unsure what to make of it all. As he contemplated, he couldn't help but notice her rubbing her side where the gunshot still healed.

"You really should go lie down. If Tara comes back and sees you up and about, she may actually have one of the brothers carry you to bed." Though it was meant to be a joke, they both knew there was an air of truth to it.

Melinda softly chuckled before grabbing the sides of his face. Her dark eyes dug into him, as though they rooted themselves in his soul as she spoke. "You are still here, Ezra Watson. I know that things are hard, but you've endured."

"I just...don't know how I fit in with all of you."

"Not everyone has to be a trained assassin," she chuckled. "There is strength in resilience and mercy. It doesn't make you weak. Maybe *that's* the root of your magic. But you have to be kind to yourself, first."

A long sigh passed through his lips, closing his eyes to shut out the world. "But I don't want to be a liability."

"Then don't go out looking for a fight. Leave that to me and

Tara. And Winnie, I guess, if she ever decides to come back. Make sure you can defend yourself just in case, but leave the rest to us. You'll find your place, I promise. Now all that's left is to make the conscious choice to stop being so hard on yourself, and finally let yourself live."

Offering him a quick hug, she returned upstairs. He turned, sauntering outside to have a seat along the grass.

The others will probably think I'm mad, but I don't care, he thought, feeling a strange sense of connection to the soil beneath his fingertips.

For a few wavering moments, he tried to settle his thoughts. A strange concoction of panic and hope stirred in his chest, tears burning the backs of his eyes knowing that someone other than himself had witnessed the beast who relentlessly stalked his every waking moment.

"Okay fine. I haven't been the praying type for some time, but I'll concede. Is anyone out there?" He sent his thoughts into the void, though nothing seemed to answer.

Just past his closed eyes, the sun peeked through the clouds. Shining down on him, the rays peppered his vision with spots of red and black. A symbol began to form in his mind's eye, though nothing clear enough to determine what it was.

"Is…someone trying to show me something?"

Though he may have thought such an internal conversation was silly in the past, he wasn't sure what to believe now. Since discovering the truth about Winnie and her family, he was painfully aware that anything was possible.

Still, nothing answered.

"Dammit, show yourself! If any of you actually exist, prove it!" The words bellowed through his mind, almost stinging as anger nipped at his soul. A warm breeze caught him off guard, replacing the icy chill from Chicago's winter momentarily.

"Choose life." An oddly familiar feminine voice, more

comforting than he could explain, startled him.

When he opened his eyes, he still remained alone outside the orphanage.

"Who's there?" Calling out to the nothingness before him, the warm breeze ceased.

Several blocks away, the sounds of gunfire caught his attention. For once, panic didn't course through his bones. Worry, yes, but not debilitating fear. Attempting to stand, a vine caught his foot. Falling to the ground, he couldn't help but examine the root that hadn't been there only moments before.

"Stay here. Sit with your trepidation, and trust that your friends will be okay. You must learn to settle your mind for what comes next." Again, the woman's voice rang through his mind.

"Who are you?" he asked, wondering if he was communicating correctly.

"You will come to recognize me soon enough, darling. For now, simply heal." A motherly lilt and soft chuckle reverberated through his entire being as she spoke.

With a huff of frustration, he did as she asked. Taking a seat along the ground, he waded through the panic. Listening to every gunshot as it echoed through the streets, he counted them until there was only silence. The fear creeping up his spine threatened to drown him before her voice anchored him to the earth once more.

"You are protected, Ezra. But that doesn't mean you are sheltered from your own mind. Remember to choose life. Never accept Death's call again."

"I can't do this. Can't do this...forever." Somehow his thoughts came out as whimpering cries, even as it echoed through his head.

"It doesn't have to be. For now, just heal."

With a final gust, the woman no longer loomed in the comforting breeze surrounding him. He was alone, but not quite the same as before.

TARA

The low growl pulsed through Tara's body first. Then the scream of someone nearby ripped through her ears as he was torn in half, the blood splattering across the surrounding buildings. A hellhound had waited for the opportune moment, ready to strike. Without warning, a herd surrounded the innocent workers of Chicago. Joining the fight without hesitation, Cricket stood at her side ready to attack.

The shuck's hackles raised and eyes deepened to a blood red as the first set lunged toward them. The man with the sledgehammer swooped in beside her, the two of them working as an unlikely pair. When the last of her bullets emptied into a nearby hound, Tara pulled out her dagger, and readied for close-combat.

One of the beasts circled back, lunging at her blindside. The man with the sledgehammer stepped forward, hammering into the skull of the hound. Over and over again, he swung until there was only a heaping pile of blood and bones.

As he finished off the beast, another lunged toward them. Tara sliced at the hound before Cricket knocked into it. With a yelp of pain, he fell to the ground. The moment of disorientation was enough of an advantage for Tara to drive her dagger into the creature's skull. With only moments to spare, she realized her beloved furry friend wouldn't put pressure on an injured leg. Whistling a quick command, she ordered the shuck to return to the orphanage's safety.

Obeying, Cricket took off. A hellhound's attention snapped toward the running creature. Tara immediately saw the intense stare of the beast, following every movement with careful consideration. Another hound jumped in front of her, morphing into his human form before she could go after her pet and ensure he made it back safely.

"Not so fast," the hound tsked.

Ducking, she avoided a near collision. As he reached for a blade at his side, Tara used this to her advantage. Swinging her leg beneath him, he toppled to the ground before she plunged her weapon into his chest.

Her unlikely partner returned to her side, kicking another oncoming hound before jutting his chin in the direction of Cricket. "I got this one. Go get your dog," he yelled over the nearby sounds of fighting cries and gasps of pain.

Without hesitation, Tara took off after the hellhound hot on Cricket's tail. He turned down an alleyway opposite the direction of the orphanage. With only a few yards to go, a pained yelp made her heart sink into the pit of her stomach. Another yowl rang through her ears, rounding the corner and unsure what to expect.

Slowing to a walk, she cautiously approached the situation. Cricket cowered in the corner, blocked in by a hound. The beast's midnight fur shone in the sunlight, a low prowl stalking toward her beloved shuck. Behind them, Alaric creeped forward unnoticed. A dagger in hand and ready to strike.

Ready to cry out, Tara could only suck in a sharp breath as the hellhound's leader threw himself onto the beast, driving the dagger into its side. The creature morphed back into the body of a woman, a tear rolling down her cheek as violet eyes glared at him.

"Why?" she managed to choke out. Her voice was sweet and innocent, similar to one Tara had heard in London the night of Ezra's attack.

Alaric said nothing. Running his fingers over her eyes, he closed them as she took her final breaths. Only a moment passed before he gently set her aside, covering her with rubble. He stalked toward Cricket, next. With hunched shoulders and a blade still in hand, she couldn't tell what his intentions were.

"Stop!" Tara bellowed, the shuck still cowering from fear. It was as if he could sense the beast that lurked beneath the man's skin.

Alaric's attention flashed in surprise toward her just a few feet away.

"Please don't hurt him," she cried, placing herself between Cricket and the hellhound leader.

"I wasn't," he began, holding his hands out in front of him. His voice was a low growl, the beast within him daring to be set free. He placed a lightly bloodied knife down on the ground, kicking it to her feet.

Teary eyes softened as she realized what was happening. "Did you just?" There didn't seem to be an end to her sentence.

"I'm not going to hurt either of you." An unseen war seemed to battle beneath his skin, his glittering blue eyes luminescent as his inner beast waited for another fight.

Endless thoughts raced through her mind as she warned, "We're leaving." Firmly, she held the dagger out toward him before whistling to Cricket once again. The shuck obeyed, leaping to her side with his tail between his legs.

"Dammit, I just want to talk to you. Give me a chance to explain. Please," he grumbled through panting breaths, quietly following them as they backed away.

"Thank you for saving Cricket. I won't forget this act of mercy." A tear rolled down her cheek, realizing how close she'd come to losing the only consistent love she'd ever had in her life. At the end of the alleyway, she glanced over her shoulder one last time.

Alaric only stood, pacing, glancing back and forth between the hidden hound and Tara. *I don't know why he did it, but I doubt it comes without strings attached,* she thought. Rounding the corner, the last of the attacking hounds were slain by the Falke brothers. Shivering bodies lined the ground, surviving workers sharing bewildered looks amongst themselves as the hellhounds turned back into their human forms while drawing their final breaths.

Pockets of conversations spread throughout, Tara picking up on a few as she passed.

"I thought they were wolves..."

"Am I drunk on absinthe, or did those creatures turn into humans?"

"Did you see those two? They have wings. Bloody hell, do ya think they're angels? I better start going to church again."

At last, she stood before the Falke brothers and the trio that hounded her only moments before.

"Excellent work. What's your name?" Thoren asked, shaking the hand of the man with the sledgehammer.

"Danny," he replied, setting his weapon aside and shaking the siren's hand.

Thoren introduced his brother before pointing to Tara as she approached. "And this is Tara with Cricket at her side. Though he looks like he's seen better days."

"Thank you for taking care of that hound so I could save him," she said, glancing over her shoulder to see if Alaric would make another appearance. *If he's smart, he'll hide,* she thought nervously. As the words flitted through her mind, she couldn't help but wonder why she cared what happened to her enemy.

"You're welcome. Sorry about my sister, earlier. She doesn't always know what's good for her. I think we're all a little on edge," he added before heading off to check on her.

Tara's gaze followed him, realizing the woman sat on the ground clutching a crimson shoulder. She approached with caution, peaking to try and getting a better look at the wound.

"Make sure it's not a bite," Tara ordered.

Danny glanced back at her, nodding in reassurance as he tended to his sister.

"Here." Reaching into her pocket, she pulled out a vial of Milicent's healing ointments. "Use this; it'll speed up the healing."

He nodded in thanks, curious brows examining it with

skepticism.

"Just trust me," she chuckled. "Your brother hasn't introduced either of you."

"Riah Borderick," the woman said through gritted teeth as Danny applied the magical concoction. "And that's Spencer," she said, pointing to the youngest who stood silently, eyes fixed on everyone's mouths.

A shy wave followed, though he didn't say a word. Riah's hands motioned again toward him before he softly said, "It's nice to meet you."

Tara watched curiously as the siblings spoke using only their hands, never having seen such a language used.

Noting her confusion, Riah added, "He's hard of hearing. We use sign language to communicate. If you want to speak to him, make sure he can read your lips."

Tara offered an equally shy wave with a smiling nod before asking, "Where are you all from?"

"New York, originally. We came here for work. Heard of the buildings needing to be fixed. Thought we could help out," Danny explained, still tending to Riah.

A sigh of relief escaped the woman as her pain began to lessen. "What is this stuff?" she cried out, clutching her shoulder in relief.

"Just some ointments..."

"How does it work?"

"I'm not sure to be honest. I just know it does. Some herbs and whatnot. Who knows!" A nervous chuckle escaped the redhead, worried she was talking too much about the magical properties Milicent perhaps didn't want to share.

Spencer's hands moved with furious speed. Tara's eyes flashed back to Riah as a wry laugh escaped her.

"He says we've seen stranger things." She jutted her chin toward the dead hounds littering the ground that had been in their wolf forms only moments before.

"No matter how it works, we thank you," Danny added at last before ushering his siblings after him.

As she watched them enter one of the nearby tents for workers, Tara felt the hair on the back of her neck stand in attention. Cricket beside her sat whimpering, nudging at her. *He probably wants to go home. I need to take a look at that limp,* she thought before scanning the area again. Down the street, she made eye contact with *him* again.

Alaric.

Standing within the rubble. Eyes locked on her and watching. No one but Tara noticed him as he escaped. She was grateful he'd saved Cricket, but equally confused. *Why do I feel so guilty for not letting him speak? He's the enemy,* she thought. *I'm sure that wasn't the last time I'll see him. Next time, I'll try to listen.*

14

WINIFRED
MARVIVIA - 1861

After stopping at a few air-filled buildings along the way to catch a quick breath, Winnie and Oslind finally arrived at the largest structure in Marvivia – the palace. Her body pushed through the pearly white walls, feet landing on the other side gently before removing her goggles and staring out over the magnificence of it all. With a few heavy coughs, she eventually caught her breath and wrung excess moisture from her braid.

"Whoa," she whispered, a glittering gaze taking it all in.

The inside of the underwater palace was the perfect balance between royal elegance and oceanic beauty. Towering ceilings were made of see-through glass, showcasing the surrounding corals teaming with life. Various areas housed small pools of water, rich with tiny fish and other little creatures.

The same material as the other buildings made up the walls and floors, shimmering teal and brown like an abalone shell. Glowing orbs illuminated the cold structure, her glowing wetsuit responding to the nagging cold by heating her core.

Small pockets of reefs and underwater plants covered the edges of the sparse furniture throughout, mostly adorning the gargantuan thrones at the center. The king and queen's chairs looked to be straight out of a fairytale. Made of coral as well, the sitting areas were padded with salmon pink cushions. Sea anemones and underwater flowers decorated the corners of the thrones, moving as though still blissfully surrounded by water.

Around the room, merfolk discussed business and other official matters. The low murmurs ceased as Winnie entered behind Oslind, noticing an outsider amongst them. Their attention remained fixed on her selkie clothes.

"She's not a selkie," Oslind announced, raising his hands in submission. "She's a human who just needed warmth."

Mermaids nearby scoffed, a few muttering to each other. *They really don't like outsiders,* Winnie thought as she overheard a nearby group wondering aloud how a human had managed to find their hidden paradise.

Ignoring their gawking stares, her attention returned to the room. "This is…"

"Overdone? I know," he mumbled, crossing his arms over his chest.

"I was going to say incredible." Roaming eyes took in every tiny detail, noticing schools of jellyfish swimming outside the domed ceiling. She shuffled over to one of the small pools of water, sticking her hand in as the tiny fish nibbled at her fingertips. A booming voice from the opposite side of the room distracted Winnie from her new, tiny scaled friends.

"Oslind! It's about time. What brings you here?"

Winnie turned toward the incoming voice, an older man sauntering toward them with a scowl on his face.

"Father," Oslind muttered plainly, lips in a tight frown and posture a little too straight.

The man's stride was cocky and exuded arrogance, a cold gleam to his eyes as he approached the two of them. She'd expected him to embrace his son, or even shake his hand. Instead, he patted him on the back, the young man's face only grimacing at the unwanted touch.

"King Aalto Maddox," he announced, turning his attention down to Winnie.

Panic coursed through her as she glanced toward Oslind. "Um, do I bow?"

The king let out a sardonic cackle, waiting to see what she'd do as she scrambled to understand the court customs down at the bottom of the ocean.

"Bowing seems unnecessary. I doubt my father deserves such respect," Oslind mumbled, his voice muted and face void of any love Winnie would've expected to see between father and son.

The king ignored the comment with a mere eye roll before offering his outstretched hand to Winnie. She took it, offering a polite curtsy. Deep brown eyes watched her carefully, plump lips curving into a feline smile as he offered a head bow in return.

The two men didn't seem to share many features, Aalto's sharper and more pointed. Oslind's face was soft and welcoming, whereas his father appeared more brutal. A lack of skin pigment and silky white hair were about the only thing they had in common.

"No need to bow, my strange little friend." King Aalto continued to examine her as if wondering the same thing as everyone else in the room.

With a gulp, she introduced herself at last. "Lucille…"

"You're not a mermaid," he noted, examining her up and down. "Not a selkie either, as far as I can tell. Though wearing that outfit is near blasphemy in my court."

"No," she chuckled nervously. Pausing for a moment, she was unsure how to answer. It occurred to her she'd never had to tell someone 'what' she was.

"Siren? I sense something…strange about you." The king continued to guess, his gaze only digging deeper and deeper into her essence.

"She's a seer," Oslind interrupted, noticing her hesitation.

"Long way from home, aren't you?"

Winnie's eyes flashed toward the prince, hoping he could help explain it all.

"I visited land the other day, and she came to me with visions of the future. I have a letter I need you to take a look at before I send it. It may be a huge asset to us in the war," Oslind explained, once again straightening his spine and messing with the weapon at his side.

"Son, a word?" King Aalto eyed her suspiciously, pulling Oslind out of Winnie's earshot. Still, she could make out most of their conversation.

Wandering off, she returned to the small pool of nibbling fish to ensure their privacy. As she looked over her shoulder, Oslind hesitantly offered his father the letter. The man read it over once, then again. One more time. He glanced up at Winnie, though she quickly evaded his eye contact. *Don't want to seem like I'm spying,* she thought anxiously.

In an attempt to look busy, she walked toward the pearly white doors. Before she could place a hand on the wall, a set of merfolk startled her as they entered seamlessly. They looked just as surprised as everyone else to see a land-dweller in the palace.

At last, she held a delicate hand toward the gelatinous wall. It felt like touching a block of ice. Pressing a little harder, her hand disappeared through the barrier. Frigid waters rushed past her fingers on the outside, wiggling them and calling forth Gali's magic. Pulling a handful through the barrier, a small ball of water levitated above her open palm.

Gali's chuckles reverberated through her mind as she played with the glittering liquid. *I didn't realize how much I've missed my element,* she thought, the stir of Aelius's fire moving within her soul. His fire had nearly consumed her, tethering Boudicca's essence to her own. But feeling the playful splashes against her skin helped bring a piece of her old self back to the surface.

"Are we sure she can be trusted?" King Aalto asked, his voice barely carrying itself to her ears. "How did she get all the way down here? We're miles from shore. You and I both know you don't visit land for fun."

"She teleported in," Oslind guessed with a lazy shrug.

Only a half lie, she thought.

"She found me at the bar. I have no reason to believe she'd be lying. If what she claims is true, this device could really help us out." His tone turned desperate, though she wasn't sure why.

"Seers don't teleport. Even fewer work with water magic," he mumbled, eyeing Winnie carefully. "Very well. Against my better judgment, we will send it. But I want this 'Ernest Fox' under constant supervision while he's here. I don't want to take any chances with more spies."

Winnie turned to see the King with furrowed brows, clutching the tiny letter in his hands as though he were ready to crumple it up and toss it into the ocean.

"Of course, Father," Oslind muttered, offering a strained head bow. The tension was almost tangible in the air as he walked away. Approaching Winnie, he handed her the paper. "Send it."

She nodded, closing her eyes and envisioning Fox Manor. The connection formed, though it was weak at first as the distance was great. Being surrounded by her element, however, a small surge of power rippled through her as the letter disappeared. Oslind watched in curiosity as she reopened her eyes, offering him a soft smile.

"It's off! I think you promised me a watery tour of Marvivia," she reminded.

He nodded at first before something just beyond caught his attention. Glancing behind herself, she noticed a curious dolphin peering into the windows as though it searched for him specifically. It circled around the entire palace twice before landing back at the window, round pupils locked with Oslind's.

"Is that a friend of yours?" she teased.

He cleared his throat before rushing her toward the door again. "We need to get back to my place." His words were sharp and quick, ready to pull her into the sea without so much as a warning.

Winnie took a rushed breath, entering the water faster than she'd anticipated. She'd barely had enough time to pull the goggles over her eyes before the icy chill spread over her, once again surrounded by water.

On the way to the throne room, he'd stopped a few times so she could catch her breath. It seemed that whatever the 'dolphin' meant didn't allow for such luxuries. It wasn't long before her lungs burned with the familiar sting of breathlessness, wishing he'd take a moment to drop her off to recapture the oxygen she so desperately needed. She tried to hold on; tried to keep the liquid from entering her body. But the distance was too far.

"Relax." The voice of the Gali sloshed through her mind.

"I'm about to die!" she thought, sending the goddess spears of panic.

"Relax," she said again.

Oslind continued his darting swim, nearing home.

Winnie knew she was running out of time. Seconds stood between her and a watery death. *Relax,* she tried to tell herself. *Take deep breaths…oh wait. I can't! How am I supposed to calm down when I can't take a deep breath?* Instead, she shifted her focus. Trying to envision something to help settle herself, only one image stood at the forefront of her mind.

Kane.

His hazels peered back at her; wide smile, scruffy face, silky hair. As she pictured him, she could hear his voice in her mind. His eyes turned sad, his siren song sounding through her like an alarm. The pull of him searching for her was overwhelming, desperate to find her. Nearly succumbing to his siren song, mesmerized and filled with peace, she found herself able to breathe. Her eyes flashed open in a panic as they neared Oslind's home.

Clutched her neck, she wondered if perhaps this was the last few moments before Death would come to claim her at last. She was overdue at this point for a final meeting with the entity. Wanting to cough or even choke on water, she only seemed to meet air. Pulling away from Oslind's grasp, Winnie floated in the open seas.

Turning toward her in a panic, he mouthed unintelligible words. The water in her ears ensured she didn't hear a thing, though she could read his panic like a book. Winnie grasped for her face again in wonderment, realizing a small bubble had formed around her nose and mouth.

"What is this?" she asked Gali, though the Element didn't respond this time.

"A gift," an unfamiliar male voice hummed. *"Shared with your siren. Momentarily."*

"Caelus?" she thought, though only a slight chuckle answered her inquiry.

Glancing around, she could suddenly take in the full beauty of this underwater world. Looking from a window was one thing; being in the midst of the watery paradise was another.

Oslind urged her to hurry, grasping her hand firmly and pulling them toward his home.

Barreling into his flat, his gaze flashed around the room. On the floor lay a heaping pile of fur and skin. Winnie grimaced in disgust, unsure what it was that lie there. She bent to touch it, though he stopped her. Peering up, the naked body of an unknown female sauntering toward the door.

"Where are my clothes?" she asked. It wasn't until she saw Winnie that she squealed, and hid in the bathroom.

Winnie gasped, covering her eyes out of sheer respect for the stranger.

"Who is that?" the young woman called out, peeking from behind the door. She looked scared at first, though her gaze softened when she noticed Winnie's face. "Hey, you look familiar. Didn't we meet yesterday?"

It took her a moment to put the pieces together. At last, she managed to ask, "Brenna?"

The young woman was nothing like the creature that saved Winnie the day before. She still had similar wide-set, coal eyes, but her face looked far more human now. A thin layer of short seal fur no longer covered her, but rather regular smooth, silky skin wrapped around her bones. Auburn hair lay down her back, wet and tangled.

"I'm sorry, I borrowed them. They're on the couch!" Winnie rushed to bring them back to the selkie.

When Brenna exited, Winnie couldn't help but notice how incredibly human she looked. Glancing back at the pile of fur curiously, she wondered how the magic of it all worked.

"Don't touch those. They're my ticket home," the selkie teased with a small smile. She revealed larger canine teeth, though not nearly as long and pointed as they'd been in her selkie form.

"What are you doing here?" Oslind urged, grabbing her by the arms and pulling her in for a tight embrace.

"I had to warn you – had to make sure you could stop the selkies from the attack they're planning," she whimpered, doe eyes gazing up at him.

The two of them took a seat on the edge of his bed, in their own little world. Winnie glanced around awkwardly, unsure what to do with herself. Eventually she took a seat on the couch, facing the two and listening to their conversation. *Why does it feel like I'm intruding on the two of them?*

"They plan to attack Fort Monroe. And soon! A few have been picking off soldiers these last few weeks. Now they want to take out the entire fortress, including confederate Hampton just outside of it." Her eyes pleaded with him for help.

Winnie noticed a softness in him she hadn't seen before, the love evident between the two.

"What are the odds that you come here looking for Fort

Monroe, and now there's a planned attack?" he mumbled, rubbing his face in worry.

"Please, Os. You have to help," she urged. "Winnie, you can help too, can't you?"

"I think that's the whole reason I'm here," she confessed, grabbing her leather-bound book and flipping through the pages only to find nothing. *As usual,* she thought. "We can tell your father I had another vision," she suggested, sensing his muddled mind.

"That's a good idea. That way they don't suspect..." His eyes roamed Brenna in worry before flashing around the room to ensure the blinds over the windows were closed.

"Do you come here often?" Winnie asked, directing her question back to the selkie.

"No, only in emergencies. We often meet in other places," she said, though he shushed her.

His attention darted to Winnie in mistrust.

"I hope you know I won't say anything about you two..."

"I'd feed you to the sharks if you did." At first, Winnie thought he was teasing. But his stoic face told her there was no humor in his words. "How did you do that thing with your mouth, by the way?" Oslind moved his finger in a circle around his own.

"You have your secrets, I have mine. But it looks like I'll be able to get to Fort Monroe after all," she said happily.

He cocked his head to the side, still trying to figure her out. Turning his attention back to Brenna, he cupped the side of her face. Her big, round eyes softened at his gaze, melting into his touch.

"Can't I stay?" she asked, leaning in to offer him a delicate peck. He let out a long sigh, pulling her in close for a deeper kiss.

"It's not safe, you know that."

"I don't think I care right now," she mumbled.

Winnie turned her head awkwardly, thinking: *Maybe I should throw myself back out into the ocean so I can give them the room.*

Clearing her throat, she hoped they'd remember she was still there.

Oslind groaned, looking back at her. "I'm going to make sure she gets home safely. Will you be alright staying here?"

"Safety, huh?" Winnie mused, watching as they sauntered toward the door. "I'm sure that's definitely your top priority. But yes, I'll be fine."

Brenna grabbed her seal skin, pulling it over her body like a wetsuit. Winnie watched as her face and body returned back to the familiar animalistic features. Oslind helped her through the door, waving as he exited. The grin on his face told Winnie exactly why he was following her home. She chuckled, pulling her legs up around herself. She looked around the small home, wondering what to do with her time.

For the next few hours, she rested and meditated. Trying to recreate those same image of Kane in her mind, she wanted so desperately to hear his song again. His search for her seemed to vibrate through her entire being, every second apart eating away at her mind.

When boredom at last took over, she wandered toward the pearl doors. Sticking her head out into the ocean, she practiced creating that small bubble of air around her nose and mouth.

The first few tries were sloppy and inconsistent. After all, air was never an element she'd worked with before. But an hour turned to several and eventually it was all she could do to distract herself from the constant siren song echoing through her mind. Training the ability like a reflex, it at last became second nature the moment the water touched her skin.

15

---•‹‹●●››•---

TARA
CHICAGO - 1871

A few days passed before Tara and the others determined it was best to just stay in Chicago. Miss Leona had kindly offered the men a room to share while she stayed with Melinda. It seemed the hellhound attacks were only spiking more and more every day with the number only rising.

Darkness loomed outside, a heavy moon lighting the sky with its warm glow during such a frigid evening. Cricket sat at Tara's feet, panting as nervous eyes watched the children run playfully back and forth in the hallway.

"I know you want to play with them," she lulled, patting the shuck on the head gently. His paw was still wrapped up, healing from the encounter with Alaric. It seemed Milicent's ointments didn't work on a creature that wasn't even a little bit human. For some reason, not even the siren song could fix the minor injury.

Melinda shuffled through the door at last, releasing a heavy sigh before removing her coat and laced up boots. Her gaze landed on Tara, offering a soft, greeting smile before slouching down on the adjacent sofa.

"The mayor's council again?"

Melinda offered a contemplative nod. "They're begging me to be at the check-ins every morning, looking for anyone hiding out amongst the newly arriving workers. They need all the help they can get, but it seems that the hounds know exactly when to strike.

Usually when one of us isn't there, or the Broderick trio are away. They have a knack for recognizing a threat, and waiting for us to leave."

Tara's mind raced for a moment before Melinda continued.

"At least I can make myself useful." With a soft shrug, she started to head toward her room.

"I'll come with you tomorrow. Keep an eye on the workers, and help where I can."

Offering a thankful nod, she walked to their shared room at last. Tara thought about following her up, knowing rest was much needed. Yet, her body refused to move.

Her attention remained fixed outside, glancing up toward the moon. An endless stream of thoughts continued to crawl back to the encounter with Alaric, wondering why he'd risk it all just to save her pet. Just to talk to her. *The next time I see him, I'll hear him out,* she decided before getting ready for another night filled with restless sleep.

The following morning, Tara ordered Cricket to stay put. "It's your job to protect the kids while we're out. You know that!" A demanding finger pointed back toward the door.

The shuck's eyes landed on the orphanage. With a heavy sigh, he took a seat outside the entrance. A moping frown watched her leave, pulling at Tara's heartstrings with every step she took away from him. *He and I have always been the same – we don't feel useful unless we're helping the ones we love,* she thought.

Melinda waited along the street, rubbing at her side.

"Everything alright?" Placing a hand along her friend's shoulder, Tara anxiously awaited an answer.

"Just a little sore. I'll be okay," she reassured before walking toward the closest work site. Pulling her thick fur-collared coat closed, she shivered at the cold.

During their slow trudge, Tara couldn't help but notice Melinda's hesitation. Occasionally glancing back at the orphanage, her friend's mouth seemed to open and close a few times as though she wanted to speak but couldn't.

"Out with it," Tara teased with a playful nudge.

"I keep thinking about Winnie. No one seems worried about her except Kane, but I'm beginning to wonder if maybe he's right. Where the hell is she?" Melinda's head drooped low, fiddling with her hands before crossing her arms over her chest.

"Milicent swears she's safe. I know it's hard to believe, but I tend to trust what she says."

"Okay, so she's safe. But why isn't she here? She's the whole reason we're in this situation. And yet she just leaves so that we get to clean up her mess?" A huff of frustration puffed in a cloud before them, the cold morning wind rushing past.

Tara paused for a moment, thinking of anything she could say to ease Melinda's mind. Truthfully, she didn't know what would help. "Let's just hope she's back soon, and can explain what she's been doing. Hopefully she has a good reason for why she's left us. Though I must warn you, she's done this before. She never gave me a good explanation for the incident two years ago. I wouldn't expect an apology."

Melinda nodded, though a simmering, slow rage seemed to burn in her eyes as though she had a lot more to say, yet no words to properly articulate her thoughts.

The two ladies walked through rows of buildings, this side of Chicago thankfully unaffected by the Queen's treacherous fires. Any housing was bustling to the brim with life, workers from all over the United States awaiting their duties for the day. Before Tara and Melinda could make it to the rubble, the sound of music caught their attention.

"That sounds merry," Tara mumbled, searching the streets.

"What's going on down there?" Melinda asked a nearby worker, hustling in that direction as well.

"Ya didn't hear? All work's been canceled for the day. Everyone's to take the day off to get some rest, and hopefully enjoy a little holiday celebration," the young man explained, a glitter in his eyes before skipping off toward the sound of a party.

"Seems odd to have a celebration now, doesn't it?" Tara asked, eyeing her friend sideways.

"It does, but I welcome the break. These last few weeks have been hard on my soul." Melinda sighed before a smile graced her lips. One that made Tara, too, smile in excitement.

Down the street, lively music came in waves of welcome. Tents decorated with wreaths, pine cones, and garland stood around an open square. It had only been a year since the United States declared Christmas an official holiday. Though it was still a few short weeks away, it seemed the people of Chicago were ready to forget their troubles for a little while.

Nearing the masses, Tara took in the sight of the vendors and merchants set up along the outskirts. An occasional church group handed out free soup, others offering hearty treats and warm sandwiches to those with enough coin to afford it.

Cider stalls and lit fires were strewn throughout as well, a swirl of delightful smells and sounds surrounding the two young ladies. For those that wanted a more lively event, they danced at the center as a few musicians played fiddles and other instruments.

Melinda made eye contact with two of the Broderick trio, Danny pouring himself a cup of cider before waving them over. Riah, fully healed, sat on the outskirts snacking on bread as she watched their younger brother, Spencer, dancing with a few young ladies in the middle.

"This is so exciting!" A girlish squeal escaped Melinda, tugging at Tara's arm to go join the three siblings.

"I had no idea such a festival would take place here!"

"I've never been to one like it. Other than Samhain but…" Her words came to a halt, unable to choke from her throat.

"Did Miss Leona not let you out very much while you were growing up?" Tara questioned as they slowly made their way over to the siblings.

"None of us orphans were allowed to leave, really. That wasn't Miss Leona's doing, but rather an order by the church. They didn't want us galavanting through the streets."

"And yet you were out the night of the fire?" Tara cocked her head to the side in curiosity.

"I was never one to follow the rules," Melinda mumbled with a small giggle. "My uncle showed me a few spots that were good places to sneak out. To this day, I'm not sure Miss Leona knows how I got out all the time."

"You haven't said much about your uncle. Why were you in an orphanage if you had family?" Unable to control her anxious mind, Tara caught herself scanning the crowd as they walked, waiting for something bad to happen.

"He worked for them: the church and those before Miss Swan, the current matron. But he was very, very ill. I think he knew he'd never make it to see me into adulthood. So he worked at the orphanage, knowing that I'd have a place to stay should he lose his life. And he was right." Sad eyes dropped away from the redhead.

"I'm sorry," was all she could muster, placing a sympathetic hand on Melinda's arm.

"He always said our family was cursed to live short lives. Knowing what I know now about Boudicca, I wouldn't be surprised if he was right."

"I sometimes wonder if my family is cursed as well," Tara confessed, glancing down at the pendant around her neck.

"You've never mentioned them before."

Tears strung the backs of her eyes as she relived the last

moments with her family. The cold crack of waves into their ship. The screams of her younger sister. The haunting melody of the seal-like creatures slithering their way onboard.

"There's not much to say. We tried to travel to America. Got caught by selkies on the way out. I'm the only one that survived the wreck."

Placing a delicate hand on Tara's shoulder, Melinda mumbled, "I'm sorry, friend. I know how hard that is."

Across the crowd, Melinda's name echoed toward them. Spencer, much to Tara's surprise, waved excitedly at the two ladies, though his doe-eyed gaze remained fixed on her friend.

"Go!"

"You won't come with me?" Antsy feet shifted weight, Melinda eyeing the young man beckoning her to dance.

"I'll be out in a little while. Go have fun." She offered an encouraging smile before gently pushing her friend toward Spencer. Watching for a moment, she noticed his charming smile light up even brighter as Melinda approached. "Oh you sweet, hopeless fool…"

To her left, Riah appeared. "He does seem to have taken a liking to her."

"What's not to like? She's a wonderful person. Beautiful girl. Kind soul. If he's smart, he'll tell her before someone else snatches her up."

Riah chuckled softly under her breath before turning back toward the redhead. "I wanted to thank you again. Whatever you gave me the other day worked wonders. I've never healed so quickly in my life."

Tara offered a nod before asking, "Do you dance?" She couldn't seem to stop herself. Admiring eyes took in Riah's impressive height and muscular physique, hoping for a positive answer.

"Never been one to have any sort of talent for the arts. I find I'm better suited… elsewhere." She patted the pistol at her side.

Even standing beside her, Tara had to crane her neck to look up at the Amazonian woman. *People usually tell me I'm tall. Wonder what they'd make of her,* she thought with a chuckle.

"Then why are you here? Seems if you're not here to dance, you could be off doing something you actually like."

"Perhaps I'm just here to enjoy the company," Riah said with a feline grin, playfully glancing down at Tara. "Someone came by early this morning and dropped off a letter for you. We never would've known who it was for had he not said it was for the plucky redhead with the big mutt. He left a cupcake too, but I'm afraid Danny may have eaten it by mistake. Sorry."

Her blood ran cold. A careful hand reached out and took the paper, too afraid to turn it over. As Riah sauntered back toward her eldest brother, Tara examined the outside. There were no markings on it to indicate who had dropped it off. Nothing other than a nickname on the front. *'Little fawn'* was written in swirling font, her heart dropping at the sight of it. She tore at the paper eagerly, unsure what to expect. The words inside looked to be carefully etched, reading:

I saved your dog. The least you can do is meet me for a drink.

Tara scoffed, looking out over the crowd. Approaching a nearby fire where workers huddled, she threw the paper inside. *There's no way in hell,* she thought, disregarding the promise she'd made to herself the night before.

Just as the words passed through her mind, Tara felt a tap on her shoulder. Turning, she was surprised to see the face of Alaric waiting. Jumping back, panicked eyes flashed to Melinda to see if her true sight would notice the beast among them. Her friend was too busy dancing her heart out, eyes closed and spinning wildly to warm herself with the company of others.

"I had a feeling my little fawn would ignore my letter," he

crooned.

Assessing the situation, she wondered if she should yell. Scream. Anything to alert the people of Chicago of the danger they were in.

"Don't say a word," he warned, as if reading her mind.

Sauntering toward a nearby pub, he never looked back to see if she'd follow. Against her better judgment, Tara shuffled in behind him. *I'm being foolish. I know it. But maybe I should just hear him out,* she thought helplessly.

"Taking an awful lot of risks just to talk to me, aren't you?" she asked, entering the pub. Shivering from the sudden warmth, she loosened her coat without taking it off entirely.

"I figured you'd be stubborn, so I came to fetch you myself," he explained, taking a seat. Alaric pointed across from him, ushering her to join.

With a quick glance around the bar, she realized it was wholly deserted. Not a soul sat within, most enjoying themselves at the small festival. Only the bartender stood behind the wooden counter, grimacing at her. The hellhound's leader offered him a quick nod before the man exited, snagging his coat on the way out.

"You know each other?" she asked, wondering what sort of alliance the bartender had if he knew a hound. *Perhaps that's why so many people keep dying.* A shudder escaped her as the thought crossed her mind.

"From before, yes."

"Before what?"

"Boudicca got to us. You forget we were normal people once. Many didn't have a choice about changing."

Lazily sauntering toward the bar, he poured a drink for them both. She glanced at it suspiciously, sniffing it. He chuckled, taking a small swig before handing it back to her.

"Not poisoned, I promise."

Hesitant fingers took the glass, sipping slowly as the alcohol heated her insides. "If you want me to believe a word you say, you'll have to first explain why there's been so many attacks."

His brows scrunched upward, cocking his head to the side to examine her carefully. "I'm not responsible for all hellhounds. You must know that."

"Do I? From my friends' accounts, you're the leader of the whole bunch," she spat. "You're Boudicca's right-hand-man. Surely you must hold more sway than most."

"I'm the leader of a small group, yes. But there's thousands of us. Surely you can't think I control them all." An amused scoff escaped his lips. "After Boudicca was defeated, many of us stayed near London where we're from. Some came here. Others have traveled West, trying to make new lives for themselves."

"So your disease is spreading all over the world? That's grand..." She took a long, hard sip of the drink in hand.

Alaric flinched at her words, but said nothing.

"How did you all get back here?"

"Boudicca opened a portal between Chicago and London. It was accessible for a little while after her defeat. But it's closed now, so I'm stuck here and can't get back unless I want to take my chances with the sea. Though I think I'd rather deal with Chicago's residents trying to kill me over the selkies hunting those waters," he explained, a tight frown across his lips as he nursed his own drink.

She raised her eyebrows. *I know exactly how deadly those beasts are,* she thought, memories of her lost family tugging at her tear ducts. For a moment, second nature kicked in. Wondering how she could help, she had to remind herself: *He's your enemy. You're getting a little too comfortable.*

"You're not how I expected you to be. Thoren describes you as bein' violent and cruel."

"The sky rat? Like he's one to talk. The things I know about his kind, not to mention his brother, would shock you," he said, taking one last gulp before setting the glass down.

"You know them? The Falke brothers?" Her curiosity peaked, thinking back to all the times Alaric's name had been mentioned in conversation. Not once had they claimed to know him in return.

He smirked but maintained his curated silence, grabbing the whole bottle from behind the bar and rejoining her. Offering another drink, he leaned in across the narrow tables. The smell of campfire wafted off of him, a familiar scent that Tara couldn't help but ache for. The same smells of a life on the road, wandering and never tied down.

Placing her hand over the cup, she muttered, "Better not."

"Suit yourself."

"You brought me here to talk, so talk. I'm not here at leisure. Tell me what it is ya need to say, or I'll go outside and alert the others of your presence," she threatened, resting her hand along the dagger strapped to her thigh.

He leaned back, a cocky grin plastered across his face. "You'd sell out the man that saved your precious beast? I'm shocked." Removing her hand from the cup, Alaric poured her another.

"Speak," she commanded, begrudgingly taking another sip.

"I needed you to understand why we took the mayor, and why you're not getting him back," he began. She opened her mouth in protest, though he shushed her. "You told me to speak. That means it's your time to listen."

With a grumble, she sank into her chair.

"He's not who you think he is…"

"You already said that! Give me somethin' new to work with!"

"I've told you I don't command all hellhounds, yeah?" He waited for her to nod. "There's more moving pieces here than you realize. An ancient battle between packs; ones that believe hellhounds are superior, and ones that believe we should be cured. Somehow, my group got mixed up in all of this.

"Which do you believe?" She cocked her head to the side,

awaiting an answer.

"I think a hound should have the right to choose. Don't you?" His stare dug into her, examining every movement she made with careful consideration like a predator ready to pounce.

"Well, sure, but how is the mayor wrapped up in all of this?"

"He has information. There's rumors he may know more than he lets on." His brows furrowed as the words escaped his lips, leaning in toward her as if telling secrets.

When she glanced up from the rim of her glass, she couldn't help but feel the pierce of his stare, noting the scar along his eyebrow. *Why is it that the pretty ones are always evil?* The thought came out by accident, making Tara straighten herself to try and fix her wandering mind.

"Why would he know anything about hellhounds? Are you tryin' to insinuate he's one of your kind or something?" With a scoff, she finished her second drink. Turning her head to the side in annoyance, she wondered, *Is he just wasting my time? This feels ridiculous.*

Swirling the liquor in his glass, he added, "Not insinuating anything. I know for a fact he's had his own little group of beasts murdering anyone who dares share the truth about where the hellhound curse came from."

"The mayor isn't a hound. Melinda would've seen his true face."

Alaric's eyebrows shot up. *Shit,* Tara realized. *They didn't know that about her.*

"So the descendant of Paulinus has special gifts? Interesting…" Finishing his drink, he added, "If you saw what I did, my little fawn, you would be infuriated."

"Tara," she corrected. "Stop calling me that!" Anger roiled inside her at the mention of that ridiculous name.

A smile curled at the corner of his mouth in response. "I like mine better."

"I've seen you murder plenty of people. Namely Augustine,

the lycan I was with the night of Samhain," she recalled, throat bobbing at the memory.

A pensive stare fell away from her. "Yes, well, that's the nature of war isn't it?" Tapping his empty glass, he seemed to ponder his words. "I still feel bad – taking that moment away from you. You seemed to be enjoying yourself immensely before I cut in."

There's the beast I was expecting, Tara thought with a huff, trying to block out the memory of the gurgling sounds she'd heard that night.

"That right there is why I'd never even consider entertaining a hound like you," she grumbled.

All he did was smile into his glass before taking another hard sip.

"Return him to us. Let the people decide what to do with Medill. If he really is a so-called murderer, bring him back. We will ensure justice the proper way, assuming you can prove it."

"Can't do that, sorry. We need him. He has information, and he's not going anywhere until we get some answers."

"Why is this so important to you? I figure you prefer to be a wolf. No one likes being powerless." Her gaze fell away, wondering who she was really talking about.

"Right now, we're hunted," he answered in astonishment. "By you and yours. By the people of Chicago. By other damn hounds. We just want to live! We can't even try rebuilding this city without Medill's watch dogs jumping on us."

"You're trying to tell me that the hellhounds pretending to be workers – that keep killing innocent people, by the way – are just trying to help?" She scoffed again, unable to believe his story.

He nodded. "Different groups, remember? Believe what you want, Tara, but we're not all monsters. Some of us just want to start a new life. For many, that's not possible with the curse still coursing through their veins."

"Can't you just hide your true form? Not turn?" With a roll of her eyes, she thought: *Why am I still sitting here, entertaining any of this in the first place?*

"And where's the fun in that?"

With a shake of her head, she asked, "Why don't you just come to an agreement with Medill? It sounds like he's still alive. Perhaps you can make a deal with him."

"He says he won't do it. His only focus is on fixing Chicago, and ridding the city of our kind." Alaric glanced down at the empty cup in hand with a deep sadness. One she almost felt sorry for.

"Return him safely. We can try to persuade him if you bring him back unharmed," she tried to convince.

As if by accident, she found herself placing her hand over his. His whole body seemed to tense as their skin made contact. Desperately, she tried to ignore the sensation of pin pricks beneath her fingertips. But she couldn't seem to ignore the all-over warmth that spread through her as her hand retreated.

There was a long pause.

"I can't do that," he said at last. "I may be in charge, but I can't be seen as weak. He's not going anywhere until we see this through."

"Then my friends will come after you." For a moment, she felt as though she were pleading.

"Unless you stop them…" Alaric's piercing blue eyes dug into her soul, grabbing her hand and playing with the freckles speckling her skin.

Tara sat speechless as his eyes roamed her.

"They don't listen to me," she whispered. "They never have, and never will."

"I'm sure a pretty little thing like you could change their minds if you wanted to. Not to mention, they have a woman capable of leading armies at their disposal, and yet you aren't given the time of day. Doesn't that piss you off?"

Her cheeks flushed cherry red with embarrassment, avoiding his gaze. All she could do was shake her head in denial.

"A tongue like a whip and now you lose words? Didn't think I'd manage to make you speechless. Perhaps I should try complimenting you more often." A hunger sat behind his words, leaning in toward her as his pale eyes seemed to darken with need. The way he looked at her, like she was a snack to be devoured, made her snap out of it at once.

Snatching her hand from his grasp, Tara stood. "I need to go! I didn't come here for compliments. I came for answers, and you have yet to provide me with anythin' believable."

Preparing for the cold, she walked toward the door. Alaric grabbed her arm, turning her back to face him. Instinct took hold, reaching for her dagger and pressing it just below his jaw. Just as before, he didn't flinch. *One of these days, I should just stab him,* she thought.

"At least think about what I said. You have the power to stop all of this. To bring peace to Chicago. To cure our affliction," he said softly, tucking a strand of red curls behind her ear. Still, he ignored the blade held to his throat.

She gulped, wanting to pull away but equally wanting to lean in toward his touch. His hand lifted, carefully removing the weapon from her loosened grip. With a wolfish grin, he sheathed it back to her thigh, careful fingers grazing her leg as if he wanted to see what he could get away with.

"I already told you – my word is useless to them."

"Just try. You are more powerful than you realize. Perhaps Winnie can help you," he mumbled, offering her hand a delicate kiss before stepping away so she could leave.

She took a moment to examine him, feeling like she'd memorize this moment. The way his electric blue eyes looked her over in admiration as he pleaded for help to save his people. The fire that roared behind him in a hearth, those smells drawing on fond memories of her past surrounded by the heat of a flame.

Can I do it? Can I help cure an unstoppable curse? I don't know that anyone would take me seriously if I brought this to them for consideration, she thought. But alas, she said nothing. Straightened her coat, turned toward the door, and headed out into the frigid December winds.

16

WINIFRED MARVIVIA - 1861

A few days passed when Winnie sat on Oslind's sofa once again, flipping through the pages of her thick, leather-bound book. He was away as usual, attending to business in the city while she waited aimlessly for her father to respond to the letter they'd sent days ago. Attempting to read the scribbled, unknown language for the hundredth time, she could only sigh before walking to the doorway.

Sticking her hand through the strange surface, the cold water rushed past her finger tips. Calling on Gali, she brought the swirling liquid through the entrance and into Oslind's flat. A booming voice paraded through her mind, making her wince as the water sloshed to the floor.

"Why are you wasting your time? You have a job to do!" Aelius's fire stirred in her chest as the words coursed through her veins.

"You and I need to have a talk!" she grumbled, taking a seat along the ground.

She could almost feel the deity's eye roll as she meditated, attempting to access the same place she'd met with Gali days before. It took a few minutes, but at last the fire god conceded, and Winnie's essence floated to the unknown realm.

When she opened her eyes, darkness surrounded her just as before. The same strange piercing glare of invisible beings made her skin crawl. Even the warmth from her wetsuit was not enough to escape their chill. At last, Aelius appeared. The room turned to molten flame, surrounding them in a dome of privacy just as Gali had with her ice.

"What do you want, Winifred?" His scowl was disapproving, a swirl of flames along his skin igniting with every word.

"You need to stop being so damn jealous every time I use Gali's gifts!" An accusing finger pointed toward him, Winnie's blood boiling with rage. Being around him wasn't as nurturing as being around the water goddess.

"You have become selfish, witch. You should be on your knees thanking me for bestowing you with a secondary power!"

Winnie took a deep breath, trying to think through her response. "Every time I use water magic, I can feel you and Boudicca in the back of my mind. It's like you're constantly judging me!"

"We are. Fire is a highly coveted power, yet you continue to waste your time with her," he hissed.

Though she couldn't quite tell, Winnie thought she saw the outline of Boudicca's figure just past the surrounding flames.

"Are you asking me to give up my water powers? Wouldn't that make me weaker? Less likely to fulfill your vague plans?" Propping a hand on her hip, Winnie waited for a response.

Aelius circled her like a viper, glaring at her entire body as though she made him sick to his stomach. "Why are you wasting time sitting in the mermaid's flat when you should be out completing your task?"

"I am working on my task! I'm waiting for my father to respond to my letter!"

His mouth turned into a snide smirk, shaking his head. "I imagine Gali told you to go with a more passive route. But there are other options. You don't have to simply wait around. Start exploring a little more. You'll recognize your purpose when you see it."

"Are you saying I shouldn't be trying to secure an alliance?" she asked, his words only adding to her pre-existing confusion.

"No, you still need an army. But how you get it, remains to be decided." He waited, his temper seeming to settle as her attitude simmered as well. "Speak with the king. See what he wants in exchange. You may not even need those silly little contraptions."

With a nod, Winnie prepared to leave. Before she could, he stopped her.

"I'm surprised you haven't asked about your brother," he almost sneered.

Her attention snagged onto his words, turning back toward the fire god. Playfully, he stood with large arms crossed over his chest.

"Gali said I already saw him."

"Did you? Let's see…"

Aelius raised his hand, a frame of lava forming as flickering images appeared inside. Winnie approached with caution, her eyes squinting from the heat of the deity. She couldn't quite get close enough, but a few images caught her attention.

He walked down an alleyway, face blocked by a puff of smoke. She likely wouldn't have known it was him had she not recognized his coffee-brown hair. Behind him on a brick wall were splatters of paint in a strange pattern. The word 'outsider' was scribbled in those same colors, unlike anything she'd ever seen. The view of him backed away, only to reveal a strange city skyline with buildings in shapes Winnie had never seen before.

"Where…is he? That's not what I saw the other day." Backing away from the living flame, Winnie's mind continued to race.

"Finish your tasks, and you'll find out." A playful lilt sat in Aelius's voice as he lowered the dome of fire around them. With a groan of annoyance, he added, "Great. The lovesick songbird once again."

She cocked her head to the side in confusion. It wasn't until she heard Kane's voice musing around her that she realized what he meant. His song circled her, a strange daze taking control of her movements.

"I need to go back…" Her words came out a mere mumbled.

Aelius took a step forward, snapping his fingers. "Get it together, witch. You have work to do!"

Only a moment passed before Winnie felt her essence tumbling down again, landing back in her body along Oslind's floor.

Later that evening, Oslind finally offered to show her around Marvivia. They visited a few places, making frequent stops in case her strange new air bubble faltered. First, the palace once more to get a better look. Then, the statue protecting the city. Before retiring to the bar, he showed her the community hub where large events and gatherings happened. Each place was more magical than the last, covered in corals and shimmering seashells.

As they shared a drink at the underwater pub, Oslind confessed, "I was meant to visit 'you know who' tonight."

At first, disappointment washed over Winnie. Then she asked, "Can I come with you? I'd like to get to know her better. Plus I don't think I can stay another night in your flat. Alone. No offense."

He contemplated for a moment. A slow nod followed before he chugged down the last of his beverage. "You think your air bubble will hold up for a while? We have a long way to travel."

Eagerly nodding, Winnie finished her drink before hustling toward the exit.

"Hold on tight," he seemed to tease, pulling Winnie through the pearl-white doors and into the frigid ocean.

Anxiety festered in her chest the longer they swam. Paranoid she'd lose the connection with Caelus, she couldn't help but memorize every turn, every rock, every coral. Until eventually he led her to a cave a few miles from his civilization, dimly lit with glittering bulbs of verdant welcome.

They entered through similar doors as those in Marvivia, though the inside of the rocky cavern reminded Winnie of others she'd found near Fox Manor. Rugged and barron, the only thing inside was a cot, some chairs, and glowing bulbs of light. Brenna sat waiting, doodling in the sand.

He sauntered over to her casually, an almost automatic reaction before leaning down to offer a sweet, tender kiss. Her gaze flashed to Winnie, glowing in welcome.

"He didn't tell me you were coming! What a pleasure!" Brenna's voice echoed through the rocks, her warm welcome almost intoxicating.

"I had to beg on my hands and knees, but he eventually agreed," Winnie joked, though Oslind rolled his eyes.

"I'm shocked you made it here! It's quite a trek," Brenna said softly, pulling a chair around for Winnie to have a seat.

As she sat before the glowing orbs at the center of the cave, Winnie couldn't help but reach out. "It's…warm! How do you do that?"

"You'd think a witch would recognize magic when she sees it," he mumbled, lounging beside his love. She swatted him, though they both chuckled.

"It's quite simple, really. It's basic conjuring. Try it with me," she offered, reaching for Winnie's hand.

Their fingers laced as Brenna talked her through the steps. It only took a few tries to create a mimic flame, though Winnie's was a little more fiery thanks to Aelius's cackling laugh.

"You're a natural!"

Winnie shook her head. "I don't know about that."

"You witches are so limited by what you believe. Perhaps that's for good reason; if you knew what all you could do without the limitations of your coven, you'd be unstoppable." The selkie carefully eyed her, offering a warm smile.

She took a moment to consider those words, unsure what to make of them. At last, she asked, "Why does Oslind wear that suit, and you wear one like me? One that's heated?"

"Most selkies need it to stay warm in their human form all the way down here. Unless they're...well insulated," Oslind teased, nudging Brenna.

With an eye roll, she added, "The mermaids, if you can't tell, are quite cold blooded. Much like the fish they swim with."

"No wonder everyone's been so rude to me! I'm walking around dressed like their enemy."

As if sensing her discomfort, the mermaid mumbled, "We can tell the difference between a human and a selkie, don't worry. I suspect they just don't like you."

Ignoring his comment, Winnie continued. "Was there ever a time when your people weren't at war?"

Brenna nodded, sad and contemplative. "For hundreds of years, Marvivia was a place welcome to all sea creatures. Even other species. But Aalto was put on the throne and everything changed. There were a few good years, but it quickly came to an end."

"What happened to make the merfolk and selkies hate each other so much?" Winnie inquired as they passed around a bottle of tropical, amber liquid that reminded her of better tasting gin.

"My people," the selkie began with a pause. She seemed to choose her words carefully. "Some have very different opinions on humans. The merfolk have always believed that they have no business being in the waters. Therefore they avoid them. The selkies are a little more..."

"Aggressive," Oslind blurted, causing Brenna visible discomfort.

Her eyes shot toward him in slight anger as the words seemed to bite.

"You know I'm right. They also think humans should stay

out of the waters. But rather than avoid them, they take down their ships, attack them on land, or sing songs that drive them to madness to send a message. And somehow the merfolk always get the blame. We even get confused with sirens, somehow. You'd think sailors could tell the difference between feathers and scales."

"So this is all because of humans?"

Brenna shook her head. "When they couldn't agree, my people wanted to take it to a vote. But the King wouldn't have it. Then the question arose: Why do we have a king? Why not a democracy like America?"

"My father did not take it well. He saw it as a sign of rebellion and slaughtered anyone who supported the idea." Oslind's attention rested sadly on his love for a moment.

"Even my own family," the selkie whispered, avoiding both of them. "Oslind's mother, Afissa, was very close with my mother. That's how we got to know each other as kids. But after King Aalto slaughtered them, everything changed."

"My mother doesn't look at my father the way she once did," he added, placing a hand of solidarity on Brenna's knee, stroking it lovingly.

"We've been at war ever since." With a half-hearted shrug, a look of despair fell across her face.

"Where do your people live now? Now that you've all lost your home?"

"After being exiled from Marvivia, we've had to make our own dwellings. Some live on islands, hiding their skins from poachers. Others have caves like this scattered throughout the sea."

"Why not go somewhere else? Surely you could create your own version of Marvivia?"

With a scoff, Brenna explained, "That city took decades to build. We can't just snap our fingers, and make a new one. Some have tried to find asylum elsewhere, but the trip is too dangerous. Between the freezing temperatures, beasts lurking in the waters, and pirates wanting to poach our skins, very few survive the trip."

Winnie waited a moment, contemplating what to say.

"Truthfully, we're homeless. A people divided with no real leader. Everyone is out for themselves, and willing to kill to survive." She glanced around the cave before adding, "I'm lucky I got into this one when I did. Otherwise I'd be homeless like so many others."

And to think this will still be going on in ten years, Winnie thought, unable to bring herself to look at Brenna.

"I wouldn't say there's no leader amongst the selkies. You've had quite some sway with your people these past few months," Oslind retorted, a glimmer of pride beaming.

"Let's be realistic; they don't listen to me," she huffed. "I know they're planning on attacking Fort Monroe. When I tried to tell them to stop, they excluded me from the plans. I think they suspect me of being a sympathizer."

A panic spread across Oslind's face, likely thinking of the danger this put her in. "As long as we have each other, everything will be okay," he whispered, placing his hand on her cheek in comfort.

"And what about you, Mrs. Winifred-Lucille? Now that I've bared my soul to you, tell me something no one knows about you." Brenna's cheeks turned to a sad smile, forcing herself to appear happy.

She thought for a moment. "There's not much to know," Winnie lied, knowing there wasn't much she could tell them of her time.

"Where do you live when you're not appearing in random bars under the sea?" Oslind questioned, brows quirked curiously.

"Bethnal Green – over the sea in London. It's not much, but I have a small flat there. Yours is definitely nicer than what I have back home. Between the vermin that scamper about, and the spirits that roam the streets, I'm beginning to prefer Marvivia," Winnie chuckled.

"And is there anyone back home waiting for you?" Brenna's hand rested on Winnie's dainty moonstone ring. When Winnie flashed her a strange look, she explained, "I can sense the love behind this gift. I assumed someone special bought it for you."

Winnie released a long, hard sigh. "There is. I miss him terribly."

"What's his name?" the selkie pushed as though it were just two girls discussing crushes on a summer afternoon.

"Kane." The mere mention of his name twisted her heart into knots. "Like both of you, we've been friends for years. We officially began courting before I was pulled away here. I can tell he's looking for me. I hear his siren song day and night, drawing me home."

"A siren?" Oslind scoffed. "Tricky creatures, those ones. Why don't you just leave? Go home to him?"

Brenna shot him a look. "That was rather rude, you urchin."

Winnie chuckled, understanding what he meant. "I've been sent here on an assignment. Until I've done what I'm meant to, I'm not allowed to return home."

"We'll help you with whatever you need," Brenna assured with another of many sweet smiles. Between the two creatures, Winnie was beginning to think she preferred selkies over mermaids.

17

THOREN
CHICAGO - 1871

Heavy boots thudded along the stairs of the Chicago Orphan Asylum. Thoren marched toward the exit with Ezra just behind him before his attention landed on his brother. Kane sat in the window, eyes rested on the sky as though he were deep in thought, and trying to make sense of their situation.

"Still just staring..." Ezra mumbled, motioning with his chin toward the lovelorn siren.

"What are you doing just sitting here, moping?" Thoren called.

Kane jumped, startled by their sudden presence. "They called off work for the day. There's a festival. I was just listening to the music."

"You'd hear it better if you'd come out and join us. There's no use sitting here staring off into the distance like some lost puppy." Though he didn't mean for them to come out so harsh, Kane seemed to flinch at Thoren's words.

"I can't. Not until I know Winnie's safe."

Releasing a heavy sigh, he handed his brother a small slip of paper. "That's her spell. Our Mum's. I'm basing it all off of memory, so hopefully it's accurate. If for some reason it doesn't work..."

"Don't." Kane's words were sharp, a bitterness to them as the muscles in his jaw twitched in hidden anger. "It'll work. It has to."

"Just...be patient. It may take a few tries. I don't want you to completely lose it if nothing comes of it."

Ezra shot his love a confused glance. Thoren shook his head, as if to say *"I'll tell you later."*

"We'll be patrolling for a little while. Then we intend to go to the festival. I hope you'll join us," Ezra added before turning toward the door as he and Thoren exited the orphanage.

The cold December wind swirled around them in a cool welcome. They passed Cricket on their way out, on guard and waiting for Tara to return. Thoren noticed his love's eyes rested on the sounds of the festival, though they turned and headed away instead. At least for the first half of the day. *I don't want to risk missing any beasts that may ruin this for the locals,* he thought as they walked.

"We should just skip the patrolling, and have some fun," Ezra said, pulling Thoren from his thoughts. That beaming smile was an enticing enough offer for him to almost change his mind.

"Later, moró mou," he crooned, pulling Ezra in for a quick peck on the cheek.

His love's gaze flashed around in a panic, noting whether anyone around them would notice. Only Thoren saw the anxiety. Rather than use words to calm him, he pulled Ezra in for a firm embrace. Thoren cupped his face gingerly, planting plump lips on his love's. Ezra welcomed the affection, their tongues intertwining and heat coursing between them.

"I keep telling you that we have nothing to hide. I will not be ashamed to be seen with you."

Ezra released a beaming smile before leaning into Thoren's touch. He turned, their fingers still interlaced, pulling him along through the streets of Chicago.

"Your brother seems so lost without Winnie."

Thoren shook his head. "I don't know what more I can do to reassure him that she's fine. Or any of you for that matter."

"How are you not more concerned? She's been gone for more

than a week now. Whatever she's doing, it's not like her to just abandon us like this without so much as an explanation." Ezra's gaze dropped heavy to the ground, kicking at a nearby rock.

For a moment, Thoren was too stunned for words. Through all of this, he didn't realize that in trying to be the rational one, he'd end up seeming the most heartless.

"I'm worried about her, of course. But we all seem to forget that she's an incredibly powerful witch. One that can take care of herself. Rather than worry myself to death, I'd rather trust she knows what she's doing, and will come home when the time is right. Besides… She is one to just abandon people. She left me for Samuel. Then her entire family after Kane and I were banished. Somehow, everyone likes to overlook that side of her."

With a slow nod, Ezra continued. "I see your side of it, but I've only known the 'witch' Winnie for a few months now. I've known her longer as simply my best friend. I'm terrified something happened to her."

"She'll be okay. And if she needs help, we'll find a way to make sure we're there for her. Nothing's going to happen…"

"I refuse to lose anyone else." Ezra's face turned to a scowl, anger replacing what had been fear and sadness in the weeks following Samhain.

"You won't, Ez. Trust that she'll be okay. Have faith in her abilities." A gentle hand stroked Ezra's blonde waves for a moment until he seemed to still beneath Thoren's touch, anger simmering down.

"What's Kane trying to do? With the spell you handed him?"

"He's attempting a ritual our mum and dad used to send visions to each other. It's old magic from our family. I'm petrified to think it won't work, and he'll completely lose any bit of sanity he has left," Thoren explained with a sigh.

"Why wouldn't it work?"

"It requires the connection between the two people to be

incredibly strong. Soulmates, to be exact. Our parents were fortunate to share such a rare bond." Thoren continued his saunter down the streets, his hands in his pockets to brace the cold chill.

Ezra's brows scrunched in confusion. "You don't think they're soulmates?"

Thoren scoffed. "You do? They only just went on their first date. Soulmates are incredibly rare. Most never meet theirs in their lifetime, and hope they can try again in the next. Your soulmate is more likely to be someone who you never even fall in love with."

He hesitated a moment before a curious gaze landed back on the siren. "Do you think we're soulmates?"

This feels like a trap, Thoren thought. He paused for a long, hard moment. "I think they're too rare. You're the love of my life, but soulmates aren't as abundant as people think."

With a grunt, Ezra's face turned to a cynical glare. "Seriously?" Hurriedly, he walked off as if suddenly looking for a fight.

Thoren slouched, dropping his head low and immediately realizing he'd messed up. "I didn't mean it like that," he tried to say. "I love you, but I just think that…"

"Sometimes I feel bad for you," Ezra began, that same slow anger bubbling to the surface again. "One of these days, I hope you'll explain why you have such a lackluster view on love. In the meantime, I will hold true to the fact that I do think we're soulmates. Nothing you can say will change my mind. Perhaps one day, you'll agree."

Thoren couldn't tell if he was still angry or if humor laced his words. Regardless, Ezra attempted to march down the street.

"Kane mentioned something else," Thoren added hesitantly, thinking back to his brother's talk.

Ezra stopped, his cheeks flushed. He waited, Thoren unsure how to bring up what he needed to say. "He mentioned how you're having trouble in fights. How you tend to freeze up."

"Wonderful. First Tara, now Kane? At least Melinda isn't fixated on my inabilities. I tried to warn you all – I'm not a warrior!" His cheeks flared red hot, pacing before the siren.

"There's something we can do, but it's risky. It would take away the pain of that first kill. Maybe help you heal from it all." Thoren's gaze avoided his love's, unsure he wanted to be the one to perform that kind of dark magic.

"Explain."

"It's a simple siren song," Thoren lied. "It can help you to see that first kill with less…feeling. If you want. Make you accept it a little more, so you won't feel as guilty for it." Nerves bubbled in his stomach, feeling the anger broiling from his love.

"Do you honestly believe I'd want that? To not feel?" Ezra paused for a moment, searching for the right words. "I didn't think you could manipulate people like that."

"There's a lot we can do with our siren songs. Magic and powers we don't tap into unless we have to." Trying to avoid Ezra's piercing attention, Thoren turned away.

"Because it's evil?"

The question caught him off guard. "No! It's not…"

"You're a terrible liar, Thor. Be honest with me." Ezra braced his arms over his chest, a scowl printed across his face.

"Manipulating someone like that, it's… darker than any magic we typically use. Most siren cities have such practices banned for good reason. I've known very few who went that far, and live to tell the tale," the siren admitted at last.

Ezra released an almost manic laugh. "And you thought it appropriate to offer it to me like it's no big deal? What's gotten into you? Honestly? And you mean to tell me Kane suggested this?"

"He's done it before. It's a rather long story but…he was technically successful. It took him almost two years to recover, but he did. You don't have to do it, but it's there as an option if it all becomes too much." Thoren felt as though he were suddenly back tracking, wishing he could take back those words. And perhaps the ones before, too. *Somehow, I'd planned on bringing up Sezen in this conversation. Now is most definitely not the right time,* he thought.

"Let's just focus on patrolling," Ezra scoffed before heading off down the street.

I should never have opened my mouth, he realized with a heavy sigh.

18

KANE
CHICAGO - 1871

Kane still sat in the window of the orphanage, watching his brother and Ezra down the street. At first, he'd nervously wondered if they were discussing him. But as the blonde's face shaded pink with anger and his brother's stance turned apologetic, he assumed they weren't discussing him at all. His attention turned back toward the sound of the festival music. *Winnie would've loved going to such an event,* he thought with a heavy heart.

Though he'd considered going by himself, it didn't feel right while worry sat in his stomach like a pit of rocks. Weighed down by nerves, his mind raced endlessly thinking of all the worst possible outcomes.

Thoren could be right – she could be dead. Though strangely, Kane felt like he'd know if that were the case. Something deep down in his chest would ache. He'd feel her absence in this word like a missing limb.

She could be injured, needing help. Lost and alone; no friends or family to help her. *But she's strong and capable. Stop undermining her,* he scolded himself.

Then, an even worse thought occurred to him. What if she just didn't *want* to come home? What if she'd simply run away from them? Away from *him.* Just as Thoren suggested. What if she had no intention of ever returning? Perhaps all the worst qualities he saw in himself were ones she'd realized too, and now she never wanted to come back to him.

Deep down, despite it all, he had to remind himself that when Wesley died, so did a part of her. Since the funeral, her light had dimmed. Winnie's usual sunshine was clouded now. But it wasn't just her; every member of the Fox family was affected. And because of what happened, it seemed to turn her against him.

And now she was just *gone*. Not a trace left. Every night since the moment she disappeared, he attempted his siren song. Sending out tiny explorers of energy looking for his lost love, Kane was desperate. If she heard the song, she'd have no choice but to return. Yet still, she somehow managed to evade him.

The old Winnie I knew would never keep so many secrets from me, he thought.

A badgering itch of a voice slithered in the back of his mind. *"Aren't you the one keeping secrets, too?"*

A quick tug on his shirt sleeve pulled Kane from his thoughts. He looked to his side, sending his gaze down to the small curly-haired boy.

"Yes, mikri?" he crooned, Otto being the only one who seemed to coax a smile from him these days.

"I'm bored," the boy whined. "Can we do something fun? Miss Leona won't let us go outside, and I feel I'll go insane if I stay here any longer."

"Have you finished your studies for the day?"

The boy nodded in excitement as Kane examined the list in his hand.

"I do have an errand to run. Maybe we can sneak you out for a little bit?" he suggested, getting down to the boy's level.

Otto's excitement only built higher and higher with every jump as though he'd spring himself to the moon. "I'll inform the matron!"

Kane caught his arm. "Let's tell them when we get back. Otherwise they may say 'no.' Miss Leona, especially, " he whispered.

175

It's probably not the best idea, but it's only the manor, he thought. The estate was still warded, probably safer than the orphanage itself. The boy's face turned to a mischievous grin, nodding in agreement. Otto grasped his hand firmly, Kane walking them toward the mirror portal upstairs.

"Now, in a second we're going to step through. When we do, it may feel a little funny but we're going to come out on the other side just fine," he reassured.

"I knew you were lying the other day when you said you didn't walk through the mirror. I finally get to have my own adventures!" Otto seemed to glow with excitement, the energy wafting off of him palpable in the air.

Kane could only chuckle. The boy yelped in surprise as they ventured to the other side of the world and onto the lands of Fox Manor. All at once, the siren's breath was taken away at the sight of the estate. Even Otto let out a small gasp, both of their eyes wandering the grounds.

In the short days they'd been gone, a bed of snow had fallen across the land. Chicago had only seen dry cold, windy as ever. Here, Milicent decorated the outside with fairy lights and wreaths of greenery intertwined with berries.

Kane recalled fond memories of being a kid, sharing winter solstice gifts around the many fireplaces. Those moments pulled at his heartstrings, thinking of the many chess games he'd played with Wesley over the years. And the ones he'd denied.

Otto shivered, unprepared for the cold in his everyday clothes.

"Let's get you inside," Kane rushed, the two running toward the manor's sunroom. As they entered, they shook off their shoes and hurried over to the fireplace to warm themselves.

"Kane?" Milicent exclaimed, looking surprised to see him back so soon.

"Afternoon," he said softly, pulling Otto in front of him. "I hope you don't mind. I know we said we'd be gone for a while, but there was someone who needed to get out of the Asylum for a while. I thought this was the perfect place to show him."

"And who might you be?" she chirped, kneeling down to meet the boy at eye level as her black dress sprawled around her.

"My name's Otto. I'm six." A confident hand reached toward her, a beaming smile revealing a missing tooth.

"Is that so?" she giggled, taking his tiny hand in her own. "I'm Milicent, but you can call me Momma Millie." She offered Kane a quick wink before straightening herself back up.

He chuckled, glad to see some of her warmth returning. The last time he'd been here, she'd seemed so void of any and all emotion. He worried about leaving them alone without...

"I came to fetch some supplies for a spell. I hope you don't mind." Kane offered her Thoren's list.

"Not at all. What exactly are you trying to do? Aphrodite? Eros?" she questioned, brows furrowed as she scanned the list. "I've never seen a spell like this before. These are deities I've never tried to invoke."

"I'm trying to get in contact with Winnie."

Her eyes dropped, nodding a little in understanding.

"Have you had any more visions of her?" He waited, hopeful that she'd open up. But she stood for a long moment in complete silence instead.

"No, I'm sorry. I know she made it to her destination, but I haven't seen her since."

"Do you actually not know, or are you keeping secrets again?" He hadn't intended to be rude, though the words came out too quick to stop.

Otto looked back and forth between the two, confused.

"I truly don't know," she repeated. "If I could tell you any new information, believe me I would. I hate seeing the strain this has on you and the others."

Kane nodded, accepting that he had to simply trust her.

"Where's Ernest? I figured he'd be plowing the snow and removing it from your flowers out front."

A sad smile graced her lips, staring past them toward the door. "He's in London with Horace looking into some grave robbings Ezra warned us about. I doubt they'll find anything, however. I suspect it's pure gossip."

There was a moment of pause before Otto chimed in. "Momma Millie?"

"Yes dear?"

"What are those?" he asked, pointing toward a bowl on a table nearby.

Milicent took a cookie and handed him one. "These?"

His eyes widened in bewilderment, like he'd never seen something so amazing.

"They're cookies. An old family favorite. Have one."

Otto took a hesitant bite, Kane's favorite almond cookie crumbling in the boy's mouth. He squealed in joy as though he'd never experienced anything like it.

"Has the boy never had a cookie before?" she questioned in disbelief.

"I doubt the orphanage celebrates solstice," Kane teased, taking one for himself. It'd been years since he'd enjoyed the taste of nutty vanilla, bringing back more and more memories with every bite.

"Come with me," she commanded, pulling them both by the hand into the kitchen.

Kane followed diligently behind. Reaching into the cupboard, Milicent pulled out a bar of chocolate, then a jar of milk from the icebox. Placing a pot on the gas stove, he watched as she asked Otto to pour the milk into a pot. A look of concerned confusion lay plastered across the boy's face, though he did as she asked.

"A Momma Millie specialty?" Kane already knew the answer. He remembered the steaming drink from his teenage years. During the winter, they always enjoyed a cup of hot drinking chocolate after a day of playing in the snow.

"Of course. The boy needs to try it!" At last she smiled, the first he'd noticed in over a month. "Feel free to take anything you need from my study. We'll be here," she said, turning the gas stove on and shredding the bar of chocolate with a grater.

Otto looked between Milicent and Kane in worry.

"You'll be alright. Stay here. I'll be back in a second," he reassured.

Walking up two sets of creaking stairs, he arrived at Milicent's attic study. As he entered, he instantly recognized the peaked ceiling, dusty and covered in cobwebs. He hadn't been up here since he was fourteen, after Wesley dared him to sneak into her workspace. He laughed thinking of those memories, Momma Millie's stern tone of disappointment that he would try to do anything without permission.

It was exactly as he remembered it; walnut wood lining the walls and ceiling. Rich colors of red and navy in an intricately woven rug. A large podium at the center, a thick book sitting on top.

The walls were covered in shelves, stacks of magical texts and ingredients for potions lining them. She didn't keep plants up here as the small round window only let in a little bit of light. It was just enough to make his way toward the gas lamp on a side table before turning it on to illuminate his way.

Grabbing one of the cloth bags that hung on a nearby shelf, Kane collected the supplies he needed. Candles mainly, though he also required rose petals and basil. Why those things, he wasn't sure, though he didn't question his mother's spell. Most of the work came from simple visualization and meditation, as with most magic.

Just behind him, a small groan in the floorboard caused panic. Kane turned, not seeing anything. Another creak sounded, this time closer. He spun around, more and more alarm spreading as he felt the presence of someone nearby that he couldn't see.

He heard one final wooden squeal just in front of the shelves before a vial of cloves fell to the floor. He picked it up, examining the contents before checking his list again. Cloves weren't on it. Placing the glass container back, he turned to go back downstairs. Before he could even make it through the door, the vial fell again.

"I take it, I need these?" he asked the void.

Around him, a strange sensation seemed to swirl and dance. A familiar scent filled the air, transporting him back to childhood. Freshly baked bread and all manner of flowers; a floral sweet and light with just the slightest hint of earthy notes that made his heart ache for a home that no longer existed. He took a deep breath, tears stinging the backs of his eyelids.

"Mum?" he whispered softly. He didn't hear anything in response, though the smell of her perfume got closer for a moment before disappearing until only the musty smell of attic remained.

"Thoren must've forgotten these," he chuckled to himself, wiping away a silent tear as he headed back down to the two giggling in the kitchen.

Pangs of grief hit him as he saw her at the stove making drinking chocolate with Otto. It reminded him of all the times he'd seen her do that with Wesley. Those memories brought on others. Before he knew it, a waterfall of grief flooded him. There was no strength left to withstand the sorrow.

Milicent turned in time to see Kane crumble. "Oh my dear," she whispered softly, rushing toward him.

Pulling him into an embrace, they both fell to the ground in a heaping mess of heartbreak and sadness. Otto ran to Kane's side, offering an equally affectionate bear hug.

A few moments passed before the boy whispered, "There's a lady here."

With a sniffle, Kane straightened and followed the boy's gaze.

"She's saying something strange. I don't know what she means.

She says Thoren did forget the cloves. Does that make sense to you?" Otto cocked his head to the side with a confused scowl.

"You can see her? You can see my mother?" Kane asked, his desperate eyes flashing around the room.

"She had to go, but she said she loves you. And is proud of the man you've become. She seems like a very nice lady. She's also *really* pretty," the boy said with a blushing smile before his gaze fixed permanently on the siren once more.

Kane turned to Milicent, seeking answers.

"The boy sees...spirits. Like Winnie did when she was little," she said with a huff of surprise, wiping away a tear. "You're very special, you know that?"

Otto giggled. "I'm usually told I'm creepy, but thanks anyways."

Kane crumbled once more into Milicent's arms, the tears feeling like they'd never stop.

"Otto, will you stir the pot? I think we need a minute," Milicent asked gently, a calming hand stroking Kane's head as his weeps slowed and fizzled out.

The boy nodded, hesitantly walking away.

"I'm sorry for my behavior," he whispered at last when the tears dried up.

"What behavior? This is grief. Nothing more. There's no need to apologize. We've been through literal hell the last few months. Years even. We all need a good cry," she said, wiping away another runaway tear.

At last, Kane got back up to his feet. Glancing back toward the doorway where Otto had seen his mother, he felt Milicent place a delicate hand on his arm.

"I know you're not a child anymore, but a part of me will always imagine the scraggly little boy you were when we first welcomed you into our home. Running around, causing absolute havoc. They remain, to this day, some of my fondest memories." Her smile was soft and sincere, holding back more tears. "One of my greatest regrets in this life is sending you boys away when you needed us most."

Kane didn't know what to say. He could only offer her a soft nod as years of memories spent here with his parents threatened to send him into another tailspin. Years of longing for family, only to vanish the moment he'd let his emotions get the better of him. The moment she'd banished them.

"I say we take this outside and enjoy it in the snow," she said at last, trying to hide the lingering sorrows.

With a snap of her fingers, a thick winter coat surrounding Otto as he yelped in surprise. Kane hadn't warned the boy, or Milicent for that matter, that he wasn't accustomed to magic. The boy didn't seem to mind, his eyes wild with excitement.

They sat in chairs amidst the snow, looking out at the frozen lake while Milicent told tales of Kane as a young boy. Otto giggled at many of them, staring at him in disbelief only to discover how much of a hooligan the siren had been.

The two took some time to explore the woods briefly, the little boy picking up all manner of treasures and shoving them into the pockets of his coat.

"We should probably get back. Miss Leona will have noticed your absence by now, I'd imagine," Kane shouted across the glistening white field.

Otto came running, though he passed Kane to offer Milicent a bear hug. He glanced up at her, then back at the siren, before ushering her down to his level.

Though Kane couldn't tell what the boy said, she seemed to giggle and nod. With a snap of her fingers, something thin and spindly appeared in her hands. She offered it to the boy who shoved it into his jacket before running back toward the siren.

"Bye Momma Millie!" he called, grasping Kane's hand firmly.

Before they could leave, Ernest appeared at the door of the

sunroom.

"One second. I need to talk to him," Kane mumbled, urging Otto back toward the field. The boy didn't put up a fight, happily skipping off to play.

"You've made a new friend," Ernest chuckled, watching the child jump joyously in the icy snow. Pain sat behind his eyes, though he smiled nonetheless.

"Still looking into those grave robbings?" Kane asked, leaning against the edge of the house.

The man nodded before rubbing his head. "Have you heard from Winnie? Any news on my daughter?"

"I wish I could say 'yes,' but sadly I have no idea where she is." He shook his head, glancing down at the ground. "I'm trying to find her, I promise. I won't stop until I know she's okay."

A solemn frown moved across her father's face before he added, "Do me a favor…"

Kane nodded, turning toward him in curiosity.

"Make her tell you the truth. Don't be a fool in love like I was all those years ago. Your partnership is only as good as the honesty between you two. If she can't tell you what's going on, save yourself the trouble of heartbreak, and end it quickly. You don't want to end up an old man like me, desperate for answers from a wife who won't give you any."

The siren took a step back. The shock of Ernest's words moved through his mind, needing some time to process.

"I could never break your daughter's heart like that…"

"Then I pray she'll tell you what she's doing. Otherwise it'll be your sorry ass that gets hurt." Ernest peered toward his wife before offering her a careful wave.

Otto came running back toward them, jumping up and down in excitement. "Kitchen duty starts soon! I need to get back!"

Kane nodded, offering Ernest one last look of concern before bidding farewell.

19

TARA
CHICAGO - 1871

A cool rush of wind met Tara as the bartender offered a nod and entered the establishment again. She glanced inside, seeing Alaric hand him a handful of coins before turning to exit. She rushed off, back to the celebration where Melinda now sat by a fire talking to the Broderick trio.

As she approached, her friend's face lit up in joy. "You're back! I was wondering where you ran off to." Melinda peered behind Tara, though didn't seem to pick up on Alaric's presence.

"I was just," she began, though truthfully didn't know what to say. "It's a long story. I'll try to explain later."

With a quick glance over her shoulder, she couldn't figure out where the hellhound had scampered off to. It wasn't until she saw his broad-shouldered silhouette walking down the street that she realized she could breathe easy once again.

Taking a seat with the group, Danny offered her a cup of cider. She declined it, feeling the effects of the alcohol she'd shared with Alaric. Instead, Tara reached for a loaf of bread and nibbled hungrily.

"So you know where we're from. What about you both?" Danny asked, jutting his chin toward Tara and Melinda.

The redhead watched curiously as Riah translated every word into hand signals for Spencer, who's eyes jumped back and forth between the mouths of whoever spoke and his sister's signs.

"I'm from here," Melinda said with a shrug and half smile, gesturing around them at the city.

"You can probably guess by my accent where I'm from," Tara noted with a chuckle, tossing a chunk of bread into her mouth.

"Our mom was from Ireland, too," Riah said with a faint smile, eyes wandering as if recalling memories.

"You don't have accents yourself," she noted, examining them curiously. She saw small signs similar to her own family – the freckles peppering their faces and reddish tint to their hair. But overall, had they not mentioned it, she would've just assumed they were American.

"Dad wasn't Irish. He was a freed man, trying to make a living in the city. Met our mom fighting for work, living in the same slums. Told us he fell in love with her the moment she gave him attitude," Danny explained, a hazy smile across his lips.

Melinda seemed to sense the moment of hesitation before asking, "Are they not around anymore?"

Spencer's gaze fell away from the conversation, fists clenched and cheeks reddening in anger.

"Yes and no. Mugging gone wrong," Riah muttered plainly, pulling apart a piece of bread in her hands as though it were the muggers themselves. "They're thankfully still alive, but our family desperately needs money. That's why we came here."

"Sorry to hear that," Melinda mumbled.

Riah signed to Spencer, though his eyes still avoided the conversation. She nudged him with her foot, fingers moving rapidly as he simply nodded in response.

At last, he finally mumbled, "I'm fine," though still refused to look at the group.

In an attempt to change the topic, Tara asked, "Was it hard to learn sign language?"

She shook her head. "We were young, and it was a necessity. You learn quick when you have no other option."

Melinda prepared for an incoming question, though quickly seemed to decide against it. Danny's head dropped as if understanding the nature of her curiosity. Spencer's eyes traced her expressions carefully before explaining himself.

"Scarlet Fever," was all Spencer said before once again averting his gaze.

"It hit New York like a train when we were kids. Everyone had it. If you didn't have money for a doctor, you either died or survived within an inch of your life and hoped your hearing wasn't impacted. Our brother wasn't as lucky as us, being the youngest of the group," Danny explained.

"I can hear some sounds. But I mostly feel. The music especially," Spencer said quietly, pointing out toward the crowd. "Damn fever didn't take everything from me." He shot Melinda a shy smirk which she returned with blushing cheeks.

"The three of you have really been through it, haven't you?" Tara mumbled.

"That's life in America, I suppose. Apologies. No need to put a damper on the festivities. Let's discuss something of less weight," Danny joked. When he began to discuss the gossip of the town, his sister seemed to shrink back into her chair with an eye roll.

As the group sat around the fire, the Broderick trio took turns pointing out various workers and townsfolk. They discussed who had issues with whom, and for what petty reasons. Who was enjoying the neighbor's wife a little too warmly, or who had recently ended secret flings.

Struggling to concentrate on the conversation, Tara found herself caught in a storm of her own making. *Is Alaric right? Or is he just lying? What does he stand to gain from my help?* The questions tumbled around in her mind until other thoughts surfaced instead. The way his hand had so casually grazed along her skin. The slight quirk in the corner of his mouth when she pressed her blade into his skin. The hair tuck behind her ear. The assurance that her word was worth more than the others gave her credit for.

Tara's mind seemed to wander Chicago, her soul searching for him. Whether it was to question him further or understand his motives, she wasn't sure. *Either way, I know I'm being foolish,* she thought with some resignation.

Eventually, the sun in the sky slowly set. The horizon was a warm sherbet swirl of blues and oranges, though the party wasn't over. It seemed the workers would milk the festival for all it was worth. Even some of the refugee families who stayed at the Chicago Orphan Asylum were in attendance, childless for the night. For once, there were no attacks. Only festive joy and laughter.

"I think I'll retire," Tara announced as a lull passed through the conversation.

"You won't stay? I heard there will be a big performance later with more musicians!" Melinda grabbed Tara's hand.

"You can tell me all about it tomorrow." Offering the Broderick trio a polite smile, she pointed to Spencer. "You'll take care of her, won't you?"

His face paled before blushing cheeks turned to a grin, offering her a quiet nod.

"We'll make sure she gets home safe," Riah assured, swatting Danny who dozed off in his chair.

Leaving at last, Tara felt like she was wandering rather than heading home. After some time, Cricket's tapping paws outside the orphanage welcomed her. Panting heavily, the shuck's face turned to an almost human grin as she offered him a quick scratch. Walking through the threshold, the warmth of the house radiated through her, as she removed her coat and headed upstairs. *I may sleep at Fox Manor tonight if Milicent will have me,* she thought.

"Go back to Milicent and Ernest. I'll be right there," she ordered Cricket. The mutt's face seemed to drop once again, as if pleading to stay. "I know you have to potty! Go and wait for me," she insisted, pointing at the mirrored portal once more.

Cricket let out a deep, depressed sigh before stepping through at last.

Standing in the hallway, the sounds of shouting alerted her. Coming from their shared room, she could hear Thoren and Kane yelling at one another. *They'll wake the children,* she thought with a grumble.

Tara knocked on the door, her eyes jutting around the room anxiously. Fallen candles lay in a semicircle, Ezra on the couch rubbing his head as the brothers stood in fuming anger.

"What's going on?"

The three men in the room turned, their heads snapping to her sudden intrusion.

20
WINIFRED
MARVIVIA - 1861

After yet another seafood dinner, Winnie found herself sitting along Oslind's floor meditating as Kane's siren song swirled through her mind. Every ounce of strength she had was used to resist the enticing call. *I wish he would stop so I can focus on my work,* she thought begrudgingly. It wasn't until a set of hands shook her shoulders that she was pulled from the trance.

"Your father finally responded." Oslind tossed the letter onto her lap as she rubbed the daze from her eyes.

Realizing he was upset, she asked, "What's wrong?"

"He says he won't help. He's suspicious of us; wants to know how we learned about his family." His tone was sharp, back to that same heartless version that she'd originally met.

Dammit, she thought. *Of all the stories my parents told of their involvement with Afissa's people, they'd never mentioned my father's initial refusal.*

"Maybe I can talk to him. Do you have a portal to..." She stopped herself. *The portal to Fox Manor hasn't been created yet,* Winnie realized.

"At some point, you have to let me in on what you're thinking. I understand you're trying to help, but without the full picture, you're just growing tiresome." His arms were crossed in front of his chest, lips tight in distaste.

"Do you possess any earth or air magic? Or know anyone who

does? I need help to create a portal. I can wield water and fire. I'm just missing those final elemental components, and then I can confront my father myself."

He shook his head. "The best you'll find down here is water or air. My father has one mermaid on his council who can wield fire, but I'm not bringing him anywhere near this situation. Brenna can use air, but earth remains unspoken for."

"Brenna has air magic?"

"All selkies do. That's how you're breathing right now."

A moment of clarity hit her. "You mean to tell me selkies helped build this place, and yet your father still exiled them?"

"Long ago, yes," Oslind nodded, his brows scrunched in confusion as if unable to understand how she lacked such basic knowledge. "There's plenty of valid reasons why I hate my father."

"Can you get her here? We'll have to make it work, I guess. But I'll need you both to try opening a portal home."

Truthfully, she didn't know what she was saying. All the way at the bottom of the ocean, she didn't know what phase the moon was in, or if it was even nighttime. She didn't have all four elements or offerings. But she'd have to make it work somehow. Thinking back to what Brenna told her of the coven's limitations, she hoped the Elements would work with her.

"It's not safe for her to come here. I'm not risking the love of my life for your vague mission." Leaning against the wall, he glared at her.

"She snuck in here the other day undetected. I'm sure she can do it again," Winnie countered.

With a heavy sigh, he said, "I'll send word, but I make no promises. If anything happens to her..."

"I know. I'm sure you'll kill me like every other lovelorn man."

Later that evening, Brenna darted into Oslind's home. Spearing through the door, she hid behind the wall to avoid being seen through the windows. Removing her selkie skins, she covered her body with shivering arms.

"What's wrong?"

"Nothing – it's okay!" Winnie reassured, rushing to bring her a blanket to cover and warm up.

Nodding in thanks, the selkie asked, "What's the emergency?" Staring past Winnie, her attention remained fixed on Oslind.

"I just need your help. I need to create a portal."

Brenna's eyes darted back to her angrily. "The dolphin signal means 'emergency!' And you need me to help you with a simple portal? That's not life or death!" Her shouts echoed through the flat.

"I know, I'm sorry, Bren. I needed to get you here." Oslind stroked her arms in reassurance. "You might as well get back into your skins; we need to get going."

"Did you say 'simple' portal?" Winnie asked, caught off guard. *My family struggles to create portals and she thinks it's easy?*

Brenna nodded, her face pinched in annoyance. "Patrols will be out again in a few minutes. They're switching shifts. If you want to create some damn portal, we better go now."

Sliding back into her skins, she transformed into the selkie Winnie had initially met. Preparing to enter the frigid waters, Winnie pulled her goggles down and asked Caelus for help just as before.

This late at night, the darkness was terrifying. In the shadows, anything could've been lurking. And it felt that way, too. Winnie glanced around the area, looking for signs of danger. She wanted to believe Oslind when he said no predators entered within the city's limits, and yet she'd still see the occasional shark. The octopuses freaked her out even more – terrified to get caught within their gangly tentacles.

Brenna turned back, grabbing Winnie by the hand and dragging her through the water. The sheer speed of the creature was unmatched. *No wonder the mermaids are losing the battle against them. They can't even keep up,* she thought as the waves pelted her goggles.

Oslind joined them on the outskirts of Marvivia shortly after. Opening her eyes, Winnie couldn't see two inches in front of her. It was pitch-black there, a strange feeling of claustrophobia spreading over her. She was out in the wide open ocean, and yet never felt more trapped. Should her magic fail – which was a real possibility – she wouldn't make it anywhere in time to survive.

As if reading her mind, Brenna motioned for her to calm down; breathe. She and the mermaid seemed to have some sort of conversation, though Winnie still couldn't hear a thing. Water filled her ears, making her skin crawl hoping the liquid wouldn't get trapped in them again.

Pointing down to the bottom of the ocean, she gestured toward a good spot to create the portal. Oslind nodded, throwing a dimly lit orb down to illuminate the area a little, though not too much to draw unwanted attention.

Winnie paddled toward the bottom, her body fighting not to float up. *When my father makes the suits, they need to be weighted so that swimming isn't quite such a fight,* she thought. *Trying to navigate this underwater world is exhausting.* With her feet planted on the sandy floors, she reached for the others.

"Elements! I have no offerings. I don't even have all four elements. But you have to help me. We need to get to Fox Manor," she pleaded, sending her prayers through the void.

As her fingers grasped Oslind and Brenna's, a small jolt of energy coursed through her. It took a moment before she realized that it was coming from the selkie, more power than she'd ever felt before in her life. *She's stronger than Thoren and Kane combined. No wonder King Aalto feels so threatened.*

Both nodded to Winnie as she closed her eyes, attempting to visualize Fox Manor. The strange sensations of claustrophobia engulfed her once more, feeling like the water might officially drown her. Though she could see the house clearly, she wasn't feeling the connection to the Elements.

Motioning to the ground, Winnie attempted to bring forth a ball of fire. Nothing appeared, so she turned to Gali instead. The others nodded in understanding, sending their own elements into the earth. Tiny shimmering blobs of magic nestled into the sand, awaiting their destination.

A wave of energy spread around them. Oslind's orb dimmed, the sandy surface seeming to brighten in molten flame. For a moment, it looked as though the ground would split in two as scorching lava rose higher and higher from beneath the earth's crust.

Brenna reached out, smoothing the surface. Placing her energy into the creation of the portal, the embers seemed to settle and turned back to the familiar sandy texture. It swirled below like quicksand, ready to drag them below, hopefully toward their desired location.

Cringing, Winnie thought of the sand that she'd likely be pulling from her ears and nostrils for the next century. Brenna grabbed her hand, guiding them down. Before they made contact, she turned back one last time. With a hopeful smile, the selkie motioned as though to tell Winnie to hold her breath before they finally pushed through the gritty abyss.

21

KANE
CHICAGO - 1871

Sitting in their shared quarters at the Chicago Orphan Asylum, Kane moved makeshift mattresses aside to make room for a large circle of candles. Jittery and anxious, he memorized Thoren's spell, double checking the ingredients. Then, he practiced visualizing Winnie in his mind. *Everything has to be perfect,* he thought.

Before beginning the spell, he tried his siren song one last time. Summoning her as hard as he could, still nothing happened. *It doesn't make any sense. If she is anywhere nearby and can hear me, she'd have to come.* When that didn't work, he pushed a little harder. Sent his search out wider and more commanding, using a certain kind of magic he'd been explicitly told to avoid.

Tonight wasn't the first time he'd tapped into the darker side of his siren abilities to lure her. The haunting melody of their favorite song had escaped his lips several times, intending to draw Winnie home. He tried and tried, his voice almost hoarse from the constant strain as he repeated the song.

With a heavy sigh, he whispered to himself, "Time to put our relationship to the test." *Can I really call it that when we've only gone on one date and shared a few kisses? Perhaps I'm making a fool of myself, after all,* he thought as he glanced down at the spell. Despite the hesitation, he settled his mind. *I can't have doubts before even starting…*

Kane walked to the door, and peaked down the hallway. The entire house was still, only the sounds of little snores just down the hall from the children's quarters catching his attention. Usually there were some conversations lingering throughout, but all of the adults had gone away to enjoy the festival while the few remaining orphanage staff agreed to stay behind and babysit. A set of shuffling feet paraded down the hall.

"Good night," he called out to Miss Leona.

She paused to examine him without saying anything. Cautious steps approached before she finally asked, "What's got you so glum?" Her inspection pierced through his soul, something only a mother or grandmother could perfect.

Kane's head dropped, a small huff escaping him. "I'm worried about my friend, that's all."

"The short one? With the dark hair and strange markings on her arm?" Miss Leona motioned to roughly Winnie's height before bracing her hand back on her hip.

Kane nodded.

"I can say a prayer for you, if you'd like. I've gathered that you and yours don't share my faith, but it can never hurt having more than one person looking out from above."

He fought back the urge to smile. "And here I thought you didn't care for us."

Her wrinkled lips turned to a grin before placing a delicate hand along the side of his face. "I never said I didn't like you, Kane. But I'd appreciate it if you didn't kidnap one of my children to go galavanting through the forest."

With a gulp, his face paled. Words weren't necessary. She could clearly read the expression on his face.

"No worries, Mr. Falke. It's probably the most fun Otto's had in a long time. It's good for the boy to get out and see the world. Perhaps when things are safer, you'll stick around. It would be good for him to have a positive male figure in his life."

"Not sure I qualify," he scoffed.

"The boy thinks the world of you. If you're not a man you'd want him to look up to, then this is your call to become one." A soft smile forming. "Don't let the darkness win." Offering the side of his face a quick squeeze, she walked to her own sleeping quarters beside the children's.

Kane turned, a glimmer of hope sparking in his chest. "Don't let the darkness win," he repeated softly, returning to the circle of candles along the ground.

At last, he prepared for the first step. Mixing together the ingredients, he sprinkled the crushed rose petal, basil, and cloves alongside pink candles. The sweet smell of autumn cloves wafted to his nose, mingling with the floral of petals. Turning off the gas lamps, only the flicker of candlelight illuminated the room.

Sitting in the center of the circle, he placed Winnie's dagger along with a pair of her favorite earrings before him. Silently, Kane prayed to the deities of love. First, he tried Aphrodite. Pleading to the goddess, though she did not respond. Then, he turned his attention instead toward Eros.

"Please, Eros. God of passion, desire, and love. Help me see her. Help me see my beautiful Winifred." He waited, several minutes of meditative visualization passing. Nothing happened, only his own mind creating scenarios where she'd run off with someone else as though he were her new Thoren, or worse: died. His search seemed futile, as though she didn't even exist anymore.

Looking over the spell, he mumbled, "Am I doing something wrong?" Defeated, he closed his eyes again. *Maybe I'm not focusing hard enough,* he thought to himself.

Once again, he called upon Eros.

"I don't know what I have to do to prove my love for her, but I'll do it. Please! Show me she's okay. Wherever she may be in this universe or the next, show me!"

At last, a glimmer of something started to form.

Vague images appeared, too subtle to make out any details. Pausing his meditation, he tried to understand them. Glittering waves washed up ahead, a soft and subtle blue hugging his essence. A muffled voice in the distance called out, though he couldn't turn his head in search. As if pushed out by an unseen hand, nothingness replaced the shimmering blue.

Is this…the afterlife? His thoughts raced, stuck in some strange void.

With a sharp sting, he returned to his body. The cold water made his bones ache, though the warmth of the orphanage soon returned. As he reopened his eyes, it hit him. *The spell didn't work.* Clutching his head in his hands, anger simmered in his gut until all he could do was knock over the candles.

"She said she'd never lie to me. Said she was safe. And now all I see is darkness when I try to find her." His words came out a pained mumble to no one in particular, wondering if perhaps he could somehow usher her spirit to join him.

Or maybe that wasn't her. The intrusive thought bubbled to the front of his mind, setting his entire body ablaze with rage. Picking up a nearby chair, he hurdled it at the wall with a heavy crash. A gentle knock rapped across the room as the last of the wood clattered to the floor.

"What?" he snapped, ripping the door open. Thoren and Ezra stood on the other side, curiously looking in.

"We, um, came to check in," Ezra began. "We wanted to see if we could convince you to take the night off and come with us."

"I'm not going to some fucking festival!" Kane yelled, ready to slam the door.

Thoren jutted his arm out, wincing as the wood struck him. "Careful how you speak to him. I know you're upset, but that's no way to talk to the people who care about you."

"I can't find her," Kane bellowed, pacing around the room. The candles extinguished themselves as he walked toward the gaslamp, and turned it on so they could see the bare outlines of the sparsely decorated room.

"It…didn't work?"

"No, it didn't fucking work," he spat.

"So then you're left with two options. Well, perhaps three. One, she may be dead." Thoren's words were plain as Ezra drew in a sharp breath, refusing to look at the siren brothers.

"Stop," Kane warned.

"Two, the spell is wrong. I could be misremembering, you never know," Thoren continued, two fingers waving in the air.

"I said, stop!"

"Or option three…"

"Don't you dare finish that fucking sentence!" Kane spat, lunging toward his brother with fists aching to punch something.

"Or, she's not your soulmate."

At last, his little brother uttered those dreaded words. The ones he knew were coming. Backing away, Thoren put his hands in the air in surrender with a tight frown. Ezra rushed to have a seat on the small sofa, a cool breeze picking up around the room. Caelus's powers swirled through Kane's body. Though, something else seemed to ignite. An unfamiliar power he wasn't used to.

"What our parents had was rare. You know that. Right now, I need you to focus on calming down," Thoren said softly, placing a calming hand on his brother's shoulder.

"I don't accept that," Kane growled, the surrounding air swirling, though simultaneously heating as though it suddenly turned to summer.

"Let's revisit option two," Ezra cut in. "The spell could've failed. Though he doesn't like to admit it, Thoren isn't right one hundred percent of the time."

"Stay out of this!" he yelled, returning his gaze back to Thoren. "Mum came to me at the manor. I know the spell worked. I saw something, just not her!"

"Brother," Thoren seemed to hiss. "You either calm down, or I'm going to knock your ass out. You are approaching a dangerous level of anger. Take a look at where you stand."

Kane did as he said, though hesitantly. Small tornadoes formed along the ceiling, ready to morph into something that would destroy the entire orphanage.

"I need to find her!" His voice came out as more of a cry, at last letting go of the festering rage. The wind around them settled, though his insistence did not.

"You sound like a damn lunatic," Thoren spat, Aelius's fire stirred in his eyes. "She can take care of herself! She doesn't need you. Driving yourself insane won't do us any good. You're acting just like Dad right now! And I'm sorry, but I'm not willing to let you consume yourself with this. I'm not willing to lose the only family I have left over some obsessive little crush."

"Thor, take it easy," Ezra sighed from the couch. He seemed unsure whether he should intervene, and instead chose to stay seated.

"Obsessive little crush?" The words escaped Kane as a mere whisper with a sardonic laugh before turning back toward his brother.

"You've been obsessed since we were banned. Don't even try to deny it! You saw what happened to her that night, what Samuel did, and it drove you to complete madness. Let's not forget everything that happened after we were told we were no longer welcome at Fox Manor. All because of you!"

Ezra leaned forward, clearly desperate for more details. He looked to Thoren, though the siren dismissed the incoming questions.

"You are constantly using that time against me! In every argument; every time you're upset with me! I made a mistake. When are you going to let it go?"

Thoren scoffed. "Mistakes don't almost kill a man. Or worse…"

Before he could finish his sentence, Kane stormed toward his brother. One hand grabbed his shirt, the other ready to strike.

Behind them, the door creaked open slowly. A head of red hair poked through, a nervous glance passing over each man inside.

"What's going on?" Tara asked, their attention snapping in her direction.

"Nothing," Kane snapped, releasing Thoren's shirt and shoving him back.

"I was hoping to talk to you lads for a moment, but I'm wondering if now may not be a good time."

"Seriously, Tara? Right now?" Kane's arms crashed in front of him with a scowl on his face.

"Stop being an ass to everyone," Thoren snapped. "Go sit over there and shut up for a few minutes."

Kane grumbled, stalking toward the couch. Before he sat down, he grabbed some gin from his bag and took a sip straight from the bottle.

"I doubt alcohol will make this conversation any better," Ezra mumbled, glancing at the drink.

"Can't make it any worse." Begrudgingly, Kane offered him some. He accepted cautiously, taking a hard sip.

"What is it, Tara?" Thoren asked with a sigh, motioning for her to have a seat in one of the remaining chairs. He took his pistol and dagger off his belt, setting it on the edge of the table before joining her.

"Before I say anything, I need you to just hear me out," she began, though she was met with strange looks from all three men. "I met with someone today, and he told me some information about the mayor. Something I thought you should know."

Thoren rolled his eyes before asking, "And who is this person you spoke to?"

"I don't want to say any names," she said hesitantly. The room seemed to still, waiting for her to continue explaining. "The hellhounds are trying to find a cure for their disease."

"You've got to be kidding me," Thoren scoffed. "You seriously expect us to believe that?"

"It's not so unusual to believe. They're human, too! They just want to be like everyone else!" The reds of her cheeks heated in quick anger, realizing no one was on her side.

"They stopped being human the moment they became infected with that curse. They're no more human than that wretched queen they served!" Thoren pressed two fingers over the bridge of his nose in distaste.

"Boudicca was just as human as any one of us. She was misunderstood and in pain. Just as I believe the hellhounds to be," she defended.

"Making excuses for the enemy are we?" Kane mocked, passing the bottle back to Ezra.

"Not excuses," she tried to say, her own anger increasing with every interruption.

"Who the hell is selling you all of this?" Thoren cut in once more. When she didn't answer, he slammed his hand down on the table and repeated, "Who is it? I'm growing tired of these games."

There was a long pause before her voice came out a mere whisper.

"Alaric."

Kane's attention darted to his brother. *He hates Alaric. This ought to be good...*

"Alaric?" Thoren seemed to whisper, getting up out of his seat. Only a moment passed before he repeated his question, his yell tearing through the room. "The man who nearly got Ezra killed, *Alaric?* The leader of the hellhounds, *Alaric?*"

Tara jumped back in surprise. With tense shoulders, she doubled down on her statement. "Yes! I spoke with him. And I don't really care what you think of me for it."

"You can't be this bloody stupid."

201

"Watch your feckin' mouth," Tara warned, getting out of her seat to meet Thoren face to face. "He saved Cricket the other day. I don't think he's the villain you make him out to be."

A small, manic laugh escaped the siren's lips. "Are you being serious?" He looked toward Kane and Ezra for backup. "The man murdered countless people. Tried to kill that man right there," he said pointing to Ezra. "He attacked you the night of Samhain. And you think he's suddenly changed?"

"I never said he was a good man, but I know that there are many hellhounds who just want a life. Boudicca forced them to work for her."

"I do remember Winnie talking to one of them after the battle," Kane added. "Many of them felt they didn't have a choice. Who knows how they ended up cursed in the first place."

Tara's eyes softened as he spoke, thankful that at least one person wasn't entirely against her.

"I see what's happening here," Thoren mumbled with yet another cynical chuckle.

Tara glanced at him sideways, huffing in frustration.

"Any man or woman that pays you any sort of attention is one you'll believe, isn't that right?"

She stepped back from him in disbelief. "What the hell does that mean?"

"You know exactly what it means. You reek of desperation and immaturity. You'd do anything for attention, even entertain the likes of him." A glowing fury sat behind Thoren's eyes, scanning her entire body in disgust.

"I'm not desperate," she insisted, clutching the dagger at her thigh as though she'd stab him in the chest. "I just want to help those that are hurting."

"He's manipulating you! And all you care about is keeping your bed warm," he spat.

Tara released the dagger, but landed a right hook across his jaw regardless. "How dare you speak to me that way! I know I may fight like you boys, but at the end of the day – I am a woman who will not be labeled as some common whore."

"Could've fooled me," Thoren retorted with a grimace, rubbing a bruising jaw.

She seemed speechless, gaze roaming around like she tried to decide what to do. Kane noticed the sliver of tears welling in her eyes before she announced, "I'm leaving."

"Where are you going?" Ezra called out as she ran out the door. When she didn't answer, too far away to be heard, he turned back to Thoren. "Did you really have to say all that?"

Thoren shrugged. "It's the truth."

"I don't know what's gotten into you lately, but it was cruel and you know it," Ezra added, heading out the door to find their friend. Thoren took a seat next to his brother, grabbing the bottle of gin and taking a swig himself.

"Was I too harsh?"

Kane shrugged his shoulders, realizing he was too drunk to care. "You have been awfully testy lately. Everything alright?"

Thoren moved his shoulders in anxious circles. "I don't know, honestly. Aelius is particularly vocal lately. Always nagging away in there." He hit the side of his head as though something were stuck.

Kane didn't know how to respond, comforted by the sudden silence. As the two passed the bottle back and forth, they first heard the sounds of Ezra's feet pacing downstairs. When the door to the orphanage opened, Thoren seemed to pause.

"Did you hear that?"

"Hear what?" Kane asked with a grunt.

"A strange noise... I should probably go make sure he's okay."

Thoren stormed out, heavy boots thumping down the stairs leaving Kane alone in brooding silence. All he could think about was the failed attempt to call on his soulmate who he thought was Winnie.

22

WINIFRED
FOX MANOR - 1861

Pushing their way through the sandy portal to Fox Manor, Winnie cringed. *This is the most disgusted I've ever felt while traveling,* she thought as the sand encroached on every inch of her body. The prickling of tiny specks pushed against the lenses of her goggles and into her ears as though it tried to turn her inside out.

The hand that fell through to the other side could feel warm water surrounding each finger. As the magic attempted to push her back one last time, Winnie's hope to see her family was enough reason to keep going. Not only was she eager to see them, but her body ached for solid ground. For the first time in over a week, she'd be on land again. The thought threatened tears to break free just as she pushed one last time, completely surrounded by the murky water of her family's lake.

For a moment, darkness waited all around her. Not a single light shimmered down at the bottom, an area of her home which she'd never visited before. She waded around aimlessly, unsure where Brenna and Oslind had ended up. A rush of movement circled around her feet. Small and quick, something darted past before more slithering movements surrounded her. Something gangly wrapped itself around her ankle before she kicked violently, preparing to swim toward the surface. Fingers wrapped around her wrist, the touch familiar compared to the strange creatures slithering in the dark.

A small glowing orb appeared, illuminating the area. For a second, dozens of piercing, empty eyes appeared before scattering away from the light. To Winnie's right, she realized Oslind was the one holding her wrist. His face revealed panic, pointing toward the surface as if they were using borrowed time.

In the dim light, tiny snake-like beings weaved themselves around her legs. Avoiding the illumination, their pale eyes glared at the trio as they moved upwards. Razor sharp teeth sat in sets of three or four, chomping toward Winnie's feet. Oslind pulled her up, though her attention seemed fixed on the creatures below as though she were hypnotized.

Ripping her arm free of his grasp, she obediently sunk back down with every tug and pull of the bony beings. Something inside Winnie seemed to still. For a moment, the water surrounding her turned frigid, mimicking the feeling of an approaching spirit. *Move you damn fool,* her mind screamed at her, though nothing happened. Instead, curious fingers reached for the chomping jaws, the light growing dimmer and dimmer the further down she went.

Time seemed to still. The water in Winnie's ears ceased their calming hum. Her breath slowed. Only those eyes – still dozens of blank stares – peered back at her. Their teeth open and ready to devour.

"Don't stare too much longer. You'll be their next meal."

The tattoo etched into Winnie's forearm glittered, mimicking the soft haze of the orb above. It took her a moment to recognize the playful lilt of the woman's voice that rang through her mind.

Before she could put the pieces together, a rush of movement seemed to pull Winnie from her trance. Brenna shot toward the bottom of the lake, the selkie's mouth expanding as waves of screeching sound ripped through the hold of the tiny creatures. They scattered, the selkie dragging Winnie to the surface.

Making her way up, Winnie noted her arm still shimmering

like embers in a fireplace. *"How are you speaking to me?"* she asked, wondering if the wicked woman in her subconscious was still around to hear her.

Sinister laughter echoed through her mind, the familiar voice of Queen Bouicca ringing through her entire body. *"Aelius thought you might need a little push."*

At last, Winnie's head broke free through the surface of the lake. She gasped, enjoying the feeling of familiar air before removing her goggles. Wading in the water for a moment, she took in the sight of Fox Manor. Never had she expected to be *this* excited to see her home.

The light on the side of the house turned on at once, glittering in the moonlight in warm welcome. Winnie continued to paddle toward land, desperate to put her feet on solid ground. When she finally felt the rocky shore, she couldn't help but roll onto her back and stare at the night sky, peppered with stars.

A slow, almost manic laugh escaped her as she cried out, "Land! Finally!"

Brenna and Oslind came up beside her, one removing her skins and the other allowing his fins to change to a set of scaly legs. They took a seat as well, giving her a moment to acclimate to the surface again.

The same all-over ache writhed through her body, her muscles screaming and head pounding. Winnie attempted to sit up, though Brenna stopped her. "Trust me, take a minute. Coming up from the surface that quickly isn't good for you."

"I can help with that," Oslind mumbled, placing his hand along Winnie's temple. It only took a split second before her body felt at ease again, the sting of the transition slowly leeching from her body through to the mermaid's fingertips.

Rolling onto her stomach, Winnie examined the estate. Around the sides of the house, she saw the rye fields freshly harvested. *I miss having those,* she thought, remembering her childhood spent running through mazes with Wesley.

In the next few years, Mum will insist on getting rid of them in an effort to look less like farmers, she thought begrudgingly. *If the fields are freshly harvested, that means they must've just celebrated Lughnasadh. It must be early August.*

Brenna stood, pulling on the wetsuit Oslind brought from Marvivia.

"Good thinking," Winnie muttered before attempting to stand.

"Can't let my beauty meet your parents naked," he said with a shrug and a grin.

Behind them, the sound of the sunroom door slammed open. Milicent stood in the frame. Her arms were outstretched, a protective mother bear waiting to meet their intruders. Ensuring the seashell necklace was tucked away beneath her bodice, Winnie hoped nothing would give away her true identity.

The trio walked toward the house before a set of vines snapped at their wrists. Holding them in place, Milicent stalked toward them. Across the field, she shouted. "State your business!"

Winnie fought back every instinct to cry out to her. *It's me, Mum! I'm here!* The words echoed in her mind, heart aching to be told everything would be alright, but instead she remained silent.

"We don't mean any harm!" Oslind called. "We come from Marvivia! I sent a letter recently. Ernest will know of me."

Realizing Oslind was pulling at the vines, Winnie snapped, "Don't tug! It'll only make it worse."

But it was already too late. The green slithering hands gripped his wrists harder, pulling him to his knees with a soft groan of pain.

A familiar voice pulled Winnie's attention back toward her mother. "Who is that, Millie?"

"Ernest!" Winnie shouted. "We contacted you the other day! We've come to ask you for help!"

She wanted to explain further; wanted to tell them who she was. But instead, her heart dropped. As her parents discussed quietly, a small head poked out from behind their figures.

Little Wesley.

He was ten years younger, only seven. Big round green eyes peered down at the lake, a look of terror in them. Something in them seemed to soften when he noticed Winnie; as if he could see her for who she was, not the facade the necklace put on.

Little Wesley tugged on his mother's sleeve, pulling her down to his level. He whispered something in her ear, Milicent's eyes flashing toward the trio in concern. Her panic eased for a moment as unsteady breath slowed, and her shoulders loosened up.

Barely audible, Winnie made out a few words as Wesley turned and spoke with Ernest. "Not here…to hurt…need help."

Unable to focus, her grief threatened to drown her. Desperately, she wanted to race toward them. Scoop him up into a tight hold and never let go. Every squeaky syllable tore at her heart and mind, knowing what was to come.

You're getting him back, she reminded.

Milicent's vines eased, slithering back into the ground.

"I supposed you lot should come inside then," she announced, eyes narrowing in on them as the group approached. Her mouth sat in a tight frown, looking each of them up and down skeptically.

As they entered the sunroom, Winnie couldn't help but hear it – herself, giggling. She would've been nine at the time, only a few months from meeting the Falke brothers.

"Who're they?" nine-year-old Winnie asked. She curiously examined the three of them, not recognizing her older self.

Milicent turned back toward them. "Visitors from…where did you say again?"

"Marvivia," Ernest interrupted, leaned against the doorframe with arms crossed over his chest and brows furrowed. "I believe I said I wasn't going to help. Or did that message somehow get lost in translation?"

"We wouldn't have come unless it was really important,"

Winnie began, though her words were cut short. She couldn't help but notice the way her mother's piercing gaze narrowed in on her, judging every word, movement, and sound.

"Winnie, take your brother upstairs. We need to discuss this matter," she ordered.

Nine-year-old Winnie groaned, grabbing Wesley by the hand and leading him upstairs. Twenty-year-old Winnie wanted to reach out and strangle her. Wanted to yell in her face; tell her how precious these years would become. How much she needed to soak up every ounce of time with him.

And yet…she could only watch. Her throat bobbed, eyes welling up. But she needed to keep a brave face. She couldn't let her parents see such weakness and become suspicious.

"So who are you?" Ernest's tone was harsher than she'd expected. Not the same loving version of her dad she'd always known.

Oslind and Brenna introduced themselves first. "I'm Lucille," Winnie said last.

Milicent continued to scrutinize every inch of Winnie before adding, "That's my daughter's middle name."

"What a coincidence!" With a hard sigh, she threw her hands in the air. *Shit, I didn't think this through.*

"And you're here for…" Ernest's voice trailed off, arms out in front of him as he shrugged.

"Didn't you read my letter?" Oslind's familiar attitude reared its ugly head.

Winnie only glared at him as if to scold, *'Be polite!'*

Her father huffed a short laugh. "I read it. I think you have me confused with someone else. I can't make such a contraption. I'm not an inventor."

"I'm a seer! I had a vision of the future and in it, you made such a device. It helped to end the war between the mermaids and selkies." Winnie took a step toward them, though Milicent's power simmered between her fingertips as the house rattled a bit. Taking a step away from her mother, she recognized the distrust immediately.

"If you're a seer, I'm a duck. Who *are* you?" The words hissed from Milicent's mouth, still glaring at her daughter. The longer they spent in the same room, the more her suspicions seemed to multiply.

Ernest chuckled at his wife's comment before adding, "We don't want to be a part of your war."

"All we want is peace. And you can help make that happen!" At last, the selkie finally spoke.

Brenna and Oslind took a few moments to explain the severity of the war and the threat to the human lands. Told them tales of the rogue selkies who ravaged the surrounding towns and islands along the coast of Virginia, specifically focused on Fort Monroe and Hampton. When they were finished at last, Milicent's skeptical glare narrowed in on Brenna. She seemed to look the selkie over, landing on the wide-set eyes and fangs.

"Aren't *you* a selkie, yourself? Why turn on your own people?"

"I'm not turning on them," she countered, a surprised hand clutching her chest. "I just want to protect those who want to do the right thing. And ensure no other human lives are lost because of a few stray selkies who are giving all of us a bad name. I'm not sure how the contraption helps with all that; Oslind hasn't quite told me the entire plan. But I know I have to do something."

Ernest turned toward Oslind, cocking his head to the side curiously. They seemed to share a quiet conversation, one no one else could hear, before Oslind shook his head toward her father. No one seemed to notice the exchange but Winnie. And it was then that she remembered what they'd written in the letter.

He hasn't told Brenna that the purpose is to bring in more soldiers...to take out her people, Winnie thought with a shudder.

Ernest paced the room for a moment, no one daring to speak

as the trio awaited his answer. "I'll need some time," he added at last. He rubbed his head nervously before turning back toward them.

"We don't have much of it. The selkies are planning an attack on Fort Monroe within the next few days. They want to wipe out the entire fort and surrounding cities," Brenna urged.

"Three days," Winnie interjected at last. This time, less nervous. Less awkward. More demanding. "In three days, we'll come back, and I'll test out the gear."

"That seems dangerous," Milicent began.

Ernest held up a quiet hand, stepping between her mother and the trio. "Fine," was all he said. "Now please leave, and take your stinking lake puddles with you. I don't want to hear a word for the next three days while I work."

Oslind glanced back toward Winnie, sharing a silent conversation. "We...intended to take you with us to Marvivia," he said at last.

Her father scoffed. "I'm not following you to the bottom of the ocean without the ability to breathe. I work on it here, or not at all."

Winnie nodded, knowing this was likely their only option. "I'll contact you through letters."

The group turned toward the door, ready to go back to Marvivia when she stalled for a moment. The sound of children's laughter pulled her gaze toward the hallway. She wanted so badly to go upstairs and give Wesley a big hug. Wanted to cherish a few more moments with him before returning. But that wasn't an option.

The group exited the sunroom, standing along the edge of the lake. Winnie enjoyed a few moments of solid land one more time before preparing her air bubbles.

"When we're down there, keep your eyes closed. Those little devils can hypnotize you if you look into their eyes too long. Though I suspect you've already learned that," Oslind mumbled, a mocking chuckle following before offering Brenna a hand into her skins.

Winnie said nothing, only nodding before venturing back toward the bottom of the family's lake. Pushing her way through the sandy portal, the cold ocean waters surrounded her again. At the bottom of the sea, the heavy weight of the water held her down. Her head throbbed and for a moment, all went dark.

Her vision blurred, and all she could see were the flickering of candles before her. When her eyes opened once more, she saw him. Across from her, illuminated by orbs, Kane floated in the water.

His body didn't seem corporeal; not entirely at least. Sad eyes gazed around in front of him, reaching out, though he didn't seem to notice her. She swam toward him, but with every inch she got closer, his image seemed to get further and further away. Calling out in her mind, she hoped he could hear her.

"Kane! I see you! Look at me!"

But he still didn't notice her. His attention remained fixed above him, examining the water as everything slowly faded to nothingness. Within moments, he was gone. Every piece of his image faded, a sliver of her heart breaking a little. He'd been right there, and yet couldn't see her. Couldn't recognize that she was reaching out to him, trying desperately to connect. Instead, he was just gone.

23

MILICENT
FOX MANOR - 1871

Milicent sat on the porch of Fox Manor, looking out at the stars. Beside her, Mohini nursed a cup of tea, chattering away about their most recent trip to Italy. Truthfully, she couldn't hear much of anything. Her mind raced, thinking back to the last few months. The visions she'd had of Ezra and Wesley played on a loop at the forefront of her mind, a constant reminder: *I was not strong enough to save my own son.*

Ernest and Horace stepped out, joining them. Her husband leaned against the wall, eyeing her carefully before offering a warm smile.

"Find anything today?" Milicent snapped her fingers, a cup of tea appearing for herself.

Horace shook his head. "I'm beginning to wonder if these rumors that boy heard were just that. Rumors."

"I had a vision the other night. In it, I saw bones. I didn't see much of anything else. It seems Fate and I are a bit disconnected right now, so the message was rather jumbled. Surely the two have to be connected. People don't just go digging up remains for fun." Twirling a strand of dark hair, she looked back out at the night sky.

"We'll keep looking," Ernest reassured, placing a kiss on her forehead.

"Mohini and I need to get back to the pack soon," he added. "The full moon's coming up, and I can promise you one thing: your hospitality does not extend to my beast form."

Milicent chuckled. "You'd be correct about that."

The familiar 'whoosh' of the portal alerted her, wondering if Kane had come back with his funny little friend from the orphanage. She sighed realizing: *It's just that damn shuck.* The creature ran toward them, nudging each as anxious paws tapped on the porch.

"Cricket without Tara? That's odd," her husband muttered.

"Do you think we should go to Chicago? Check on them?" Placing her cup down, Milicent stood.

"I'm sure they're fine. Let's enjoy one last drink before we head out," Horace insisted, grabbing Ernest and Milicent and dragging them inside the manor with Cricket whimpering outside the door.

————◦((●●))◦————

TARA

It only took a few moments of pacing around the halls before Tara decided she'd had enough. *Thoren has no right to speak to me that way,* she thought. *I'll teach him a thing or two about messin' with a Quinn woman.* Bursting through the door, only Kane remained inside. He was seated on the small sofa, staring off aimlessly.

"Where's your brother? I have more to say to him!" Her cheeks were flushed with anger.

He shrugged before taking another long, hard sip from the bottle.

She sat next to him before asking, "What's the matter with you?" Grabbing the bottle, she tried to catch up to his level of intoxication.

"It didn't work. Winnie's not my soulmate…"

"Whatever that means." She slouched back to make herself comfortable. Hot tears still stung the backs of her eyes, replaying Thoren's words in her mind. *But I will not let myself cry,* she scolded. "Do you think I'm desperate?"

Tara glanced sideways at Kane as he stared around the room in a drunken haze. "I think we all are," he finally admitted. He glanced back at her lazily, his hazels wild.

She took another sip before handing him back the bottle. *Who knows…maybe I am a little desperate,* she thought begrudgingly.

"Thank you for siding with me earlier. Mentioning that about the hellhounds. It's nice to know someone still has my back." She turned her body toward him, pulling her legs up onto the sofa.

"What do you think Winnie would make of your little…pet?" he asked, staring down at his hands where the alcohol waited.

"My pet?" It took Tara a moment to realize who he was referring to. "What are you trying to imply?"

"It seems awfully calculated that Alaric just so happened to save your mutt. Then, managed to suss you out to speak with the one person in our group who would entertain him in the first place. Quite convenient, if you ask me."

With a huff of frustration, she couldn't help the words that slipped from her mouth. "Almost as convenient as Samuel going missing after you had a word with him at the pub?"

All color drained from his face. "Wh–what do you mean?"

With a soft chuckle, she explained. "You didn't realize I was there that night, did you? At the pub. Saw you drag him out into the alleyway, then into the sky. Never saw him again, did we?"

He remained stoic at first, staring around the room. "You weren't there. I would've seen you."

"You all underestimate me. Every single feckin' time. If there's one thing a Quinn woman knows best, it's how to hide." Snatching the bottle from him, she took another sip. "I saw what you did that night. Or at least what you started. What do you think Winnie would make of *your* little pet?"

Kane opened his mouth, though she didn't let him get a word in. Fire coursed through her veins, an unstoppable rage bubbling to the surface. She silenced him by shoving the bottle back into his lap.

"I think you've done enough talkin' for one night. You and your brother both. If Winnie does come back and didn't leave your sorry ass, I think I may just have to tell her everything myself. Then you can stop playin' high and mighty like you're some feckin' savior whose above reproach. Everyone needs to stop acting like they're feckin' saints, and accept that we've all made questionable choices. Gods forbid I want to try and save some people along the way."

The moment the words came out, she regretted them. And when a cool breeze turned to funneling storm clouds above them, she knew she'd made a massive mistake.

"I will not let you be the reason Winnie hates me," he hissed, taking the bottle of gin and throwing it across the room. The glass clattered to the floor as he turned back toward her.

"Maybe you should've thought about that before you killed a man!" Removing her dagger from its sheath, she was ready to defend herself – even if it was Kane who would pay the price.

"I didn't fucking kill him!" he bellowed, his head in his hands as though he'd rip off his own face. When he looked back up at her, there was a wildness in his eyes that she'd never seen before; an unbridled rage simmering deep within. "I want you to leave. We will manage just fine on our own."

Tara turned toward the door, though she paused. When she looked back at him, she tried to think of what to say to make it even a little better. Her thoughts slithered in her mind: *Do I even care what they think of me?*

"Get out of here!" Heavy footsteps paced after her, slamming the door in her face.

Tara let out a rumbling groan, running for the stairs. She needed to get out of there, and fast. She couldn't stand to be in the orphanage for one more second.

Passing Thoren on her way down, he asked, "What just happened up there?"

Though he tried speaking to her, she simply ignored him. Desperately, she tried to calm her racing heart. At the bottom of the stairs, she sprinted outside. Stepping onto the porch, it was entirely still. A strange deafening quiet surrounded the orphanage. Not even the sounds from the festivals were audible.

To her right, a strange gurgling caught her attention. Then, a soft whimper. Her vision played tricks on her as she stared out into the darkness, the city's street lamps extinguished. Something was watching her. Their eyes were piercing, though not a single soul was visible in the dim moonlight.

Before she could turn to close the door, she heard it. A low growl. Something prowling in the darkness. She looked out one last time, when at last her heart sank. A cool December breeze swirled around her, several sets of luminescent eyes revealing themselves. At last, the deep snarl turned to snapping jaws, dozens of hellhounds waiting for her to exit the Chicago Orphan Asylum.

24

WINIFRED
MARVIVIA - 1861

Just up ahead, Brenna and Oslind wadded for a moment before going their separate ways. Winnie swam toward the mermaid before he snagged her wrist and pulled her toward Marvivia.

"Do you think they'll ever tire of dragging you around, and just leave you out here to die?" The voice of the queen sounded through Winnie's mind, an alarm alerting her to the intrusion.

"How the hell are you in my head?"

There was a lull before Boudicca finally responded. *"We're bound by blood, darling. I will always be in your head."*

"I've felt you waiting for months. Why wait until now to speak to me at all?"

All was quiet again, as though Boudicca were waiting for incoming answers. It took a few moments before she finally admitted, *"Aelius and I both felt you needed a little push to get things moving in the right direction."*

They swam for several miles before approaching his underwater flat. Three mermaid guards waited for Oslind to return home. They conversed with a mix of strange hand signals and haunting underwater noises, though she couldn't decipher much. All she could do was admire their angelic armor.

They wore sets of chest plates that looked to be carved from shimmering pearls. Their helmets were intricately designed with a halo of spikes around their heads, similar to the statue that guarded the city. Their fins remained unprotected, glistening scales glittering by the light of surrounding orbs. Strapped to their waists, each carried a glowing, ivory-handled sword and a trident spear in hand. Swirls of teals and pastoral greens decorated every square inch of them, a true beauty to behold.

Oslind turned back toward her, a look of despair written across his face. Though she couldn't hear him with the water in her ears, she could almost feel his grumbling displeasure as he pointed toward the palace. It wasn't long before she was stepping foot into the throne room.

"Everything alright?" Winnie noticed King Aalto sitting on the coral throne just beyond a set of guards.

"My father has requested a meeting with you. Alone. I'm to remain outside, under guard. Nowhere near your conversation." Worry laced his words, though she couldn't tell if his concern was for her at all.

"No, he's not worried about you. He's worried about his little secret," Boudicca snapped, seeming to answer the question at hand before Winnie could even finish her thought.

With a nod, she hesitantly moved toward the king. Oslind peered back one last time before exiting the throne room. As she approached, the guards moved aside with ease as though she were nothing more than a harmless starfish, here to pay a visit to the king. King Aalto sat lazily on the throne, Afissa entering from the left wearing a beautifully crafted silken white and gold gown, her hair braided down her back with a tiara of shells.

She took a seat beside her husband, the King and Queen of Marvivia. *I've never seen Afissa this dressed up. Whenever she comes to our house, she always wears her swimming gear. I never would have guessed she was royalty,* Winnie thought in admiration.

Bowing before them, she lowered her head. "King Aalto. Queen Afissa. It's a pleasure to see you both tonight."

"No need for such formalities, dear. We're all friends in Marvivia," Afissa sang, her arms urging Winnie to stand.

With a gracious nod, she waited for the king to speak.

Aalto cleared his throat, shifting in his throne to examine her more carefully. "Seer: I bring you here this evening to uncover the truth. I believe you may be visiting with ulterior motives. I demand you explain your real reason for coming to Marvivia at once. The human world has never known the location of our civilization, and we wish to keep it that way." His voice managed to bellow through the hall even though he wasn't shouting.

"First, tell me your name." Afissa interrupted her husband, eyes softening as though she recognized the panic stirring deep in Winnie's chest.

He shot her a look of disdain, one that could kill if it wanted to.

"Lucille," she managed to say.

"How did you learn of Marvivia?" King Aalto repeated.

"That question is a difficult one to answer," she began, wondering how much the Elements would allow her to say. "I come from a land far away. A land where people know of your existence and your home because you don't feel the need to guard it."

Afissa and Aalto shared nervous glances before the king's eyes plastered back onto her, intense and unyielding.

"This place – we don't wish to harm you. I swear! We have a good relationship with the merfolk. One day." A small ring in her ears warned she was sharing too much information.

"One day?" Afissa asked curiously, cocking her head to the side.

Winnie nodded. "You will find yourself close friends with these people. The Fox family. They will help you win your war."

"With your contraption that Oslind mentioned the other day?" King Aalto questioned.

"Yes! It will change the course of history, I suspect. Ensure you have the numbers needed to win this fight against the selkies."

They don't need to know that the fight will continue for another ten years...

"Very well. And what is it that you want in return?" The king's eyes narrowed in on her.

"There will come a time when these people–the Fox family–will ask for your help. They will have their own war, and will need men and women to fight." Her words came out awkward and greedy. They sat in her throat like a stomach virus, unwanted but unstoppable at the same time.

Aalto scoffed. "That's an awful lot to ask of a stranger."

Afissa placed her hand on his as if to convince him. He shrugged her off, before murmuring, "Leave Lucille and I alone for a moment. I need to discuss this in more depth."

Afissa glanced nervously toward Winnie before finally vacating the throne room. Aalto whistled, the remaining guards exiting as well until it was only the two of them left.

He didn't say much at first, merely rubbing his chin as contemplative eyes examined her. Eventually, he mumbled, "You're awfully brave to stand in front of a king, and demand an army."

"I don't mean any disrespect! I'm just trying to help my family!" Her words tumbled from her mouth, face red hot with embarrassment.

He chuckled. "Relax. I'm willing to help. For a price."

Winnie waited, unsure what to say.

"My son. I know of his dalliances with the selkie. Brenna has been a sore spot of conversation for my family for many years now."

Her face paled, thinking of what Oslind would say if he knew the truth. "I'm not sure I know what you're talking about," she bluffed.

"Bullshit. I saw you three together the last few days. I'm the king. You must know I have eyes everywhere. My son has gotten sloppy. He used to be better about hiding it."

"What will you do to them?" Unsure she even wanted an

answer, she folded her arms across her chest.

"Not me. You. My court was already suspicious of him. Now that word is spreading that he's a selkie sympathizer, they grow restless. I need Brenna taken care of."

A rock fell in the pit of her stomach. *Take…care of her?*

"As in kill her, yes," Boudicca retorted.

"I'm not sure I can do that." She took a step forward. "I'll do anything to secure this alliance, but I can't harm her. She's become my friend the last few days. She truly means well! She doesn't agree with what the other selkies are doing!"

"Her opinion doesn't matter. The selkies as a whole will never stop until they have Marvivia. The beliefs of one selkie bitch does little to help me when it's only causing alliances to stir and weaken within my own court."

Winnie winced hearing his foul words. *If Oslind knew what his father was saying about his love,* she began, though her thoughts were interrupted.

"And you will say nothing. You're here for an alliance. You will do what is necessary," Boudicca insisted, an unlikely coach Winnie hadn't expected.

"Since when are you on my side?" she thought, hoping the blood queen could hear her. Focusing on Aalto, she asked, "Can't I get her to leave? Go somewhere far away and never return?"

The king shook his head. "Oslind would never stop looking for her unless he knew she was dead. He's a stubborn bloke like his mother."

"Then what would you have me do?" she asked, once again afraid of the answer.

"Kill her. And bring me her skin as proof. I'll need them to convince Oslind to give up his search, and join my side." Aalto once again slouched back in his seat, arms folded across his chest and examining every tiny detail of Winnie's face.

"And if I do this, you'll swear to help my family in the future?"

"When?"

"Ten years from now. No matter what is going on in your time, you must swear to me that you'll help." Deep in Winnie's soul, she felt something stir. Not Boudicca, but rather an Element. A feeling of dread settled over her, suddenly worried she was making the wrong choice.

His eyes seemed to widen at the thought of this long-term commitment. "Bring me her skins, and I swear it."

Getting up from his throne, Aalto approached. He drew a knife from his side, Winnie backing away in caution before he slid the blade across his own palm. Offering it to her, a devilish smirk fell across his face. And then, he simply waited. Winnie's mind continued to swirl anxiously, unsure what choice to make. *Is this really what the Elements want me to do?* Not a word came from any of them, only silence in her mind.

Hesitant fingers grasped the handle of the blade. "I will bring you her skin. You will help me ten years from now." She nodded, about to slice into her palm.

At last, a small voice appeared in her mind as Aelius whispered to her. *"You cannot change what has already happened. Ensure he does not help one moment sooner, or you risk erasing your future entirely."*

"Ten years from now," he repeated with a nod.

"After November. Not a single day sooner," she clarified.

With a look of confusion, he nodded again.

Slicing into her unbranded palm, crimson dripped onto the floor of the throne room. He held out his hand, embracing hers as their blood mingled and their pact solidified.

Did I just agree to kill Brenna? A shiver ran down her spine at the realization.

"If you wanted to get technical about it, no," Boudicca added with what Winnie could only imagine was a smirk.

Winnie wiped her bloodied palm on the pants of her wetsuit.

A guard poked his head through the doors, gaze locked on the king.

"Sir, there's trouble! Word from guards near Fort Monroe came – the selkies are attacking!"

Oslind barreled through the door, snagging Winnie's hand before even noticing her injury. "We have to go! They're attacking early! They weren't supposed to go for a few more days."

He pulled her aside, the walls giving way to shimmering armor which gleamed like the shine of a pearl. Handing her a set that matched the Marvivian warriors, Winnie placed the chest plate over her wetsuit and fastened the sides.

"Take this. Not sure how much you'll be able to fight in the water, but you should at least be prepared." A trident spear landed in her hand, Oslind sheathing a sword at his side while pulling armor over himself.

"They're fast. You know that. Use the length of the spear to keep them at a distance. Aim for the gut if you can. Whatever you do, don't let go of your weapon. If you can, get to land and fight where you're more useful," the mermaid coached.

With a careful nod, Winnie exited the throne room. Wading through the frigid ocean, it occurred to her that she was headed into a skirmish without proper gear to fight creatures in their natural element.

25

Walking through the halls of the orphanage, Thoren continued to search for Ezra. He thought maybe his love had hidden himself away in one of the empty classrooms, looking for somewhere quiet to reflect. His attention perked up at the sound of broken glass shattering against the walls of their quarters. Racing back toward their room, he saw Tara exit in a frenzied anger.

"What just happened up there?" he called out, though she ignored him rushing out of the orphanage. The door stood agape behind her, an icy chill swirling through the halls.

"Ezra?" he called out again. *I can't yell too loud, or I risk waking the children,* he thought with a shudder, knowing he didn't want to face the wrath of a sleepy Miss Leona.

Thoren sighed, leaning against the wall for a moment to collect himself. Seeing his brother that way, the wildness and anger... It brought back memories of their time away from Fox Manor. Of a time when Kane had plunged himself headfirst into darkness like a fool without a care as to how it would affect his little brother. A shudder wracked through him as he thought, *What lengths is he willing to go through in order to get her back?*

When he opened his eyes, he glanced down at the open door. *She'll let all the warmth out,* he thought with a grumble as he made his way downstairs. Nervous butterflies fluttered in his stomach, realizing how still the house was. It almost felt unnatural without the sounds of soft conversations, squeals of iron sewing machines, or giggling children filling the halls. The only noise throughout the entire house was the wood groaning beneath his feet.

About half way down the stairs, a sudden warning washed over him. The hair on the back of his neck stood. A twin creak of wooden planks echoed down the hall where the children's quarters were. Rushing to shut the front door, he turned back to investigate.

"Is someone out of bed?" he whispered, hoping not to scare an unsuspecting child.

Silence returned his question, entering the children's quarters filled with soft snores and gentle dreams. Thoren's gaze darted around, carefully inspecting every movement. At first glance, all of the children appeared to be accounted for. Not a soul stirred out of bed, the shadows dancing with only a small glimmer of moonlight spilling inside to subtly guide his search.

Otto sat up in bed, leaning over to his nightstand to light a small candle. Rubbing sleepy eyes, he mumbled, "What's going on? I thought I heard something."

"I'm sorry, that was us. Everything's fine. Just go back to sleep," he soothed as the shadow from the flame created dancing images on the walls.

"Not you guys. I heard something else." A sure finger pointed across the room where only darkness waited.

The boy's words nearly chilled him to the bone, but upon examination he didn't see anything lingering. "There's noth…" Thoren began to say, though he stopped. His eyes locked in on *something*. Unsure, he squinted and moved toward the strange heaping mass. He inched closer and closer when suddenly the air in the room seemed to vacate.

There.

Crouched.

A figure unidentifiable, but obviously hovering in the corner like a demon awaiting the children's souls. A low grumble fell across the room when the candle extinguished. A chill in the air, no thanks to Tara, slithered its way toward Thoren as he continued careful steps forward.

A few of the children slowly woke, rubbing their tired eyes. Thoren tried not to wake any more of them. *The last thing I need is panic,* he thought, knowing in his gut that something wasn't right.

That's when it moved.

Surrounded by darkness, a set of gleaming yellow eyes revealed themselves. An almost serpentine grin gave way to razor sharp fangs. It glanced around the room, licking its lips in delight. Prowling forward, it stopped at the foot of a little girl's bed. A taunting gaze fell from the child to Thoren as if daring him to make a move.

"Otto…"

"What is that?" the boy whispered, getting out of his bed.

"Get the others out! Find Miss Leona! Now!" Thoren lunged at the hellhound lurking in the shadows.

As if waiting for him to attack, the hellhound lunged. Its fangs were deadly, awaiting flesh to bite down on. Thoren seemed to be of little concern to it, pushing past him to snap at a little girl who sat wailing in her bed.

Only seconds stood between the girl's demise and his rescue effort. Kicking the beast in the jaw, it whimpered before turning back to the siren. Thoren only had a few moments to snatch her up, tossing her toward Otto. The boy managed to stabilize her just in time, ushering the rest of the children into the hallway. Acting in protective brotherly instinct, he snatched the youngest from a nearby crib, carrying the tiny toddler sloppily on his hip as they all darted toward Miss Leona's room.

"Leave them alone! You have me to deal with!" Thoren watched as the hellhound regained its composure. He reached for his side, ready to withdraw a pistol and end things. But that's when he remembered… *Shit,* he thought, thinking of the gun and dagger sitting in their shared room.

He scanned the area for a weapon. It was too dark to see much of anything, only the moonlight shining through the windows to cast more shadows. It seemed that the beast knew how to hide. Backing up to the threshold of the room, he glanced down the hall. The children pounded on Miss Leona's door. It swung open in a fury, her terrified eyes connecting with Thoren's.

"Barricade the door! Don't let anyone in!"

The woman rushed a quick nod, snatching the children inside.

The beast growled, getting closer and closer with snapping jaws. Thoren grabbed Otto's candlestick, thankful he had at least something to fight with. Swinging at the approaching beast, it simply jumped back. Rather than attack, it continued to prowl in the shadows.

"Enough of your games," he shouted, balling his fists and calling on Aelius to engulf his hands in molten flame. Careful not to hit any furniture, he tried to avoid setting the whole orphanage on fire as he waited for the hellhound to make a move.

Attempting to strike the creature, it avoided his blazing fists and continued to skulk in the darkness. It didn't attack; merely seemed to wait.

"Why are you just standing there?" As his hands continued their blazen flame, the pull on his energy only intensified.

That kind of power needed a target.

His stomach sank when the sound of a feminine scream just outside pierced his ears. "Shit! Tara!" he mumbled to himself, eyes flashing over his shoulder.

Thoren turned to run. Before he could produce a single thought, the hellhound stood before him ready to fight. It stalked forward, the siren taking careful steps back into the room further and further. Another scream rang out just in front of the building, and suddenly he knew he needed to make more aggressive moves.

"Get out of my way!" he bellowed, swinging molten fists at the beast.

As the hound snapped, Thoren grabbed ahold of its jaws with flaming hands. A razor sharp tooth dug into the skin of his palm, but that didn't stop him. The flames consumed its flesh, the beast yowling in pain with every lap of Aelius's deadly gifts. A minute passed, and all that remained of the hellhound was a pile of ash. Behind them, clumsy footsteps were on the move.

Kane, with wild eyes and panic across his face, stood in the hallway. "What…the fuck is happening?"

"You idiot," Thoren grunted, wiping ash onto his pants. "At least you had the common sense to bring weapons."

He snatched his pistol, leaving Kane the dagger. Outside, more screams pierced the night.

"Go check on Miss Leona and the kids. Make sure nothing gets through. Somehow the hounds got past our wards."

"How…is that…even possible?"

Thoren shook his head, unsure he wanted to know the answer to that question. Pointing down the hall, he shoved his brother toward Miss Leona's room. He didn't wait before racing down the stairs. Stepping foot into the chill of the December night, Thoren followed the distant sound of the nearby festival mingled with blood curdling cries.

———◄•《《●●》》•►———

KANE

Kane clutched the dagger in his hand with blurry vision, racing toward Miss Leona's room. The world felt like it could fall around him, spinning at a speed that felt inhuman. The moment he'd heard screams and children crying, he'd regretted everything. Every sip of alcohol. Every moment he'd let his guard down. He could only hope that his own poor choices wouldn't be the reason more lives were lost.

Lifting his hand to knock on the door, something big barreled into him. Falling face first into the door, he turned to see the figure of a man waiting. From inside Miss Leona's room, the children screamed. A sudden clarity washed over him, sobering up enough to fend off the incoming attack.

The man carried a dagger, waiting to slice into Kane. Holding his hands out, the siren called on Caelus for strength. Though all of his effort focused on his power, nothing happened. The hellhound flinched, awaiting a deadly elemental strike. When nothing happened, he released a mocking cackle.

"Gone lame, have we?" The hellhound's lips curled into a sinister smirk, prowling forward.

Kane didn't have much time to think before the beast was swinging a dagger toward him. Landing a quick hit on the man's wrist, the weapon dropped to the floor. He kicked it aside before moving his own blade high into the air. With feline grace, the beast snatched the dagger from Kane's hand and swung it inward. The sharp metal met the siren's shoulder, digging deep into his flesh.

Crying out in surprise, his gaze remained fixed on the protruding blade. Parting his lips, Kane prepared a devastating siren song. But before he could muster a single note, the beast had already delivered a swift punch to the throat.

Coughing, his only option was to fight. Tearing the blade from his impaled shoulder, Kane's vision turned woozy as blood spilled onto the floor. The hellhound lunged for his fallen weapon. Before he could make contact, the siren sliced at the beast's arm. He backed away, clutching the wound. Barreling into the hound, Kane slammed him into the ground. It didn't take long before the blade in hand plunged into the hellhound's chest, over and over again until all movement ceased.

Standing, dizziness overwhelmed the siren. Blood poured freely from his shoulder, vision growing darker with every passing second.

Offering Miss Leona's door a soft rasp, he muttered, "It's me. Open up…"

"Mr. Falke?"

Furniture slid from behind the door as speckles continued to cloud his vision. Her eyes were wild, darting from Kane's bloodied shoulder to the body in the hallway. Terrified children huddled in the corner of her room, fear tangible in the air. Otto stood, running with outstretched arms toward the hallway.

"No! Stay in there!" Kane ordered, turning the boy at the last second. *I remember what seeing Death at this young of an age did to me,* he thought.

"Come," Miss Leona urged, pulling him inside and stacking furniture back against the exit. "You're hurt?"

"Just a little…" He'd meant for it to come out as a joke, but his words slurred as stumbling feet refused to keep him upright.

"Otto, help him," she ordered, replacing the last of the barricade.

"No, don't." Kane held out his hand, guiding the boy away. "Go sit with the others. I'm fine."

"I want to help," the boy pleaded, his eyes weary.

"You can help me by keeping the others safe." He nodded in reassurance, motioning for Otto to go back to the other children.

Miss Leona crouched beside him, her nightgown ballooning around her. "Why won't you let him help you?"

"I know what this kind of thing does to a boy. I don't want him feeling like I did," he mumbled.

Miss Leona' brows furrowed as she examined his wound. Applying pressure, he winced in pain.

"Thank you for saving us. That thing would've gotten through the door if you hadn't showed up."

"That's what I'm here for," he said with a half-hearted smile. The world faded, overwhelmed by euphoric darkness.

"Mr. Falke?" she asked, seeing the way his head drooped before him. "Kane, look at me!"

"I think I'll take a small snooze if that's alright," he whispered, the weight of the world crashing down on him.

"No!" Panicking, Miss Leona shook him. "Don't close your eyes!"

26

WINIFRED
MARVIVIA - 1861

Focused on the swim ahead, Winnie noted the schools of mermaids organized in lines similar to the Roman formations from Boudicca's memory of her final battle. Fort Monroe awaited their rescue as they swam for several miles. She could only hope they'd get there in time. Each soldier was adorned in the same intricate and oddly beautiful shimmering pearl armor. With the surrounding darkness, they were almost invisible within the waves.

"How do you expect to survive this?" the queen taunted.

"If I die, you'll lose your tether to this world. Quit mocking me, and be quiet. Unless you have anything useful to say," Winnie snapped back, trying to focus on their journey. Slithering movements below her in the depths of the ocean caught her attention, the group speeding up their swim to avoid a mass of reaching tentacles.

At last, they arrived in the Chesapeake Bay. Selkies darted across the shoreline, unaware of the newly arrived mermaid fleet. Bullets rained down into the water as soldiers from Fort Monroe fired up ahead, tiny torpedoes of Death spearing into the water.

Desperate to see what was happening above, Winnie paddled her way to the surface. Lines of union soldiers stood on the banks of the fort, firing aimlessly into the darkness. Some threw bottles of flaming oil at the selkies, managing to hit a few despite their speed.

On the edge of the water, their attackers snatched unsuspecting soldiers as they reloaded their weapons or commanded others. When Winnie looked below the surface, she watched in horror as the creatures tore the men apart like ravenous paranas. When yet another innocent soul cried out in pain below, she knew she couldn't stand by any longer.

Paddling toward a set of rocks, Winnie flared her fingers and called on Aelius. Flames protruded from her hands, her tattooed arm glowing like embers as Boudicca's soul stirred in excitement. A pair of selkies leaped from the water, aimed right at another group of unprepared soldiers. Before the mermaids had a chance to arrive in rescue, Winnie shot two flaming spears toward the creatures. Shrieking, they fell back into the water.

Two of Oslind's soldiers positioned themselves before the humans, narrowly avoiding being shot by the terrified men. "We're here to help you!" one of the mermaids hissed, the soldiers in too much shock to know who to trust.

When the selkies attempted another spearing lunge toward them, they were met with the sharp end of the mermaids' blades. It was then that the soldiers of Fort Monroe seemed to release a long exhale, aiming their weapons beyond their strange saviors, and back toward the water where the selkies hunted.

Winnie turned, trying to decipher where or how to help. Stranded on the rocks, she felt utterly helpless. Then, her mind alerted to a pair of eyes plastered to her. She didn't have a chance to see the identity of her attacker before a firm hand grasped the back of her neck. Just as her face was about to be smashed into the rocks, she called on Gali. A pillow of water lessened the blow, barely missing the protruding rocks.

Sending her elbow back, she managed to hit someone in the nose before that same hand grasped her leg and pulled her below the surface. A moment of panic threatened to take hold, the air around her mouth not forming at first.

"Caelus? Where are you?" she cried out in her mind, though the god of air seemed unavailable for the moment.

Trying to remain calm, she called on the god again and again. The air finally formed around her mouth and nose with mere seconds to spare. That familiar burning feeling in her lungs no longer threatened to send her to a watery grave as the selkie continued dragging her down.

At last, it ceased its swim and turned back toward her. Winnie tried to call on Aelius, though this time the surrounding water subdued her flaming magic. Without enough strength to call on the fire god, she clutched her trident spear instead. The selkie examined her with a smirk, noting Winnie's air bubble. Its mouth moved as though to speak, but she couldn't hear anything as the water filling her ears drowned out the noise.

Thrusting her spear toward the creature, her movements felt weaker than usual. The water around her slowed her speed, feeling like she was swimming through molasses, fighting a losing battle.

The creature laughed, darting below. Winnie tried to look down, but the water's darkness made it impossible to see anything. In a panic, she paddled toward the surface. A few feet away from the edge, she felt the creature barrel into her. Had it not been for the armor surrounding her torso, the hit would've probably knocked the wind out of her lungs entirely.

Hidden in the darkness like a master of disguise, the selkie was nowhere to be seen. Barreling into Winnie's side, the trident spear in her hand almost loosened its grip, though she clung to it like life itself.

The creature grabbed a hold of her body, torpedoing them straight toward the rocky banks. Her gaze darted toward the incoming wall before finally getting some sense. Focusing on trying to spear the beast, she managed to knick the selkie's torso.

Blood clouded the area. Within seconds, it retreated back into the watery depths.

Knowing that fire was her strongest weapon, Winnie kicked as hard as she could to climb the rocks jutting from the water. As her head breached the surface, she gasped for air. It didn't take long before a wet hand grasped her ankle once more. Salty water gushed into her mouth, accidentally swallowing some. Unable to take a full breath, Winnie was pulled under yet again.

Turning, she attempted to impale the beast. The selkie snatched the trident spear, hurdling it into the open ocean. *I'm... defenseless,* she panicked. The moment of pause was enough for the selkie to thrust her head into the rock formation.

For a moment, Winnie couldn't see anything. Her vision clouded. The sounds of water all around her. The air that protected her up until now, dissipated as she attempted to regain her vision. Dark spots blocked incoming attacks.

Desperate hands grasped at her face, trying to call on Caelus to bring her air back. Hazy eyes looked back to the surface, realizing she was mere feet away and yet seconds from drowning. The selkie grasped her hand tightly, dragged Winnie farther and farther away from salvation. Kicking and screaming, Winnie couldn't match the sheer strength of the selkie; a beast in its own element.

Calling on Aelius, she thought, *"Even though I'm surrounded by the sea, surely you can help me!"*

Boudicca's essence swirled inside, anxious and excited.

"I told you my gifts would prove more useful when used correctly," the fire god purred.

With every last ounce of strength she could muster, she created a flaming ball. The surrounding water boiled, singing her own skin as the flames rioted toward the selkie. Wide eyes stared back at Winnie, the last thing she saw before flames consumed the creature.

When the selkie's grip no longer held her down, she attempted to paddle back to the surface. It felt like she'd been dragged miles below, kicking as hard as she could. No matter how much she tried, the air surrounding her nose and mouth ceased to exist. Caelus wasn't responding. At last, her swimming stopped. Slowed. Before ceasing all together.

Weightless, the deafening sound of water-filled ears was almost hypnotizing. A peaceful calm surrounded her. All she could do was stare out into the darkness. A sense of euphoria encompassed her, one she'd heard all too much about. A few moments passed before the darkness gave way to a new entity approaching.

"Death?" she called out. Wondering. Curious.

But it was not Death who waded before her. The outline's glimmering shape subsided until the figure of a man floated up ahead. Dark waves and hazel eyes examined her carefully, realizing she was underwater. The figure tried to call out to her, though she still couldn't hear his words.

At last, the man reached out. Cupping the sides of her face, he planted a delicate kiss on her lips. Only moments passed before her hazy vision cleared, realizing Kane hovered before her. Eyes wide and concerned, he examined her. He wasn't exactly *there*. Though Winnie couldn't place her finger on it, the nearby water felt several degrees cooler – near icy.

A sudden realization sent panic radiating through her spine, the bubble around her nose and lips bringing back the precious air she desperately needed. Looking Kane over, she watched his ghostly hands grasp her face tightly. A sad stare noted every inch of her body, looking for wounds or anything out of place.

In her mind, his words rang loud and clear. *"Come home to me, love. We need you."*

Before she could say or do anything, he offered her a careful nod. Raising his hand, she speared toward the surface. Though she tried to fight, she couldn't get back down to him. Just below, Kane floated with an outstretched hand. As though he didn't have a care for his own well-being, he at last disappeared. But not before sending one final kiss as her head jutted through the water at last.

"Kane?" Her voice pierced the night sky, glancing below the surface once more. But he was gone. Utterly distraught, his name escaped her lips before releasing a cry to the heavens.

"Get yourself together!" Aelius insisted, a strange sensation washing over her.

Winnie looked over her shoulder, realizing another selkie waited to drag her back down to the depths of the ocean. Sending another flaming spear through the creature's head, it was dead within moments as ashes lay on the surface. She paddled toward the rocks, leaning back on them as a wave of exhaustion washed over her.

A head of light hair popped out of the water to her side. Ready to shoot another flaming arrow toward it, she thankfully turned in time to see the blonde hidden amidst the waves.

"Just me! Not a selkie!" Oslind rushed, arms resting on the edge of the rocks.

Winne peered around the water, realizing only mermaids remained. "Is it...over?"

"For now. I think we may have temporarily scared them off. They didn't bring as many as we'd expected."

Winnie coughed, feeling the remnants of ocean water deep in her lungs. Oslind pulled himself up onto the rocks, placing a hand on her forehead like he'd done several nights before. The burning in her lungs eased, a calming warmth spreading over her.

"I half expected to find you dead, if I'm honest. Glad to see you made it out alive. Though I take it, something got to you?" he asked, examining her head when he noticed the blood trickling down the back of her ivory armor.

Her eyes remained fixed beyond, thinking back to the images of Kane.

"Winnie? Everything okay?" Oslind's words barely pulled her

from her trance.

"I saw…Kane. Below. In the water. The figure of him… I think he's…" She couldn't bring herself to finish her sentence.

Oslind followed her gaze before cocking his head to the side curiously. "Can he astral project?"

She shook her head. "I think it was his…soul." Winnie covered her face, weeping into the palms of her hands.

Oslind offered her back a comforting pat before adding, "I'm sure your siren is alright. He's probably just sending you a sign. I've heard stories of their abilities to connect with the ones they love."

"Really?" She barely managed to choke out the word between sniffles. "But I…I know a spirit when I see one."

"I pray, for your sake, that you're wrong." He gave her a moment before jutting his chin toward Fort Monroe. "Come on, let's go introduce ourselves. They're probably incredibly confused."

Grabbing her by the hand, Oslind guided them toward the shore. Lines of rifles pointed at them, ready to fire. With their hands above their heads and weapons dropped, the mermaid called out to the soldiers awaiting orders.

"We mean you no harm! We've come to help!" the Prince of Marvivia shouted.

"Drop 'em!" A voice sounded behind the lines waiting to shoot at any sign of danger.

At once, the barrels lowered, and Winnie felt she could breathe again. Inside the parting crowd, a puffy faced man with a balding head stood examining them carefully.

"Major General Benjamin F. Butler. And you would be?" Reaching a hand out toward the mermaid, he grasped it in a firm handshake.

"Mr. Oslind Maddox. Prince of Marvivia," he announced, straightening his shoulders.

"Daddy wouldn't like his little boy announcing the name of their civilization to a herd of humans," Boudicca taunted.

239

Before the general turned toward Winnie, his eyes narrowed in on Oslind's face. "What's wrong with your skin?"

"Not sure we have time to explain. Just know my people came to save you tonight. Had we not arrived, the selkies would have killed your entire fort." Though he likely didn't mean to sound smug, it was hard not to take it that way.

Speechless, the general turned toward Winnie. "And you are?"

"Ms. Winifred Fox, Sir. Here to aid in protection as well," she said, taking his hand in her own with a small head bow of respect.

"I don't know where you came from, but we appreciate your help this evening. It was as if the heavens opened up above and below." Butler's eyes widened, as if reliving the events.

Winnie's gaze darted around the remaining soldiers, wondering how many were injured during the attack. Or worse-lost their lives. "Happy to help. We can come back soon. Offer more protection, if needed."

Oslind's attention flashed toward her in anger. It took a moment to realize she'd volunteered his army for the cause without consulting the king first.

"If that's alright with you, of course...prince," she almost mocked.

He rolled his eyes before nodding. "Anything you need, you have it. We'll be in touch soon. We must return and inform my father of what happened. Rest assured, if those monsters attack again, we will be at your aid."

General Butler nodded, though he stopped them before they could head back to the sea. "Where did you say you're from again?"

Oslind offered a muted chuckle. "Marvivia. A world below the sea – where my people are from."

"You mentioned...selkies?"

Winnie and Oslind both nodded. "My scales; I'm sure you can guess what my people are." He offered a wry smile, as if taunting the man to play along.

"Surely you can't be…"

"Mermaids." He motioned toward the soldiers wading in the water. "Here to protect you and your men as you focus on your war."

"What do you get out of all this? Protecting us?" Butler's eyes narrowed on each floating figure.

Oslind offered a lazy shrug. "Nothing, really. But we'd much rather be your ally than your enemy. Is that not enough?"

"Very well," Butler mumbled, still seeming to process the information.

Bowing their heads before parting ways, Winnie and Oslind returned to the sea. He graciously pulled her through the water, her muscles screaming from exhaustion. When they returned to Marvivia, she waited behind in his flat as he informed the king of the attack.

Lying on the sofa, Winnie stared up at the ceiling. She felt like she was still in the water, the room moving around like a living wave. *Kane,* she thought, her heart aching for him. Closing her eyes, she pictured his face as she'd seen him in the water. *Things have been strange since the funeral. But it's my fault they got that way,* she confessed internally.

Begging for a vision, she hoped she'd get some sort of sign as to whether or not he was okay. But nothing came.

"You and I can both recognize a dead man when we see one," Boudicca whispered.

Winnie groaned before holding a pillow over her head as if to block out the incessant queen. She thought for a while, wondering how she could get Kane a message.

Ripping a piece of blank paper from the Element's leather-bound book, she wrote. One way or another, she needed to warn him to be careful. Until she could figure out what happened, she could only hope that he'd somehow find the letter just in time to ensure his safety.

When she was done, she envisioned Fox Manor. Hiding it in a place where she knew he'd find it, the paper disappeared. She could only pray the letter would make it ten years, and not be found by anyone else by accident.

One way or another, I'm coming home to you, she thought as she drifted off to sleep.

27

THOREN
CHICAGO - 1871

Carefully exiting the front door, Thoren's attention remained peeled for anything. The cries he'd heard were now silenced, only the sounds of the festival's lively music echoing through the streets. Soft laughter rang in the distance, the occasional hooping holler from a lively group of pedestrians walking home. Up ahead, the gas lamps flickered in and out as though someone tampered with the beaming light. It was just enough to obscure the siren's visions as he searched for Ezra. Then begrudgingly, Tara.

Before he could step off the porch, he came to an abrupt stop. Something hid amidst the shadows; he could feel their eyes watching him. Every inch of his body alerted, spine tingling knowing there was danger nearby.

"Show yourself!" he shouted into the void.

The gas lamps above ceased their flickering dance, several hellhounds appearing out of thin air. Their frothing jaws snapped toward him, teeth glimmering in the moonlight. He scanned the area, realizing suddenly – there weren't just a few of them. There were dozens.

With a gasp, Thoren cocked his pistol and fired at the prowling beasts. They retreated, the break in their lines enough to see just beyond them for a moment. Down the street, two bodies were dragged down an alleyway. One red haired. Tara for sure. And then…blonde hair. Thoren's heart sank to the pit of his stomach, feeling queasy with panic.

"Ezra!" There was no answer as the beasts dragged his love away.

Tara seemed to awaken, kicking at the hound whose teeth sunk deep into her ankle. Thoren watched as she tried everything to break free of the grasp, sending one solid kick after another toward the hound's sturdy jowls.

The beast shook its head, regaining some composure before turning back into its human form. Only moments passed before the woman grabbed Tara by the shoulders, thrusting her head into the ground. The fight ceased, dragging her limp body into the same alley where Ezra had disappeared.

"Let them go!"

Thoren attempted to run after them, but the hounds reformed their blockade. One managed to kick at his knees, taking him to the ground with a cry. Forming a circle around the fallen siren, they attacked. Nonstop, vicious and unyielding. They did all they could to keep him on the ground.

Thoren raised his pistol, firing the second-to-last of his bullets. Stumbling to his feet, he managed to retreat to the porch. Searching for Ezra, he saw nothing. They were too far gone now. Only the hounds and their tentative watch remained.

Last resort, he thought, glancing down the street to see if any pedestrians were nearby. When he was sure the door to the orphanage was closed, he drew on the only power he knew would ensure that many hounds dropped within seconds so he could run after his love. Reaching within himself, he pulled on the angelic siren melodies. As his mouth opened and the vibrations slipped from his lips, he waited.

And waited.

But nothing happened. He dug a little deeper, pulling on older, darker magic. How the hounds were resisting his songs he wasn't sure, but they could only withstand it for so long. Still, they seemed unphased by his siren magic.

"We came prepared this time," one of them yelled, pointing at his ears.

Thoren couldn't tell what he was getting at, the evening too dark to see clearly.

"Beeswax works wonders. Guess the tales of Odysseus were right," the hound called out.

Thoren didn't recognize the beast at first, though the cockiness in his voice mimicked that of their leader – Alaric. Instead of the dark, gorgeous disaster he was expecting, the hound before him stood tall and slender, a set of glittering verdant eyes waiting for the siren to make a move.

"Bring them back now!" he shouted, holding his pistol toward the man. *One bullet left,* he thought.

"Get comfortable, sky rat. You'll be here for a while," the man sang, a smug grin on his face.

Thoren didn't hesitate, squeezing the trigger. The beast clutched his chest in surprise, falling to the ground as nearby hounds dragged him off before the siren could make another move. Others filled in the empty space, a stone fortress trapping the group inside the Chicago Orphan Asylum.

He tried his voice once more...nothing. Not a soul was impacted by his song, the baritone notes reverberating through the air; the power looking for a host to claim victim. He only ceased when the sounds of footsteps came from behind the opening front door.

"Brother? Is that you? We need to get help. They have Ezra and Tara!"

Miss Leona stood in the doorway with a bubble of solemn silence surrounding her.

"Mr. Falke...something happened..."

The siren rushed inside, shutting the door before pushing a

nearby dresser in front to barricade them in. "What is it? Are the children okay?"

"The *children* are fine. Your brother protected us. But he's... Thoren," she paused, her eyes searching the orphanage for the words to explain. "I don't think he'll make it. You need to come quickly, and prepare your goodbyes."

"He's still alive?" Thoren's words came out rushed and sloppy, darting up the stairs toward her quarters.

"Yes, but barely." Her tiny feet puttered along behind him, trying to match his pace.

"If he's alive, I can save him," he mumbled, realizing that Miss Leona didn't have any idea how powerful he truly was.

His heart raced, searching the room as he entered. The children huddled in the corner, soft whimpers and wailing cries of fear escaping their mouths. Otto lay across Kane, weeping as the boy begged. His eyes seemed locked onto something in the room that Thoren couldn't see.

"Go away! You can't have him!" A small brown trinket of some sort was clutched in his hand, laid on Kane's chest as though it were a protective talisman.

Thoren's gaze darted to where the boy glared, though he saw nothing. But he knew that look. Had seen it on Winnie's face enough to recognize the being the boy likely saw.

"Stand back," he said gently, placing a hand on Otto's back. "Don't worry. I won't let Death take him."

He watched for a moment as the boy moved aside, his eyes never losing sight of the nothingness he pleaded to. Thoren's lips parted, humming the soft lullabies their mother used to sing them. Soft tenor notes of healing encompassed Kane's shivering, lifeless body.

"What are you doing?" Miss Leona asked, scooting in next to them.

Thoren shook his head, moving his index finger over his pursed lips to silence her and avoid breaking his concentration. The songs continued, pushing a little harder as Kane's body seemed to fight the magic. *Does he not want to be healed?* he wondered, though he continued to push.

He stopped for a moment, placing a hand on Kane's neck to check for a pulse. "Come on, brother!" he begged, pumping Kane's chest a few times before resuming the siren song.

"Keep trying," Otto commanded with the most might a six-year-old could muster.

Thoren nodded, Miss Leona grabbing the boy and stroking his hair in an attempt to sooth him. Clutching the cross necklace around her neck, she said a mix of soft prayers as though it would ease her own worry.

The boy pushed her aside, grabbing ahold of Kane's hand as he perched beside him. "Come back to us, Kane! We need you!"

At last, his brother's eyes flashed open. With a loud gasp, he shot up. The wound on his shoulder dissipated, the flesh healing around it.

"You're alive!" Otto cried, hugging him tightly.

Miss Leona let out a soft whimper, crouched beside the little boy and ready to offer Kane a hug of her own.

"Winnie..." was all he mumbled, looking to his brother for answers.

"Come here, you idiot! I thought I lost you!" Thoren pulled his brother into a tight embrace, clutching one of the last remaining family members he had left. *Even a second later, and it would've been too late,* he realized.

"Pretty sure I was dead," he managed to mumble, rubbing the spot on his shoulder where he'd been injured. "Winnie... I saw her. She's alive. She was in trouble, but I think I managed to help her."

"You astral projected?" His brother's face cocked to the side in curiosity.

"No, not quite. I really think I was dead. There was something hot on my heels the entire time I was looking for her. As if it didn't want us to find each other." Kane's eyes remained fixed on nothingness, staring blankly around the room as though he tried to remember. "The longer I sit here, the less I remember."

"But she's alive?" Thoren took a seat beside him, one hand on his brother's back.

"She's alive." A lovesick smile fell across his face.

"Only you would be worried about a girl instead of your own life," he teased, offering his brother a gentle push.

Kane chuckled before focusing on the little boy in front of him. "I heard what you said. I followed your words back here."

Otto wiped away a rolling tear before his face broke into a beaming smile. "I helped?"

Kane nodded, pulling the boy into his arms and hugging him tightly. "Whatever you said to Death must've stuck, because I saw that figure run screaming when you yelled at it."

"Maybe this had something to do with it," he said, grinning ear to ear.

In his hand, he offered Kane the small brown trinket Thoren had noticed when he first walked through the door. His brother took it, examining the delicate thing before his own face broke into a smile.

"Where did you find this?"

"I found the acorn at the manor while we played in the woods. Momma Millie gave me the twine. Death told me what to carve into it for protection. It was supposed to be a Christmas gift, but you better take it now," Otto explained as Kane laid the necklace around his neck, and patted it close to his chest.

"You took him to the manor?" Thoren interrupted, awaiting Miss Leona's reaction.

"We may have had a little adventure," he confessed, eyeing the woman as well.

"Don't give me that look! I would have told you it was okay

had you merely asked! You act as though I want the boy to suffer!" she retorted, flustered and cheeks reddening.

Thoren's mind raced back to their lingering issue outside, setting aside momentary happiness. "I hate to rush you, but we do have a bigger problem to worry about."

Groaning, Kane stood.

"There's dozens of hounds out front. They took Ezra. Well, and Tara, but…"

"Don't finish that thought," Kane warned.

He knows me too well, he thought, knowing he was about to say something unseemly regarding the redhead. "We have to find a way past them."

Both sirens walked toward Miss Leona's window, realizing the entire orphanage was surrounded. Not a single opening or door stood unguarded. Their eerie howls formed in unison, letting the group inside know that they weren't going anywhere.

28

MELINDA
CHICAGO - 1871

Melinda stared out at the sea of angry faces glaring back at her. A mix of tears and petrified eyes from worried parents awaited answers. After entrusting the orphanage to babysit their children for the night, no one could have expected the attack. Only a half an hour before, they'd all casually enjoyed the festivities. Sitting with the Broderick trio, the sounds of bullets firing down the street sent everyone into a panic.

The masses ran toward the howls, only to scatter at the sight of hellhounds surrounding the building. The parents had been promised a night off, the children safely left behind. But they now stood inside one of many boarding houses for workers, worried to death that their babies were in danger.

"What are you going to do about this?" The voice of an angry father boomed across the room. If looks could kill, his surely would have speared her.

"I need everyone to calm down!" Melinda pleaded, unsure what to say to make the situation better. *Can I tell them the truth? Would they even believe me?* she wondered.

"My children are locked inside *your* orphanage! Do something!" Another angry mother yelled, her first shaking in the air.

The orphanage isn't mine, she thought begrudgingly, though she knew it wouldn't help to clarify.

"What are those things?"

Finally, a question I can answer, she thought with a sigh of relief. "Do you want the truth?" She waited for a moment as all went silent in the room. "The creatures you see surrounding the orphanage aren't wolves."

"Then what are they?" Another man interrupted, stepping closer as if he planned on getting in her face.

At her side, she couldn't help but notice Spencer tense. She glanced toward him, an unspoken question written across his face. One that seemed to ask her: *Do you want me to intervene?* She released a quiet huff of frustration, turning her face to a scowl as she returned the man's anger.

"Get out of my face, and I'll tell you!"

With a huff, he backed down. He motioned for her to continue, impatiently crossing his arms over his chest.

"Those things are called hellhounds. Without going into too much detail, they're incredibly strong. And fast. They aren't beasts that you want to face without a plan of attack."

"I thought I saw one of them turn into a man!" a mother cried in the crowd.

Melinda paused, glancing to her side at the Broderick trio. A part of her wished one of them could answer these questions. *What I wouldn't give for Milicent to be here to help me,* she thought.

Beside her, Riah nodded with an encouraging smile. "Whatever it is, just tell us. We need to be prepared."

Melinda took another deep breath. "You're correct – they can turn into humans. That's what makes them so dangerous. In wolf form, they can easily overpower you. In human form, they have weapons. Some can even…wield the elements. I know it's hard to understand but…"

Laughter erupted throughout the crowd. It seemed they didn't want to believe her wild tales.

Danny stepped in, a booming voice cutting through the

chatter. "Quit your jabbering! She's telling the truth! We've all seen it! Every one of you has been there for an attack. Stop pretending this isn't real!"

All went still again.

The same angry father from before finally added, "Then tell us how to stop them! We want our kids back." His rage seemed to simmer down, replaced by hopeless worry.

"We need time to assess. Figure out what they're planning. Thankfully we have friends on the inside to keep them safe for the time being. I think we should take turns keeping watch, discovering their weaknesses," Melinda began.

"We can figure out if they have some sort of rotation. Hit them when they're least expecting it," Danny suggested.

"They don't seem to be attacking now, thankfully. They're just…waiting." Riah's arms crossed over her chest as she spoke.

Melinda nodded. "I have no idea what they're doing, but it can't be good. Whatever they're planning, I'm sure it has something to do with…" She wanted to finish her sentence and mention the dreaded blood queen's name, though she quickly realized no one in that room would know what she was talking about. *I don't have anyone who knows what happened back in October…* she thought, a cold chill running through her.

Spencer took another step forward, leaning down to quietly speak to her. "Just let us know how we can help." When he straightened himself back up, he offered her a shy smile before placing a gentle hand along her back.

"I'll take the first shift. Anyone care to join me?"

Almost all raised their hands, worried parents eager to keep an eye on their children.

"Why don't we take the first shift, just you and I?" Riah offered. "Too many people and we'll be spotted immediately. The others can join in later."

"So we're just supposed to wait around?" a mother asked.

"While we're gone, I need everyone to gather supplies and weapons. As many as possible." Melinda offered the concerned women a gentle smile.

At last, the group before her scattered. Only the Broderick trio waited.

"I saw them take two of my friends," she mentioned, turning toward Riah who waited for her at the door.

"Should we focus on them first?"

On the other side of the room, Spencer caught his sister's attention. His hands moved with fluid speed, her eyes examining each movement carefully. Melinda waited eagerly for her to translate.

"He knows where the camp is," Riah explained. With a huff of frustration, she added, "And how the hell do you know that?"

Spencer took a few careful steps forward. "I followed one of them into the woods the other day with another worker."

"Seriously?" Danny looked at his brother in annoyance. "You can't keep running off like that!" he urged, his hands moving in a fury as their youngest brother chuckled.

Spencer shrugged his shoulders with a smirk, leaning against the doorframe casually. *I admire his spirit. That's exactly what I would've done,* Melinda thought.

"The camp is huge. We'll never save your friends unless we sneak in," Spencer added, glancing toward her.

Rubbing her head, she said, "Let's take care of the hounds around the orphanage, first. With the help of the Falke brothers, we stand a better chance."

The trio nodded before Danny asked, "Are they hellhounds, too? They seem too strong to be…human."

She chuckled. "Not beasts, but not humans either. I'll explain another time."

"Let's go," Riah urged. "We don't want to miss anything important."

The two women exited the boarding house, trudging toward the orphanage. Hiding in the shadows of alleyways, the two snuck up until they could see the building clearly. The hounds still surrounded the Chicago Orphan Asylum, nearby streetlamps low and flickering. Melinda searched the area for any sign of a weakness on their part, but they seemed to have every square inch of the place covered.

A tap on her shoulder startled her, turning to see Riah mouthing unintelligible words.

"I don't know what you're trying to tell me," Melinda whispered.

With an eye roll, she muttered, "I was trying to ask if they have super hearing. I didn't want to talk if they could hear me."

"I honestly have no idea. Maybe?"

Riah seemed to huff a small amused laugh before jutting her chin toward the orphanage again. "Isn't that one of the brothers up there?"

Melinda followed her line of sight, noticing Kane in the window staring out covered in blood. *Hopefully not his own,* she thought. He looked over his shoulder, talking to someone behind him. Only a moment passed before Thoren peered out. They seemed to be in a heated debate, Thoren's face twisted with anger. *He's probably worried sick about Ezra,* she thought, hoping that he and Tara both were okay wherever they'd ended up.

"I need some way to get his attention," she mumbled, more to herself than anything.

"I could try throwing something," Riah suggested, picking up a small pebble.

"That may cause suspicion. Super hearing or not, they'd notice something thrown at a window for sure."

"I'll be right back," Riah whispered, a devilish smile across her face running toward the boarding house.

Melinda waited a few minutes, unsure what the plan was. At last, she heard the sounds of music flowing from down the street again, as though the festival were still on. When Riah returned, Spencer trailed behind her.

"He insisted on coming..."

"Music. You're a genius!" Melinda added, trying desperately to hide a blushing smile from the young man who joined them.

Riah shrugged off the compliment, turning back toward the orphanage. Spencer scribbled something on paper before showing it to Melinda for her approval. On it, he'd written *'Look outside.'* She nodded before he tied the paper around a medium sized rock, and handed it to his sister.

"Let's hope I don't accidentally hit one of them in the head," Riah muttered before standing. She waited a moment, listening down the street for the perfect timing of the music. Just as a rowdy crowd cheered alongside booming drums, she hurdled the rock toward an orphanage window.

Kane and Thoren both darted away from what they likely thought was an incoming attack before peering outside with caution. Melinda offered a quick wave before crouching back down behind the alleyway. A few of the hellhounds glanced around in suspicion. When she looked back, she noticed Kane writing something. Within seconds, the paper appeared back in front of them.

Riah and Spencer both jumped back in surprise as it appeared, looking to Melinda for answers. It took her a moment to remember the magical letters the Fox family seemed to use often before she snatched it from where it floated.

On the paper, he'd written *'Melinda, our savior! What's the plan?'*

She took a moment to think of a response.

'No plan yet. Trying to figure out a weakness. Looking for any sort of rotation or moment when there's less of them. Also gathering supplies and weapons. Am I missing anything?' She scribbled the words down quickly before thinking back to Wesley's

instructions.

Closing her eyes, she envisioned the inside of the orphanage, thinking of all the tiny details that surrounded Kane where he stood. It only took a minute before the letter disappeared. A small squeal of excitement escaped Melinda as she peered back up where he stood, holding the paper in hand with a proud smile.

"Are *you* human?" Riah asked, cocking her head to the side with playful fascination.

Melinda didn't know how to answer that question as they waited for Kane to respond. To her side, Spencer tapped on her shoulder. Pointing to the top of a nearby building, he whispered, "I can climb up there, and keep watch. They won't see me."

She offered him a careful nod before he trudged off, hunched to avoid detection. Melinda couldn't help but watch anxiously, worried someone would hear the creaking of a metal ladder on the side of the building. Thankfully, the music still raged on down the street to cover any sounds they made.

"My brother sure does fancy you," Riah mumbled, a half smile on her face.

Her cheeks flushed, glancing back toward the young man now shimmying his way across the roof's shingles until he lay comfortably to watch the hounds.

"He's too shy to say something. But as his sister, it's my job to intervene after all. And embarrass him if I can," she whispered again, noticing the reds of Melinda's cheeks.

Before she could respond, the paper reappeared.

Kane had written, *'I couldn't have planned it better myself. We'll keep watch here, too. They have beeswax in their ears. Use that to your advantage. Hang on to this paper, and send it back when you have any updates. Tara and Ezra?'*

She sighed, worried sick about her friends. On it, she scribbled back, *'I saw them taken away by hounds. They were still alive at least. We're trying to locate their camp in the meantime.'* She closed her eyes and sent it back.

Looking toward the window, he nodded before returning the enchanted paper. *'Thank you, Mel. We owe you big time.'*

She stared at the paper for a moment. No one had ever given her a nickname before. She'd never been around people long enough to afford them the closeness required, it seemed. Even Miss Leona stuck to formalities. *I think for the first time in my life, I might actually have true friends,* she thought hopefully. *Let's keep it that way,* she decided at last before settling into their hiding places for the remainder of the night.

29

WINIFRED
MARVIVIA - 1861

That evening, Winnie tossed and turned all night. Memories of Kane's ghostly figure floating in the water haunted her every thought. Whenever she closed her eyes and drifted to sleep, she could only feel him reaching out to her. The way his sturdy hands had cupped her face, giving her the gift of air with mere seconds before she'd end up beside him and off toward Death's portal.

"To anyone listening – please. Tell me if he's alright," she begged, after waking from another nightmare where she traveled home with no love to return to.

For quite some time, nothing happened. Only a static silence waited for her pleas, not a single entity willing to answer her. Until she found herself yet again sitting in her old familiar pub.

It took a few moments for Winnie to figure out where she was. She'd fallen into another nightmare, this time one where Kane's face had contorted into a strange grimace, his arms replaced by tentacles that seemed to attack his body, and eat him alive. Kicking and screaming, she'd blinked and found herself... *here.*

Winnie's eyes moved over the familiar pub, though something

didn't feel quite right. Just like her last visit to what Wesley called 'Between,' small details seemed off. Softer, more angelic. Almost like an oil painting this time. Quiet murmurs surrounded her, though not a soul sat before Winnie as she waited.

Across from her, a glass of red wine stood, though no one seemed to step up and claim it. The hair on her arms stood as the murmuring souls surrounded her, curious about the newcomer that didn't belong with them.

"Why am I here?" she called out, hoping someone would answer.

It was then that a flash of bright light made her wince in surprise. When her vision regained, a head of dark hair strode toward her. Tears welled as Winnie watched the approaching siren, those deep eyes examining her affectionately like they'd done years before.

"Mrs. Falke..." Winnie's words came out a mere whisper, surprised to see the woman sitting across from her.

"My beautiful Winifred," she beamed, grabbing ahold of Winnie's hands. The wide smile and heavy Greek accent brought back a flood of memories that were almost too painful to remember.

"What are you doing here?"

Seeing Kane's mother like this... in her prime again. Before the illness took her life. Before her body withered away, hair fallen in clumps and mind lost. The look of fear in her eyes when she didn't recognize her own sons, much less the love of her life. Winnie remembered it all, pushing back the urge to leap forward and scream, *"I'm so sorry my family's magic couldn't save you!"*

"I waited for a while to see if anyone else would answer your prayers, but it seems they've all gone silent. So I took it upon myself to come tell you," Mrs. Falke reassured, gently stroking Winnie's hand.

"Kane? Is he alive?" She sat forward in her seat, awaiting an answer.

The siren offered a soft smile and nodded. "He is. Thoren healed him just in time."

A sigh of relief escaped Winnie, a heaviness in her chest easing all at once. "How do you know? You're...not dead yet."

She offered a delicate smile. "Time works differently on the other side. You'll see one day."

A shudder wracked down Winnie's spine, realizing she wanted that day to be a long time from now.

"I always knew you two would share this connection. Even in my final days, I could see it. The act of dying is a curious thing, you know. You don't just see Death, itself, come to usher your soul. Sometimes others come to get you. And often, secrets are revealed as well."

Winnie leaned forward, resting her elbow on the table and propping up her chin.

"When you go through something like I did, it's hard to put into words what it's like. On one hand, I knew all of you were there. Trying to help me. But my physical body didn't want to cooperate. My greatest regrets are that I spent my last few months unable to tell my husband and sons how much I cherished them. I never got to tell them that they were my whole world. Maybe you can go back and tell them for me, yeah?" Mrs. Falke continued to squeeze Winnie's hand, both fighting back tears.

"Of course," she said with a sniffle, guiding away a small tear that threatened to call forth more.

"These next few months will be...hard. But if you could see everything I do, you'd know that the fight is worth it. I know it's difficult right now, and it'll only get more strenuous moving forward. But I promise you... From the darkness, you will find so much love and light. It's all waiting for you."

Winnie nodded, unsure what to say. A strange sensation washed over her, a dark looming presence awakening as though Death realized the medium had snuck in again.

"I think I have to go," she whispered, getting up from the table to offer Mrs. Falke a quick hug.

"I know. One last thing... Tell my sons to be careful. I'm not allowed to say much, but please. Ensure they don't turn out like their father and charge head first into any altercations with lovesick hearts."

The siren offered her a final hug before guiding her back toward the glowing portal at the entrance of the pub. Before Winnie could ask any other questions, she found herself sitting upright on Oslind's couch, sweating and panting as though she'd just gotten done running laps around Fox Manor.

------•((●●●))•------

MILICENT
FOX MANOR - 1861

*N*ervous *eyes darted around the area.* Where am I? *Milicent wondered. A ruckus went on behind her, the sounds of terror and screams overwhelming. Her heart ached, the feeling of complete despair suffocating. Threatening to take her under entirely. Just across from her, a hazy image appeared. Faint outlines of wooden planks and ornate columns.*

My house. This is my porch, *she realized.*

The image cleared slowly, vague outlines of others revealing themselves. Wherever I am, whenever this is. It's a long time from now, *she decided, trying to decipher the vision.*

Two beings highlighted themselves as she hesitantly approached. One of them cleared, though his face remained partially hidden. Blonde hair fell around his features, the glimmer of foggy blue eyes outlined and staring to the heavens.

At once, she was overwhelmed by a sense of adoration. She didn't know who he was yet, but could feel enough to know that he was dearly cherished by the family. His blood shot gaze remained fixed to the sky, a tear rolling down his cheek.

"He saved me..." The words tumbled from his mouth with a sob, each one a stab to the gut. Something didn't feel right.

Who saved you? *She wondered, trying to make out the features of the person in this young man's arms. Still, the identity of the other evaded her.*

Behind Milicent, an arm grasped her shoulder. She turned, seeing a being made of glowing sage green hues. Fate stood behind her, pale vacant eyes glittering with more human emotion than she'd ever seen before.

"I'm sorry to show you this," Fate whispered, ushering Milicent to turn her attention back toward the young man cradling the other figure.

"Who's in his arms?" She inched her way toward the two.

Turning her attention back to Fate, the being never answered the question. Behind them, the blonde haired man continued his chant.

"He saved me. Why would he do that? Why didn't I save him?" The despair and sadness in his voice was tangible, thickening the air with grief.

"Who is he holding?" This time, her question came out as a poignant demand.

Those glimmering pale eyes only stared back at her. Fate opened their mouth, though the voice that came from them was not the one Milicent had heard time and time again. Instead, the voice mimicked her own.

"Stay with my son."

Her entire world collapsed. An icy chill ran down her spine, settling into her gut as despair washed over her in waves. Nausea crept up her throat, her heart heavy and limbs going numb.

"Wait. No... Is... Is Wesley going to die?" Mere stutters managed to form, not a single coherent thought evident.

Glancing down at the body cradled in the blonde man's arms,

Wesley's face cleared just enough. The face of a teenage version of him showed through, the same mossy green eyes staring blankly out at the ceiling of the porch.

Fate held their finger to their translucent lips and shushed. "You mustn't tell anyone. For this passing you cannot stop. Death will have this boy, no matter what you do."

Fate snapped their fingers, sending Milicent back to her body. Expelled from her trance, Milicent glanced down at the little boy whose head lay cradled in her lap. Her thunderous heart worked to slow its beating, though nothing could stop the pure panic she felt.

Looking down at Wesley, her darling baby boy, she took a moment to memorize him. The sleepy eyes, closed and covering the beauty that matched the grassy fields just outside. The deep brown hair like her husband's, the small ringlets around his ears and at the back of his head where a cowlick lay. The curvature of his nose; the way it buttoned with tiny specks of freckles many didn't notice. Small details, ones only a mother would see.

Tears welled, stinging the backs of her eyes as her throat bobbed and burned. A nurturing hand ran down the length of his back, attempting to wake him gently. They hadn't meant to fall asleep on the sofa, though their lake adventures with Winnie from earlier had worn them both out. The fact that her daughter still dared enter that lake to begin with shocked her. After the most recent incident...

When Wesley didn't wake, she carefully slid from under him and placed his head back on a pillow with care. Seeing him sleep so peacefully, Milicent couldn't help but replay those images in her mind.

"He saved me." The blonde man's words stuck out the most. Despite what Fate said, she'd find a way to ensure Wesley would never get the chance to save some stranger who'd be the reason her baby boy was killed. One way or another. She'd stop it all.

After a few moments of silent contemplation, Milicent turned. Following the sounds of voices coming from the family library, she entered to see Ernest and Lucille discussing the contraption he was meant to build.

Milicent still didn't quite trust Lucille. Something was off about that one. A familiarity surrounded her, though who she was seemed unclear. How she came to know of such devices and contraptions was also unclear. Milicent knew better than anyone that Fate would *never* allow such forwardness in regards to discussing visions. There was no way Lucille was clairvoyant. That could only mean one thing… there were greater beings involved.

"How's it going, you two?" she asked, leaned on the doorframe, examining them working.

"Slowly. Lucille here thinks that I'm more talented than I am," Ernest said with a half chuckle.

"I know you can make this! I'm telling you! I've seen it!" Her enthusiasm seemed to be wearing off on him. "There's a few key pieces we need. I recently came face to face with a selkie underwater and know first-hand how important these will be."

Ernest offered the girl a nod before preparing to leave. She paused for a moment, examining her husband. The vision tumbled around in her mind like a nagging marble, relentlessly reminding of future tragedy.

"Can I tell him?" Milicent asked in her mind, hoping Fate was still listening.

"No. You cannot tell anyone what you saw. If you do, it will change the course of time. No one can know," they responded, the familiar warmth of Fate's grasp firm on her shoulder.

"I don't know how I can keep this to myself," she admitted, tears once again threatening release.

"If you must tell someone, tell Lucille. She will not impact your timeline." At last Fate's presence disappeared.

Examining the girl curiously, Lucille sketched images on a

sheet of paper for Ernest. That strange feeling of knowing washed over Milicent again, though it still remained unclear how. *I'll just need to get her alone to be sure,* she decided.

30

TARA
CHICAGO - 1871

Tara wouldn't remember much from the night of the attack when she woke days later. Flashes of the empty street's gas lamps fluttered in and out of sight, realizing she was being dragged away by a hellhound. The razor sharp fangs that dug into her ankle burned, infectious saliva of the beast mingling with her blood. After managing to get a solid kick to her attacker's face, the last thing she remembered was the beast's sturdy grip on her shoulders as she thrust Tara's head into the ground.

Darkness plagued her vision, consciousness fading in and out. She remembered being dragged for a while, glimpses of an alleyway surrounding her as a head of blonde hair lifelessly trailed behind them. A sudden howl interrupted her opponents. Then a small skirmish.

Yelps and fired bullets drowned out her panicked thoughts. Before she knew it, she was being carried off. No longer dragged by her bleeding ankle or thrown around like a ragdoll. But at last, someone handled her with care.

"Thoren? Kane?" Tara's guesses came out a strained whisper, trying to rub her eyes clear so she could see her new savior. Only the smell of campfire smoke filled her senses as they walked for what felt like miles.

"Shh, it's okay. I've got you now, little fawn."

That nickname sent her body into a complete and total panic. "Put me down," she slurred, unable to focus on anything specific.

She was utterly helpless, the throbbing in her head so intense she almost didn't feel the sting of the bite around her ankle.

"Get them both inside," she heard him say. Flickering lights peaked through her cloudy vision.

With a heavy sigh, she'd fallen into a strange sleep. Several hours passed, unable to wake. Her body gave up, though her soul seemed to sense the nearby beasts that guarded her comatose body.

I need to wake up. I need to get out. I need to save myself. The words rang through her mind like an alarm, though she could do nothing to pull herself from a dreamless sleep.

A t last, Tara shot up. The heavy daze faded as her vision adjusted, realizing a chilled breeze surrounded her. The sounds of chirping birds just outside summoned her attention. She'd woken in a tent, lying in a cot with a thick blanket draped over her. A smoldering fire simmered just across, though there were no signs of anyone else. Only her thoughts remained.

With a wince, she tried turning her head to the side. Along her neck and cheek, a burn of sorts was slowly healing from where she'd been dragged. Small cuts and bruises peppered her freckled skin. Beneath the blanket, a dull ache surrounding her ankle sent her mind into a tailspin as bits and pieces of the attack came to her.

Moving the blanket aside, she gasped. Though gauze covered the injury, Tara could feel the stinging throb without ever having to look beneath. Still, curiosity got to her. Moving aside the white ribbons, she nearly began to weep at the sight of a feral bite.

Her flesh was stained with purple bruises, the blood cleaned off and small purple flowers tucked into the teeth marks. *I need to get out of here,* she thought as she swung her legs off the cot. Attempting to put some pressure on her injured foot, she winced in pain.

"Dammit," she mumbled, eyes darting toward the exit as figures moved just outside.

She scanned the area, looking for any sort of useful tool or weapon. The tent was bare, likely on purpose. Rubbing the back of her head, she felt a heaving knot from where she'd been knocked out. Attempted to get up, the pressure on her ankle was excruciating.

Ignoring the pain, she picked up her shoes. Trying to hide the whimpers that escaped her lips, she scolded herself: *I can't risk being heard.* Carefully, she pulled on her boots. The mere touch of leather against her shredded ankle made fire course through her entire leg. Just outside, the sound of heavy boots warned of an intruder.

A shadow appeared at the tent's entrance as she hobbled toward the door. She hid against the side, ready to ambush whoever came through. A head of dark hair peered in before she swung with vicious intent. Tara managed to get a solid punch in, though the pain of her ankle made her lose balance enough to lessen the impact.

"Good morning, little fawn. I see we're as lively as ever," Alaric said with a slight grimace, holding his bruising cheek. "You shouldn't be walking on that foot."

With more care than she'd expected, Alaric grabbed Tara by the arm and slowly guided her toward the cot. "Let me go!" Adrenaline pumped through her veins, the pain momentarily forgotten.

She prepared to swing at him again, though this time, he caught her fist before she could make full contact.

"Stop. Fighting. I'm trying to help you." He raised his eyebrows in a sort of playful judgment she wasn't expecting.

"If you truly mean to help me, let me go!" She swung again, her fist meeting with the open palm of his hands.

She stumbled a little, Alaric sweeping her off her feet and

carrying her back to her cot. He tossed her on top of it, the makeshift bed almost falling from the sudden weight.

"Ease up for a second and just listen," he insisted. Crouched in front of her, he met her at eye level. Rearing her head back as if to deliver a headbutt, he repeated, *"Stop.* Fighting. I won't keep repeating myself."

With a frustrated huff, she ceased her attempted attacks. "What the feck happened last night?"

"You mean three nights ago?"

Her eyes flashed in terror. "It's been three days?"

Her first instinct was to stand and pace, though Alaric pushed her back down on the cot. "Stop walking on that ankle. It needs rest." He paced to the corner of the tent, grabbing a stack of kindling to get the fire going again.

"Cricket! My friends! They must think I'm dead! What the hell happened? Why did your hounds attack us?"

"I keep trying to tell you, Tara. Not all the hounds are mine." The words came out through gritted teeth. He took a seat across from her on the ground, cross legged and casually slouched back.

"Bullshit. I don't believe for one second those weren't your hounds," she spat.

"My hounds are the ones that saved you and your friend from getting dragged off for dinner. Thanks to us, you two are still alive." His words came out with a grumble, avoiding eye contact.

"My friend?" Tara thought back to the attack. She could hardly remember anything, the memories fuzzy. She only remembered the outline of Thoren on the porch, firing out at the surrounding frenzy.

"The blonde one. Seems quite cozy with your siren friend." His tone was frank, stocking the fire carefully, welcoming warmth back into the tent.

"Ezra! Is he okay?" She leaned forward on the cot in worry.

"He's okay. He's healing and unconscious, but he'll be okay. The

Wolfsbane is still working its magic."

"Wolfs...what?" She examined her ankle once more, realizing the flowers stuffed into her wound glowed with a strange iridescent shine.

"We began experimenting well before Boudicca was defeated. If applied early enough, it'll sometimes stop the change. If applied too late, it's more likely to kill a new hound. We're still ironing out the kinks."

"Wait...am I going to turn?" Her hand cupped her mouth in horror, dizziness overwhelming her senses again.

"No, Tara," he said with a smirk, head cocked to the side playfully. "Not unless you want to."

"Why would I want to be one of *your* kind?"

He only rolled his eyes at her disgust. "We aren't all monsters like you've been led to believe. It can be quite fun actually." His eyes lowered again, leaning forward toward her as if eager to share.

"Show me Ezra. I want proof he's okay," she insisted.

Alaric nodded, getting to his feet to help her up.

Tara swatted the hand that offered support. "I can walk on my own!"

"Suit yourself. Though the more you move that ankle, the less likely it is that the Wolfsbane will work." Alaric backed off for a moment, watching as she stumbled and winced toward the exit.

Tara tried to contain the whimpers of pain that escaped her lips. She leaned down to walk through the tent flap, losing her balance. Falling forward, a strong hand caught her.

"Just let me help you," he grumbled in annoyance.

Hoisting her up, he pulled her up by the waist. To her surprise, she found herself clinging to the support. Even the slightest bit of relief on her ankle was welcomed. Wordlessly hobbling beside him, she was careful not to put too much pressure on her ankle.

Tara stared out over the camp, a web of leafless tree limbs covering them. A thick blanket of snow coated the ground now, the sun shining in the sky and warming her ever so slightly. Her breath puffed in front of her in clouds as they continued to march forward. Shivering, she couldn't help but lean into him. Savoring another's body heat, she took in the smell of campfire again.

A shiver ran down her spine. Not because of the cold, but rather the hellhound leader's breath which brushed her neck as he glanced down at her. His brows furrowed up as if to silently ask, *'Are you alright?'* as they walked. So sincere, she could almost believe he was actually concerned. Regardless, she trudged forward thankful for the support he offered.

"Where are we?" As they continued, she caught herself counting the tents silently.

"Just outside Chicago." Seeing her eyes darting around the camp, he added, "You can stop surveying. There's a lot of us. Just know you're safe. Stop thinking that we're going to hurt you."

She opened her mouth to say something, though truthfully didn't know what she was trying to get at. They approached another larger tent, two wolves waiting outside on guard. Alaric nodded, the pair moving aside to allow entry.

"If we're safe, why have hounds on watch?" As they entered the tent, her eyes widened in surprise, realizing who was trapped inside.

Ezra lay flat on a cot similar to hers, eyes closed and unconscious. Small vines jutted from the ground below him, wrapping themselves around the bed's legs. They seemed to reach for him, though a strange haze blocked their path.

In the corner, Mayor Medill sat strapped to a chair. His mouth was gagged, face bruised with healing cuts. Freeing herself from Alaric's grasp, she limped to Ezra first. His chest rose and fell steadily, minimal damage done to him aside from the wound on his midsection. *Thank the Gods he's alive,* she thought. Turning toward the mayor next, Alaric blocked her path.

Medill's muffled cries for help rang through her ears. Every instinct told her to save him, but the hellhound leader wouldn't let her past. She glanced over his shoulders, Medill's eyes widening in fear. They pleaded with her, likely wondering why she was just standing there.

"You're here to see your friend. Not the mayor." His face was stern, the scar over his blue eye glinting in the nearby light.

"You expect me to believe I'm safe when these two are clearly prisoners?" Attempting to push past him again, the hellhound remained steady.

"I keep telling you; he's *not* who he says he is." His voice was low, an almost whisper, as he glanced suspiciously over his shoulder.

Tara sighed in defeat before returning to Ezra to examine his sleeping body. Just like her ankle, his bound midsection was stuffed with those same purple flowers. The vines surrounding his bed moved curiously toward her, though retreated at her touch.

"Not sure that those little things are. Every time we cut them, they reappear. I thought he was human?" Alaric asked quietly.

Her panic was too great to comprehend his question.

"I need to get him back to my friends. The sirens can heal him!" Kneeling before Ezra, she glanced back at Alaric with pleading eyes.

With a shrug, he said, "There's too many hellhounds surrounding the orphanage. We'd never make it."

"You clearly have enough people here at your camp. If you really mean well, help me get him back!" she demanded, hobbling back to her feet. As she stood before him, she had to fight the urge to lean in closer. *What must it be like to count the starlight speckles of those beautiful blue eyes,* she thought.

He glanced down at her, head cocked to the side as if studying her face. The corners of his mouth turned to a smirk, placing his hands on her shoulders in an almost endearing manor. "If we move him in this condition, the Wolfsbane may not take effect. His bite was far worse than yours. I doubt your friend wants his lover returned to him as a hound. Since we're such awful brutes."

"We can't stay here! They'll think we're dead. They need to know we're okay."

"We can find some way to send word. But going up against the hellhounds surrounding that place is not an option. Definitely not in your condition." Alaric motioned for her leg as he spoke. Pointing back toward the exit, he suddenly urged her to leave.

"I want to stay here with him." Tara held fast next to Ezra, grabbing his hand. The pendant around her neck glowed for a moment. Curiously, she glanced down at it and wondered: *What magic could it be warding against right now?*

"You can't stay in here with the mayor," he insisted, grabbing her hand and pulling her toward the exit. "You don't have to believe me when I say he's a dangerous man, but I won't allow you near such a monster. Not in my camp."

As soon as Ezra's hand dropped from hers, the glow of her pendent ceased.

"Can't you move my friend to my tent then? That way I can care for him. It would be less work for you and your hounds." Resting her hands on his forearm, she pleaded.

Any hope she had vanished as he shook his head.

"It's too risky to move him. I'd love to ease your mind, but moving him isn't an option."

With a sigh, she nodded. *Thoren already dislikes me enough as it is. If I'm the reason Ezra is turned into something he hates, he'll never forgive me,* she thought.

Alaric's eyes flashed to the Quinn family necklace in curiosity as he pulled her from the tent. "What does that thing do anyways?"

"You should know. You tried to steal it the night of Samhain." She avoided his gaze, still studying the campsite for any sort of upperhand.

"Boudicca wanted it, but wouldn't say why," he explained,

nodding to hellhounds as they passed. None of them said a word, glaring at the redhead on his arm.

Ducking, she groaned as they entered her tent. "It wards against magic."

Alaric guided her to the cot beside a slow simmering fire, stocking it to bring forth its life again.

"Any magic?"

Tara examined him curiously, trying to get a read on his body language as he took a casual seat across from her on the ground. "So I'm told."

"Where did you get it?"

"Why do you want to know?"

"Can I not make conversation with you?" He chuckled as his lips curved into a devilishly handsome half-smile.

"We don't know each other well, but I'm very aware that you're always scheming. Why are you so interested in a trinket around my neck?" Crossing her arms over her chest, she waited.

He seemed to huff a little, though she wasn't sure if it was from amusement or frustration. He raised his hands in the air as if to surrender. "Fine. Necklace – off limits. I won't try to make conversation with you."

For a moment, neither said a word.

"I can't stay here." Her stomach grumbled, realizing she probably hadn't eaten in days.

"We just have to figure out how to take care of that little hound problem, and then I'll get you back to your demented little pet and the friends who take you for granted. Don't worry." He stood, ready to exit the tent.

She scoffed, refusing to look his way. "You know nothing about my friends."

Though she couldn't see him, she heard his steps stop just in front of the door flap. Turning back toward her, his gaze dug into the skin of her back. A beckoning call urged her to look at him, realizing how devastatingly distraught he now looked.

"Thanks to Boudicca, I've spent a great deal of time watching all of you interact. There isn't a person in that group who values you as they should."

She said nothing, only looked back at the fire simmering just as her anger singed her soul.

Carefully, he stepped back toward her and placed a gentle hand on her back. "Aren't you tired of being used as a fighter, and then discarded when it comes time to contribute with your ideas?" His face was soft and gentle. A side to him that was entirely new to Tara. Almost unsettling: a stark contrast to how the Falke brothers had described him, or even the arrogant enemy she'd shared a drink with at the bar.

She waited, unsure what to say. Nervous hands fiddled in her lap before she finally added, "It's not all of them. My best friend, Winnie, doesn't take me for granted."

"And where is she? Hm? Last I checked, she disappeared the night we snatched the mayor. She hasn't returned, has she? At some point, Tara, you have to accept that you're all alone." Without another word, he left.

His absence was a surprise knife to the gut. *I am alone, aren't I?* Her thoughts raced, thinking back to the last three years since meeting everyone. The memories of her lost family crept into the forefront of her mind, though she pushed the painful images of sunken ships and selkie attacks aside to focus on happier memories.

However, she couldn't help but recall the night the Falke brothers were banished. The day after she'd watched Kane drag Winnie's ex-lover into the sky with a vengeance she'd never seen in any kind-hearted man. She'd arrived at the manor to check on her best friend, only to find Winnie had vanished. No one knew where she'd gone off to. Tara didn't hear from her supposed 'best friend' for two years until she was once again *needed.* For a fight, no less.

"Perhaps he's right," she mumbled, poking the fire with a stick.

"I'm good for a brawl, and then I'm discarded like trash."

Half an hour passed before Alaric returned with a few slices of bread, some cheese, and a tin of water in hand. "It's not much, but it'll do for now. They'll cook up some stew later this evening, and then I can offer you something with more substance."

Cautiously, she took what he offered. Looking it over, suspicion laced her every move.

With a dark chuckle, he asked, "Still think I'm trying to kill you?"

The sound of it sent a wave of heat through her body as she attempted to focus on the offering of kindness, rather than the teasing lilt of his voice.

"I don't think there's anything you can say to convince me otherwise," she admitted. Offering everything a quick sniff, she still eyed him carefully. *What am I doing? I doubt I'd be able to tell even if it was poisoned,* she scolded herself.

"Why would I go through all this trouble to save you, just to poison you with some cheese?" Just as he had with the alcohol the other day, he took a small nibble from each item before handing it back to her.

"Fair enough," Tara sighed, at last taking a bite. Her stomach twisted in knots as an overwhelming hunger awakened deep within.

"Rest up. You'll need your strength."

"I still don't trust you…"

The words seemed to spear him in the back as he turned. A sad gaze morphed to a devilish smirk before he took a careful seat beside her on the cot.

"That's fine. You don't have to trust me. Not yet. But one day you'll see." A gentle finger ran over the wounds on the side of her face before he dug into his pocket. Showing her a vial of ointment that looked similar to Milicent's, he asked, "May I?"

Unsure how to respond, Tara nodded in silence. He spent a few moments carefully applying the salve along the freckles of her skin, the tingling sensation of healing magic lessening the sting.

"Thank you," she mumbled, unsure what to do – who to trust.

"Can't let that pretty face of yours scar up like my ugly mug," he joked, a wry laugh escaping him as he stood.

"You and I both know you're far from ugly." Her cheeks flushed, wishing she hadn't said those words.

He turned, hiding a bashful grin. "Seriously, get some rest. I'll come get you when it's time for supper."

All she could do was nod, finishing off the last of the bread and cheese. Taking a sip of water, she watched him exit in silence. Tara's hand cupped the side of her face, thankful to have one less part of her body aching and sore. She played with the fire for a short time before exhaustion overwhelmed her. With nothing else to do, she lay back on her cot. The tent around her seemed to spin as she drifted back to sleep.

31

WINIFRED
FOX MANOR - 1861

Winnie's heart raced in her chest. The muscles in her legs screamed, a bead of sweat dripping down her temple. They weren't far behind her. They'd catch up soon. Ducking behind a nearby tree, she waited. Slowing her breaths, she squeezed her eyes shut. *I hope they don't find me,* she thought.

"Gotcha!" little Wesley yelled, jumping around the side of the tree.

Winnie let out an animated groan, hunched over to finish settling her skittering breath.

"Again!" the boy yelled, tugging at her arm.

"One sec, Wes! I need a minute to breathe!" Laughter came out between each word, soaking up every minute she could spend with him.

A few feet away, slow steps approached. She peeked around, seeing nine-year-old Winnie kicking at nearby debris. "I'm tired, Wes! I don't want to play anymore!"

Something broke in Winnie's heart, hearing those words. Knowing what she knew. A look of hurt fell across the boy's face, looking between his sister and 'Lucille.'

"Why don't we take a break and play more later?" she suggested, knowing Ernest would need her shortly.

"Okay…" His sigh was one of the last things she heard before he trudged off with his head drooping low.

"Finally," little Winnie groaned with an eye roll.

Fighting back tears, she waited. Unable to look at her younger self, thoughts raced through her mind. She wanted so badly to grab the young girl by the shoulders and shake some sense into her. *'One day you will lose him! And you will find yourself an adult who's sad and angry. Willing to give everything to come back to these moments and play on the lake, or hunt for fae in the woods! Just do it!'* The words screamed in her mind, though she never allowed them to form.

"Why don't you head back, too? Your mother will want to see you for meditation practice, soon." The words choked from her mouth, wanting to say so much more than she was allowed.

Her younger self nodded, turning toward the house again.

Spending time around her family in its youth was an odd feeling. The memories she had from this time were hazy from age, bits and pieces coming back to her with every second they spent together. The last three days at the manor had been a welcomed break from Marvivia. She was thankful to sleep in an actual bed, feet firmly planted on solid ground that didn't move with the neverending tides.

Strolling along the edge of the lake, Ernest waited. At last, it was time to test his invention. The intense August sun beamed down on her, gnats and other tiny insects buzzing along the water. Her father held the breathing device he'd one day boast about, never mentioning the 'Lucille' that helped him. A fact she'd realized begrudgingly.

Winnie stood beside him, examining the contraption. It didn't look quite how she remembered it, though her parents never allowed her to try it out in their time. She cringed, thinking of having to wear it in the water now. *It looks obnoxiously heavy,* she thought. Around a collar sat a large see-through dome. Runes of water and air signs were carved into the golden edges, power radiating off of it in waves.

"You said you needed weight because you were constantly fighting the current. It's certainly dense. You won't be floating up unless you're trying to. I just hope the magic doesn't fail." Ernest shifted from one leg to the other, rubbing his forehead nervously.

"I have backup magic, if needed," she reassured.

"That's comforting, at least. The last thing I want is to be responsible for your death should this fail. I can't handle another drowning in my lake." His eyes rested across the water, lost in thought.

"Another drowning?"

"She's fine now, thankfully. I'm not sure what happened. One moment my daughter was swimming peacefully in the water. The next, she felt something drag her under. Winnie claims Gali helped her escape. We're curiously waiting to see if her elemental powers come in from the whole ordeal."

With a deep exhale, Winnie paused. *I...drowned? In the lake...when I was nine?* "I... Winnie. Did she fully..." the question never completely formed.

With a hesitant nod, Ernest continued. "She was dead for a few moments before Milicent was able to revive her, and get the water from her lungs. We thought we lost our daughter. When she came to, she only spoke of Gali."

A familiar presence loomed in the atmosphere.

"Why do I not remember this?" she asked the goddess.

"Some things, a young mind need not remember," Gali said with a sigh, her voice faint and barely audible.

"Shall we?" he ushered, pointing toward his invention.

With a nod, Ernest helped her into the flippers, pulling the golden breathing apparatus over her head. It was even heavier than it looked. She expected the dome to fog at her breath, but it seemed to almost disappear immediately. Caelus and Gali's magic felt like a welcoming hug with the contraption on, allowing temporary access to anyone wearing the device.

"Once you're down there, it should automatically start working. I don't know the limits of it yet, so make sure you come up to the surface every once in a while just in case. Don't go too far down. After what happened with my daughter, I worry there may actually be something down there." His voice was muffled through the dome surrounding her head.

Winnie offered another nod before shuffling awkwardly into the lake, tripping on the flexible material extending off her feet. She turned back to her dad once more, offering him a careful smile. *I don't know why I'm so nervous. I already know it works!*

Ernest rubbed his head before calling out. "Please don't go too far! And don't get yourself killed…"

His words trailed off as she submerged herself underwater. The moment her face slipped beneath the green lake, the air immediately began to work. She took careful breaths at first, testing it out before blindly trusting her father's magic. The weight of the breathing apparatus was surprisingly lessened once submerged, the flippers helping her glide through.

She didn't see much of anything at first, pushing through the murky water. *That's something we need to add – lights,* she thought, struggling to see through the thick darkness. Farther below, a glimmer of something shined. As she approached, she realized it was the portal to Marvivia. The glittering outlines of symbols and runes lined the bottom of the lake, illuminating the area enough for her to see what was nearby.

A strange heaviness washed over her, as though she were being watched. At these depths, it could have been anything. She shivered, thinking of the tiny slithering creatures who had wrapped themselves around her ankles days before.

It was then that Winnie noticed it. A set of red eyes stared at her, a flowing gray mane washing over its animalistic face. At first, she couldn't make out what it was. It wasn't until the creature turned that she noticed a set of hooves and a long tail. There was a monster circling, with razor sharp fangs. Waiting. Ready for her to make a move.

"So you must be what attacked little me…" she mumbled into her breathing apparatus.

Reaching for her side, Winnie withdrew a borrowed Marvivian dagger. The figure darted, flashes of a dark fish-like tail slithering around her. *I'm outmatched,* she panicked. *I don't have the skills necessary to fight a beast like this underwater!*

Still, she had to try. For the sake of her little self and brother, she needed to rid the lake of this beast. They'd spend many summers in these waters; she couldn't risk it remaining down here to kill one of them or the younger Falke brothers.

A rush swam past her, quicker than lightning. The water monster was gone in moments, disappearing into the darkness of the murky waters that surrounded her. At once, it barreled into Winnie. The mane of the beast nicked her exposed skin, sharp as razors and as deadly as the red eyes glaring at her. In a matter of seconds, it disappeared once again in the dark abyss. Winnie waited, trying to anticipate its next move.

But instead it lunged into her once more from behind, her body thrust into the bottom of the lake. When her body made contact with the muddy lake bed, the slithering of those strange little fish made her skin crawl. Their vacant eyes gleaming at her, glowing in the darkness and threatening to once again mesmerize her.

Squeezing her eyes shut, she pushed off the lake bed. Only a moment passed before the underwater monster barreled into her back, slamming her into the thick clay below. The dome of her breathing apparatus smacked into a nearby boulder, cracking with a sharp hiss as water trickled in. Calling on Caelus for help, she took a final breath before attempting to open her eyes. The water stung as she tried to remain vigilant, her vision clouded.

Below, a glowing light caused the slithering fish to scatter away. The portal to Marvivia opened, two figures appearing a few feet away. Expecting to see Oslind followed by Brenna, Winnie was surprised to see two sets of mermaid tails instead. It wasn't long before the creature appeared behind them, ready to pounce.

One of the figures held up their hand, a glowing white light protruding from their fingertips. Fighting back the sting in her eyes, Winnie finally realized who it was. Afissa floated, wearing the outfit she recognized from her aunt's many visits. An abalone shell colored corset with tiny beads of pearls covered her torso, the queen's hair braided down her back and interwoven with seaweed.

The creature hovered in anticipation, huffing as the water around it stirred. Its red eyes softened at the sight of the mermaid, their glow simmering to a luminescent orange as though it had calmed down. Afissa approached the creature, placing her hand on what looked to be a horse's face. With a gentle smile and careful strokes, she nodded to Oslind who guided Winnie back to the surface.

Winnie's head speared through the surface, the water housed in her helmet finally escaping and eyes no longer stinging. Removing the dome and rubbing her face, she gasped for air realizing that despite Caelus's gifts, she'd been holding her breath. Oslind checked her over with surprise care, ushering them to the shore where he changed to his human form.

"I take it that the device didn't work?" Ernest huffed, frustration tangible as he snatched the domed helmet before tossing it to the ground.

"It did work. Brilliantly actually! But I met…something down there. It damaged the glass. Otherwise it would have been fine," she reassured, wringing excess moisture from her hair.

"So there is something in the lake?" His anxiety was evident, crossing his arms over his chest and pacing warily. "What was it?"

Before anyone could answer, the sounds of splashing water caught their attention. Afissa rode from the lake on what looked to be a dark-coated horse, wet grey hair curled and laying down its neck. Atop the creature, she rode with human legs, her corset glittering in the August sun.

"A kelpie. Truly misunderstood creatures," she called down confidently.

"That thing almost killed my daughter the other day," Ernest countered, stepping forward toward the duo as they rode onto land.

The towering beast snorted the closer he got, its head bobbing anxiously as tapping hooves moved away from the man. Afissa offered careful reassurance, patting its neck.

"I'll be happy to take him off your hands."

"You'd better. If my wife sees an animal on the property, she'll have a fit. She's never been fond of pets, and even less for an aquatic one that could kill our children." Ernest rubbed his head in worry before picking up the breathing apparatus.

"I have some ideas for how to fix a few flaws," Winnie added before he disappeared back into the house with a nod. At last, she turned back toward the two mermaids. "What are you doing here?"

"I wanted to meet the infamous Fox family that we'll be helping one day," Afissa explained, getting off the kelpie's back.

"My mother knows more than my father does," Oslind added, offering her a warm smile.

At least he has one parent he can trust, she thought. "Does she know…"

"About Brenna? Of course. She shares very different views from my father. Clearly. He would have killed this beast, and mounted its head in the throne room." Oslind patted the kelpie's neck before leading it over to the side of the house.

"My son has just as kind a soul as I do. Neither one of us agrees with my husband's choices. I'm beginning to wonder, myself, if perhaps the selkies had the right idea. Maybe democracy is the way to go…" Afissa's sad eyes dropped to the ground before glancing back at her son.

"I doubt King Aalto would appreciate that…"

With a shake of her head, Afissa continued. "He'd have me killed just for uttering those words if he knew. I want to trust you and this family you speak so highly of. I just hope they can help my people break free of my husband's control. This war has gone on for far too long. And if they can help, I want to know them."

Guilt stirred inside Winnie, recalling the timeline that lay ahead of them. "The Fox family may not be of much use for now, but one day their daughter will help you. I swear it."

"Isn't she a bit young?" Afissa chuckled, noticing a head of curls poking out from the sunroom door as little Winnie examined them.

"I can't explain it, but many years from now, the girl will do whatever it takes to help you and Oslind gain control. I don't know if you'll get your democracy, but one way or another, you or your son will sit on the throne at the very least."

"And what will this Winnie want from me in return?" She squinted in suspicion. "People don't usually help unless there's something in it for them."

"In exchange for overthrowing your husband's control, Winnie will need *your* help. With an army."

"I overheard your conversation with my husband. You've already struck a deal with him. Those are incredibly difficult to break free of." Afissa raised a brow, cocking her head to the side.

"I'll figure it out…" she mumbled. "Can I count on you *instead* of him? To keep such a long-term promise?"

"How long are we talking here? My people can only hold on for so long," she asked, a sad gaze finding her son as he patted the kelpie on the neck.

I can't tell her the truth, she thought. "A few years from now…I can't say how long."

With a heavy sigh, the queen contemplated. "If that little

girl truly helps me overthrow my husband one day, I will gladly provide her with an army. One of mermaids *and* selkies. It'll be the best defense she can ask for."

Hope sparked in Winnie's mind, realizing perhaps she could get what she needed peacefully rather than having to kill the woman she'd grown fond of.

"Don't get your hopes up," Boudicca mocked. *"One does not simply break a blood oath. You should know that better than anyone."*

"Then it's a deal. But you mustn't say a word until *after* Winnie turns twenty. I know it's quite a bit of time from now, but…"

"Twenty?" Afissa cried. "That girl is a mere child! We're meant to wait that long?"

At first, she didn't know what to say. Contemplating, she at last thought of what the Elements had told her. "Everything is already fated to happen. Though I can't tell you the specifics, just know it will happen in your favor. The Gods won't have it any other way."

"I guess it'll have to do," Afissa conceded. "I suppose at least having hope is better than nothing." The two walked toward the sunroom before the queen asked, "I take it you're Winnie?"

Panic sent electric waves down Winnie's back before realizing the woman was talking to her younger self. A small, delicate hand reached for the mermaid with caution, only for the little girl's face to erupt into a smile. "You're the most beautiful woman I've ever seen!"

With a blush, older Winnie added, "She's a mermaid!"

"My name's Afissa. Is your mother around? I'd like to meet her." The queen crouched down to meet the young girl's gaze, who's eyes wandered the pearls and seaweed woven into her intricate braids.

Little Winnie ran off only to return with Milicent's hand in her own. Her mother's feet dragged across the ground, approaching in caution.

"Lucille – you must stop bringing strangers into my home.

Especially sopping wet ones," she scolded playfully as her daughter introduced them.

"I've heard so much about your family. I'm truly honored that you would help us in our fight," Afissa added as she shook Milicent's hand.

"I've recently had visions that make me hesitant to help. But regardless, I know my husband is working hard on his inventions for you."

Afissa's gaze darted back toward older Winnie who nodded in understanding. *One way or another, I'll have to find a way to help them when I get back,* she thought as the mermaid's attention landed back on her mother.

"I'll fix us some tea and biscuits," Milicent said at last, ushering the group into the family's main sitting room where the start of a ten year friendship began.

"You think breaking a blood oath is that easy?" Boudicca mocked once more. *"Good luck, Winifred. You'll need it."*

32

MELINDA
CHICAGO - 1871

Three days later, Melinda and Spencer sat atop the roof once again. Dusk hung heavy in the sky, soft blue and tangy orange streaking up ahead as the sun began to set. By now, the hellhounds had grown comfortable. Day and night, they'd kept a watchful eye on the orphanage.

It was only within the last day that they'd began to do regular rotations, scheduled and prompt. Previously, they'd switched at random. Almost as though they didn't want any sort of pattern that would provide Melinda and the others with a chance to attack when they were at their weakest.

"Just like we thought; every six hours," Spencer mumbled, pointing to the group as they rotated out.

"Finally a pattern." Melinda turned, noticing his eyes glued to her lips. "We have another six hours to prepare the others; get everyone ready. Then we can finally get my home back."

His eyes seemed to soften as their gazes met, offering her another of many shy smiles. "I brought you something," he added, reaching into his pocket.

She sat up, giddy excitement making her cheeks flush. He handed her a small square of wrapped chocolate. With a gasp, she asked, "Where did you find this? Please tell me you didn't spend your hard-earned money on me!"

He said nothing, only offered her the sweets.

"I can't accept this," she tried to say, though he shook his head. When he still didn't say a word, she added, "At least share it with me."

The corners of his mouth quirked again, watching as she opened the wrapper and split the square in half. As Melinda handed him some, their fingers brushed against one another. Her heart stalled, warmth spreading through her chest despite the icy Chicago winds. For a moment, her breath quickened as he held her gaze. When it dropped at last, she watched as dark lashes fell over his heavenly eyes.

"Don't tell Riah I spent my money on chocolate. She'll kill me," he teased as they both savored the delicious treat.

Melinda and Spencer sat silently for a few minutes, their attention fixed on the hellhounds as they swapped shifts. Counting every passing second, they timed the transfer. When all were settled into their designated spots again, he turned back toward her.

"Do you remember the signs I taught you?"

She nodded, moving her hands in fluid motions to repeat the words he'd shown her over the last few days. He'd focused mostly on fighting signals such as run, attack, look, or escape. But at last it was her turn to surprise him.

"Your sister taught me something else," she said, turning toward him and straightening herself. The shingles beneath her groaned, digging into her body uncomfortably. Recalling the small lessons from Riah, she moved her hands carefully trying to remember each motion exactly as she'd been shown. *"Hi Spencer. How are you tonight?"*

Now it was his turn to turn cherry red, hiding a blushing smile before he responded back with motions that she didn't recognize.

"I'm sorry, I'm not sure what you said." A nervous giggle escaped her, wishing desperately she knew every way to communicate with him.

"I'll teach you another time," he reassured, turning back toward the hounds.

"What did you say?" she pestered, eyes glued to his flushed freckled cheeks, the setting sun spreading a warm glow over his dark skin. She repeated her question as soon as his eyes landed back on her.

"You'll just have to learn sign, I guess," he mumbled before jutting his chin back toward the hounds as if to tell her to 'focus.'

A rush of heat washed over her, watching the flirtatious quirk to his smile as he glanced away from her. Knowing he fancied her made it that much more endearing, but she didn't want to reveal what his sister had said. There was something far sweeter about letting things build, slowly and in their own time. She was never one to rush head first into anything other than a fight. Surely this would be no different.

"They're done moving." Spencer pointed to the last of the hellhounds.

"We should head back. Go over the plan with everyone. Make sure they're ready," Melinda said quietly, turning to shimmy down the ladder.

Back at the boarding house, the parents prepared themselves for a fight like they'd never expected. Several of the workers joined as well, ready to protect their fellow members of Chicago. It took little to convince them once they were aware that children were in danger.

The late hours of the night fast approached as Melinda readied herself, too. She'd snagged a pistol from the loot the others managed to scrounge up, but wanted to have something else as a backup. She knew all too well that pistols weren't the most reliable of weapons.

Claiming a long broom, she snapped off the end before attaching a large kitchen knife with waxy twine. She'd easily spent over an hour ensuring its hold, nervous fingers checking the blade over and over again to be sure it wouldn't break the moment she entered into a fight.

"You look rattled," Danny commented, standing to her side with his usual sledgehammer braced across his shoulders.

"If this fails, it'll be my head on the chopping block. I'm the one who came up with the plan, after all." Melinda held up the blade, pushing it against the wall to see if it would budge.

"It won't fail. Have faith. You're an excellent fighter from what I hear, and this plan is solid. It's going to work." He placed a gentle hand on her shoulder, pulling her attention away from her makeshift weapon.

"I hope you're right."

"Time to get ready. Let's go over the plan one more time before we head that way," Riah interjected, strapping guns and bullets along her sides and across her chest.

Melinda offered a nervous nod before standing on one of the tables to get everyone's attention. "Alright, listen up! We have to execute this perfectly. One mistake in the initial attack, and we will be overpowered."

The groups of parents and workers listened, weapons in hand. Anxious fathers and angry mothers waited, prepared to fight. More than ready to be reunited with their children after three days of tortuous waiting.

"The musicians will begin playing again, giving the illusion that we're celebrating. They may not even think twice about it, but we can't be sure. That's why we have to hide! We'll sneak up, get as close as possible, and use our guns at a distance to take out as many as possible before they realize they're under attack."

"If you're a weak shot, give the gun to someone else," Riah began, glaring at one of the men standing before them with a rifle in hand. She snatched it, holding it up to offer someone else. "We can't have any weak links."

"No one can shoot early. You risk the entire group's success if you mess up our timing. Wait for the signal!" Melinda's eyes narrowed on each person carrying a gun, awaiting their acknowledgement. At last, she showed them one last time what the signal would be before they secured their weapons, and filed out of the boarding house.

Nodding at the waiting musicians, they began their festive tunes. Melinda was thankful they were willing to help, even if they weren't able to fight. After almost fifteen minutes of music, they at last snuck down the street toward the Chicago Orphan Asylum.

"The Falke brothers know we're coming?" Riah whispered, crouched alongside Melinda.

She nodded. "I sent word an hour ago. They're armed and ready, awaiting our arrival."

To her right, Spencer and Danny joined them. The group snuck ahead of the rest, the parents and workers not far behind. They kept their distance, awaiting the signal to get in place. When they arrived, she took a moment to count the hounds.

There were fewer than earlier. Shift change – she'd planned it perfectly. The small window where a few of them left to refuel their bodies still left almost two dozen behind. But, it was enough of an advantage that she didn't want to waste.

She signaled to her fighters wordlessly. Slowly, they began to creep. Three days of tortuous waiting had led to *this* moment, and Melinda was ready. To reclaim her home. Her family. To protect the children helplessly waiting inside. Every day since the battle of Samhain, she regretted sitting on the sidelines. But this was one fight she would not miss.

33
WINIFRED
FOX MANOR - 1861

Standing at the sink in her family's kitchen, Winnie slowly washed the dishes. Such a simple task; one she didn't realize she'd missed while being away in Marvivia. This would be her final meal at Fox Manor before returning to the sea to find a way out of her deal with King Aalto. While her mother sat and gabbed with Afissa, her father had anxiously gone off to the lake to test out the device for himself.

The food wasn't as good as it would be ten years from now. Milicent hadn't met Mrs. Falke yet. Nonetheless, her daughter enjoyed some semblance of home even if she couldn't truly be herself around the people she loved and missed dearly.

"You didn't have to clean up." Milicent joined her at the sink to drop off another stack of plates. "I've enjoyed speaking with your friend, Afissa. She's truly a remarkable woman."

With a simple nod, Winnie continued the chore in silence.

"She says there's another woman she wants me to meet. Acacia Falke. Do you know her as well?" Curious eyes examined Winnie in surprise suspicion.

Winnie's brows scrunched in confusion before it all clicked into place. *They haven't met the Falke family yet. But…how would it have happened had I not traveled here?* The thoughts swirled through her mind like an endless storm.

"I've heard of her. She's likely more remarkable than Afissa."

Her cheeks turned to a smile, wishing she could be there when they all met. When the boys would stumble into Fox Manor, lacking the manners of a proper English lad as their father would lovingly say. When they'd inevitably touch every piece of priceless porcelain in her mother's space.

What she wouldn't give to be there, watching Milicent's heart pound, trying to subdue the anger she'd feel when little Thoren would knock over her beloved statue of Ina, shattering it to bits. So many little moments she'd forgotten, blocked by age but slowly coming back the more time spent around this young version of her family.

"You do that often, you know? Retreat into your mind." Motherly affection washed off of Milicent as she tilted her head to the side, examining 'Lucille.'

"Being around your family brings back memories of my own." *Is she starting to suspect something is off about me?* she worried.

"Do you not have a family of your own?"

Winnie placed the last plate down to dry, turning toward her mother. "I have a family, but…it's broken now. Everyday I wonder how I can possibly fix it all. Take us back to who we once were."

"I know that feeling all too well," she admitted, picking up the dripping plate and running a towel over its edges.

"Your family isn't broken," Winnie blurted. *I probably shouldn't have said that,* she thought as a small ringing in her ears began.

"Not yet. But it will be one day. Fate has once again bestowed me with more information than I wish to receive. It's cruel, really. Why they feel the need to torture me so terribly, I'll never know." Sad eyes examined a small painted portrait that hung on the other side of the kitchen, all four members standing in regal positions.

"You may not be able to stop his death, but there will be a way to fix it. That I'm sure of," she said as the ringing intensified. It made her jump, the Elements warning her of words that could potentially get her in trouble.

"Hmm. I assumed you knew what was to come, but wasn't sure how to bring it up. It seems you've answered my question for me." Suspicious eyes narrowed in on 'Lucille.'

Winnie said nothing, only avoided her mother's all-knowing gaze.

"When I asked Fate who I could confide in, they only said you. For some reason, your knowledge of my son's fated death will not impact the timeline we're on. I'm not even sure what that means, if I'm honest." Square shoulders turned toward Winnie, one hand propped on her hip in distaste.

"I'm not sure what you're getting at..."

"I know you're not who you say you are. Lucille." The way she spat that name felt like daggers to the back, sharp and protruding with blame.

"Perhaps I...I should leave," Winnie stuttered, the ringing in her ears growing to near blinding pain.

"There isn't much you can hide from a clairvoyant, my dear. You should've picked a better name. My daughter has her tells when she lies, and a mother would recognize them no matter how old she became." An angry foot tapped along the ground. "Explain this instant! Are you some sort of mimic? Or are you truly...my Winifred? Somehow here, all grown up? How did you do that to your face?"

The questions were rapid fire, almost endless. Winnie's head still spun out of control, a strange concoction of panic and overwhelm from the Elements making her unable to rationalize anything.

A plate slipped from her hands, crashing into the sink. The seconds that passed felt like a millennia as it shattered to tiny bits, her eyes glued to her mother's angry scowl. She attempted to answer a few times, but all her mind could do was scream: *What do I even tell her? I can't be honest!*

Suddenly, Milicent's eyes glazed over and her face went slack, falling forward with only seconds to spare as Winnie caught her. She cradled her mother, the figure of a small boy appearing behind them with an outstretched hand.

"Sounded like you needed a little help," little Wesley squeaked, revealing a devilish smirk. His wild curls looked even more unruly with youth, green eyes glittering in the light of the setting sun.

"Wh…what did you do?" Carefully setting Milicent down, Winnie's attention turned to the archway. *What if the others come in and see my mum unconscious? They'll think I did something to her!*

"I just put her to sleep for a few moments. When she wakes, she'll think you merely said your goodbyes and left. She won't remember her suspicions." His little voice chirped through the kitchen, warming to her soul remembering how mischievous he'd been as a boy.

This must be during his particularly naughty phase when he even rivaled the Falke brothers, Winnie thought. "Do you know… who I am?"

He nodded, nervous feet tapping as he fidgeted. "You're my big sister. Aelius told me so. Said you were coming, and that you needed some help."

A single tear rolled down her cheek. "How much of our conversation did you hear?"

"All of it. Even what mother said about…me. But don't fret, Wimmie. I'll be alright. The Elements have assured me of it."

Wimmie.

Her heart broke hearing that name. The one he used to call her before his speech had sorted itself with age, and he confused his letter 'n' with an 'm.' The nickname that stuck for years to come. One they'd often tease her of as a teenager that would make her cringe.

One she so desperately wanted to hear again, realizing how badly she'd missed it all. The simplicity of childhood. The ease of merely having to grow up. How simple it all was, and yet thinking back she knew all she ever wanted was to be exactly where she was now.

How naive it is for young children to think they want to be adults, she thought. *What I wouldn't give to slow down time, and just stay here. Absorb it all. Take it in, and savor these little moments.*

"Can I…give you a hug? Before I go?" Cautious feet stepped toward him, hoping not to scare the boy.

"Of course. I'm not afraid of you. You're my big sister after all!" Leaping into her arms, the little boy wrapped himself around her.

The moment she held him, heat in the back of her throat threatened to close it entirely. Stinging her eyes, Winnie was overcome with grief. This was all she'd been wanting to do the last few days, and she was finally *here.* Clinging to her little brother, she savored every second possible. She took in the smell of the lavender shampoo her mother still made him use. The lake water lingering on his skin. Memories of childhood rushed back to her, bombarding her heart with such remorse she could hardly stand it.

"You have to hurry, though. She'll wake soon, and you can't be here when she does." Carefully, he pulled back and wiped away a stray tear. "It's alright, sis. Aelius said you'll fix it. But you have to go now."

With a small nod, she backed away. Glancing back to her mother, she took one last look at her little brother, in all his boyish charm, trying to capture this memory for good. Never wanting to forget this little life that she was working so hard to save.

"Wait – take this!" He held out a small vial before him. "You're going to need it for your friend."

Curiously, she nodded and took the healing ointment, pocketing it for later. "Thank you, Wes." At last, she offered him one final hug before darting for the door.

Glancing out over the lake, Winnie pulled on her swimming gear. While Ernest tested one of the contraptions, he'd left the other one at the edge for Winnie to use. Removing her gown to reveal the wetsuit beneath, she slipped into the flippers. Before pulling the breathing apparatus over her head, she tied her hair up into a tight bun.

Curiously, she looked for her father before stepping into the water. *Perhaps he's deep in the lake,* she thought. *Maybe he's making sure there aren't more monsters down there.* She wasted no time before swimming toward the portal. Pushing through the sand, Winnie appeared on the other side, the water cooler now that she was at the bottom of the sea.

When she arrived within Marvivia, she glanced between Oslind's flat and the palace. *I need to speak with the king,* she thought with a grumbling sigh.

"Do you honestly believe he'll let you out of your deal?" Queen Boudicca asked, snide as ever.

"He has to! I can't do it. I can't bring myself to kill Brenna when we've become friends. Afissa says she'll give me an army by siding with them," she countered, feeling the spirit stirring anxiously beneath her skin.

"And how do you know he won't find out about his traitorous wife and leave you with nothing? No army. No selkies. No one to stop my hellhounds." The woman's voice was a softening hiss, fading slowly the longer she spoke.

With an eye roll, she chose to ignore Boudicca. *"You're a spirit floating in nothingness, somehow stuck to me. The second I find out how to rid myself of you, this will all be over."*

With greater ease than before, Winnie swam toward the throne room. Pushing past the gelatinous walls, she stepped forth and marveled at the sight of the beauty of it all. No matter how many times she visited, she couldn't get over the magnificence of the palace. The pinks, blues, and corals that decorated the room were a beautiful depiction of the sea, peaceful and angelic. But alas, her eyes met with King Aalto, whose stoic anger simmered away on his throne, reminding her this place was not a sanctuary afterall.

Lugging the helmet off her head and placing it near the door, Winnie approached the king. "May I have a moment of your time?"

He carefully bowed his head before dismissing the nearby guards. Only the two of them remained in the throne room.

"I wish to discuss our deal again…"

With a fiery anger she hadn't expected, King Aalto shouted in discontent. "What is it now, seer?"

She paused for a moment, unsure how to continue. "I…can't do it. I can't kill Brenna for you. She'd become my friend, and I don't wish to impose any pain on her or your son."

King Aalto stretched out his hand with a grumbling roar. Winnie clutched her neck as unseen pressure pushed down around her esophagus, making her fall to her knees.

"How dare you try to break a blood oath with me, witch. You should thank the Gods that I even considered an audience with you to begin with. Now you mean to tell me you would disobey my orders? You are a guest in my court, may I remind you." Fire blazed within his sharpening pupils.

Gasping, Winnie continued to clutch at her neck. "Please…" she choked out, feeling the grasp only tighten with every attempted meager word.

"You're a fool," he bellowed, throwing his arm to the side and discarding her like an unwanted doll.

Winnie's body slammed into the wall, coughing as she attempted to regain her breath. Across the throne room, King Aalto continued to simmer in his rage.

"Might I remind you of the debt that must be paid to break a blood oath?" His head tilted to the side with a sort of wicked playfulness.

Beneath her skin, every inch began to burn. What felt like

thousands of tiny, crawling worms made their way through her veins. As if they were trapped, they pushed against the muscles in her forearms sending radiating shocks of pain through her entire body.

"Should you forsake our deal, it will cost your life. Should something happen to me by your own hand, it'll cost you even more. Is that not enough to persuade you to complete the task you started?" His words came out as a bitter hiss, cocking his head to the side in disdain.

"I...I can't do it!"

"We did not come this far for you to be killed! Fight back, dammit!" Boudicca roared in her mind. Deep down, she could feel Aelius stirring anxiously in agreement.

With a heavy sigh, Aalto continued. "I had a feeling you might say such an idiotic thing. That's why I had a backup plan. Since your own life means so little to you," he spat, an outstretched hand pointing toward the side of the room.

Though her vision blurred as the beings beneath her skin slowly eased, a muffled cry sharpened her attention. She saw him suddenly. Her father, Ernest, wrapped in seaweed and eyes panicked as he watched 'Lucille' gawk at him with pity in her eyes.

"Should you fail me, I will throw this sorry sap into the ocean without his fancy contraption. Drowning is a truly horrible way to go. That's if my eels don't get to him first." A wicked grin smeared across the king's face as her father squirmed against the confinement.

"Let him go!" Winnie's screams echoed through the domed hall, inching her way toward them on her hands and knees.

"It's simple, really. You either bring me that selkie bitch's skins, or you both die. And when I'm finished with him, I'll go through that nifty little portal you created, and drag the rest of the family down to the bottom of the ocean as well, starting with the children. I know how to keep them alive long enough to use for chum before finally ending their miserable existences. Do you understand me?"

With a slow and shallow nod, Winnie raised back up to her feet. "This is the reason your son hates you. This is why everyone hates you."

"Careful what you say now," Aelius warned. *"You still need him."*

Anger flared in the king's face again, his free hand forcing her down onto the ground once more with a heavy thud. Her face was next, slammed into the abalone shell floors, her own reflection staring back at her. When the pressure eased up, she struggled to stand.

"You will fail, Aalto Maddox," she began, wiping away a line of blood pooling from her nose. "You may win this small fight between you and I, but I promise you the death of Brenna will not lead to your victory. When the others see the poison of your rule, you will be executed like the monster you are!" Her words bellowed from deep within, Boudicca's own soul stirring in glory watching the young witch find her voice.

Leaning forward to the edge of his throne, Aalto hissed, "Is that a threat?"

"It's an oath, actually." Spitting blood at his feet, she turned and slowly stalked toward the exit.

Once again, that familiar unseen hand of King Aalto's grasped the back of her neck tightly. "No one speaks to me that way in my own court!"

Shooting a spear of ice, his hold loosened to block the incoming attack.

"Enjoy it while it lasts, cryptid. If he's dead when I return, you'll have me to deal with," she warned, allowing balls of flames to form in the palms of her hands.

"You wield...two elements? How?" He stared in morbid fascination, as if to steal the abilities for himself.

"You're lucky one of the Elements chose you. You're not worthy of two," she spat, snatching the helmet off the ground and securing it back onto her head. At last, she stepped through the doors and darted for Oslind's flat, hoping that he'd be there. Somehow, she needed to get to Brenna.

Alone.

34

KANE
CHICAGO - 1871

For days, the Falke brothers tried to escape without success. Thoren had tried the rooftop, though it ended miserably with chomping jaws waiting below. Bullets hadn't caught him, so one of the hellhounds' air wielders sent storm winds to bring him down. Kane barely caught his brother's hand in time before gunfire started again.

Thankfully, they still had the portal back to Fox Manor when weapons and supplies had run low. Though it had only been three days, the hounds had timed it perfectly for when they'd need to replenish food and other necessities.

"Can't we bring the children here?" Thoren had asked on the first night after checking in with Mr. and Mrs. Fox.

"No," she'd insisted. "I don't know why, but Fate tells me that the children should not come here. I'm afraid we can only help from afar."

They'd, instead, chosen to research stronger warding spells. Even Ernest couldn't understand his wife's reasoning, though never dared ask her to explain.

The time had finally come. Just outside, Melinda led a group of fighters closer and closer toward the orphanage. Kane ushered his brother over before adding, "We should cause a distraction. Get them to pay attention to us so they can get closer."

"So I can get shot at again? No, thank you," Thoren grumbled.

"We could try our songs, but I suspect it would just put the others in danger."

"Not an option. Sorry, brother." Kane shook his head, flaring his wings in the window to give Melinda the signal that it was time to go. As they walked toward the entrance, he called out, "Miss Leona?"

She poked her head out from her sleeping quarters, shuffling over to the two sirens. The children were once again asleep in her room, too afraid to be alone in their beds. "I see them creeping behind the hounds. Is it time?"

With a nod, Kane ordered, "When we walk outside, barricade the front door. Then your own. I don't want to take any chances that a hound gets in during the fight."

"What of you two? Will you be okay?"

"At this point, I thought you'd be happy to get rid of us," Kane chuckled.

The woman's small wrinkled hands grabbed his own as gray brows furrowed in worry. "I keep telling you that I never disliked you, Mr. Falke. I've been thankful for you rowdy lot since the first day you barged through that door. Please be careful." She offered his hand an encouraging squeeze and a careful smile, though a layer of worry clouded her kindness.

His gaze softened for a moment. Leaning down, he offered her a quick hug. Some part of her reminded him of Milicent, her stern but nurturing ways slowly growing on him. *She might pretend to be a stickler, but I can tell who she truly is,* he thought.

"Keep them safe."

"With my life." Offering him one final squeeze, Miss Leona waited to barricade the door.

The two brothers exited the orphanage before she swiftly blocked the entrance with a dresser nearby. Kane listened for a moment to the sounds of small thuds running up the stairs, back toward the room to protect the children.

The hellhounds outside snapped to attention, glaring at the two sirens who now stood armed and ready to start a fight. Half remained in their beast forms, the other half turning back to humans. A mix of men and women snickered at the sight of the brothers, armed with swords, pistols, and outstretching wings. Their eyes lightened to luminescent amber as they always did before a fight, primed and ready to win. Snow peppered the hounds who shivered from the cold, taunting them with their howls and slurs.

"Gonna sing us another song are ya?" one sneered.

Upbeat melodies echoed from down the street, as though another festival were raging on without a clue that beasts were haunting this orphanage. It masked Melinda's group perfectly, coupled with the beeswax in the beasts' ears.

"Thanks for coming out finally. We're eager to end this!" another yelled.

"Delicate little birds, aren't they? I think I'll use those feathers to stuff my pillows," a woman cackled.

Thoren snarled, ready to fight.

"Hold it," Kane mumbled.

Only a few more steps.

"We've been eyeing that little redhead of yours. The blonde looks rather tasty too," a man yelled.

"They're still alive at least," he mumbled again, Thoren nodding his head in agreement.

A few more steps – mere seconds before the fight would begin.

"When we're done with you two, we'll be sure to pay our respects to the residents inside," another hound howled.

Kane flinched, the anger in his stomach seething. The mere mention of the children was enough to send him over the edge.

"Don't," Thoren warned this time, recognizing kindred rage. "You and I both know we won't let that happen."

"We'll take our time, won't we, hounds?" a man called out, the group belly laughing and howling with putrid amusement.

Almost there, Kane thought. The group was just behind them, the hounds completely oblivious to the quiet approach.

Melinda's fighters lined themselves a few feet behind a row of hounds, guns and other miscellaneous weapons ready to go. They quietly aimed, looking between each other for the right moment. Even a single second before and the first deadly blow wouldn't be as effective. Melinda held her hand up, a silent command to wait as the last of the workers got in their places.

Her hand dropped, a symphony of gunfire racketing through the street. The back row of hellhounds fell in an instant, a line of bullets riddling their skulls. Anyone with a gun fell back, a hoard of fighters ready with knives, daggers, sledgehammers, and anything they could possibly use. The gunsman prepared to fire once more, flanking either side of the building and ready to end the hounds that came from the back.

Without hesitation, the brothers joined the assault with outstretched wings. Thoren took to the sky, raining down balls of fire as Kane stood along the ground swinging and slicing through anyone that dared to come near.

To his left, Melinda was fast approaching through the crowd. Her makeshift spear sliced into the belly of a beast, another ready to attack her from behind. Kane shot a forcefield of air between them before she turned and smacked the beast across its wolfish spine. A deadly blow landed next.

With Kane's attention fixed on Melinda, another beast lunged forward. The glint of metal caught him off guard, Danny's sledgehammer slamming into his would-be attacker's skull. Another ran toward the eldest of the Broderick trio, though Kane stepped in before they made contact. With a thrust of his sword, the hound crumpled toward the ground turning the snow crimson.

Calling on Caelus, Kane shot a wall of storm winds at another barreling toward him. With an artful turn, he slashed his sword through the hound's midsection as graceful as though he danced with Death itself. Only seconds passed before another approached him from behind, nicking his wing with a sharp end of a blade. He turned, though a bullet from a nearby pistol landed right between the creature's eyes.

He glanced over his shoulder, seeing Spencer offering him a cocky nod. Kane offered one in return, noticing Riah glued to his back in the battle, both raining bullets around them, just as lethal as their brother. While one reloaded, the other fired. When it was time to switch, they seemed to nudge the other to let them know it was time. And so the two continued with their deadly dance.

"Kane!" Melinda yelled over the chaos. Only a few hounds remained from the original pack, though a panicked finger pointed toward a small group that attempted escape. "We can't let them warn the others!" she yelled as she stabbed the end of her knife into the belly of a nearby beast.

The siren nodded, taking flight. The beasts didn't make it far down the road before he landed just in front of them. They met a wall of cyclonic wind before falling to the ground.

"And here I thought you cowards wouldn't back down from a fight?" the siren crooned with a wicked smile across his face.

Thoren landed behind them, ensuring no one would escape. Both held their swords in hand, bloodied from the lives they'd already taken. The four hounds glanced between one another, knowing they had no option other than to fight.

The four hounds split in half, each attacking one of the Falke brothers. Leading his two away from his brother, Kane attacked head on. Knocking them off balance with Caelus's magic, the two hounds regained themselves before lunging simultaneously toward the siren. He plunged his sword into the male hound's chest. The creature clutched his wound as he fell, gurgling and taking his final breaths.

A blonde female stood before him, ready to survive. An unfamiliar gust of power similar to his own knocked him on his ass, dodging a head on attack from above. As he evaded her incoming strike, he jumped to his feet, slicing as he moved. The blade cut into her thighs, making her drop to her knees before plunging the sword through her chest.

To his side, Thoren finished off his two attackers. They came at him together just as the others had, but he didn't retreat. Instead, he sent a wall of fire toward them with a swinging blade. Shallow cuts made them retreat, through Aelius's magic caught up to them almost immediately. It wasn't long before the snow beneath the hounds was dark with ashes.

"I don't see anyone else," Thoren added, wiping blood off the blade of his sword.

"Nice job," Kane beamed, patting his little brother on the back.

"We should get back to the others."

Lifting themselves into the air effortlessly, they landed in the front yard of the Chicago Orphan Asylum with roaming eyes that took in the carnage. Most of Melinda's fighters clutched bloodied injuries, minimal damage at best. Though at least two or three fatalities were laid to rest, grieving family members closing the eyes of their deceased.

As the crowd parted, Melinda came running toward them. With outstretched arms, Kane ushered her in for a quick hug. "You're a genius!"

She leapt to his side, hugging Thoren as well. Her body quickly tensed, attention locked in across the field. Kane followed her line of sight, realizing a hound was trying to inch their way from the crowd unnoticed.

"Not on my watch," she seethed, throwing her makeshift spear like a javelin. The beast cried out, shifting back into its human form as it took its final breath. "Is everyone inside okay?"

"Yes, thanks to you." Thoren offered her a smile, following her toward the porch.

She knocked feverishly, waiting for someone inside to open

up. "Thanks to you. I'm so glad you were here the night of the attack!"

Miss Leona opened the door, embracing Melinda without hesitation.

"Bless you, child!" Tears glimmered along the woman's water line, cupping Melinda's face gingerly. "I've never been more thankful for your rebelliousness."

She couldn't help but laugh, embracing the frail woman tightly. Behind them, the Broderick trio approached.

"Glad you're reunited with your family," Danny said softly.

Kane turned toward him, offering an outstretched hand. "I take it you three had a hand in pulling this off?"

"We helped a little," Riah said with a modest shrug.

"They did more than just a little. Thanks to Spencer, we know where the camp is," Melinda added before waving to Miss Leona, who began letting concerned parents back into the orphanage to reunite with their children.

Thoren's eyes lit up in anticipation. "Well let's go! I can't stand the idea of Ezra being stuck in that camp. Let's get him back!"

"And Tara," Kane added begrudgingly, though his brother merely grumbled.

Spencer stood along the outskirts of the orphanage, ushering them toward the street. He signed something to his sister, who turned and said, "He'll show us to the camp."

Melinda glanced at the Falke brothers as they walked. "Did I miss something? Why are we suddenly anti-Tara?"

"I'm tired of Tara always making terrible decisions, and us having to pay the price," Kane muttered.

"What price did you have to pay?" Even his own brother glanced at him sideways, eyeing him carefully.

"Doesn't matter…"

"Well, we can't storm the place," Melinda began. "Spencer said there's too many. We need to sneak in to get them out."

The young man's hands moved furiously, Riah's face pinched in confusion.

"What's wrong?"

"He saw Tara the other day...hanging out. Like she was a part of the group or something," his sister explained.

"That can't be! She's a prisoner," Melinda retorted, crossing her arms over her chest.

With a heavy sigh, Thoren asked, "Or is she?" The group looked at him in confusion. "She's the one who's been going on and on about what the hellhounds *want*. We have to be prepared that she might have switched sides."

"She wouldn't do that." Melinda shook her head, swooping down to retrieve her makeshift spear from the belly of the dead hound.

"You don't know her like we do," Kane mumbled.

"She's a good person; she would never knowingly help the hellhounds if she knew what they were doing to us!"

"We'll see." *After threatening to tell Winnie about Samuel, I almost hope she's wrong,* he thought.

Thoren's hand paled as he gripped his sword tighter. "If she joined them, I'll kill her myself."

Everyone in the group turned to him in shock. Even the Broderick trio seemed to think it was harsh.

"She didn't switch sides!" Melinda yelled. "And you won't be doing anything to hurt her, or you'll have me to deal with."

All conversation ceased as they continued down the streets toward the outskirts of the city. After quite some time, they finally reached the edge of the snow-covered woods. The darkness of the night made it difficult to walk, branches and other obstacles hidden beneath a layer of snow.

"Stay sharp. They could be hiding anywhere," Danny whispered before they continued their descent into the forest, following the glowing light of fire to the camp nearby.

35
WINIFRED
MARVIVIA - 1861

Winnie twiddled her thumbs anxiously, waiting for Brenna to arrive at Oslind's flat. He'd signaled her not long after she'd returned from Fox Manor, though it was obvious he didn't want to.

"I hope you know how dangerous it is for her to come here," he'd scolded after sending the dolphin her way.

Roughly an hour passed before she'd barreled through the doors of his home, ducking behind the entrance as though she'd been followed.

"What's wrong? Why did you need me?" Panting, she removed her skins and covered her body, awaiting an answer from either of them.

"I was hoping you'd help me get to Fort Monroe, and speak to the soldiers there. Get some non-magical people to test the breathing apparatus, and ensure it works properly," Winnie lied, avoiding both their gazes.

Brenna's attention darted toward Oslind with a grimace. "You and I need to have a conversation about the meaning of the dolphin signal!"

Oslind sauntered toward her, offering a tender kiss before covering her with a blanket. "Agreed," he said at last, glaring at Winnie.

"Why not bring Os? He could help you get there just as well

as I can."

"I suspect his scales may scare any potential participants away," Winnie teased, though it wasn't entirely dishonest.

"True," she sighed. "Humans aren't accustomed to seeing scales lining such a pretty face." Brenna smirked, the corners of her lips curving up to taunt the mermaid into another peck.

Oslind's face flushed before peeking outside. "You two better get going. Shift change is about to end. And don't forget a suit. Can't have the soldiers at Fort Monroe telling tales of my naked, red-haired beauty."

With a slight huff, Brenna turned back to the exit. Pulling on her skins begrudgingly, she rushed to say, "Meet me just past the statue." With that, she darted through the door and was gone in mere seconds.

Winnie equipped Ernest's contraption, thankful for the flippers that would now guide her through the water with greater ease. Before she exited, she turned back to Oslind. "I'll...see you later."

He cocked his head to the side, examining her carefully. "Everything alright? You don't seem like yourself."

She looked away, fighting back the sting of tears that lined her eyes. "I'm ready to go home, that's all."

"Not too much longer, right? Though I've grown accustomed to your presence here, I would enjoy having my flat to myself again," he added with another of his many teasing chuckles.

"I appreciate all your help, Oslind. Thanks to you and Brenna, I'll be able to save my family." Her gaze still avoided his own. *I can't stand to look at him, knowing what I have to do,* she told herself.

"You're no better than I am," Boudicca hissed.

"Watch her back, will you?"

Winnie nodded in silence, solemnly exiting into the frigid ocean just beyond.

Wading in the water, Brenna was nowhere to be seen. Lines of soldiers with trident spears and shimmering armor guarded the outskirts of the city, waving to Winnie casually as she swam past them. Though her initial arrival had been unwelcomed, they'd grown used to the strange little witch that found herself at the bottom of the ocean.

Regardless, she pressed on in search of the selkie. She swam for several miles on her own until Marvivia was a mere glimmer in the water. The weight of the contraption coupled with the rubbery fins on her feet aided in a smoother swim, though her muscles still ached. *By the time I return to my time, my muscles will be so defined, the others won't even recognize me,* she thought with a cynical chuckle.

When the underwater civilization was far out of reach, a figure darted behind Winnie. Before panic could set in, Brenna appeared at her side with a gleaming smile. Though she tried to speak, not a single word was intelligible. The selkie seemed to giggle before grabbing Winnie's hand and pulling her toward Fort Monroe.

The swim began leisurely, though it didn't take long for Brenna to torpedo them through the ocean. The sheer force made Winnie feel as though she could hurl. Past corals and rock formations, they swam through the dark depths with all manner of slithering creatures darting below.

Slowly, the icy waters warmed. A glimmer of moonlight peeked through as they neared land, ascending to the surface at last. Before them, the sandy shores of Hampton, Virginia, waited. As Winnie's head speared through the water, the peppery August heat warmed her body, and chased away the nagging cold of the sea. A muggy cloud of moisture hung in the air, sticking to her skin and making her sweat. Nagging gnats swarmed the surface, tiny fish darting away from their presence.

"Over there!" Brenna pointed toward a small island of rocks, snatching seaweed and other ocean debris. Removing her skins, the selkie hid them amidst the wet rocks. She covered them in greenery before pulling on a wetsuit to match Winnie.

Both swam slowly toward shore, unsure what awaited their arrival. Brenna wrung excess moisture from her hair as Winnie removed the contraption with a sigh of relief. Winnie ran her fingers through her dark curls, getting caught on every little knot and tangle. She pulled it up into a tight bun before asking, "How do any of you maintain your hair when you're constantly underwater? I fear mine will never recover from the salt."

"We don't come up to shores often," Brenna confessed. "Why come up here when we can live beneath the sea?"

"I suppose if that's what you're used to, it makes sense. I, however, miss land more than I care to admit," she confessed. "Thank you for bringing me here." Guilt continued to stir deep down in her soul, her mind restless as she was reminded what she needed to do.

"You're better at buttering her up than I thought you'd be," Boudicca mocked. *"Perhaps when we get back to our time, you'll consider joining us after all."*

The selkie approached her cautiously, a careful hand reaching out to touch the throbbing bruises on Winnie's face. "Who did that to you?"

"The *beloved* king."

Brenna stood for a moment in silent contemplation. "He's a cruel man. It's a wonder Oslind has even an ounce of humanity in him after being raised by that monster."

"Thanks to his mother, I'm sure." Winnie jutted her chin toward the fort before adding, "We should go."

The two walked carefully to the fort's gate, hands up over their heads to show the soldiers they weren't armed. They stood at attention, awaiting recognition.

"We're here to see General Butler," Winnie announced. The men standing with muskets in hand glanced her over before ignoring the request entirely.

"He's not taking visitors at the moment," one of the men grumbled.

"Excuse me?"

"He's got better things to worry about than what a couple of trollops have to say," he spat, something in his gun clicking as though he were ready to fire.

"Trollops?" Winnie gasped. "You bite your tongue! We helped save your asses the other night. Let us speak to the General."

Brenna shot her a strange look; one that seemed to scream, *'Be nice.'*

Clearing her throat, she attempted to sound as proper as possible. "Won't you please help two lost young ladies?" It came out a little more sarcastic than she'd meant.

Another of the young soldiers up front shot his comrade a glare, lowering his gun away from them. Without so much as a word, he beckoned Winnie and Brenna to follow through the gates into Fort Monroe.

"Yelling initially was rather unladylike," Brenna mumbled, hiding a smirk.

"If there's one thing I cannot stand, it's being undermined by tiny men who think they're superior just because they have a..."

"General!" The soldier's announcement came at just the right time.

Butler turned, the same stunned look on his face as the night they'd met. "We've met, haven't we?"

"Ms. Winifred Fox. This is Ms. Brenna..." Suddenly it occurred to her she didn't know the selkie's last name.

"Ronan. Ms. Brenna Ronan." She stretched her hand toward the general, shaking it graciously.

"You two haven't met yet, but I assure you, she was vital in stopping the attack the other night."

Butler avoided looking at their bodies before adding, "I've

never seen women in such…revealing attire. Did you come straight from the sea?"

Brenna chuckled. "Yes, sir. This is what everyone wears in the water."

"I doubt corsets and crinolines would do us much good against the waves." With an awkward chuckle, Winnie waited for him to respond.

At last, Butler grinned. "What brings you two fine ladies to Fort Monroe this evening? It's awfully late, don't you think?"

"We'd like to speak to some of your soldiers. Have them try out a contraption we've created to see if it could assist in…"

The pause in her sentence immediately caught Brenna's attention, squinted eyes trying to read Winnie like a book. "Assist in what?"

"Your war, General. We thought these may come in handy during your naval battles," Winnie lied, though truthfully it wasn't the worst idea she'd come up with.

"This…contraption," Butler began, motioning to the helmet in her hands. "What does it do?"

"It allows one to breathe underwater, and swim like the creatures who reside below. I've been in the ocean for weeks now without any issues."

His eyes widened in fascination. "You're welcome to speak with our soldiers in the barracks. Perhaps I may even try it myself!"

Winnie nodded in thanks, turning toward Brenna once more as the soldiers on guard dismissed themselves, taking their muskets with them.

"In all the conversations we've had, you and Oslind never mentioned wanting to help the *humans* with their war. What's actually going on?"

Winnie's mouth opened a few times, her mind racing as she tried to think of any possible explanation that would make sense. Anything other than, *'Your love is trying to kill your people, and*

I sort of have to kill you to save my family. You understand, right?

"What is the actual plan? Tell me this instant!" An angry foot tapped along the ground as the selkie's eyes flared in anger.

"The intention behind making the contraption," Winnie began, too afraid to finish her sentence. "Please don't be upset with Oslind."

"Just spit it out already!"

"We intended to create it to aid in the war against…you. Your people. We hoped that by having more soldiers in the water, the mermaids would have a greater chance of winning." She released a heavy sigh, the weight of kept secrets lifting.

"That is the most idiotic idea I've ever heard, Winnie. Do you realize what that does? It only puts humans in *more* danger! The mermaids barely stand a chance against the selkies. You want to take innocent people, and add them to the mix? All it will do is give them extra targets to aim for!" Brenna rubbed her head, pacing in a circle as her mind seemed to race. Above them, the wind picked up and Winnie felt the rush of warm and cold air swirl around.

"Are you making that happen?" she asked, motioning for the sky.

"Give me a second to calm down before speaking to me again." The selkie sauntered off toward the edge of the fort to look out over the water, a swirl of questions visible on her conflicted face.

Winnie waited, unsure what to do. She could start asking for volunteers, but truthfully it seemed pointless now. *Brenna's right,* she thought. *I'm only putting more people in danger. Perhaps this is why my father rarely talks about his invention.* It wasn't until the winds above calmed that she finally approached Brenna again.

"Hey," she said gently, if only to keep from startling the selkie.

"Why would Oslind keep this from me?" Sad eyes and furrowed brows turned toward Winnie, a small tear rolling down Brenna's cheek.

"I think he probably felt helpless. He didn't want to hurt you, but also wants to save the merfolk." Winnie wracked her brain, thinking of what to say that could possibly make the situation better.

"He wants to hurt *my* people. We promised each other we'd never do that unless there was no other choice."

The two stood in silence for a few moments, staring off across the water.

"We have a new plan, if that makes you feel more at ease. One that doesn't involve bringing in human soldiers," she added, turning toward the selkie.

There was a long pause before she asked, "And what's this new plan, then?"

"I can't say much, but I can promise you this: years from now, Aalto will not be on the throne." *She doesn't need to know she won't be alive to see it,* she thought as Boudicca's soul riled up deep down.

"Won't you tell me the details?"

"I don't know if I can. Just know that I *am* trying to help. I promise. But right now, King Aalto has the upper hand. And I can't quite figure out how to get out of his grasp," Winnie admitted, staring at the crusted cut across her palm which slowly healed.

Brenna's gaze shot curiously toward her. "If you don't intend to bring the humans into the mix, why are we here?"

Once again, Winnie didn't know what to say. "I'd still like to see if the device works for non-magical folks. I have some friends back home who are human. You never know when one of them may need such a contraption."

Brenna faced the fort, peering across the stoney fortress. "So strange, don't you think? Two worlds separated by water, yet an almost identical fight. I never thought this would be my life."

"I didn't think I'd be here, either..."

"When I was little, I always assumed Oslind and I would rule together. It seemed the most natural thing in the world. Until Aalto..."

Seeing the hurt in the selkie's eyes, Winnie attempted to distract her. "How did you and Oslind actually meet? You two have spoken so fondly of growing up, but never mentioned the beginning of your love story."

"What are you doing, you fool? You have to kill her! Don't get to know her! That's the same mistake you made with me." Boudicca shouted in her mind.

Regardless, she pushed aside the throbbing headache from the queen's voice, and tried to focus on her friend.

"We were very young when we met. I was ten when I first saw him. We were on the run from our previous home, and my parents met with the king to plead for asylum. Oslind was tasked with entertaining me."

Winnie couldn't help but chuckle as the selkie glanced at her sideways, head slightly cocked as if trying to read the expressions on her face. When she didn't respond, the story continued.

"At first, he hated it. I could tell. He simply rolled his eyes and swam off. When I didn't follow, he turned around and held out a begrudging hand." Her eyes seemed to spark from the memories, reliving those precious early days.

"Why was your family on the run?" She sucked in a sharp breath, realizing that question was perhaps a little too personal.

"That's a story for another time," Brenna mumbled, playing with a rock at her feet.

In an attempt to change the subject once more, she added, "I didn't realize there were other civilizations underwater."

"Oh yes, there's quite a few. Did you seriously believe there's only one small city, when there are thousands of human cities?" Brenna chuckled, shaking her head playfully. "Unfortunately, not many accept selkies. Oslind showed me around and eventually we became more comfortable together. Shortly after becoming friends, he showed me that cave we visited the other day."

"I didn't realize it had been your hiding place since you were little." The corners of Winnie's mouth turned up, thinking of how cute tiny mermaids and selkies could be.

"Mhm," she mumbled, facing the sea again, though her eyes peered up toward the sky in wonder. "For years, we would sneak off to play there. As we got older, we snuck off to do other things." A sly wink followed her words.

With a blush, Winnie tried to hide a giggle.

"I'll never forget the first time he kissed me. The way I trembled, so afraid to ruin the friendship we'd built. But when he pulled away and all I could see was his smile, I knew. I made the right choice." A warm breeze drifted off the ocean water as the words escaped her lips.

"I know that feeling all too well," Winnie admitted, thinking back to her first kiss with Kane. "Kane is home waiting for me to return. We had a moment like that only a month ago. I keep trying to find my way back to that kiss, hoping it'll feel like it used to."

"Ahh yes, the best friend you mentioned."

Winnie nodded. "We've been thick as thieves since we were young. Just like you and Oslind. We've spent the last few years apart, and only reconnected a few months ago when I made a terrible mistake. My brother...passed...in October. Since then, I haven't felt the same. Haven't been the same person I once was. I worry the girl he fell for doesn't exist anymore."

"I can remember what that felt like," Brenna admitted. "I remember the numbness I felt after my parents were killed. It eventually boils away and anger replaces it. Just don't let any of that destroy your love. One way or another, you'll find your way back to one another," she assured.

Winnie looked down at her hands, wondering how the hell she was going to go through with this. To save her father, save herself. Save her brother. To have to kill such a kind and gentle soul...

What will happen to everyone from my time should I fail?

Brenna continued telling tales of her and Oslind as children, but Winnie couldn't hear a word she said. The noises around her grew faint, goosebumps prickling her skin. Only the voice of the queen was clear, slithering toward her with desperate urgency.

"You're running out of time," Boudicca hissed. *"You need to finish what you started, and get home to those dear friends of yours."*

Winnie's heart sank. *"Do you know something I don't?"*

"Being a spirit has its perks." The queen's voice ceased at once, an absent void leaving behind a gaping wound.

"Boudicca? Answer me! What do you know?"

But alas, the queen remained silent.

36

TARA
CHICAGO - 1871

Sitting on her cot, Tara shivered as she stoked the fire before her. She'd been stuck in that tent all day, unable to leave or visit Ezra. It seemed Alaric was too busy to escort her to the area which still sat heavily guarded by hellhounds. Moving her ankle in circles, she winced as a sharp pain shot through her entire leg and up her thighs.

Hesitant fingers reached for the white gauze, moving the purple flowers aside to look at the bite. Though it appeared nearly healed, the area felt like thousands of tiny bees sat beneath her skin. *It's healing rather quickly,* she thought curiously. Feeling woozy, she clutched the edge of her cot. *When will my head stop throbbing?*

Tara remembered reading about Wolfsbane long ago, though truthfully herbology wasn't her strong suit. There was something odd about the delicate flower, but she couldn't quite remember what it was. She removed the bloodied flowers and set them down on the cot, dipping a clean rag into a pail of fresh water. After cleansing her ankle, she reached for new bandages.

As she reapplied fresh Wolfsbane, the Quinn family pendant glowed a soft haze of orange. *That's odd,* she thought. *It's never been that color before.* She set the flowers down, lifting the necklace from her skin. In the past, it had only ever glowed red to block spells or warn her of danger. This was new.

She shrugged, unsure what it meant. As she picked up the

flowers again, the necklace glowed the same copper color. The light only got brighter as the Wolfsbane neared her healing skin.

"Are you trying to tell me something?" she wondered aloud, placing them down. Her suspicions were correct, the necklace ceasing its glow. "Guess I'll skip those."

Just as she finished wrapping her ankle, Alaric peered a smiling face into the tent. "Supper's ready!"

"I'm not going," she protested, turning her back toward him.

With a sigh of frustration, Alaric entered her tent and took a seat beside her. "I was patient your first night here. Didn't insist anything of you; even brought you food when you refused to come out. Why do you keep fighting our hospitality?"

Unwilling to look his way, she was worried she'd do anything those gorgeous blue eyes told her to. "You forget you're still my enemy."

A deep, dark chuckle escaped Alaric as a careful hand grasped the base of her chin, pulling her gaze toward him. A shudder ran down her spine as his unwavering attention pierced her very being. Reaching into the depths of her soul, that stare was capable of pulling out her insides to reveal the ugly truth: *I don't want him to be my enemy.*

"I can read your mind, you know."

Her eyes widened in terror before she realized he was joking. *Hellhounds can't actually read minds...right?*

"For someone who considers us the enemy, you sure did spend quite a bit of time around the fire the last few days getting to know everyone."

She thought back to the treacherous days spent at their camp. Though she'd fought at first, Alaric didn't seem to take no for an answer after that first night. If she wanted to eat, she had to leave the tent. And leaving the tent meant allowing the guilt to eat her alive as she listened to his people.

At first, she'd listen with a mask of disdain. She didn't want to feel sorry for them; it was easier to hate. But as they told her tales of their lives before, remorse stirred in her chest like a living being. Without a cure, they couldn't fathom a way to be a part of their old communities. Their kindred longing for something now lost was one she could sympathize with.

"What are you thinking about?" His velvet-smooth voice pulled Tara from her thoughts.

It was curious how much he'd changed since they'd first met the night of Samhain. Around others, he put on a show. Cocky and gruff, like he was constantly fighting for alpha. But here, just the two of them, he was gentler than expected. Not the same beast her friends spoke so terribly of.

"Why did you let them hurt Ezra? The night Boudicca attacked us in London." *I wonder if a part of me wants him to be a good man,* she thought, trying to understand the cocktail of emotions that swirled through her heart.

He let out another heavy sigh. "There will come a day when you, too, will have to make hard choices. Ones that will dictate whether you live or die. You might not be proud of what you have to do, but you do it nonetheless to ensure your family is safe."

Sorrow threatened to summon tears from her eyes, thinking of the family she hadn't been able to protect. "So you were... protecting someone?"

"Boudicca found my sister and me first. We were already hounds, to be fair, but she forced us to use our curse as a way to build her army." His attention dropped away from Tara, staring blankly into the fire. "We're responsible for all of the suffering that the queen caused these people. That's why I fight so hard to make it right." A tender hand reached toward her, tucking a stray lock of hair behind her ear.

"Don't," she whispered, pushing him away. *Do I actually want him to stop?*

With a nod, he sighed. "Come on, I'm starving."

She said nothing, only stood to join the hounds around yet another campfire. As they exited, she looked toward the tent where her friend still lay unconscious. "How is Ezra?"

"He's doing alright. He opened his eyes for a moment today. I'm hoping that means he'll be awake in the next few days," Alaric explained, looking ahead of them.

"Can I see him?"

"After dinner perhaps," he offered, the light of the nearby fire reflecting in the electric blue of his eyes.

Tara took a seat across from an older woman, her hands wrinkled and hair grey. A weary face peered at the new guest, stirring a large pot of stew.

"Runnin' low on supplies," she grumbled, glaring at Tara with disdain before handing Alaric a bowl.

"Some for her too," he insisted, passing his portion over before stretching out his hand for another.

A moment passed, the woman's breaths quick and angry. A low growl escaped him before the woman finally fixed a second helping. Shaking hands handed the soup over before retreating to bring some to others nearby.

"Thank you," Tara mumbled, watching as the few hellhounds around the fire stood and left. "Guess they don't want to be around me, either..."

"We're enemies, remember?" Alaric's words fell flat, void of emotion as he stared blankly into the bowl of stew.

"Any word from the orphanage?"

"We can't get past the hounds on guard. We'll have to figure something else out," he explained between bites.

Tara took a bite herself, a mix of potatoes and venison swirling in her mouth. "This is delicious!"

Alaric only nodded, hunched forward as he finished the last of his portion.

Tara ate in silence before asking, "Why are you so kind to me?

I know this isn't who you are. I've heard the stories from the others. You're treating me differently, and I want to know why."

With a look of shock, he asked, "Why wouldn't I be kind to you?"

"I'm serious, Alaric. Why are you treating me like this? Ezra and the mayor are clearly prisoners in a guarded tent. If you're truly benevolent, why not let my friend stay with me?"

He leaned back in his chair for a moment, rubbing the base of his chin. The wheels in his brain seemed to turn before his gaze landed back on her. "I see a lot of myself in you. Feisty, protective. Both terribly beautiful," he said with a sly smile. She merely rolled her eyes. "Both desperate to protect the ones we love. I suppose I want to ensure you're safe because…"

She motioned for him to continue, leaning forward with anticipation.

"Because…I care for you, Tara."

"You can't care for someone you don't know," she seethed, leaning back in her chair with a huff of frustration.

"Wrong. I haven't stopped thinking about you since the night of Samhain. The way that woman's mouth trailed your body. The way I want my own to…" He once again didn't finish his sentence, his eyes roaming her. At last, they landed on her ankle. Alaric grabbed the base of her chair and scooted her toward him. "Where's the Wolfsbane?"

"I must've forgotten it," she lied. "So that's all I am to you? That's why you're kind to me? To get me to bed? Trust me, you wouldn't be the first person to use me." Despite her words, her breath turned shallow. Never had they sat this close to one another, where she could feel his breath dance along her skin.

"No, Tara." He let out another sigh, brows furrowed as he examined her carefully. "I don't *just* want to bed you. Though that is on my list of things to do." The corners of his mouth turned to a wicked smirk. When she didn't return the favor, he continued.

"You always assume everyone is out to get you. I want to…know you. Be someone you don't want to call an enemy. Someone you can trust."

She said nothing, only looked him over carefully. Traced the scar on his face with her eyes, wishing to reach out and touch it. Though her fingers trembled too much to try. A few moments of silence passed between them before he leaned back in his chair, allowing space for her breaths to return to normal.

"All in good time, little fawn. Make sure you reapply the Wolfsbane. The last thing you want is to turn into one of us," he mocked, the light of the fire casting shadows over his face.

With a small shrug, she mumbled, "The hellhounds don't seem so bad."

"Coming around are you?" His smile lit up her insides, a wolfish grin intoxicating as he leaned forward in anticipation, one hand rested on her thigh.

"I want to talk to my friends again, and try to get them on our side." *Shit,* she thought. *Did I just say our? I didn't mean to phrase it that way.*

"Joining the hellhounds, are you? How daring," he grinned, eyes darkening. "What will you tell them?"

"Not joining you, no. But I want to tell them everything. How you've treated me with kindness. Worked to heal Ezra. The stories of the hounds I've met. If there is truly a cure, no one should be denied its access." *For my sake, I hope he isn't lying,* she thought.

"I'm glad you're finally coming around," he whispered, reaching for her empty bowl and setting it on the ground beside them. "That is truly the best news I've heard in a long time."

Somehow, he managed to pull her in even closer. With one hand still rested on her thigh, the other reached up and cupped her face. Tara's treacherous eyes couldn't help but glance down at his lips, wondering what they'd feel like across her own. With a racing heart, she felt like she couldn't breathe.

"Your eyes are the most beautiful shade of green I've ever seen," he mumbled, running his thumb along her cheek.

Attempting to look away, she thought, *I shouldn't be doing this.*

"I," she began, unsure where she was going with her sentence. "I…want to trust you. I want to help even more. But I don't know if you're genuine or not."

His fingers pulled her chin up to meet his gaze, heat exploding beneath her skin as he did so. Mere inches sat between them, the smell of campfire and something else – something sweet and fresh like Yule cider and cinnamon – overwhelmed her senses. She couldn't help herself from taking in the scent, closing her eyes to regain some sense.

"Ignore what your mind is telling you. What does your heart say? Haven't I given you reason to believe me?" As he whispered, dangerous lips grazed her cheek in merciless teasing.

She looked back at him, unsure what to say.

"I think I know you, Tara. Maybe even better than you know yourself. You've got a massive heart that puts others first, no matter what your needs are. And you have a chance to make a difference here." This time he was the one to glance down at her lips, the corners of his mouth turned up into a charming smile.

"I…" Her heart continued to pound in her chest, a wave of lightheadedness washing over her as though the world itself was spinning off its axis.

"I would never lie to you…"

Unable to stand the distance between them, Tara leapt forward. As though she'd lost all control of her body, she placed her lips along his own. Running her fingers through his hair, along the stubble on his face, she wrapped her arms behind his neck. Alaric grabbed ahold of her legs, pulling her into his lap with a suddenness that made her squeal. A soft chuckle reverberated through her, though she wasn't sure if it was from joy or pleasure.

It didn't really matter as he ran his hands along the curves of her body, not an inch between them.

"I knew you'd be a good kisser," he hummed between pecks.

"Feck off," she ordered playfully, silencing him with another kiss.

A set of cautious steps approached at once, so quick she didn't even have time to think.

"Tara?"

I know that voice, she thought in a panic. "Melinda?" Without hesitation, she jumped off Alaric's lap and straightened herself out like a teenager caught in the act of something devious.

"I came here to rescue you, and this is how you're spending your time?" A glimmer of tears welled in Melinda's eyes, disappointment riddled along her angular face.

"Please...let me explain!"

"What the fuck is this?" Alaric asked, his voice once again returning to the gruff hellhound leader she'd previously known. "How the hell did you sneak in here? Do I not have any security?"

Melinda didn't hesitate to reach for her pistol, aiming it directly at Alaric's head.

"Wait, don't!" She stood between them, placing herself in harm's way.

"You're choosing *him?*" Melinda spat, her gaze filled with a fiery rage Tara had never seen before.

"I'm not choosing anyone. This is all a huge misunderstanding. Please just give me a moment to help you understand!"

A howl echoed through the camp, hellhounds alerted of the unknown intruder amongst them.

"I stood up for you. When they said you would choose the enemy, I told them there was no way you could do this. They killed Wesley. Tried to kill *me.* For no reason other than who I happen to be related to. How could you do this?" Her friend's voice quivered but her grip did not, the gun still pointing at them.

"Melinda, please!"

"This betrayal cuts too deep, Tara. Don't even try to come back when this all goes to shit," she hissed, turning her back on them as if intending to leave.

"Wait!"

"You're dead to me," Melinda spat, shooting a final shot at Alaric without hesitation.

Tara's heart sank, unable to move. Her friend glared one final time before running away from the enemy's camp. The words rang through her mind, along with the deafening shot just fired. Too afraid to turn toward Alaric, she was unsure what to do. *Do I want him to live? Or die? If I run after her now, I can try and persuade the others that I wasn't just sitting in his lap*, she pondered. A muffled cry made her turn toward him, relief washing over her realizing the man wasn't dead.

"Tara, please. Help me!"

At last, she made her decision.

"Let's get you somewhere to take care of that wound."

"You don't want to go after her?" he wheezed, clutching his shoulder where the bullet was lodged in his skin.

"You heard her... I'm nothing to them. I guess you were right." Tara fought back the urge to cry, as she thought: *For once, I wish someone would just choose me.*

In the distance, she realized Melinda wasn't alone after all. The Falke brothers and the Broderick trio followed her friend. Ezra lay limp in Thoren's arms, head bobbing and arms flailing with each step. The mayor ran clumsily in the middle, each member of the group armed and ready. They didn't stop to look for her; didn't even bother to turn one last time.

They just...left me here. "Where to?" Pulling Alaric's arm over her shoulder, they hobbled forward.

"My tent. I have healing supplies." Pained groans escaped him, crimson spilling down his arm.

Pointing toward a tent not far from hers, they entered. Oriental rugs, trunks of clothing and weapons, and a surprisingly cushy chair awaited inside. Tara guided him to take a seat before the fire, urging him to remove his shirt.

"And here I hoped that when we'd undress each other for the first time, it would be for fun reasons, not medical." He sucked in a sharp breath, wincing with every movement.

"I ought to slap your bullet wound for that comment," she scolded, examining the damage. Her fingers traced down the side of his arms, then his chest noticing more scars to match the one across his brow. "Who gave you all of these?"

"My father. I took it all so my sister would never have to." His gaze dropped away from hers before her hands cupped his face gently.

"Let's take care of this bullet, and then we can chat. Shall we?"

"There's a knife over there," he groaned, jutting his chin toward a stand with weapons.

Tara grabbed one before holding it in the fire for a moment. Cleaning the blade of any debris, she hesitantly held it to his skin. "I'm sorry in advance," she whimpered, digging the sharp end into his shoulder and fishing around for the tiny piece of metal.

He covered his mouth, though a muffled growl still managed to slip through. "Stop fucking around, and get that thing out!"

"Aha!" she cried triumphantly, her hands bloodied holding up the small bullet.

He pointed toward his dresser again. "There's healing ointment in the first drawer."

Tara rushed to grab it, examining the contents. *This looks like Milicent's,* she thought curiously. As she applied the salve, she was surprised to see the wound heal unnaturally quickly.

"That was fast…"

"Perks of being a hellhound," he grumbled as the last of the wound closed and he was able to breathe normally again.

Pretending to put the vial back where she'd found it, Tara slipping it into her pocket.

"You don't have to steal it," he muttered, standing behind her. "You could just ask. Though if you want to avoid turning, I'd recommend not using it on your bite." Reaching into her pocket, he grabbed the small container and placed it on the table.

Her cheeks turned cherry pink with embarrassment, though she didn't respond.

Pulling her in for a tight embrace, he nuzzled his face into her neck. "You put yourself in danger to save me. Why?"

"I don't know," she admitted. "It seemed like the right thing to do."

"What will you tell your friends?"

"Apparently I don't have any." The realization hit her like a punch to the face. *First Winnie abandons me again. Now the others all turn on me. I truly have...no one,* she thought.

"Join me. Join us. You were meant to help lead this fight."

She paused, thinking of Melinda's words. *'You're dead to me.'* They left a sour taste in her mouth, like she'd vomited and hadn't had a chance to get water.

Meeting his gaze, she leaned in and planted her lips on his again. When she pulled away, the words "I will" escaped her.

Alaric's mouth turned to a wolfish grin, grabbing Tara by the waist to hoist her up. A squeal of surprise made him chuckle again as she wrapped her legs around his hips. Running curious hands through his dark hair, she trailed kisses along his jawline and down his neck. A soft moan escaped him before carrying her toward his bed. With a gentle toss, she landed on the cushioned surface before he prowled toward her.

"You're incredible," he mumbled, trailing a line of kisses down her chest.

Tracing the scar that ran down his face, the light of the

campfire illuminated the tent. His lips continued to dance along her skin, moving up her chest and toward her collarbone. As his cheek grazed the Quinn family pendant, he retreated with a hiss. The light of the necklace shone through the dimly lit room, Tara sitting up in surprise.

"Feck, I'm sorry!" She whimpered, pulling him toward her once more. "It won't happen again, I promise!" In her mind, she calmed herself. Reminded her nerves that she wasn't in danger and hoped her ancestors would get the message.

When his skin made contact with her necklace again, it no longer burned him. Tender kisses resumed as Alaric caressed her body. Exploring the muscles previously hidden, she admired the hellhound leader for who he was.

"Still think you can't trust me?" His eyes darkened, a wicked playfulness hiding in his voice. His hands ran teasing lines over her legs, moving closer and closer toward her center.

"I don't care right now," she whimpered. "I want you. All of you."

He tugged at her corset laces, removing them devastatingly slow. At last, she shooed him away and removed the garment herself. It wasn't long before more clothing fell to the floor of the tent, scattered like autumn leaves in a storm. Only her necklaces remained.

"Do you ever take those things off?"

She shook her head before realizing how exposed she suddenly felt. Her red hair fell around like a drape, hiding her curves. Alaric kneeled before her, hungry eyes devouring every inch of her body.

"Forget the Gods; I'd rather worship you," he whispered, moving hair aside before his lips made contact with her ivory skin. They explored every inch of her body, just as he'd promised, until she couldn't wait any longer. As the night went on, she found herself ready to devour every inch of him, his passion for her equally matched. It was like nothing she'd ever experienced before;

aggressive and fueled by fire. As though some strange new hunger had awoken deep within.

It was all she could do to forget Melinda's words.

37

WINIFRED HAMPTON - 1861

Panic raced through Winnie's body, trying to process what the queen had whispered in her mind. Though she tried again and again, Boudicca either couldn't or wouldn't answer her. Her attempts only seemed to produce a throbbing headache. Brenna still stared out over the water, telling tales of her and Oslind as children before realizing Winnie wasn't really paying attention.

"We should probably head back. It's getting quite late, and you look like you could use some rest. We can come back tomorrow to talk to the soldiers then," the selkie suggested, hooking their arms and pulling them toward the water.

"Maybe we can stop at one of the pubs before we leave." When Brenna turned back in suspicion, Winnie added, "I'm sorry. I'm just enjoying being on land. Not everyone is cut out to live under the sea. And as kind as Oslind's been to me, I've enjoyed some female company for a change."

The selkie chuckled, opening her mouth to respond before a strange sound caught their attention not far from shore. Something echoed through the night, slithering toward them and wrapping itself around Winnie with animalistic intensity.

"Plug your ears!"

"What's that…" It was all Winnie could muster before her mouth fell agape, losing all control of herself.

It was too late. Like leeches, the song engrained itself into every part of her. Just as fluid as the water before them, the melody seethed through her body and took root in her mind, a cloud of dark magic wrapping itself around her. Losing all control of her body, Winnie wandered toward the noise.

She walked through shallow banks until her feet met the other sides of the shore where the city of confederate Hampton waited. A group of selkies sat on nearby rocks, their melodies bringing out dozens of citizens.

Winnie thrashed against the control, trying desperately to free herself. A strange feeling of familiarity washed over her; a sort of kindred plea for autonomy as though she'd gone through this before. But as hard as she tried, she couldn't break free of the haunting selkie songs.

The creatures looked over their shoulders, surprised by her arrival from the sea.

"Where the hell did you come from?" one of the women sneered, her sharp fangs gleaming by the light of the moon.

A few of the others continued their songs, luring more and more confederate soldiers from the dwellings of Hampton.

"Keep singing. I want as many as possible," another selkie announced, his voice deep and sultry.

"What are you doing?" Brenna cried, running from the water beside Winnie.

"We're putting a stop to their madness," the man spat. "Their fighting is beginning to bleed into our waters. This ends tonight."

"You know as well as I do that we cannot interfere with the human wars! They have their own battles to fight. We have to stay out of it!"

"False. We are going to take out all those who fight, from both sides. I don't care if they're confederate or union. If their weapons have touched our waters, they will die," he bellowed, the other selkies around him continuing their hypnotizing song.

Winnie's mind raced, kicking and screaming internally

for anything to break free. *"Okay Boudicca! You always have something smart to say. Help me out here! What do I do to break free from this?"*

There was a pause before she at last responded. *"The answers are inside of you, dear Winifred. Use your brain for once, and call on your strengths."*

Though she couldn't move her body, her mind flared in a violent fury. She thought back to Brenna's words. *"I suppose I have been numb lately. My family has been torn apart, thanks to you: Boudicca. I've been ripped from my friends during a time when they need me. Kane hasn't stopped searching for me since I vanished. This selkie is right. This ends. Tonight."*

It was time to let rage take control. No more holding back.

"Yes," Boudicca hissed in her mind. *"Finally."*

Beneath her skin, Winnie felt the embers reappear. Aelius's soft chuckles echoed through her entire being, wicked and endearing. The more she thought of her friends, the more they riled up. The heat continued to build, her eyes fixed on the singing selkies before her. As her tattooed arm slowly blazed hotter and hotter, the entirety of her pupils turned luminescent amber, mimicking the flickering flames of a fire.

"What's wrong with her?" the male asked, withdrawing a weapon.

With a smirk, Brenna unsheathed her own weapon. "You pissed her off; that's what happened."

The two females ended their tantalizing melodies, both Winnie and the confederate soldiers slowly regaining control of their bodies. The humans scattered in an instant, retreating back toward the city of Hampton.

Shaking herself free of the lingering magic, Winnie shot a ball of fire toward the seated creatures. Darting into the water, they narrowly avoided the blaze. Aelius's magic shot past them, landing on a building not far from shore.

"Shit," Winnie mumbled, running toward the selkies.

Not far off, pangs of gunfire popped rapidly before the men shouted and reloaded their firearms. She glanced their way, noticing a line of men running with torches.

"This one's already lit. Keep going!"

Winnie ran toward them, ready to pull on Gali's magic to subdue the inferno she'd created. "What are you doing?"

"By order of Brigadier General Magruder, Hampton will burn!" One of the confederate soldiers threw his torch toward another building nearby as he shouted.

Ready to retreat to Brenna's side, Winnie was surprised to see an attacker standing just behind her. The selkie knocked her to the ground, sand under her dark curls swallowing her whole. The creature continued to push, the gritty texture embedding itself into her hair and ears. Sending out a ring of crimson flame, Winnie's attacker ceased their merciless grip.

Reaching for the Marvivian dagger at her side, Winnie plunged the blade into the selkie's gut and twisted. The creature fell to the ground, clutching its stomach as Winnie turned and noticed Brenna. On the ground. Surrounded.

"You could just…wait," Boudicca suggested as Winnie attempted to clear her ears of the sand.

But her friend had no intention of dying. With a firm flick of her wrist, the selkies surrounding her fell to the ground, knocked over by a gust of wind. One of the selkies flew back into a mound of nearby rocks, covering them crimson as they writhed in pain. The remaining two were quickly outdone by her swift blade, one taking the weapon to the gut and the other taking it to the throat.

"She's going to kick your ass," Boudicca sneered.

Brenna turned back toward Winnie, her panicked eyes darting between her and the burning city. "We have to stop the fire!"

Winnie nodded, running to the selkie's side. Though before she could do anything to stop the flames from eating away Hampton, the Elements sent a shrill sign of warning through her mind.

"*Don't,*" they warned in unison.

"We can't interfere," she said plainly, tugging at Brenna's arm.

"Are you insane? We have to help those people!"

Winnie avoided her gaze, ashamed of the words about to pour from her mouth. "I know you won't understand, but this has to happen. It's fated. You even said so yourself: we can't interfere with the human's wars."

With a scoff, she added, "You started the fire! Not the humans!"

"But they've chosen to spread it." Winnie's expression turned blank, peering down at the hand that held her own.

"You're not making any sense. The Winnie I've come to know would never allow these people to die!" Brenna's shrill cries echoed through her mind, a piercing reminder of what needed to happen.

"There's a lot about me that you don't know," she confessed quietly, almost too low for the selkie to hear.

Brenna paused, trying to understand as she cocked her head to the side and examined Winnie. With a swift movement, she wrapped her forearm across the selkie's neck, holding her tight against her body with a glowing molten hand.

"What are you doing?" Brenna struggled, but Winnie held her grip.

I can't do this if she's looking at me, she thought.

"King Aalto has my family. He'll kill them if I don't..." she almost couldn't bear to finish her words.

"So what? You're going to kill me? Are you out of your fucking mind?" She grabbed a hold of Winnie's arm, thrusting her hips back.

Winnie slammed onto her back, the selkie above her. Hurling another ball of flames, Brenna ducked just in time.

"I don't have a choice. I don't want to hurt you, but I have to protect my family!" she cried, thrusting her hips forward to kick the selkie off before coming to a stand.

With daggers drawn, the two women circled each other.

"Was this all some sadistic game to you? Get to know us and then cut us down?" Brenna hurled a rage of storm clouds forward.

Winnie blocked with a shield made of fire, the flames growing hotter as they mixed with her powers. She guided them toward the selkie, though Brenna ducked into the water before being engulfed entirely.

Popping from the surface, Brenna lunged for Winnie. Though she ducked out of the way, the blade still nicked her arm as a line of blood trickled out. Winnie barreled toward the selkie's legs, slicing at her calf. The selkie cried out before landing a swift kick to the face.

Brenna backed away, but not before sending another shot of air toward Winnie. Her dagger fell from her hand, onto the sandy shore. Calling on Gali, Winnie took aim for Brenna's weapon as well, freezing the surrounding area until the blade was too painful to grasp. She dropped it with a hiss before her hand could be encapsulated with ice.

"And to think I trusted you. Oslind and I both!"

Brenna's words stunned Winnie. Too similar to the ones she muttered when Beatrix had betrayed her. They left her speechless, defenseless for a moment. Her vision blurred, flashes of images invading her mind. A knocked over tree. A face contorted in fear as it burned to ash. The hellhound she'd killed after Samhain. The phantom cries echoed through her mind.

It wasn't until Brenna's firm fist planted onto Winnie's nose that the nightmare subsided and she returned to the fight. Winnie fell backwards, the selkie taking the opportunity to land above and rain down attack after attack.

A ringing in Winnie's ears intensified, every hit creating another lingering worry that she wouldn't be able to save her young family, dooming them in the future. Creating a world where none of them would even exist. The idea was enough to send her into a tailspin, calling on Gali to create a ball of water around Brenna's face.

The selkie ceased her attacks, grasping for her neck. *She can't breathe without her skins,* she realized. With a swift kick, Brenna landed on her back and Winnie was once again on top. Glancing to her side, the dagger lay too far away to use. *Reaching for it is too risky. I can't risk her getting the upper hand,* she thought as the waves pushed the blade closer and closer with the incoming tide.

Winnie wrapped her hands around the selkie's neck, pushing down on her windpipe. Brenna squirmed as her eyes turned red, tears rolling down her face.

"Please…just…tell me…why," she struggled to get out between gasps.

The grasp around Brenna's neck eased for a moment as Winnie stalled. Her thoughts raced wildly through her mind, trying to decide what to do.

"It's her or your family! You have to do this!" Boudicca's shrill scolding voice echoed through her mind.

"You sided with him! Everyone always sides with him," Brenna sobbed, her arms pinned by Winnie's knees and unable to move.

The dagger continued to drift closer to them, Winnie's eyes jumping back and forth between the weapon and her target.

"I thought you were different! Just tell me…"

Brenna's words came to an abrupt halt. For a moment, Winnie didn't understand why. A soft gurgling sound surprised her, but it wasn't until she looked down that she realized she'd sunken the blade deep into the selkie's gut.

"I…no, wait! I didn't mean to. Wait!" Panic coursed through her body as she looked down at crimson colored hands.

It wasn't until a heavy boot met her ribcage that she realized someone else had joined them. Winnie lay on her side as two more blows knocked the wind out of her. Her gaze shifted up toward a head of blonde hair, rage filled eyes checking on his love.

"I didn't mean to..." she tried to say, clutching her sides in agony.

Oslind's voice tore through the night, but all Winnie could hear was a muffled ringing. Her vision was hazy, still trying to catch her breath as she watched him pull his love into his arms. *I did that,* she thought with loathsome tears running down her face. *I...destroyed them.*

"What the hell is the matter with you?" he cried, eyes glued to Winnie. "You're lucky she's still alive, otherwise I'd kill you right now." He stood, Brenna laying limp in his arms as he rushed toward the water.

"Wait! He knows, Oslind! Your father! He knows!"

She could see the way his shoulders tensed as she attempted to pull herself to stand. Clutching her sides in anguish, face burning from Brenna's fists, she hoped he would hear her.

"What are you saying?"

"Your father has known about you two for a long time now. You haven't been as sneaky as you thought. He kidnapped my father and is threatening to kill my whole family if I don't bring him Brenna's skins!"

"My father knows about us, and you're only telling me this now? After all that I've done to help you?" Oslind bellowed. Stalking toward her, he landed another heavy boot across Winnie's face before pressing it into the sand.

For a moment, she thought she'd suffocate that way. Buried alive as the little granules worked their way into every crack and crevice. Her arms shot back in a panic, trying to swat at his leg. Calling on Aelius, she formed a ball of fire in her palms though she didn't know where to aim it. He smothered her hand into the moist sand beneath them, hissing his final words to her.

"He can't kill your family if I get to him first. The only reason I won't kill you now is because I recognize a desperate fool when I see one. I don't know why you needed an army, but I'll sleep better at night knowing you won't have one. Consider the deal you made with my mother off. There's no way in hell we would ever help someone like you. "

By the time Winnie regained herself, the two of them were gone. Lost to the sea, she screamed to the high heavens. Uncontrollable sobs sang through the night sky as shrieks echoed from just beyond, the city of Hampton burning. So much pain and suffering.

Nothing to show for it.

38

WINIFRED
LOCATION UNKNOWN - 1861

Pushing and paddling as hard as she could, Winnie prayed she could make it back to Marvivia in time. For miles, she kicked though it seemed to do little good. The faint glow of a shimmering underwater city skyline was nowhere to be seen.

"At this point, I don't know if I'm even headed in the right direction! For all I know, I'm swimming in circles!" Winnie shouted within the breathing apparatus. *I need to get back. If he won't help me, then I'll need his father alive. One way or another,* she thought breathlessly.

A mumbling groan echoed through her head, Boudicca's sigh ringing loud and clear. *"Use those handy teleportation powers of yours."*

"Are you trying to help me for once?" Winnie scoffed. *I don't know how to tap into that power though… It always just happens by accident.*

"For the love of the Gods, stop whining, and just think! Use that magnificent brain you were given, and just try! Quit giving up before you've even started!" The way Boudicca's words marched through her mind like a siren made Winnie feel like she was being scolded by her very own mother.

"Yes, ma'am…"

Closing her eyes, Winnie wadded in the dark abyss. She tried picturing Marvivia in her mind, wanting desperately to get there quickly and in one piece. In the past when she'd done so, she'd felt helpless and the jump had happened by accident. *How do I recreate that same sense of urgency?* she wondered.

That was, until she felt something dart past her in the water. Unable to see two feet in front, she padded at the shadows that threatened to swallow her whole. Unable to see the surface, she had no clue how far down she was. The nothingness mimicked the all-too familiar void when communing with the dead.

Just as Oslind had shown her several nights before, Winnie envisioned glowing light within the palm of her hands. Tiny sparks jumped from hand to hand as dim illumination trickled through the sea water. It blazed brighter and brighter before she sent it out ahead, hoping to see what was lurking in the darkness.

At first, there was nothing. But a set of reflective eyes stalked her up ahead with pinpoint accuracy. Massive fins and gray skin circled, dark, glaring pupils staring as snapping jaws waited. Oslind had warned her of the sharks that circled these waters. Otherwise harmless unless…

She grabbed ahold of her arm, still bleeding where Brenna had nicked her earlier. *Shit,* she thought.

"Now would be a good time to jump, darling," Boudicca urged.

Staring face to face with the creature, Winnie squeezed her eyes shut, picturing the glowing lights of Marvivia or the statue that protected its entrance. When she looked again, the shark approached with movements so devastatingly slow, it didn't seem to move at all.

"If I move…it might charge," she whispered aloud, unsure who she was trying to explain to.

The shark's tail hovered behind it, a toothy smile accompanying eyes that tracked every move. Slowly, she waded to the side as it mimicked her carefully. She moved left slightly, the beast once again following suit. *There's no way out,* she panicked. She'd barely escaped the selkie, much less a beast three times her size.

"Now would be a good time to try teleporting!" Boudicca repeated, as the shark prowled slowly toward Winnie.

"M—maybe I can outswim it," Winnie whispered, though she wasn't sure if she was trying to convince herself or Boudicca.

"If you can outswim a shark, then I may as well consider myself corporeal because that's the most idiotic thing you've ever said. Just teleport!" The queen's bellow echoed through her mind, causing her to wince at the on-coming headache.

"I'll take my chances…" she mumbled, taking a deep breath and preparing to push herself harder than ever before.

Darting below, she hoped that perhaps the cover of darkness would shield her from the massive creature. When she glanced back, all she saw were the snapping jaws of the shark. In an attempt to slow it down, Winnie shot a spear of ice toward it. Though it made contact, its tough skin repelled the spear as it continued its chomping dive toward Winnie.

"Fuck, fuck, fuck!" she cried out, only swimming deeper and deeper into the ocean. "Where am I even going? Gods, I'm such an idiot!"

Behind her, the shark drew nearer. Mere seconds had passed and it was gaining on her quicker than she'd anticipated. In an attempt to divert the beast, she darted to the side, shooting another spear of ice. The snapping jaws turned toward her, chomping down on the spear as it lunged forward again. It's snout barreled into her, knocking the wind from her lunges as she floated through water aimlessly for a moment. When she regained herself, she noticed the beast readying another attack.

"Jump," Aelius ordered, likely unwilling to see his latest follower die by one of Gali's creations. *"Jump now, or you're dead!"*

Winnie blinked, the shark's mouth agape and headed directly toward her. Mere seconds stood between her untimely death and its razor sharp teeth.

"Jump, you foolish witch! Do you not value your own life?"

Something below suddenly stole her attention. Thick, broad tentacles reached up, ready to wrap around her ankle and pull her even further into the depths. Before the shark could sink its teeth into her body, sticky limbs dragged it into the dark abyss. A set of glowing red eyes waited below as it continued reaching for her legs.

"You have even bigger problems to worry about now! Teleport!" Aelius's voice caused a swirling vortex of panic to stir deep within, her tattooed arm set ablaze and ready to release.

A tentacle snagged her by the foot, constricting until pinpricks numbed her leg. The shark below clouded the area in crimson, torn to shreds by devious kraken arms. More slippery limbs reached for Winnie as she tried to concentrate. Kicking feverishly, she hoped she could knock loose its hold. The glowing lights of Marvivia sat just behind the lids of her eyes. A rumbling roar sounded around her and the tentacles pulled her farther down toward the beast's hungry glow.

"Do it now!"

As though she were caught in a tornado, electric shocks pulsated through her body as she turned around and around. Releasing her breath, the water at once felt still again. That looming presence no longer grasped at her leg, ready to devour her. When she hesitantly surveyed the area, she was no longer surrounded by darkness. Instead, she could see the faint outline of Marvivia's trident wielding statue up ahead.

"Well done," Aelius praised, the words a warm caress against her aching mind.

Winnie had no time to compose herself before darting for the throne room. She couldn't get Oslind's rage-filled eyes out of her mind as she approached the pearly door that led to the king's home. What she saw next, she couldn't have anticipated.

Removing her helmet, she placed it on the cherry-red stained floor. Strewn across the abalone shell ground, bodies of dead mermaids lay slaughtered. Across from her, Oslind stood with his hands around his father's neck.

"Oslind, don't! My family! If he dies, so do I!"

His rage centered on her. "Why would his death have *anything* to do with you?"

"I made a blood oath with him. He can't die until I've fulfilled my end of the bargain!" Her eyes pleaded with him, though the corners of his mouth seemed to turn to a vicious smirk.

"You hurt one of the only people who matters to me. And you expect me to give a damn about you and your family?" Oslind tossed his father onto the throne before twisting his sword around in his hands. He held it toward her – a challenge.

"I need your father alive! Stop this now before I'm forced to do what's right for my family!" She shot her hand toward him, attempting to cover his wrist in ice as she drew on Gali's powers. However, the goddess didn't respond. As though she were unable to draw on her water magic, Winnie instead turned to Aelius.

The look on Oslind's face could rival that of the beasts she'd fought the night of Samhain, pure rage glistening in his eyes and teeth barred. "How dare you try and use Gali's magic on me! I am a creature of the sea! You're powerless here!"

Winnie knew she had moments to spare before he'd charge. And given the way her ribs ached from the sides of his boot, she didn't want to take him on in hand-to-hand combat again.

"Don't make me do this, Oslind," she warned. Before her, she called forth a set of blazen arrows.

"End him. End this now so you can get back to your family and friends," Aelius urged.

"Leave and don't come back." She stepped aside, making way for him to exit.

Still, he stepped closer toward her. Stalked, more like, as though he had no intention of letting Winnie leave alive. She glanced down, noticing his abdomen covered in his own blood, a glittering wound hidden beneath his clothes. Focusing Aelius's magic on that wound, Oslind's screams ripped through her mind as he dropped to his knees.

"You're supposed to kill him! Why did you cauterize his injury?" Aelius bellowed, a searing headache sending bolts of pain through her.

"You're hurt. Take supplies and get back to Brenna. Then leave and never come back," Winnie warned, jutting her chin toward the exit, praying to the Gods that he'd listen.

Struggling to stand, he spat, "I'm not going anywhere until my father is dead!"

She let loose the flaming arrows, stopping mere inches from his face. The flare of the fire glittered in his shimmering blue eyes, close to singeing his skin as he stepped toward her. His glaring gaze darted between Winnie's flame and King Aalto.

"You made the wrong choice," he spat, throwing his blade to the ground. "One way or another, I will kill him. And if by some miracle it doesn't take you too, I'll make sure you're next."

As he stalked toward the exit, Winnie maintained her hold on the fiery arrows. The moment he exited, she released them with a heavy sigh, rushing toward the king. She examined him carefully, noticing the deserved beating his own son had dealt.

"King Aalto?" she whispered, cradling his head.

From the side, a soft cry caught her attention. Winnie turned, seeing Afissa huddled in the corner. "My own son…" she whimpered. "What the hell happened? I thought…"

Winnie shushed her, eyes darting down toward the King who wavered between consciousness. "King Aalto, can you hear me?"

"Bring me…her skin." He hissed. "And kill my son while you're at it, or your family is all dead."

Afissa scampered over to have a seat beside her bloodied husband, mindlessly examining the wounds. The King's eyes finally closed, consciousness fading at last. Winnie checked for a pulse, noting that he was at least still alive. She smacked the side of his face a few times, before thinking: *I need to be sure he's not listening.*

"I have an idea... Take care of your husband. I'll bring him what he wants. But only if I know that we still have our deal? I promise I'll find a way to make this worth it for you."

Afissa looked out over the throne room for a moment. "I didn't think he was capable of such...violence. He's more like his father than I realized."

"He's a man in love. Hurt by someone he trusted." Guilt stirred deep in her chest, loud enough to drown out the voices of the fire god and the queen momentarily. "I will make this right. I will fix this, I promise. Do we still have our deal?"

Afissa's sad eyes dropped back to Winnie. "Yes. I swear it."

With a nod, Winnie ran for the exit. As she secured her helmet, Afissa's voice caught her attention once more.

"Please, don't hurt him. Despite what he's done, I don't know that I'd survive the loss of my son."

39

TARA
CHICAGO - 1871

"**W**ake up..."

The slithering voices faded in and out of Tara's mind as she opened her eyes. Drowsiness fell over her in waves, too exhausted from a night of indulgence to think clearly at first.

"Wake up, Quinn..."

She shot up in bed, scanning the room to locate the whispers that awoke her. Her ancestors mumbled their words of worry, though they somehow seemed to speak directly to her.

"Alaric?" Sitting up in bed, she rubbed sleepy eyes.

The fire across the room sat extinguished, a lingering cold biting as she pulled on the blanket and stood. Ready to put on her shoes, she peered down at her ankle. Turning it in circles, it no longer ached through her entire body like a disease. As she removed the bandages, the indentations of the initial bite and purple bruises were entirely gone.

She called out to him again, still hearing nothing. Seeing nothing. He was just gone. Before she could allow her first instincts to wreck her, she thought: Maybe he's out getting food like all the other mornings.

Heading for the opening of his tent, she was met with a set of piercing eyes waiting for her. As she leaned down, a wolf sat just outside the flap. Nuzzle to nose, she peered into a set of glaring, violet eyes. The beast snapped and growled, Tara backing away slowly.

"Whoa…" she calmed. "Where's Alaric? He can explain everything." Stepping back, the hellhound followed her into the tent and sat before the exit. Saliva frother around its jowls as she cried out louder, "Alaric?"

The beast ceased its snarl, but refused to move.

"You're not going to let me leave, are you?"

With a sly shake of its head, the corners of its mouth curled into an eerily human smile.

"I'm with you! I'm on your side," she tried to explain, though the hellhound simply responded with more grumbling displeasure.

She turned toward the stash of weapons she'd noticed last night, only to find it empty. There was nothing left in the tent that she could use to defend herself against this beast.

"Was this…planned?" she whispered, turning back toward the violet-eyed wolf.

"You're in danger…" the voices of her ancestors hissed. She winced, the slithering sound gnawing at her mind like an itch she couldn't reach.

The hellhound growled once more, every little movement Tara made noticed by its piercing gaze. She looked into the eyes of that beast, noting their strange familiarity. She'd only ever seen one person with such eyes…but it couldn't be.

"Who are you?" she asked, taking a seat on the edge of his bed. A piercing whine was the only response she got. "Does Alaric know you're here?" Wading through her memories, Tara tried desperately to remember where she'd seen such peculiar irises. "Turn to your human form so we can talk."

With a strange shrug, the creature stood to exit the tent.

Those eyes… she thought. "Wait!"

The figure of a woman appeared as the hound turned into her human form. With her back still toward Tara, only her dark cascading curls were visible. A scarf covered her ivory face as those same violet eyes peered over the woman's shoulder.

"You desperate fool," she mocked, a strange child-like lilt to her voice. Ducking beneath the tent flap, the woman gave orders to hounds on guard outside.

Those eyes. That voice, Tara thought in a panic. *I know who she is. I've seen her before!* The memories came tumbling down on her like an avalanche as she tried to take a deep breath. *The day Alaric saved Cricket... but, he killed her. That creature that was going to hurt him! I watched him stab the woman.*

"You didn't see him, though, did you?" An unfamiliar woman's voice roamed through her mind, foreign and unlike the ancestors still whispering words of caution.

Swatting at her head, Tara stood to pace. Panic trickled down her spine, electric shocks of worry radiating through her entire body. An odd restlessness she'd never felt before stirred in her bones, like an unwavering hunger she couldn't suppress.

"You're in danger," her ancestors whispered once more.

And then it clicked.

Her hands reached for her neck in an instant, feeling in a panic for the familiar necklaces she always wore. The one to protect her from magic; the other to get on the estate.

Both gone.

KANE

Thoren and Kane looked down at Ezra, lying atop a thin mattress on the floor of the Chicago Orphan Asylum. They never made it to the Fox family's estate, needing to tend to him immediately. Cricket had been sent ahead with a note tied to his collar, ushering Winnie's parents to come aid in healing. Their stealth mission had been a success, not a single hound realizing they snuck into their camp until they managed to get Ezra and Mayor Medill. Tara hadn't been found.

Melinda took the mayor, merely bruised and a little banged up with no serious injuries, back to his home immediately. In an effort to ensure the man's family and the citizens of Chicago that their leader was safe, she thought it was best to allow him to return to his usual security detail.

The sight of Ezra unconscious with gauze around his midsection sent Thoren into a panicked frenzy, desperate for healing. Thanks to a few siren songs and elemental gifts, the hellhounds never had a chance to chase after them. A few stray beasts appeared outside the orphanage, only to turn and run when they saw the carnage of Melinda's attack.

"I worry about what they have planned…" Kane mumbled as the two sirens took a break from their soft, healing melodies.

"I don't care about anything besides this right now," Thoren grumbled, eyes glued to his love.

"Do you think Melinda was acting strange after we got back? I thought she would have been more pressed to find Tara and bring her home, too. It seems strange she'd want to leave her behind," he mentioned, rolling his neck and preparing his magic again.

"We can always go back another time," Thoren dismissed, urging Kane back over beside Ezra.

Miss Leona walked into the room, carrying a steaming pot of tea and some teacups. Otto raced behind her, a pitcher of water in hand. The little boy tried desperately not to spill any, though his energy superseded any sort of control.

"Is he still sleeping?" the boy squeaked, his bouncing step coming to a halt as he looked over Ezra.

Miss Leona placed a caring hand on Thoren's back before asking, "What's going on? It didn't take nearly this long when you healed your brother."

"It feels like something is blocking us. Like he's under a spell or something," Kane huffed in frustration.

"Where the hell is Milicent? I sent Cricket with a note hours ago! They should be here by now!" Thoren's grumbling words echoed through the tiny room.

No one said anything in response, Miss Leona and Kane sharing concerned stares before she focused on Ezra again.

"What's that around his stomach?" Pointing to the gauze, she noted a sliver of greenery sticking out of the bandages. Her delicate fingers worked with caution to remove the strips of fabric as her brows scrunched in confusion. When the final piece was removed, exposing the wound and the strange flowers stuffed inside, she fell back onto her bottom in surprise. Kane jumped to his feet, helping her up off the ground.

"Get those off now!" Her shaking hands pointed to the purple flowers.

Rushing to do as instructed, Thoren asked, "What is it? What's wrong?"

"That's Aconite! Also known as Wolfsbane! A highly poisonous flower!"

"Why would they apply poison to his wound? That doesn't make any sense." Kane scooted forward, helping her clean the area with fresh rags and water.

His brother couldn't seem to take his eyes off Ezra's midsection. "This looks like a bite," he hissed, fire burning behind his pupils.

"A bite? What does that mean?" Her voice turned shrill, a panicked gaze jumping between both brothers.

"He would've turned already," Kane guessed hopefully, knowing just how contagious the hellhound's curse truly was.

"Wolfsbane usually kills within a few hours. He's lucky he's still alive," Miss Leona added, continuing to clean as she tsked and doted on Ezra.

"Death isn't here, don't worry," Otto whispered, clutching Kane's arm in comfort.

Thoren shook his head. "This doesn't make sense…"

"Let's try again," he suggested, getting comfortable on the

355

ground. Otto took a seat at his side, continuing to hug his arm as though the mere thought would help bring Ezra back.

When the healing melodies began again, their magic finally had somewhere to go. All previous attempts felt like hitting a wall, as though something blocked their magic from reaching the wounds on his body. Though the minor scrapes and bruises had gone away, his midsection had remained bloodied and still lay unconscious. Now, it finally felt like they were getting somewhere as the two sirens no longer struggled to push their magic through Ezra's body.

"Please wake up," Thoren mumbled, clutching his love and turning his back to Miss Leona and the boy. "I've been such an ass lately. Please don't let these last few weeks be the last we spent together."

Kane stood, Otto following close behind as they took a seat at the table. He poured everyone in the room a cup of tea, offering some to the little boy whose beaming, toothy smile waited.

"I saw your wings last night."

"You were supposed to be in bed," Kane whispered with a smirk.

There was a pause before Otto snickered and said, "I want to be a hero like you someday."

I don't want him to end up like me, he thought immediately before he'd even had time to process the boy's words. "You're already my hero. You've kept the others safe while we've been away. And for that, I'm so proud of you."

As Thoren still cradled Ezra, Miss Leona offered the siren a cup of tea. "It's probably not as good as anything you have in London, but it'll do."

Thoren accepted the cup gingerly, taking a small sip before handing it back to her. "I've made worse."

Ezra's eyes slowly fluttered open toward the ceiling. His waking was gradual, as if coming out of a deep sleep. "Th–Thoren?"

"Thank the Gods!" his little brother cried, pulling his love in tighter. Thoren planted his lips on Ezra's, a tear rolling down his cheek.

"I'm starting to think I'm like a cat. How many lives do I have left?" he somehow managed to joke between kisses.

Miss Leona's face paled. "Oh, I didn't realize you two were…" She walked toward the table to give the two their space before taking a seat beside Kane.

I can't quite read her, he thought, watching her face carefully. "Is there a problem?" Ready to fight for his little brother, Kane prepared himself for whatever answer may come next.

She paused, taking a deep breath, before saying, "No." She offered him a nervous smile and added, "The old me would've kicked you out. But then again, the old me didn't know any of this was possible." She flapped her arms at her sides as though she had wings.

"It's a lot to take in, but I appreciate your open mind," he mumbled before taking a sip of his tea. *I've certainly seen worse reactions before,* he thought.

Rubbing his face, he couldn't help but let out a sigh. Its weight was so heavy, it felt like weeks of pent up anxiety releasing all at once. His heart rose to his throat, a hot sting behind his eyes. *I will not be emotional in front of them,* he scolded himself. Defeat washed over him, the last few weeks a heavy reminder that he'd only failed since Winnie left.

Her face crossed his mind, reminiscing over her dark curls and amber eyes. Kane wished he could reach out and touch her, or hold her tight against his chest just to know she was safe. Longing for the day when she'd finally come home. *"Come back to me…"* he thought, though he felt the words escape him, searching. Reaching out into the universe looking for her.

A soft knock at the door pulled Kane from his thoughts, Melinda peeking her head through. "Everyone survive?" She took a seat on the ground next to Ezra before examining his healed wound.

"Barely," Thoren mumbled.

Ezra clutched her hand and offered her a reassuring squeeze. "Thank you. I'm alive because of you. All of you."

"That's what friends are for," she said with a soft smile before she glanced toward the ground. A strange shift in her mood was visible, not a single soul unaware of its presence.

"Are you alright?" Miss Leona asked, placing a calming hand on her back.

"Medill and his family were telling me a little of what happened while he was away," she began.

Kane motioned for her to continue, unease spreading through his chest the longer she stalled.

"According to his wife, Kitty, they received ransom notes while he was at the hellhound camp. Alaric wanted one of his daughters. Doesn't this look familiar?" Dropping from her balled fists, a small silver chain dangled.

Both brothers rushed over to have a look at the pendant, Kane immediately recognizing the symbols inscribed on the metal. "How did you get Tara's necklace?"

"It's not hers. It's Katherine's, Medill's oldest daughter. What are the odds?" Tucking it away in her pocket, Melinda crossed her arms over her chest. "She's downstairs. I have a feeling this puts a target on her back."

"Why would they want one of his kin? And why would she have an almost identical necklace to Tara's halfway across the world?" Thoren mumbled aloud.

She shrugged before adding, "That's not all. Medill was also telling me a little of what he overheard while he was there. Only bits and pieces, but I'm concerned. It involves Tara."

"Did you find her last night? I was surprised you wanted to leave without her." Kane sat forward in his chair, examining her carefully as he sipped on tea.

"I found her," she began, though anger filled her eyes as her lips pulled into a tight frown. The end of her sentence sat on the tip of her tongue, as though she didn't want to finish.

"And we left her…why?" Thoren interjected this time, awaiting answers just like everyone else.

"This is all so messed up! How the hell did we end up here?" Beginning to pace in circles, Melinda rubbed her head feverishly as her frustration only grew.

Quietly, Miss Leona excused herself and called for Otto to follow. It wasn't long before the siren brothers continued to pester.

In an attempt to be gentle, Kane asked softly, "What's got you so upset?"

"Where the *fuck* is Winnie? This is her fight that we're in! And yet she's just, what? Gone? Where is she, Kane?" Her eyes widened, rushing toward him as though she may swing on him.

I don't know that I've ever heard her use that kind of language before, he thought. "What does Winnie have to do with this?"

"Melinda, what in the world did you see? You're not making any sense." Ezra sat up from Thoren's embrace, reaching for her as though he could calm her down.

"Winnie was supposed to be here. She could've prevented this. She could've stopped Tara from…"

"From what?" Thoren's words were sharp, standing to meet her gaze.

"She was…with…Alaric." She paused for a moment, glancing between each of them to gauge their responses. "I caught them kissing."

Thoren's breath quickened, his chest heaving in anger. The room seemed to heat alongside his frustration until his love reached for his hand to calm him down. "I told you…"

"I know what you said. That's why I waited to tell you. I needed to get my thoughts straight before we talked about this." Melinda continued to avoid their stares, eyes fixed to the ground on which she paced.

"She's as good as dead." Thoren's eyebrows furrowed in anger before there was a lull in the conversation.

"What did the mayor say?" Kane asked at last, trying to change the subject. *I want to be surprised by the news of Tara's betrayal, but I honestly didn't care. The moment she threatened to tell Winnie what I did, I knew she was no more than a traitor,* he conceded.

"He heard a few of the hounds mentioning Tara. He didn't know what they were talking about, but somehow she plays an important role in their plan. Alaric needs something from her," she explained. "I think he's been manipulating her to gain her trust."

"I tried to warn her," his brother spat through gritted teeth.

"It's okay, Thor. We'll figure it out," Ezra mumbled, stroking the back of Thoren's hand.

"I shot him," she said with a quick shrug. She fidgeted with her hands as though she was worried they'd be upset with her.

Thoren let out a quick, snorting laugh. "I hope you at least killed him."

"I wish I had."

"We need to come up with a plan," Kane began, finishing his cup of tea. "Gods, I'm tired of saying that. When can we finally just get some rest?"

"If only Winnie were here to ask the spirits, or to spy on them again," Ezra added with a heavy sigh.

"Again I ask: where the hell is she?" Melinda took a seat across from Kane, pouring herself a cup of tea.

"We should check on Milicent and Ernest. We sent Cricket hours ago, and neither of them showed up," Thoren added, pointing toward the hallway.

Kane stood to exit as he rubbed his head. "I'll go check on them."

"I'll go with you," Melinda offered, jumping from her seat.

"No, it's alright. I'll manage. It's just the estate. You stay here; keep an eye out for the orphanage and the mayor. Thoren, you take care of Ezra. I'm sure he needs his rest," he said, offering gentle commands.

Careful steps dragged toward the portal, a nagging headache sitting across his temple.

"You need rest," Caelus whispered in his mind.

Kane ignored the god's plea before reaching for the portal mirror. The hair on his arms stood, something deep down alerting to an unknown threat. Regardless, he ignored the feeling. When his feet stepped through the portal and his body landed on the other side of the world, he could hardly believe his eyes.

In a panic, he realized: *Attack...they're under attack.*

40

MILICENT
FOX MANOR - 1871

Milicent awoke to the familiar sound of the portal opening. The rush of wind echoed through the house, making her jolt up in bed. Just outside, a sad howl sang before she rushed downstairs in a panting frenzy to see what was amiss. When she opened the side of the sunroom door, Cricket sprinted in with something dangling around his neck.

"Good morning, beast," she muttered, glancing at the large grandfather clock sitting on the opposite side of the room. *Almost 4:00 am. Bloody hell it's early,* she thought with a yawn.

She snatched the piece of paper attached to Cricket's collar before he nudged her leg and glanced toward the door again.

"I take it, you want to go back outside?" This time she hummed, realizing: *Perhaps this strange creature is growing on me.* His wolfish face turned into an almost human smile, nudging her for a quick pat on the head before tapping toes waited to go out. "For such a fearsome beast, you sure are a lonely little sap. We need to get your dear Tara back, don't we?"

Cricket's tawny eyes narrowed on her before nodding in understanding. As Milicent opened the door, he darted into the woodline rather than running his usual laps around the house.

"Where's he off to?" Ernest asked, rubbing sleepy eyes before stepping behind her and planting a soft kiss on her temple.

"He's gone to the woods. Do you think we should be worried?"

She glanced back at her love, eyebrows scrunched in concern before searching for the shuck again. The cold from outside crept into the sunroom, the fire across the room flickering to life.

"I'm sure he's just letting off some steam. Where else could he possibly go?" Ernest waved a telekinetic hand to shut the door before taking a seat on one of the loveseats.

"How did it go with Horace yesterday? Any leads? You got home so late, you never spoke a word to me." Milicent took a seat across from her husband. Worry made her stomach twist in knots, knowing deep down something wasn't quite right.

"Nothing. Plenty of folks talking about grave robbings, but no one's seen anything. They just keep finding disturbed graves. They did find the first empty one, however. It was unmarked; no one knew who had been laid to rest inside." Her husband snapped his fingers, two cups of steaming coffee landing on the table before them.

"I wish Winnie were here. She could've helped talk to the spirits." Pulling a blanket around her shoulders, a shiver wracked down Milicent's spine.

Ernest nodded in agreement. "It would be nice to know where my daughter is. I still don't understand why you won't tell me what she's doing."

Milicent released a heavy sigh, reaching for a steaming mug. "We've been over this already. Fate won't allow me to."

"This is absurd, Millie. We're not talking about some vague dangers, or strangers we don't know. This is about our daughter!" Leaning over the table to reach for her hand, he held it for a moment before offering her a sad smile.

Her gaze dropped away from him, unable to look at him directly. Too afraid to admit: *There are many things I haven't told you.* "You've known since the moment we met that there are things I cannot divulge."

"Since when are you one to follow the rules?"

"Since our only remaining child's life remains on the line if I reveal even the slightest of hints," she snapped, withdrawing her hand and leaning back on the couch. She covered her face with delicate hands, almost as though she could hide from the truth-seeking eyes of her husband.

"Winnie's life…is in danger? Because of what? Why haven't you mentioned this before now?" He continued to pester, scooting to the edge of his seat in nervous anticipation.

"I'm not allowed to tell you. I won't keep repeating myself!"

Ernest retreated inward, pinching the bridge of his nose with a grumbling sigh. "Do you think we'll ever recover? From Wesley's…" His words came to an abrupt stop.

"What are you saying?"

"You and I both know things haven't been the same. You've pulled away. You can hardly stand to be around me, it seems."

"It hasn't even been a full two months! Forgive me if I can't just snap my fingers, and get over the loss of my child!" Her mouth gaped open, tears welling as her heart slowly broke open to relieve the grief nestled deep within.

"I don't know how much longer I can go on living like this. Not just since Wesley's… *death*. But before that, too. Even when we're in the same room, it's like you're not here at all. You're distant. And all the secrets…the lies. They're piling up and burying us alive." Ernest stood, only to join her on the couch. "I love you, Millie, but I can't keep doing this if you won't be honest with me."

With squinting eyes, Milicent tried to block out the pain. A tear trickled down the side of her face, clutching his hands feverishly as if she could hold onto him and never let go. As though her touch could be the thing to anchor him to this moment.

"I want to tell you! I just… *can't*. You've never questioned me like this before! Why is now any different?"

"Because this time, we've lost a child. And from the sounds of it, we could lose our only remaining daughter. I won't put our children," he began, though a pained pause interrupted his sentence. Carefully, he had to correct himself. "Our *child...* is at risk. For some secrets between you and entities I've never even seen. I thought our love meant more than that." The words choked from his mouth like poison before he began to pace the room.

"I love you, Ernest. You are my entire world. I need you to understand that if I had the option I would tell you without hesitation. But at the risk of Winnie's life, my life, and even yours, I cannot tell you. I am bound. There is no way around it!"

"You and I both know that if you truly wanted to, you'd find a way. You have in the past. Though I know it's difficult, all I hear is that Fate is more important than the love we share." Ernest shrugged, heading for the sunroom door. "You're my everything, Millie. My sun, moon, and stars. But I've endured a lifetime of lies, and it has worn me down. I can't keep doing this. Talk to Fate, and figure out a way to include me. Otherwise, I'm not sure where we stand."

His hand lay rested on the door handle before the entire thing swung open, knocking against the windows behind it. The glass shattered from the force, Ernest jumping back in surprise. A cloud of suffocating purple fog filled the room, both clutching their throats in anguish.

Turning back, he grabbed Milicent by the arm and dragged her outside. The air cleared as they stepped into a soft haze of early dusk, though a wall of intruders waited beyond.

"Morning," a blue-eyed man hummed, twirling something small and metallic around his finger playfully.

Before they could even think to act, Ernest and Milicent were forced down onto their knees. *"Ina, help!"* she cried out in her mind, reaching beneath the earth, drawing on earthly vines to assist in their escape.

A hoard of incoming hounds funneled in from the treeline, just as they had the night of Samhain. Surrounding all sides of the estate, it seemed there wasn't a single area safe from their surprise ambush.

"Not so fast," a female voice hummed from behind, placing a set of cuffs around their wrists.

Milicent's gaze jumped between the female intruder and Ernest. It took a moment for her to realize Ina wasn't responding to her prayers. Vines didn't spring from the ground. Boulders nearby didn't roll in their defense.

Nothing.

"Why aren't my powers working?"

"Mine aren't working either!" her husband grumbled, tugging at the bindings.

With a teasing smile, the blue-eyed man's hand dropped to his side. "Can't allow you to escape, now can we?"

Milicent's attention narrowed onto the metal in his hands, realizing what he carried. "How did you get one of our family pendants?"

"Your daughter's little red-haired friend was all too easy to manipulate," he cackled. "By the time I was done with her, I probably could've batted my eyelashes and she would've handed it right over." A group of hellhounds not far off glanced toward their leader, laughing alongside him.

The violet-eyed woman beside him rolled her eyes, removing a blade. "Where's Winnie?"

A sharp end pricked Milicent's throat as she winced, attempting to retreat.

"Touch her and die!" Ernest hissed, though an unseen hand pushed him down toward the ground.

"I don't know, I swear! We haven't seen her in weeks!" Attempting to stand, the same hidden force pushed her back down.

The violet-eyed woman's gaze landed on Ernest before his body was pulled toward her, stretched unnaturally as he groaned in pain.

"I can assume he's Alaric," he managed to bite out. "Who are you?"

She said nothing, her strange magic contorting his body further.

"How can we work this out? Surely there's some kind of deal we can make. Is this all because of Boudicca?" At last, his body slumped back down to the ground before groaning in relief.

"We need your daughter. Where is she?" She held the knife to Ernest's throat before moving it over to Milicent again.

"I swear to you, we don't know! She's just gone!"

The violet-eyed woman turned back to Alaric, leaning in to whisper something. Though Milicent couldn't make out anything of use, she noted the man's mouth move to say the cursed queen's name.

In desperation, she cried, "Boudicca's soul was banished during the Battle of Samhain! There's nothing left of her. She's gone!"

"That's what you think," the woman scoffed. "What do we do with them? Kill them?"

"Winnie's less likely to help us if her parents are dead. We take them with us. Just in case we need more collateral damage," Alaric commanded.

"We're not going anywhere with you!" Ernest bellowed, attempting to stand again.

The violet-eyed woman rolled her eyes again, pulling out two rags from her back pocket. Her song-like voice hummed, "Enough from you two. Either you come with or you die. Truthfully, we only need one of you. So you better be on your best behavior."

Milicent attempted one final plea before her mouth was at last bound and no words could escape. Attempting to beg with her eyes, only muffled cries escaped past the gag.

"Don't give me the puppy dog eyes, witch. I lost my soul a long time ago. It won't work on me," she snapped, a wave of unfamiliar magic shoving Milicent into the ground with a thud.

It was then that Milicent once again heard the familiar 'whoosh' of the family's portal opening and closing. She searched the estate, though none of them were in view. Only the lake sat before them as she wondered who it was that was unwittingly walking into an ambush.

41

WINIFRED
MARVIVIA - 1861

Wading through memories, Winnie traced the steps toward the cave Oslind had shown her days before. Her *very* human body was of no help, however, moving three times slower than the underwater creatures since her stay at Marvivia. Screaming muscles ached for rest. When all of this was over, she'd likely sleep for a month straight to make up from sheer, utter exhaustion.

Their cave is the only safe place where they'd hide, she thought. Though truthfully she didn't know if they'd actually stay there knowing that King Aalto was privy to their relationship. Nonetheless, Winnie hoped her hunch was right and they'd be there healing their collective injuries.

"Are you going to kill them?" Boudicca whispered hopefully.

"No, I'm not going to kill them!" Winnie protested. "I'm going…to figure something out."

"Just end this already!" Aelius bellowed, his own frustration evident as the water around her heated to molten lava.

"I need everyone out of my head! Your insistence on speaking to me this way has given me a constant headache. I'm done listening to you two!"

Only small chuckles echoed through her mind as the two beings heard her complaint. She groaned, kicking harder knowing she was nearing Brenna's home. Not far in the distance, Winnie noticed the soft glow of an orb outside the entrance. *Someone has to be there; I'm sure of it,* she thought.

Before cautiously approaching, Winnie took a moment of rest. She panted inside her helmet, wishing she could master her strange new teleportation powers without needing the fear and adrenaline that seemed to trigger it. Then, some strange essence approached through the water. Oddly familiar but not at all corporeal, it was a mere feeling in her gut. Like falling from high above, or preparing to perform on stage.

"Who's there?"

No one answered at first.

Slithering whispers moved far away before leaching into her helmet, a familiar gust of wind catching her off guard. *"Come..."* the words hissed. *"Come...back..."*

The words seemed to stall, unable to fully form. But she'd know that voice anywhere. Through time and space, her soul would always recognize his.

"Kane?" Her words echoed through the helmet, never escaping into the water.

"Come back to me..." His voice – it sounded so hopeless. Not the same man she'd known since she was a child. So lackluster compared to who she'd grown to love in every sense of the word.

What's happened to you? She wondered, wishing she knew how to respond to his pleas.

"I'm coming!" she cried out, though she didn't know if he'd ever hear her. "Don't worry. I'm ending this. I'm coming back to you."

After a moment's hesitation, she pushed her way into Oslind and Brenna's cave. A dim orb flickered inside just as it had before, reminding her of a smoldering fire. Oslind was nowhere to be seen, though his love lay unconscious on a cot. Her eyes were closed, body lifeless and still. The familiar heap of selkie skins were piled near the door.

How easy would it be to just... Winnie stopped herself before she could finish her thought.

Cautiously, she approached. "Brenna?"

The selkie's eyes fluttered open, glancing around like she didn't know where she was. As if she'd been unconscious for hours. Strips of bloodied fabric lay on the ground, newer ones binding her midsection where the knife embedded itself into her innocent flesh.

"Who's...there?" Unable to maintain focus, her words came out in stutters.

She's too weak. I have to heal her, Winnie thought.

"Just let her die! Take her damned skins, and go home!" Boudicca pushed, the words blaring like an alarm.

When the throbbing headache finally eased, Winnie took a seat across from Brenna. Her eyes remained shut, groaning in pain and too woozy to realize who sat with her. Winnie took a moment to look at the wound, unsure how to help. Oslind had begun to stitch her up it seemed, though he'd left half way through.

"If only I had..." It took a moment before she remembered. "Wes!" Reaching into her pocket, she pulled out the small vial of healing ointment he'd recommended. "He said I'd need it for my friend."

Suddenly, sparks shot down Winnie's spine, feeling like someone was watching her. She turned to see Oslind hovering at the door. His face was contorted into a grimace, fists balled and ready to strike.

His voice was low and calm, pupils dilated wide until the blues of his eyes mimicked the dark abyss just outside. "I should kill you where you stand."

"I want to help. Please, give me a moment to explain," she hesitated, pointing to Brenna's wound. "I have something that will heal her quickly. Let me make this right."

Before she could blink, he rushed toward her and snatched the vial from her hands to examine it. "Why should I trust a word you have to say?"

"I'll tell you everything… from the beginning." Carefully, she withdrew her dagger. He flinched, darting for his own before realizing she was handing it over. *"Elements, I'm sorry. I have to tell him the truth,"* Winnie called out in her mind. She expected them to respond with the usual stinging ring, but instead there was only silence.

Winnie applied the healing ointment carefully before moving onto Oslind's wound next. As she cleaned it, she told him her story just as she'd promised. Starting first with her failure; the seance that started it all. As she relived the last few months aloud, she couldn't help but wonder how it was that she'd survived it all. *How can my friends forgive me for all I've done?*

At last, she explained the deal she'd made. The reason for her arrival in Marvivia; her strange powers to transport through time. He didn't say a word, those same angry eyes just examining her every movement to ensure she wouldn't finish what she started.

"Your father said he would kill my entire family if I didn't do as he said," she explained, applying the ointments on his midsection before finishing up. She examined the contents of the vial, wishing there had been enough left to treat the cuts and bruises on her own body.

"And you thought you'd do as he asks rather than seek our help? You thought it was better to try and kill her rather than find another solution?" His words came out with a bite, every ounce covered in disdain.

"I tried to find a way out. You have to believe me! Even making the deal initially, I knew it was a mistake. But I was desperate. I still am. I need an army! Not just for myself, but for the hundreds of thousands of people the hellhounds will target. Surely you of all people can understand the need to protect the innocent."

He scoffed before asking, "You didn't protect the innocent

when you dug that dagger into someone who thought she was your friend." For a few moments, he waited in silence. The ointments went to work, healing the cauterized wound along his side.

"I tried to break free of the deal when your mother offered a new one," she said at last. "I promised Afissa that I would ensure one of you would end up on the throne, but I can't help until I get back to my time. I thought I'd be able to break the pact with Aalto, and make things right. Help you overthrow him. Put you in power. But he used the blood oath as a way to control me. My father is still trapped down here, and he's threatening to kill the rest of the family, including little me! If that happens, there won't be a future to go back to."

As the gears in his mind turned, Brenna shot up in her cot with a loud gasp. When her dark gaze landed on Winnie, she stifled a cry.

"It's okay, Bren," Oslind calmed, placing a hand on the selkie's back.

"You...tried to kill me!" The selkie's hands reached for her side, realizing the wound was almost entirely healed. She stood, stomping toward Winnie.

Whatever she's about to do, I deserve it, she decided. Without hesitation, Brenna slapped her across the face. With a sharp inhale, Winnie fought back tears. When her eyes reopened, she could only see the hazy outline of the selkie's anger before her. It didn't take long before the flood gates opened and all her emotions came rushing out.

"I'm so sorry!" Winnie sobbed. "I know I royally fucked everything up, but I'm just trying to save my family!"

With a groan, Oslind grumbled, "Quit your blubbering. What exactly did you promise my father?"

"He wants Brenna's skins," she began, wiping her face dry. "And though it's not part of the pact, he now wants proof that you're dead, too."

Oslind's sad gaze looked toward his love before settling back on Winnie. "What time are you from? How long will we have to wait before you can help us overthrow him?"

Brenna's face twisted in confusion, though she said nothing. Winnie paused, unsure she wanted to answer truthfully. But alas, she had no choice.

"Ten years from now…"

"We will fight this fight for another ten years?" He stood, rubbing the back of his head feverishly as though a headache nagged him.

"I know it's not ideal…"

"Not ideal? Are you mad? Not ideal is when your favorite drink isn't available, or you stub your toe. This is complete insanity! We can't keep fighting like this for another decade!"

Brenna sat on her cot, hugging her sides without saying a word.

"In my time, the selkies pose a serious threat to the mermaids. When we asked for help the first time, they couldn't do anything because the selkies kept interfering with their everyday operations. They were under constant attack," she explained.

"Good," Brenna spat, pulling her knees to her chest as outraged eyes remained pinned to Winnie.

"We can't stay here," Oslind added. "We either end this now, or we wait." His words didn't meet Winnie at all. They seemed to bounce right over her, talking only to his love.

Her feet hit the floor, standing with both hands propped on her curved hips. "What are you suggesting?"

"We give my father your skins…and we wait. Find shelter on land, and get Winnie when the time is right." They continued their conversation as though she weren't standing only a few feet away.

"Why are you so quick to give up?" The selkie's rage continued to bubble up, a swirl of air moving through the cave in a fury.

With a defeated sigh, he mumbled, "She's from the future, Bren. Clearly it happens this way, no matter what we do."

Winnie remained quiet, glancing between the two. When the selkie didn't respond, she turned her attention back to Oslind. "Aalto wants proof you're dead. How could we accomplish that without seriously injuring you in the process?"

He pondered for a moment. "He's a sadistic bastard. He'll want to see...flesh."

"You can't possibly think..." Brenna began, though the words never made it past her lips.

"If Winnie takes your skins and a part of...*me*... he'll think we're dead. Hopefully. You can tell him the sharks or the kraken got the rest of us. Meanwhile Brenna and I will escape to land."

"We'll never be safe out there, either. They'll see your scales, and know you're not human," Brenna countered.

Winnie glanced down at the dainty shell necklace that had protected her from recognition all these weeks. "Take this. After I give him your..."

He nodded, avoiding the obvious end of her sentence. "Are you're sure we can overthrow him in your time?"

"You almost had him tonight! You would've won had I not interfered," she pointed out.

"Yes, but he'll be prepared from now on. He'll have more guards to ensure nothing like this can happen again," Oslind mumbled, taking a seat with Brenna and wrapping a loving arm around her.

"He'll think you're dead, remember?" The selkie's words were coupled with sad eyes, her lips in a tight frown as she leaned into his touch.

"I have very powerful allies in my time. They can help us. And if you remain in contact with the selkies over the years, perhaps we can use them. One way or another, the two of you will be on the throne. I know it's not what you wanted but..."

"It's hope," Brenna sighed. "What's ten years of waiting if we're together?" A sad smile formed across her face, nuzzling into his chest for comfort.

"So, uh…which of my *parts* shall we give my father?" He grimaced, looking down at his appendages.

Winnie's face turned to a revolted scowl before asking, "Will he know if it's yours?"

Brenna's attention shot to her in disgust.

"I just mean, will he have some way of knowing if it's yours or some random bloke?"

"I think I'm going to be sick…" the selkie muttered, covering her mouth.

"Yes, he'll know. It has to be from me."

There was a long pause before she finally suggested, "A finger? An ear?"

"This is the most insane conversation I think I've ever had…" he mumbled.

"Can't do finger. He'd expect the whole hand…" Brenna grumbled.

"So…ear?" Winnie asked.

"That wouldn't make sense. How would you get my ear mid-fight just for me to be eaten by a shark?"

With a deep exhale, Brenna stood. "You're not going to like it, but… a part of your fin. Something that would make it impossible for you to get away. Then the shark attack makes sense."

"But then I'm useless in the water. I won't be able to fight when the time comes, ten fucking years from now." With slouched shoulders, Oslind covered his face and groaned.

A booming presence entered the cave without warning. "Perhaps I can be of some assistance there?" The woman's voice was one Winnie recognized immediately, though she'd never heard her so corporeal before. Not even in the strange void they'd met before.

"Gali?"

Oslind and Brenna glanced at each other in confusion. At the entrance of the cave, the pearly walls rippled as the figure of a woman appeared. Before them, the Goddess of Water stood in physical form, for the first time in Winnie's life. Her navy skin glittered by the dim orbs of light, fishing nets and seaweed covering her body. Her pale eyes glanced at the three of them, a delicate smile on her face.

"Goddess!" Oslind managed to say as he and Brenna took a knee.

"No need to bow. I'm here to help," Gali hummed, ushering both sea creatures to stand.

"Thank you for coming! We don't know what to do," Winnie pleaded, approaching the goddess.

"Brenna is right. King Aalto will need something of Oslind that will render him unable to swim as proof. Anything less, and he won't believe you actually killed him. He'll never release you from your blood oath," Gali explained. As she spoke, Winnie felt the familiar rush of warmth flow through her as if it was the first time they'd ever communed.

"I don't want to be useless..." Oslind mumbled, setting aside his pride.

"If you allow Winnie to do this now, I will ensure you regain your ability to swim. When you are placed on the throne, your body will be fully restored. I swear it." Gali held her hand out toward the mermaid.

Carefully, he shook it. "So for the next ten years, we'll be stuck on land? Brenna without her skins and my fins lame. Surely there's a better option."

"If someone had made better choices, perhaps," Gali countered, shooting daggers at Winnie.

Her face heated in embarrassment, looking away from the group. The goddess turned to Brenna now, holding her hand out.

"You want me to shake on it too?"

Gali nodded. "If something happens to you, I'll ensure you're just as restored as your love. You two have important things to do in the future."

Brenna peered toward her skins before nodding. The goddess glanced at Winnie, offering her hand one final time.

"You are a part of this. You are the one to cause them this pain. It is your duty to ensure they end up on the throne in your time, no matter what is happening when you get back. You must usher in peace between the selkies and mermaids," she commanded, her icy eyes examining Winnie carefully.

"Is this part of my tasks?"

"It is now. But you need to hurry. Every moment you're away, Aalto grows more suspicious. Brenna and Oslind need to make their way to shore and then you can..." Her words came to a halt, sad eyes dropping to both of her creatures who'd soon be unable to enjoy their lives as they once were. Winnie could feel the motherly hurt radiating from the goddess.

"Let's just get this over with," Oslind grumbled, heading for the door.

After a lengthy swim back to Hampton, the group made their way toward the shore. Oslind and Brenna spent their last few moments in the water, memorizing themselves in their truest forms.

"I can't even imagine what they're thinking right now," Winnie muttered to Gali, who waited alongside her on the shoreline.

As though Milicent were scolding her, the goddess muttered, "They are saying goodbye to their other halves. For now. You made a real mess of this situation."

"I've been asking for help, and getting nowhere! I don't know what I'm supposed to be doing! And that stupid book is no help, either."

Gali took a deep breath before finally saying, "I fear someone may be interfering with our communication."

"Like who?"

"I suspect Aelius. He's known to be a tricky little wobbegong.

Has he been in your head?"

With a sigh, she admitted, "Always. Boudicca, too. They're constantly pushing me to do things I don't want to do."

"As hard as it may be, you must silence the queen in your mind. I suspect she and Aelius have a greater scheme here. They don't mean you well."

With a furrowed brow, she asked, "I thought the four of you were equals?"

"In a way, yes. But that doesn't mean each of us don't have our own missions. There are those that even we must serve in order to maintain the balance between good and evil."

Winnie took a step back in surprise. The goddess's words took a while to process. "You mean to tell me that there are Gods even you must answer to? I thought you were in charge?"

She nodded solemnly. "There are others. And Fate is a much stronger force than you realize. I'll be keeping a close eye on these two over the next decade. I've been given explicit instruction to ensure they end up on the throne. A mermaid-selkie army combined will be exactly what you need when the time comes. And these two, what their love will create. It's bigger than you can imagine."

Oslind and Brenna at last left the sea behind. Trembling hands offered Winnie her skins, folded neatly with care. Her red eyes, filled with despair, could hardly stand to look Winnie in the face. "Please make sure nothing happens to them. I don't want to be land-bound for all eternity."

"I'll do my best."

"Your best isn't good enough. Make it right, or you'll have me to deal with." Oslind's icy gaze narrowed in on her, awaiting a response.

Winnie gulped, nodding as she accepted the selkie's priceless skin.

Glancing back toward the water one last time, he muttered, "I guess it's time…"

Gali offered her two creatures a sad smile before taking them into her arms. Her towering body stood over them, embracing both in warm blue light.

"It will all work out," she said before letting them go.

"No more waiting. Let's get this over with," he insisted, withdrawing a dagger before he could change his mind.

42

WINIFRED
MARVIVIA - 1861

With Gali's help, Winnie returned to Marvivia. In her bag, she carried her disastrous prizes. The heaping pile of selkie skin. Oslind's bloodied fin. They'd removed just enough to make him useless in his mermaid form, but not enough to incapacitate him entirely. Either way, he'd never swim again.

Winnie's wetsuit was still covered in blood, a reminder of her betrayal. So much so that even the ocean water wouldn't remove the stains. Her stomach churned, feeling sick looking at the crimson stains. *You're almost done,* she thought as she neared the throne room.

"I can't go in with you. This is where we depart. As soon as you're done, you need to get back to your time. Your friends need you," Gali whispered in her mind, offering a final wave of goodbye before vanishing into a school of darting fish.

Pushing her way through the pearly white entrance, Winnie hoped this would be the last time in 1861. Triple the amount of guards and soldiers greeted her arrival, armored to the extreme and shimmering weapons at the ready.

"Let her enter," King Aalto called from his throne, a vicious gaze narrowing in on her bloodied clothing.

To his right, Afissa sat. As soon as she saw Winnie walk in with a stained bag, a whimpering cry echoed through the domed room.

"Is it done?" he asked, staring down at her with distaste. Lingering bruises lined his face, the skin around his eyes puffy from his son's beating.

Reaching into the bag, she first pulled out Brenna's skins, then Oslind's fin. "I would've brought more but we were attacked by a shark. I left when a tentacle almost snagged me. I suspect they both smelled the blood. I barely escaped in time."

King Aalto's lips curved into a devious grin, the face of the devil looking back at her. "Good. You are released from your blood oath. I thank you for your services."

Within her body, her skin began to crawl. Literally. Turning her hands over, the veins beneath bubbled and boiled. Winnie couldn't help but cry out in shock as an internal inferno threw her world off its axis. As though her blood were putrid, slithering beings wriggled their way toward her palms. As the skin split open, the king's festering blood oozed, falling toward the abalone shell floors, sizzling until it vanished entirely.

"The blood oath...is gone? You broke it?" Desperation sat behind her words, thinking of the queen still leeching off of her. He nodded before she asked, "You must simply will it?"

He said nothing, never acknowledging her question. *All this time wasted on tonics and siren songs. Somehow, I need to get Boudicca to let go,* she thought.

"Did you forget I can hear you?" the queen replied with a cackle.

King Aalto snapped his fingers, Ernest's floating body entering from the side of the throne room. The seaweed that bound him dropped, her father able to move about freely as his feet landed on the ground below.

"Lucille? What the devil is going on?" Rage turned his face to a scowl as he rubbed his aching wrists.

"All is well, my new friend. You'll be home before you know it." Aalto snapped again as a group of soldiers offered Ernest his helmet and gear back. "Put it on. Go home. We'll be in touch if you're needed."

Ernest scoffed as if to respond in some sort of a sarcastic way, though Winnie stepped between them. "Take this back to Fox Manor. Keep it safe. You'll need it again one day." Removing her set of gear, she handed it back to her father as he offered her a careful nod.

"That man better not come after my family again. I want nothing to do with this place," he whispered to her. A sort of blame lingered in his eyes as he examined his daughter, the shell necklace still cloaking her identity.

"He won't. You will see Afissa again, but she means you no harm. Quite the opposite, in fact. Avoid the king; make friends with the queen. Trust me." She nodded one last time as he fastened the helmet. The soldiers dragged him back toward the exit, ready to escort him to Fox Manor.

"One last thing," Aalto said as Winnie, too, turned to exit the throne room.

"What more could you possibly want from me?" Winnie sighed, awaiting the king's demands.

"I want you to stay for the show. I have a feeling Brenna's skins may come with other attachments. I want to ensure she's dead."

Winnie's brows furrowed in confusion. His smile once again lit up, eyes wicked with fiery intent. He pointed down at the skins as a nearby soldier reached for them. Though Winnie thought most mermaids wielded water or air, this one seemed different. There was a darkness to him, pupils blazing like flickering flames.

"Burn the skin. Kill the selkie for good. Didn't you know that?" King Aalto sneered as the soldier ignited the heap.

"You bastard!" she cried, reaching for the pile of flaming fur. Before she could call on Gali, nearby soldiers restrained her arms. *Oslind... he'll spend the next ten years alone. This is all my fault,* she thought with devastating realization.

"I had a feeling you were lying about those two," the king chuckled. "No matter. That fin proves my son can never return.

And with his love dead, I know he will live the rest of his life alone and miserable."

Afissa's cries rang through the throne room, down on her hands and knees as if praying to the Gods for mercy.

"Silence yourself, woman. You're the bloody queen. Act like it," Aalto scolded, a telekinetic hand forcing her to stand.

With his back turned, Winnie offered Afissa a knowing nod.

'My son?' she mouthed, though not a sound came out.

When Winnie offered her a sad nod, the queen hesitantly returned to her spot on the throne with a drooping head. An unspoken promise formed between the two women, the queen offering her husband a disdainful glare.

"I hate you," she spat. "I will never forget this day. That you chose power and control over your own blood."

"I could care less," he dismissed, stepping off his throne toward Winnie. "Will you teach me? Your ways of wielding two elements?" A commanding hand grasped Winnie's cheeks to force her to look at him.

Rather than speak, she spat up at him. He flinched, rage and disgust filling his face. "Throw this bitch out into the sea. Ensure the sharks get her. It won't be hard given how much blood she's covered in."

The soldiers nodded, dragging her toward the exit. Before she could be thrown into the waters, she ripped off the shell necklace hiding her identity. Reciting Gali's spell, she sent the necklace to Oslind.

"Memorize my face. Because I'll see you again one day. And when I do, this face will be the last one you'll ever see," Winnie hissed. Afissa's eyes landed on her, curiously examining Winnie's features as though she were connecting dots. *"Alright, Elements. I'm ready to go back now. Send me on my way."*

As the soldiers continued to drag her, she felt the familiar all-over buzz of the incoming jump. Her mind went fuzzy, vision blurring. A persistent ringing in her ears. At last, she released a burst of power, and then she was gone. Mere seconds turned to years as she teleported back to her time, ready to leave 1861 behind. For good.

I have vengeance to fulfill in 1871. For the sake of Oslind and poor Brenna...

When she opened her eyes again, she stood in the center of her family's stone slab altar. She wanted to sigh in relief, but it was short lived. The family's manor stood in flames. Scanning the scene, she couldn't figure out what the hell had happened. A few shadows darted into the woods before she realized they weren't human. Beasts lurked, running back to wherever they came from just as they did the night of Samhain.

Her gaze flickered up on the house once more, readying herself to draw on Gali's powers to subdue the flames.

Then her heart sank.

There, staring down at her, Kane sat at his window behind the piano. The figure of his dearly departed mother with her hand on his shoulder and Death lurking not far behind. With flames raging all around him.

43

KANE
CHICAGO - 1871

The second Kane crossed the threshold onto the estate, every one of Boudicca's hounds seemed to narrow their attention onto him. It looked like they'd brought almost every available beast. Easily a hundred. Maybe more. The siren paused, connecting with Alaric's gaze along the side of the house. Ready to run and get help, a single gunshot fired from behind. The mirror in front of him shattered, the connection to Chicago fading before his very eyes.

"Stay a while," the hellhound leader sang. His beasts stood at attention, awaiting orders. Cocking his gun, he aimed at Kane.

Scanning the property wildly, he realized he hadn't brought any weapons. *How the hell did they get onto the estate this time?* His panicked thoughts sent shock waves through his body. Muffled cries caught his attention, realizing Winnie's parents kneeled on the ground – bound and gagged. Parting his lips, Kane was ready to use his siren song to hinder as many as possible. When the melodies began, his voice faltered. Clutching at his throat, only a gargled choking came out.

Behind Alaric, the figure of a slender woman appeared. Though her face was covered by a scarf, a pair of violet-eyes gleamed back at Kane. Shooting spearing magic his way, the siren's airways tightening until not a single sound came out.

Ernest and Milicent stumbled to their feet at once, working

in partnership to barrel into the strange witch. Knocking her to the ground, the hold on Kane temporarily loosened. He flared his wings, shooting into the sky.

Knowing where a small stash of weapons lay hidden, Kane flew to the opposite side of the house. Gunshots fired at him again and again. Reaching the back of the house, he snagged a bow, satchel of arrows, and a sword. Long range and short range – both vital. *I didn't want to rely on my voice with whatever powers she possesses,* he thought.

The dark shingles creaked under his weight as he landed on the roof. Twenty arrows lay in the quiver, ready to be fired. Taking aim, he said a silent prayer to Caelus before firing. The first two missed his targets entirely. Huddled behind a nearby chimney, he took a moment to settle his breaths. Below, the sounds of orders were a muffled yell. Nocking the arrow, Kane took aim once more. Several took flight, landing in the chests of the hounds surrounding Ernest and Milicent.

"Who's the shitty archer now, Thoren?" he muttered quietly to himself as he readied another arrow. When he stood to aim, he stopped immediately.

"We only need one of them. You either settle yourself or daddy dearest dies." Alaric cocked his gun, digging the barrel into Ernest's forehead. Kane strung up another arrow, aiming directly for the hellhound leader who seemed to tsk in disapproval. "Do you want your lover's father to die? The moment that arrow leaves your bow, he's dead. Care to find out which of us is quicker? I'd wager a bullet beats wood."

Fuck, Kane thought as he lowered his bow and crouched back behind the chimney. *I can't fight them directly, there's too many...*

"Dammit!" he shouted to the heavens, wondering if any of the Gods would take pity on him and send a miracle.

"Get him down by any means necessary. And look for Winnie. We need her the most," he heard Alaric's voice command below.

He peeked over the edge of the roof again, looking at the portal. The mirror may be shattered, but others still existed in various places around the estate. Though none led to Chicago.

"*Caelus, what do I do?*" he cried out, hoping the deity was listening.

"*The house is still warded with your blood,*" he whispered, a rush of warm air ruffling Kane's hair.

"*How could I have forgotten? Thank you!*"

He peered down, half the hounds leaving to search for the siren. The violet-eyed witch stalked at the front of the pack, giving him a small window to attempt an attack below. Leaping from the roof, Kane shot his last two remaining arrows before readying his sword for one-on-one combat. As he neared, another group of hounds surrounded Winnie's parents.

Kane swooped down, aiming for Alaric first. He knocked into the hellhound as the gun fell to the ground. There were only moments to spare before the others were right on his tail. He swung his sword, hoping to slice and maim anyone nearby. A dozen or so beasts lunged forward all at once before he shot a forcefield of air in defense. It only bought him a moment of time.

The cocking of a gun caught Kane's attention again, turning to see a hellhound behind him with a pistol in her hand. Another wall of air guided the bullets away and toward the hounds behind him before he plunged his sword deep into her gut. Another set attacked from his side as he wildly swung, unsure where to aim first. It didn't seem to matter as long as he hit *something*. Never had he been surrounded by so many enemies at one time without his brother to back him up.

"Milicent!"

His words hardly carried over the carnage before him as he tried to get her attention. To buy him even a moment of time, Kane released a quick siren song to incapacitate the hoard. Without his full attention, it would only last a moment.

"The house!" he cried, jutting his chin toward the manor before driving his blade into the gut of a nearby attacker.

She nodded, turning toward Ernest as if trying to communicate the plan. As she did, Kane noticed her hands bound behind her back, a set of glowing purple cuffs around her wrists with strange runes and symbols glowing in the metal. *There must be a good reason why she's not helping me,* he realized. Kane looked back at the manor, noticing the other hounds were running from the other side of the estate with the violet-eyed witch in front.

"Fuck!" he bellowed, continuing to swing at anyone who dared come near him. *They. Just. Keep. Coming.* The panic coursing through his veins was enough to blind him.

First, he heard her cry. Then, he heard the pang of a bullet. Lastly, the thud of a body. Kane's attention snapped toward those sounds as Ernest slumped forward, Milicent attempting to scramble to her feet.

The moment of weakness – of pause – was deadly.

A warmth spread through him, turning to a blinding burn before he realized what happened. With a sharp inhale, he glanced down. The gleam of a metal blade was sunken deep in his gut, a hound's face lighting in victory.

Kane pulled back from the sword, taking flight into the sky. He barreled for Milicent, trying to reach her in time. But he flew sloppily, dipping as the sharp sting from his gut coursed through him. Gripping his midsection, he tried to keep his blood from spilling like water onto the dead winter grass of Fox Manor. His stomach turned from fiery hot to icy cold as more crimson slipped through his clutching fingers.

Moments before he could reach Milicent, Alaric stepped between them. The gun was aimed directly for Kane, narrowly avoiding the bullet that would've been a twin to Ernest's wound. When he looked back at Milicent, he saw it.

'Go,' her eyes seemed to say. *'Save yourself.'*

He let out a high pitched screech before barreling through the door of the manor. Safe behind the wards, but not safe from the bullets that riddled the home. A few hounds attempted to file in behind him, though a sharp blast of energy sent them flying back.

Ducking behind a curtain, he watched as the hounds dragged Milicent and Ernest into the woods. *Where the hell are they going?* Alaric stood for a moment, analyzing the house. He motioned to the violet-eyed witch as she raised her hand, sparks trickling from her fingertips. Before he knew it, the base of the manor was in flames.

Looking down at his stomach, Kane knew he didn't have much time left before he'd lose consciousness. The air in the manor heated as the fire slowly lapped at the wood, rising higher. Attempting to run for the exit, he realized a group of hounds waited for him outside. He narrowly avoided another shot, jumping to the side to avoid being hit once more.

I'm trapped.

Groaning from the pain, Kane darted toward the stairs. In his room, he'd hidden a few vials of Milicent's healing ointment and he needed them *now*. Clumsy feet led him up the stairs toward his familiar room, the wicked inferno below slowly creeping behind him.

Pushing through the door, he ran toward the nightstand that contained the ointments. Taking a seat at the piano, he watched the hounds outside circle Fox Manor to ensure he couldn't escape. Defeat washed over him, failure's fingers digging deep under his skin and into the very essence of his soul. Crimson dripped onto the dark floorboards below as he clutched his stomach in agony. Though, the pain somehow seemed to lessen the more blood he lost. He examined the vial in his hands carefully.

Do I even bother?

Lowering his head onto the piano, the feeling of Death's grasp tightened on his shoulder. The smell of smoke crept into the room from the consuming flames below, threatening to choke him. It wasn't until a familiar scent overpowered the fire that his head jutted up once more. Though his vision was peppered with small spots, the outline of a being surprised him.

"Gióka mou..."

His heart seemed to ease a little, recognizing that voice. That perfume. Death's grasp loosened on his shoulder, retreating for a moment. Before him, she stood. His mother.

My son, she'd said softly in their native tongue.

"M-Mo-Mom?" he whispered, his consciousness fading in and out.

"Gióka mou," she repeated. "It's not your time."

"It is," he insisted. "I'm done. I've failed one too many times. I don't have any fight left in me." Tears streamed down his face, a strange full-bodied euphoria washing over him as the pain lessened even more.

"I know you're tired, my son, but I need you to be strong just a little while longer." A gentle hand reached for his own, guiding him toward the vial that now sat on the piano.

He shook his head, turning away. *I can't stand to look her in the eyes,* he thought. "I failed you. Dad. I've failed everyone I've ever loved. I cannot recover from this."

"If you cannot live for yourself, then live for *me.* For my memory. You only fail me if you choose to give up now. You cannot let the darkness take you like it took your father." Her soft, angelic voice pulled him from his strange trance, realizing that she'd guided his hand to begin applying the healing ointment. Softly, she hummed the lullaby from his childhood, a wave of sorrow and new pain washing over him.

The sting of his wound gently eased, ever so slightly. The ointments wouldn't be enough to heal him, that he knew for sure. But perhaps it could buy him some time.

"It worked," his mother whispered. Reaching for his hand

again, she guided it toward the lid of the piano.

His brows knit together in confusion, watching as his body moved without control. "What do you mean?"

"Your spell. With Winnie. It worked. It just wasn't the right time." She leaned down and offered him a gentle kiss on his forehead. Just as she did, something slid from the inside of the piano.

Kane looked down in confusion, a letter falling into his lap. He grabbed it, recognizing Winnie's handwriting immediately. His attention sharpened, Milicent's ointments beginning to heal. The smell of his mother's perfume lessened, the smoke from below creeping down the hall and making its way closer and closer to him as he read.

Kane,

I know you said that things have felt different between us. That's my fault. I wish I could tell you everything that's happening, but there are forces at work far greater than you know. Trust me when I say – I am yours. And everything I'm doing is for my family, and the family I hope to one day have. Please be safe while I'm gone.

I hear your song every day and night. My heart aches for you, knowing you're searching for me. I can feel your essence rooting into every fiber of my being. It's as though someone has taken my soul and split it in half, leaving it with you for safe keeping. You're always with me, our hearts tied together. When I hear your voice, I can only count the minutes until I come back to you.

With you, I am home.

Your Winifred

Kane let out a stifled cry, looking back up to see his mother one last time. She squeezed his shoulder, grabbing the side of his face and guiding it to look back out the window. At last, he saw *her*. That familiar head of curly black hair, amber eyes looking up at him in a panic. His love, scheming how best to save him from the inferno.

44

·•((●●●))•·

WINIFRED
FOX MANOR - 1871

Winnie's mind raced, trying to understand the chaos before her. The last of the hellhounds darted into the woodline, likely not realizing she'd shown up at all. Above her, Kane pounded on the window in a panic. A soft glow illuminated his figure, flames creeping into the room behind him.

"Open the window!" Shouting as loud as her voice could muster, it didn't seem to carry.

His firsts rapped on the glass until he seemed to understand what she was telling him. With a shatter, the windows broke as he stuck his head out. "I can't fit! The window is too small!"

"Stay where you are! I'm coming to get you!" Racing toward the house, she called out to her goddess. *"Gali, please help me!"*

Envisioning blue lights, she tried to funnel the clear liquid trickling from her fingertips toward the treacherous fire. Balls of water shot toward the manor, one after another. As her waves lapped at the burning heat, nothing seemed to help. The inferno continued, more and more of the house slowly consumed by the blaze.

"Our water won't be enough to stop this form of magic," Gali explained quietly. *"You'll need to think outside the box. She who started the fire has tapped into the most sinister of power."*

Winnie let out a groan before coming up with a new plan. *If I can't stop the flames, I'll just have to walk through them.* Forming an encapsulating ball of water, her wetsuit proved useful once again.

Though her mind was slowly screaming for rest, overexertion wouldn't be what stopped her now.

"Caelus, can I borrow you again?" Hopefully, she waited for a response.

With what could only be described as a groan, the God of Air replied, *"Only because one of my best is trapped inside."*

Pushing her way into the burning house, the flames nearly consumed her. Though the water kept her from igniting, the heat threatened to boil her alive. Regardless, she trudged on.

At last, she reached Kane's room. The door stood wide open, Death waiting patiently in the corner. "Back off! He's not yours to take!" Her words came out gargled, but nonetheless the being seemed to get her message.

"You better hurry up or I'll claim you both." Death's slithering words echoed through her with a low, haunting chuckle.

Kane turned toward the door, eyes widening at the bubble of water protecting her body. Reaching through the barrier, blistering heat singed her skin as she waited for him to take her hand.

"I'll drown!"

Sticking her head through, she yelled, "Stay here, and you'll burn! Just trust me!" Smoke scalded her lungs with every breath she attempted.

With a cautious nod, he accepted her hand. Pulled into the water, his face contorting in fear as Kane clutched his throat. As though it were second nature, she grabbed his cheeks. Planting her lips firmly on his, her air bubble passed to him. Realizing he could suddenly breath, his expression softened before noting the incoming flames.

Just outside his room, the blaze grew hotter and hungrier. Winnie pulled him along, watching as her family's photos diminished to ash. Only one still remained, the arms of the raging fire reaching for a photo of the entire family with little Wesley standing before little Winnie. With a quick snatch, she grabbed it as they continued to fight their way downstairs.

They'd reached the stairs when Winnie glanced over her shoulder at Kane. His eyes dimmed, clutching his stomach and face twisting in agony. Tugging at his arm, she begged him silently to move faster. Her mind felt like it could split open any moment, the intensity of the flames breaking down the wall of protection she'd cast. The blaze moved like a living being, lapping at them the way Boudicca's flames once had. Half way down the stairs and only a few feet away from the exit, Kane stumbled forward.

"We're almost there!" The water in their ears made it almost impossible for either to hear the other. "Only a few more steps! Hang in there!"

Behind them, Death continued waiting patiently. Every time Winnie glanced over her shoulder, she saw the entity lurking – the familiar cloud of smoke waiting.

Kane's head drooped, feet stumbling along the ground. A limp arm fell to his side, no longer clutching the crimson stained clothes. His weight caught her off guard, both crumbling to the floor. Caelus's air bubble ceased, only moments away from drowning in her magic.

"Dammit Kane! Get up! Please!" She had mere seconds to spare. *I can't drop the water. We'll burn. But letting him stay here isn't an option either.*

"*What's your plan now, little witch?*" Boudicca mocked, the markings on Winnie's arm glowing in delight at the kindred magic surrounding them.

"*Elements! Please help me!*" she cried out, trying desperately to pull him toward the door. *He's too heavy. I can't move him...*

Clutching him to her chest, she buried her head into his body. The water surrounding them bubbled hotter and hotter, as she thought: *I will not leave him. I will not let him die alone.* The hellhound's strange flames leeched their way through her barrier, nipping at their skin like vicious little predators. Squeezing her eyes shut, she prayed for a miracle.

A moment passed when glowing azure light shot through the house like lightning bolts. Every crack and crevice filled with the strange majestic magic, the flames shrieking as they retreated. Waves crashed through the manor, chasing away the inferno for good. Placing her lips on Kane's, Winnie shared her air with him until the water ceased and air could return at last.

When her bubble of water finally cooled, she dropped her shield. Splashing to the ground, Kane was able to breath on his own again. Glancing over her shoulder, two familiar figures waited at the entrance. Glittering milky white hair and twin blue eyes stared at her, Afissa and Oslind waiting for an explanation.

"You came…just in time," she wheezed, still clutching Kane in her lap.

"We had a deal, remember?" Oslind's familiar cocky smirk was a welcomed sight as he approached. At first glance, Winnie almost didn't notice the foot he was missing, replaced by a temporary wooden one. Nonetheless, he limped toward her. "Why don't we get you two out of here? The flames may be temporarily subdued, but the smoke can still kill you."

He and his mother helped Winnie drag Kane outside onto the cold, grassless field. Winnie leaned down, feeling for a pulse. He still had one, thankfully, though his eyes didn't open and his body didn't move. They both shivered, their soaking wet bodies fighting the icy December wind.

"Kane…please. Can you hear me?"

Beside her, Afissa crouched down. She offered a familiar vial of healing ointment before adding, "Glad I always have one of these on me."

Winnie took it with a grateful nod, examining Kane's midsection. She could see some ointment had already been applied, his siren blood working to heal him. *Not fast enough, though,* she thought. Applying more onto the wound, she prayed to every being, entity, and god she could think of. In this universe and every other universe, she hoped someone would have mercy on them and save him for another day.

Regardless, his breathing slowed.

His pulse became even slower.

"No!" Placing her ear on his chest, she listened for any signs of life.

Without even thinking about it, she began to hum. Thinking back to their reunion, Winnie pictured their first hug after two years apart. The way he'd lifted her, then spun her around. Offered her love without her ever having to ask for it. Thought of their dance in the hallway; the melody she'd heard from the house as it played for only them. She mimicked the notes, clinging to that memory. The way his longing eyes had stared down at her, a sad smile across his face.

The song spilled from her lips as carefree as though it were second nature. And then, at last, she watched as his midsection slowly healed. Without asking questions, she continued her slow, quiet tune. A moment passed before his eyes shot open, darting around in confusion.

"Winnie?" he managed to wheeze, reaching for the side of her face.

"You're healed!"

"How did you..." Kane's hand landed on his stomach.

"I don't really care, to be honest. I'm just so thankful you're okay!" A happy tear rolled down her cheek as he sat up. Clutching the side of her face, he brought his forehead to hers.

"I thought I lost you..."

"I'm so sorry I had to leave! I didn't want to, I swear. I wish I could explain everything," Winnie cried, weeks of emotions spilling from her tear ducts.

"Don't ever leave without me again, Fox," he scolded, planting his lips on her own. "I'll follow you to the ends of this earth to never have to go through that again."

Gently, he reached toward her and wiped away the tears streaming down her face. Her heart fluttered as he moved closer, offering her another commanding kiss. When he pulled away, she could only leap forward and embrace him harder, never wanting to part again.

Behind them, Oslind cleared his throat.

Winnie glanced over her shoulder before helping her love off the ground. "Kane, meet Oslind. Afissa's son."

He stretched his hand toward the mermaid, shaking it in welcome.

"So you're the siren. I've heard quite a bit about you," Oslind noted, crossing his arms over his chest. "And you, Winnie, haven't aged a single bit since I last saw you. Not even your clothes. Did you just get back?"

With a nod, she teased, "You got old." Though truthfully, it seemed the last ten years had only helped Oslind's features sharpen, making him devastatingly handsome in his prime. Kane flashed a confused look down at Winnie who shook her head. "I'll explain what I can later."

"I'm ready to call in our deal."

"We don't have time for anything right now. We have to get to the hellhounds," Kane interrupted. "They have Tara and your parents! Your dad was shot right before they were dragged off. They've been harassing us for weeks since you've been gone. We only just got Ezra back from their camp this morning!"

"My dad! Is he okay?" Panic laced words slipped from her mouth.

"I don't know. I didn't really have time to sit around and find out." Sad eyes avoided her own as he spoke.

Winnie's mind began to race. "Did I really miss that much while I was gone?"

"Yes, it's been chaos since you vanished."

"A deal's a deal. I've waited ten years for this. You swore you'd help immediately, no matter what was going on when you got back. Help me overthrow my father now, and you'll finally have your army. Then we can help you with your hellhound problem," Oslind insisted.

Afissa lay a careful hand on her son's shoulder as if it could talk him out of his insistence. He ignored her, glaring at Winnie impatiently.

"Any chance you can help make a new portal? Alaric broke the one to Chicago," Kane added, glancing toward the shattered mirror.

"We weren't powerful enough with my family's full coven and just your powers alone," she reminded, staring at Afissa in worry.

"But you didn't have me."

Winnie's attention snapped to the sound of a familiar voice not far away. Her broken heart began to mend itself, realizing who stood at the edge of the family's lake.

"Brenna? You're alive?" Winnie cried, running toward the selkie. She examined her all over, not a single burn or scar visible. "Aalto burned your skins! He said it would kill you!"

"Normally it would," she hissed. "But I suppose having the favor of not only Caelus, but also Gali, helps protect one from all-consuming flames. I'm land-bound without my skins, but I'm not dead."

She released a heavy sigh of relief. "I thought I got you killed. I thought Oslind would have to spend ten years alone, stuck on land."

With a beaming smile, Oslind looked to his love. "We made a little life together off the coast of the Chesapeake Bay in a small fishing town. It's been quiet, but we're ready to go home."

Brenna turned toward the water before calling out, "It's alright, come on out!"

Two small faces poked out of the lake, dark round eyes

examining the wreckage before them.

"These are our twins, Caspian and Cordelia." Loving arms reached around both children, pulling them toward the selkie.

"Hello you two," Winnie crooned. "You look so much like your mother!" she noted, seeing the reddish hues of their hair, the wide set dark eyes. "They have scales like you, Oslind."

"They're the first ever mermaid-selkies that we know of. Pretty powerful little buggers, too," he noted, pride beaming over his face as he walked to his love's side, and put a loving arm over her shoulder.

"After you left ten years ago, I went searching for them," Afissa began. "Once I saw your true face, I knew there was more to your story. The look you gave me before disappearing told me all I needed to know."

Kane glanced down at her in confusion. "Ten years ago?"

Winnie grimaced, thinking: *How the hell can I explain all of this to him without revealing the truth?*

"I told Aalto I was simply seeing your mother, when really she was helping me find them. I've kept tabs on them all these years. Then eight years ago, they had these two beauties! It's a shame I'll never get to share with my own husband that we're grandparents." The queen's sad eyes dropped to the ground. "But it's time. His rule has only become more cruel since last you saw him."

"What say you? Ready for another fight?" Brenna challenged.

"Gods I'm tired," Winnie sighed. "Let's get this over with."

45

TARA
HELLHOUND CAMP - 1871

All day, Tara waited. Every noise she tried to decipher, hoping Alaric would return with an explanation. Completely isolated, the violet-eyed woman had left hours ago with two hounds on guard outside. *I'll never make it past them,* she knew. There were no weapons to be seen; nothing that she could use to defend herself. *If this is a trick, Alaric was smart,* she thought. *I played right into his games.*

As the sun set and the moon rose, Tara overheard strange noises outside. Pressing her ear to the lining of the tent, she listened. The clanking of metal poles or pots and pans accompanied hounds shouting orders, the entire camp on the move. Except her.

Tara took a seat on Alaric's bed, gingerly rubbing her aching temples. Her head felt heavy, with a dry mouth and clammy hands. Beneath her chest, her heart beat strange patterns as she awaited her fate. A gnawing hunger throbbed through her entire body, despite the small piece of bread a hound had dropped off around midday.

Finally, she heard him outside.

"Begin tearing down my tent. I'll get her now."

"Alaric?" Her words were rushed, jumping from his bed.

He entered, two hounds attempting to join them. "Stay outside. I'll handle this." Alaric strode forward, offering her a tender kiss. As his lips planted along her own, heat sprung beneath her chest, lowering until it hit her gut. When they parted, she couldn't help but bury herself into his chest as strong arms wrapped around her.

"What's going on?" Her words came out muffled, attempting to keep it together.

She glanced up at his dazzling blue eyes as he grasped the base of her chin. Leaning down as though he'd kiss her again, he hissed, "I figured that would've been obvious by now."

With a whimper, she pushed him away. "I... believed you. When you said you weren't as awful as the others said you were." She paused, waiting for an answer.

With a scoff, he finally said, "To be fair, I never denied your friends' accusations."

"Was all of it a lie? Everything? The hounds tellin' me their stories? The cure? What you said to me while we were..."

"Yes and no. Every truth can be manipulated to fit a certain need." A careful hand tucked a strand of hair behind her ear as he stepped a little closer.

"The cure?" Hopeful eyes looked at him, tears glittering her waterline.

"There may be one, but it's not a priority. Sorry, little fawn. The Wolfsbane method is usually effective, as I said. Unless of course you don't apply it properly." A quick glance landed on her ankle. He seemed to note the distraught written across her face, adding, "The hellhounds told their truth. All they've ever wanted was to be normal. But life has a funny way of beating mercy out of you."

"If you would've just given me a chance, I could've talked to the others. We could've actually looked for a cure. Helped your people. But now, you're no more than the monster they made you out to be."

Alaric reached for her again, attempting to rest his hand along her cheek in comfort. Tears leaked from her eyes as she swatted his hand away.

"Why?"

His face turned to a tight frown, avoiding her glaring gaze. "One day, perhaps you'll realize that this is about more than just a cure. More than just Boudicca."

"Why me?" The words barely escaped her lips.

"Your heart. Fortunately for your friends, it's one of the biggest I've seen in centuries. But unfortunately for you, it's also what makes you vulnerable to people like me. For now, I just need you to come along. Don't fight; don't make a fuss. Come with me, and you'll be safe."

"I'm not going anywhere with you after what you did!" she spat, shoving him away.

"If you don't come with me willingly, my sister will kill you. She's bloodthirsty enough as it is. Any sign of a struggle, and she'll simply end you."

With a hiss, she asked, "Why do you even care what happens to me?"

Alaric stared at her for a moment, guilt-ridden eyes examining her before his gaze darted away again. Taking a seat on the edge of his bed, he sighed. "I had no choice, Tara. I know you think I'm cruel and awful. I'd be obliged to agree with you. But if there's one thing you need to know about me, it's that I'll do whatever it takes to keep what's left of my family whole. Unfortunately, you're simply caught in the crossfires. Without your necklace, I had nothing."

Tara took a seat beside him as both sat in silence for a moment. Heat stung the back of her throat, the same gnawing hunger from earlier in the day driving her to near madness, unsure if she wanted to cry or rip his face off.

Releasing a heavy sigh, she whispered, "You could've simply asked."

He nodded in silence, pulling the necklaces from his pants pocket and twirling them around his fingers. Guilt stirred deep inside her, realizing that despite the situation, she still wanted him desperately.

"At this point, my friends hate me for siding with you in the first place. I have no family to go home to. Cricket is god knows where. I have literally nothing! I thought I had you, at the bare minimum. But now I see that's not the case either."

"I had a feeling you would've helped us. But sometimes the easiest thing to do is the most insincere."

Pointing down to his hands, she asked, "Can I at least have them back?"

"Not yet. Eventually, but not right now. We still need them." Carefully, he tucked them away into his pants pocket again, turning his body toward her.

"Whatever you do, please don't lose my family's necklace. It's all I have left of them."

Alaric nodded, cupping the side of her face. "I know you probably hate me, but for what it's worth, you still have me. I'm sorry, Tara. I wish things could've been different."

"You should be sorry," she huffed, swatting his hand away again and hopping off the bed. "Count your days, traitor."

"We have to go now." Grabbing her arm, he turned her to face him. Alaric held out a piece of cloth, motioning to extend her wrists.

"If anyone's gettin' tied up, it's you. Remember?" A dark smirk graced her lips, glancing toward the bed. "What do you think your pack would think if they knew their all-powerful leader liked giving up control in the bedroom?"

With an eye roll, he bound her wrists. "Maybe I should bind that mouth of yours, too." Pulling out a second piece of cloth, he added, "For your eyes. You can't see where we're going."

With a final glare, she conceded. "I'll never forgive you for this."

"I know," Alaric responded with what sounded like a sad chuckle before blocking out her vision entirely. "One more for the road…"

Before she knew it, his lips caressed her own. Though her insides screamed, begging for more, she instead gripped his lower lip with her teeth and sunk them as deep as she could until she tasted the coppery tang of blood. With a grunt, he ripped her off of him, though a bone-chilling chuckle rattled her to her bones. It mimicked the same laugh that rang through her ears the night of Samhain. *How could I forget the beast who stands before me?* she thought.

"I should've shot you between the eyes the moment you called me a cupcake," she hissed, spitting his blood at what she assumed was his feet.

"Just remember to stay quiet. My sister won't be as patient with you as I've been," he muttered, pulling her along, and pushing her head down to exit the tent.

The feeling of cold December winds brushed against her skin as clumsy feet carried her to an unknown location. "Where are we going?" she whispered, wondering if this mysterious sister of his was closeby.

"Sh," he snapped. "Not a word, or you're dead."

Tara groaned for a moment as Alaric stepped away. Still blindfolded, her senses felt oddly disoriented trying to track the noises around her. Not far off, she heard what sounded like a portal opening.

"Why are you bleeding? Did that little bitch bite you?" That strange, sing-songy female voice carried to Tara's ears. With a dark chuckle, she added, "She'd make a good fighter on our side if I didn't think she'd turn on us in an instant. We're not taking her!"

Alaric's voice followed suit, commanding yet playful. "I'm not done with her yet."

The woman groaned. "You are disgusting."

All Alaric did was laugh, and for a moment Tara couldn't tell which version of him was genuine. The one who'd apologized in the tent, or the one who'd diminished her down to some plaything.

"Tara?"

The sound of her name caught her off guard, moving her blindfolded face around to try and decipher who she heard.

"Tara, are you alright?"

"Milicent?" she cried out, recognizing the voice at once.

"I'm fine, but Ernest…" Winnie's mother suddenly whimpered, followed only by muffled screams.

"I should've known you wouldn't follow directions," Alaric scolded, placing a cloth over Tara's mouth to ensure her silence.

"If she causes us any trouble, I won't hesitate to kill her!" Tara could feel the sister's deadly presence directly in front of her. "I don't like you. I don't trust you. One wrong move, and you're dead," she hissed, sounding less like a deranged doll and more like a commanding warrior queen. Oddly similar to Boudicca.

All Tara did was nod, lowering her head in submission. Then, hands grabbed her arms again and pulled her toward swirling winds. Within moments, she felt the familiar zap of a portal coursing through her, landing somewhere unknown as the echoes of a sorrowful howl called in the distance.

MELINDA

Melinda paced back and forth along the hallways of the Chicago Orphan Asylum. The sounds of the children's lesson echoed alongside the pitter patter of seamstresses as they worked on their many projects to help restore some order to Chicago. A strange tingle sent shivers down her spine, a cloud of stagnant energy drawing her toward the hallway.

Something doesn't feel right, she thought, approaching Thoren. "Any word?"

He shook his head as the two walked toward the portal.

A nagging worry nestled into her mind as she asked, "Shouldn't he be back by now? It's been a little too long."

"Maybe he's gathering supplies with Milicent and Ernest." Though Thoren's words came out as a suggestion, his tone revealed a hidden question.

"I think we should head to the manor, just in case. The energy is…strange," Melinda mumbled, motioning for the mirror gateway. A cloud of that same stale magic clung to the reflective surface, blocking her view of the manor beyond.

Reaching for the doorway to the other side of the world, his fingers lay along the surface. It didn't ripple as usual. Instead, it appeared as a mundane mirror without ever revealing the hidden connection.

Stepping forward, she placed her hand along the surface as well. The haze covering it moved away from her touch, but remained nearby. "Is it not working?"

"No, it's not." He tried desperately again and again, though it appeared more ordinary with every attempt. At last, he released a deep sigh as his eyebrows narrowed in on the mirror. She could tell he was doing something magical, though couldn't exactly understand. It wasn't until the mirror before them cracked that her heart sank.

"What does that mean?"

"The portal's been closed for some reason. Something must've happened," Thoren panicked. His hand retreated from the reflection only to run through his dark hair before pacing in nervous circles.

"How do we open it again? Surely there's a way. I've seen you all do it before." Running her fingers along the cracked edges, the stagnant energy seemed to ease a little.

"I don't have enough people here to open another portal. Our only way back to the manor is by taking a fucking boat." His words came out a shallow grumble before he took a seat on a nearby chair and rubbed his head. "Winnie's gone. Her parents are gone. Now my brother, too? What more do you want from me?" Though his words initially came out a mere mumble, the last of them seemed to shout toward the sky as if the heavens could hear him.

Sauntering from around the corner, Ezra joined them. Holding a stack of clothing from the seamstresses, he placed them near the stairwell alongside other donations for nearby families. Crouching before his love, he asked, "What's wrong?"

"Kane is still at Fox Manor, and now the portal is closed. We're all stuck." Thoren's eyes darted away from his love, leg bobbing beneath him and hands clutching his face.

Ezra took a seat on the ground, rubbing his head. "I wish I could say we'll figure this out, but I wouldn't even know where to begin."

"Me either," the siren mumbled.

Ezra stood, hesitant steps approaching the mirror. He touched the cracks just as Melinda had, only this time she couldn't help but notice a radiant green glow stir beneath the surface.

"What about Alaric's camp? They had portals throughout London. I'd be willing to bet there's some there, too," she suggested.

The siren nodded before adding, "They'd likely be warded against anyone other than the hellhounds, though. I don't know how we'd get through."

As the group brainstormed, a feverish knocking rapped on the door below. Melinda ran to open it, Spencer standing on the other side with one arm braced on the frame and the other clutching his panting chest. Thoren and Ezra weren't far behind, awaiting answers alongside her.

Pulling him inside from the cold, she asked, "Spence, what's wrong?"

His hands moved with articulate speed, eyes searching between the three of them for anyone to understand.

"Slow down. Remember, I'm still learning." Placing her hands on his arms, the touch seemed to steady him.

He cleared his throat before saying, "The camp. They're

packing up to leave!"

Melinda snagged her coat off the rack as Spencer urged them all to follow. The four of them sprinted toward the woods, following after the young man whose feet thumped along the ground in a fury.

Halfway to the camp, Melinda grabbed his arm breathless and panting. "Hold on! I need a minute."

"There's no time! If we don't hurry, they'll be gone before we get back," he urged, pulling at her to continue running. With a heavy sigh, each person in the group picked up the pace again.

Eventually, the group stumbled onto the outskirts of what was once the hellhound camp. Only this time, there were no fires lit. The tents were almost all torn down. Only a few remains of the camp still stood, some wooden poles here and there or the occasional pile of wood. Not a soul moved about the area.

From the side, a shadow darted behind a tree. Spencer whistled a quick tune before two figures popped out. Riah and Danny stepped out, armed and ready in case of an ambush.

Spencer signed to his siblings who merely nodded in response.

"This way," Riah added, ushering the group further forward.

Up ahead, Melinda noticed a familiar symbol carved into the ground. "This looks just like the altar at Fox Manor."

"Can we use it to get back to London?" Ezra asked, looking toward the siren for answers.

Thoren shook his head. "Symbol or no symbol, we're still missing a complete coven to create such a large passageway."

"They hurried off through an opening over there. It looked rather strange. Like the brightest fire I've ever seen," Danny explained. "They walked through it and just disappeared. I had to rub my eyes to be sure I was awake to see the whole thing."

"By the time we got over there, the glow was gone and all we saw were the woods just behind," Riah added, bracing her hand on her hip.

"Sounds like a portal to me," Melinda sighed. "I wish I could go back to not knowing about magic." She stepped toward the area the Broderick trio noted, attempting to locate the magical doorway without success.

"I know what that feels like," Ezra chuckled, feeling along the tree trunks with her.

"I don't feel anything at all. What do we do?" Melinda's eyes jumped from one person to the other. "Right now, I'm feeling awfully helpless."

"The only thing we can do," Thoren said with a sigh as he too tried to locate the portal. "Go back to the orphanage and wait. Pray that this is just a misunderstanding, and hope that Milicent will be able to reopen the portal and get us back to the manor. Otherwise..."

"We're screwed," Ezra finished.

Melinda placed a few markings on the trees notated by Riah and Danny. As her blade dug into the wood, the sound of a sad howl startled the group. They turned as she noticed a familiar looming set of tawny yellow eyes.

"I'd know that beast anywhere," Melinda crooned, crouching down so Cricket could run to her. She offered him a few quick scratches before standing back up.

"But...we sent him to the manor. If the portal is closed, how did he get here?" Ezra wondered aloud, offering the shuck a few quick pets as well.

The beast seemed to nod, his eyes darting behind them. Getting up and running toward an opening between two trees, he disappeared at once behind a flash of bright light.

"That right there!" Danny cried out. "That's what I saw earlier! The exact same thing!"

Thoren and Ezra traced Cricket's steps, though it didn't get them anywhere. They tried a few more times without success before the shuck's head poked out. He barked at the group, as if he couldn't understand why they weren't following him.

"I don't think we can cross through the threshold like you can," Melinda said gently, patting him on the head.

"Maybe shucks are similar enough to hellhounds that their wards don't recognize him," the siren suggested.

"Not sure how that helps us," Ezra added, leaning against a nearby tree and rubbing his head feverishly.

"It might not be much, but it's a start. We can work with this."

"Come on boy." Melinda ushered Cricket to follow, patting her leg as he joined her side. "Let's get back to the orphanage. Surely Kane and Winnie's parents will return soon."

Slowly, the group began their slow trudge back to the Chicago Orphan Asylum, guided by the moon and stars hanging heavy in the sky as soft snow blanketed the forest floor.

46

·‹‹●●›)·

WINIFRED
FOX MANOR - 1871

As the group readied themselves, Winnie couldn't help but notice how quiet Kane was. She thought perhaps being separated for weeks, he'd be more happy to see her. But instead he avoided her, in a constant state of movement fussing over every little detail of his wetsuit. The skin-tight material hugged his sculpted body, making her wish they had a few moments alone together to explore the muscles beneath.

Standing in the charred sunroom, the breathing apparatuses had thankfully been unaffected by the raging flames. Handing him a helmet and fins, his eyes lit up momentarily.

"I've always wanted to try one of these suits! Since I was a child."

"Now's your chance," she said with a half-hearted smile. "You know you don't have to come with us, right?"

"Why wouldn't I? I'm not going to let you lead some attack on Marvivia without helping." The excitement on his face seemed to fade, a strange insistence replacing them.

"I know you must be terribly confused right now. Maybe even a little upset with me. And you have every right to, but…"

With a scoff, he asked, "I have the right to be? I've been beside myself these last few weeks. I honestly was beginning to think you were dead. None of us thought you were coming home. Where the hell were you? And why did you not write to me, or reach out other than that strange hidden letter?"

She opened her mouth, trying to think of a possible explanation. She set the second suit down, taking a seat on the sopping wet loveseat.

"We leave in five," Oslind called from outside the room, offering them a contentious wave.

She nodded before turning her attention back to Kane. "There's so much I want to tell you, but I just can't."

"He tried to warn me…" Kane mumbled.

"Huh?"

"Oslind said something about ten years ago." An accusing finger pointed at the mermaid waiting just outside. "How could you have helped them ten years ago? You would've been a child. He said you haven't changed at all. You better give me some answers, Winnie. My patience is running thin."

Sitting in silence, she finally thought of what to say. "My powers are growing." As the words escaped her lips, a dull ring of warning from the Elements appeared in the forefront of her mind. She winced, clutching her face in pain.

"That right there," he noted, kneeling before her. "Every time you start to tell me the truth, I can see that you're overcome by pain. What the hell is that?"

"The Elements…" Winnie muttered, their coursing magic growing more intense.

"The Elements I've prayed to my entire life would never cause harm to one of their followers." Reaching for her, Kane turned her hand over and looked at the brand on her palm.

"Then you don't know them like I do." Leaning forward, she placed her head on his shoulder.

"If you can't answer, then I'll ask them myself."

"They won't tell you, Kane. You're not…a part of all of this. This is bigger than you realize, and somehow my family is in the middle of it."

"Because of the queen?"

She nodded. "The queen. The hellhounds. Wesley's death. It's all connected, I just haven't figured out how. But with my powers growing, I'm…working for them." She'd expected the ringing to grow, but the Elements seemed to cut her some slack.

"It's alright," Caelus soothed. *"Tell him. I'll handle the others."*

"So that's what you've been doing? All these weeks? Working for them?" His face lit up in hopeful wonder, savoring the bits of information she offered.

"Yes. I have a set of tasks that I'm bound to complete for them and…I was working on the first one."

"How many do you have left?"

"I have no idea," she sighed. "They are very cryptic. They don't like to give out too many answers until absolutely necessary."

Kane grumbled. "Clearly, I'm coming with you on your next one."

"You can't," she tried to explain. Kane got up, huffing in anger as he paced the room. "I'm the only one with these new abilities. I'm not even sure I know how to control it yet."

"Does this have to do with you disappearing during Wesley's funeral?"

Winnie waited, unsure if she was allowed to answer. At last, she braved the potential throbbing headache and answered. "Yes, that's when I first met them in person. Made a deal with them."

"And you're sure it was the Elements?"

Winnie's heart began to race, panic settling in her gut.

"There are plenty of entities that can pretend to be one thing or another. I hope you made sure you were working with them and not some mimic."

"I…hadn't even thought of that." For a moment, she sat in shock. "The gifts they've given me can only come from them. I'm almost certain it's not some other creature."

"For your sake, and the rest of your family's, I hope you're right."

Before she could answer, Oslind stuck his head into the sunroom. "Time to go. Are you not dressed yet? Honestly? I've waited ten years for this! Let's go!"

With a sigh, the pair joined the sea creatures outside. Oslind handed her Gali's golden scallop necklace, offering a smirk.

"Figured you might need this back."

Placing it in her pocket, she turned toward Brenna. "I can use my air bubble. You use the helmet."

"I saw your nifty bubble ten years ago. Did you think I would let all this time pass without practicing it myself?" Brenna said with a wink, snapping her fingers and allowing a bubble to form around her mouth and nose. "My skins may be burned, but I didn't let that keep me from the water."

At last, the selkie stepped into the lake waiting for the others. Cordelia and Caspian followed shortly after, swimming and splashing one another playfully as they waited to leave.

"We're not bringing the children, are we?" Kane asked in disbelief. "They should stay here. Where it's safe."

"They're more powerful than they look. Plus, they've made some friends in the last few years that plan to help us out." Oslind's fatherly pride beamed as he spoke. "Winnie might be a good fighter on land, but she got her ass kicked quite a few times in the water, from my memory. I'm not taking any chances of failure."

Kane glanced back at her, running a gentle finger along her bruised face.

"Just because I wield water doesn't mean I can fight in it," she countered, cheeks flushing with embarrassment.

"We need to be very careful when we get there. Aalto has been counting down for years, ready for you to cash in your half of the bargain. That threat you made really stuck," Afissa explained, waist deep in the water before her legs transformed into a scaly tail.

"I don't know that I've ever heard you speak of your husband," the siren mumbled.

"There's a reason for that. You two will stay to the back, letting us go ahead. We will go in alone at first, leaving the majority of our warriors outside to protect us from an ambush. When we get into the palace, you'll be more useful."

Winnie and Kane both nodded in understanding.

"Do not go in before us. My husband has been preparing for this since you left ten years ago. The second he sees you, he'll attack. You won't stand a chance. You'll have a small group of selkies to assist you, should you encounter any dangers underwater. But I can't stress enough; *don't* go in before us."

Wading into the water, Winnie asked, "How many are helping us?"

The queen of Marvivia smirked. "Well, Bren has rallied quite a few selkies to get her and Oslind on the throne. The twins have befriended quite a few…beasts. Trust me, we have enough fighters."

"You underestimate your husband," she countered.

"You haven't been in Marvivia for ten years. You've missed the destruction and chaos Aalto has created. His tyranny has only caused more and more mermaids to side with the selkies, seeing how cruel he can be. Oslind and Brenna have been a mere fairytale to many of them, waiting for the day of their return. Children have grown up hearing stories of the missing prince of the coral throne and his selkie bride."

Winnie's eyes widened. "I didn't realize they'd have such a great impact."

"There's only so much mayhem a nation can handle before it finally decides to choose peace. By any means necessary," Brenna added, ushering the others to follow.

"Let this be a reminder to you, Winifred. You cannot change someone's fate," Gali coached in her mind.

"See you on the other side," Winnie said, pulling the helmet over her head as the sea creatures fully submerged.

She glanced back at Kane, noting his careful consideration of his helmet. Before beginning their swim to the bottom of the lake, she reached for him once more.

"Be my date?" His hand interlaced with hers, an excited grin on his face.

"Always."

Pushing their way through the sandy portal at the bottom of the lake, Winnie couldn't help but chuckle watching Kane swat furiously at the sand that surrounded him. When their vision cleared and the darkness of the ocean returned, she once again looked out across the water to see the glowing lights of Marvivia in the distance.

"It's beautiful," Kane said, his voice muffled by water. She wasn't sure how she could hear him, but perhaps in ten years her father had made some changes to the helmets.

"Wait until you see the throne room," she added, both swimming just behind the others. "Do you think my father's okay?"

At first, there was only silence in her helmet. Kane didn't seem to want to respond. After some contemplation, he said, "If he was dead, surely you'd see him. Right?"

She thought for a moment. "Surely…He has to be okay." She wasn't sure who she was trying to convince.

Up ahead, Afissa led the group. First, she motioned for a group of selkies to join Winnie and Kane. The four creatures nodded, surrounding them with protective shields and trident spears. Their seal-like bodies were covered in rigid armor, the outsides made of dark igneous rock and the insides glimmering like lava. Winnie could feel a bubble of warmth surrounding them, protecting the selkies from the cold, frigid waters.

Next, Afissa stopped at the edge of a boulder, signaling to someone far off. As she did, Winnie couldn't help but notice the sudden glimmer of dark eyes peering back at them. Hidden within the surrounding rocky caverns were dozens of selkies, waiting for orders. It took everything in her not to scream at first, her skin crawling. All she could remember were the devastatingly beautiful sounds of the selkie's songs that had almost been the death of her.

Winnie watched in awe as both children swam with mermaid-like tales, their skin covered in furs similar to their mother. Even their faces had changed, morphed to look more like seals, their eyes glowing luminescent in the darkness. Their grandmother offered them a signal, to which they both nodded.

As their mouths opened wide to reveal sharp fangs, an eerie echo searched through the icy waters. Winnie could feel the strength of their voices pulsing through her, the haunting selkie songs calling forth...something.

She glanced around in confusion as they finished, though nothing seemed to happen. It was then that she saw it. The gangly tentacles that had once held her in its tight grasp. Off in the distance, the kraken appeared. Swimming toward them at a speed she hadn't realized it could travel. Kane darted in front of her, ready to shield her from an incoming attack.

"I think it's on our side," she said, attempting to reassure him.

Wild eyes looked back at her, then glanced around at the beasts they lurked with. "My whole life, I was told tales of the sea. The monsters that dwell down here. To see it myself is truly surreal."

"I know," she chuckled. "I never realized how terrifying the ocean was until I spent the last few weeks down here."

As the kraken approached closer and closer, the twins opened their mouths again. Ordering it, the beast pivoted toward Marvivia. Within moments, the entire underwater civilization came to life. The scattered glowing orbs turned red, a sign that they were under attack. And just as the kraken wrapped its tentacles around the trident-wielding statue that protected the city, Afissa gave the final order. Even through the thickness of the deep, dark waters, Winnie could still hear her bellow.

"Attack!"

47

WINIFRED
MARVIVIA - 1871

Hidden in the darkness, Winnie watched. A line of selkies darted through the city, drawing out loyal mermaid soldiers. The kraken crumpled the trident-wielding statue at the entrance, a low, haunting grumble rippling through the water as the debris fell. Afissa disappeared amidst the masses as the others moved toward the throne room. Behind her, she felt a push as the four selkies urged them forward.

A sharp ringing caught Winnie's attention as they moved. To her right, Oslind's children repeated their wistful melodies. Something moved past her legs, emerging from the depths beneath. Eels and other strange beings slithered from the bottom of the ocean floor, headed straight for the king's warriors. She stifled a cry, watching the gangly creatures wrap themselves around the throats of unsuspecting victims.

"Will they turn on us?" Kane's voice echoed through her helmet.

"Gods, I hope not! Keep swimming!"

They pushed farther into the city when a shiver of sharks torpedoed past. The group bumped into Winnie and Kane, unaware they'd inadvertently knocked them into a nearby coral. The beasts' snapping jaws aimed for sea creatures trying desperately to protect their city. When another hoard approached, Kane pulled her out of the way.

"How many sea monsters do these kids know?"

With a chuckle, her gaze narrowed in on the palace. The twins waded in front of the entrance, waiting for their mother and father to join. A commanding scaled hand reached through the ivory barrier, dragging them inside before they could ever open their mouths to call forth their gaggle of monsters. Not far off, Brenna darted inside after her children.

"Brenna needs help! They've got the kids!" Winnie cried, urging the selkies toward the palace.

Kane scanned the carnage before yelling, "Afissa said to wait!"

"We can't let them die! We have to go in!"

Without hesitation, he nodded. Ushering the selkies forward, they didn't put up a fight to help their fearless leader. Pushing through the barrier, Winnie was unsure what she'd find when she landed on the other side, the others not far behind.

The moment her feet met the abalone-shell floor, she noticed the king atop his coral throne, Brenna and the children captured by guards with blades pressed to their throats. A mermaid stood before them, a dark gaze focused on Winnie before balling his fists. They engulfed in molten flame, ready to strike.

She recognized him immediately; there weren't many mermaids that wielded her kindred power. The barrier behind her rippled, Kane and the other selkies about to enter. The king's guard sent a wall of fire forward, only moments for Winnie to react. Second nature kicked in as she called on Gali, a shield of ice protecting them from the radiating heat. It bought her mere seconds, but it was enough for the others to join the fight at last.

Ripping their helmets and flippers off, Winnie and Kane prepared for a fight. The protective glacier began to crack, the fire-wielding mermaid sending in attack after attack. Side by side, she lowered the shield. An incoming trident spear nearly lodged itself into her chest before a gust of wind guided the weapon away.

Shooting a spear of ice toward the fire-bender, Kane's element wrapped itself around her powers, sending the spears through the chest of their attacker and skewering him into the wall. King Aalto flinched not far behind, but he merely sat atop his throne in silence unwilling to move. With a flick of his wrist, more soldiers filed in toward the group as Brenna and her children continued to struggle.

"Did you really think I wouldn't be ready for you, Lucille?" The king's words hovered in the air. He turned back toward his guards before adding, "Apparently burning those wretched skins weren't enough to stop such scum from returning. Ensure the selkie bitch and her little bastards don't leave."

The men nodded, holding fast in their positions.

A group of ten mermaids stormed toward Winnie and the others. The clanking of metal on metal and the cries of injuries echoed through her mind as she strategized her way toward the king. She dug the end of her spear into the gut of a nearby mermaid. She worked with her love in tandem, crimson clouding the shimmering floors.

To her right, Kane shouted, "What's the plan here?"

"Stay alive!"

Winnie sent another spear of ice toward the king, though he held up a telekinetic hand to use a nearby guard as a shield. The man's gurgling cry pierced her mind as she watched the king discard him.

"I thought we had a deal," she bellowed over the howls of fighting sea creatures.

King Aalto's mouth turned into a devilish smirk, his deep brown eyes narrowing in on her. "It would appear you've been able to secure an army all on your own. How did you manage to get these brutes organized enough for a coherent attack?"

Aalto's invisible hand reached around Winnie, pulling her through the crowd and toward the throne. Another small horde of selkies entered, joining the fight. Kane remained behind, blocked by near-constant attacks. He called out to her, though she could barely hear him over the on-going fight. Winnie turned back toward him, offering a careful nod as if to say *'I'll be okay.'* He huffed a loud sigh of frustration before driving his spear into the throat of his opponent.

Winnie turned back, face to face with the king. Soft whimpers caught her attention to her left, noticing the twins with tears in their eyes. Brenna spoke to them softly in a language she didn't recognize. They only responded with quiet nods, eyes fixed on the entrance to the throne room like they were waiting.

"Good to see you again," Aalto sneered, pulling her in closer. The king's unmoving grip held her tight, tracking every attempt to escape with vicious pleasure. "You didn't answer my question: how did you organize this? The selkies are known for inflicting ruthless, wild chaos. They don't ambush cities in organized lines. How did you do it?"

Winnie said nothing, only glanced at Brenna.

The king seemed to process her stare before letting loose a manic cackle. "You mean to tell me that Brenna, the dejected selkie traitor who doesn't even have skins, organized all of this?"

Caspian and Cordelia's attention sharpened onto the king, the room beginning to heat at their anger. Their sobbing ceased, though their mother shushed them softly. Again, she spoke in that same strange language.

"She's telling them to wait. To not show their breadth of magic unless absolutely necessary," Gali explained, raining down in her mind.

Aalto pulled Winnie closer until she could feel the hot air fuming from his mouth. "You're stalling. Why?"

She could only stare, realizing how much her refusal to answer infuriated him. His hand grasped her throat, constricting her airways until dark splotches of purple and blue peppered her vision.

"Don't worry. It'll all be over soon."

His unseen force pulled her up into the air above the crowd, on display for others to see. Kane's attention darted up, a moment of distraction landing a swift punch to the face that landed him on his knees. The last remaining selkies soon tumbled, too, kneeling before the King of Marvivia.

"Who shall I kill first? This traitorous bitch, or her little friends?" His gaze transferred over the crowd before landing back on Winnie. "Better start with you."

A ball of water formed around her head, the grip around her midsection moving toward her neck. She trashed in the air, hands clawing at her face for some relief.

"Caelus? Help!"

Silence sat on the other end of her pleas. Until she heard the familiar voice of her goddess. *"Let go. Trust me."*

Winnie's body went limp, a strange euphoria spreading over her. Though the grasp of Death wasn't what she felt. Gali's warm light seemed to surround her, but nonetheless she felt her soul escape, watching from above. Her body fell to the floor, a heaping pile of wet flesh and bone.

48

WINIFRED
MARVIVIA - 1871

Winnie's essence floated along the ceiling of the throne room, examining the situation before her. Her body lay limply on the floor, splayed out as though she were dead. Kane cried out, fighting against the mermaid hands that held him in place. The weapon held to his throat nicked him, blood spilling onto the seashell floor.

Attempting to reach him through the strange void, Winnie whispered her ghostly words. *"I don't know if you can hear me, but I'm okay. Stop making yourself a target."* A strange look of confusion washed over him, glancing at her body along the ground before settling himself with a grimace.

From the back of the throne room, Afissa rushed in. Wearing a dress made of cascading pearls, her hair was braided into a crown atop her head. Oceanic greenery was woven between the strands, the picture of serene beauty. *How did she change so fast?* Winnie wondered as she watched from above.

"Aalto! They're attacking the city!" She fell to his feet, sobbing before turning toward the intruders kneeling at the base of his throne.

"It's nothing, Afissa. We've already squashed their attack before it could begin." He waved a dismissive hand as one of the nearby guards plunged his trident spear into a selkie seated on the ground.

The mermaid guard moved to sink his weapon into the next selkie when Afissa straightened up. "Now, now dear. Haven't I been telling you for years that you need to adjust your attitude?" Afissa's sing-songy voice caught him off guard, a glare following her movements.

At once, the facade she'd curated melted away to reveal a warrior queen, clad in iridescent armor. The dagger in her hand sunk into his chest, a look of content washing over her porcelain features.

Aalto's words came out a fierce roar as he stumbled from his seat. "I should've killed you long ago!"

Behind them, a new hoard of selkies swarmed the palace. At the front of the attack, Oslind strode in decked to the nines in weapons and armor. The mermaid warriors surrounding the king moved as though they'd attack, but soon dropped their weapons.

More and more selkies entered the room, followed by fellow weaponless mermaids who'd switched sides. Those in the palace dropped their weapons, stepping away from the kneeling prisoners. Aalto, clutching his chest in agony as crimson spilled onto the floor, stared at his son who hoisted him up by the collar of his shirt.

"Bet you never thought you'd see my face again, huh?"

Aalto could only blink in surprise before glancing back at Brenna. "The children?"

"Are ours. Those are your grandchildren. And you will never know their love. Just as you will never know the love of your people who you've failed all these years." Tossing his father onto the ground, Oslind could only chuckle a soft, devious laugh.

A peculiar tingle spread through Winnie's essence as she watched, her soul lowering toward her slumped body lying on the ground.

Oslind crouched down toward his speechless father, continuing his final words. "I will sit on the throne with my 'selkie bitch' as you like to call her. We will rule with love and mercy for our people divided by hate. Your legacy will be one of putrid rancor. And generations from now, the only story the children will hear will be how we overcame the true monster in these waters: you."

With a swift thrust, Oslind sunk his trident into the belly of his father. He clutched his wound, backing away from his son. Pleading eyes landed back on Afissa, though she shook her head and turned away from her husband.

A sharp jolt helped Winnie awaken in her body once more. Silently, she moved behind the king. As he scooted back still clutching his stomach, he bumped into her. Turning, his face reddening at the sight of 'Lucille' still alive.

"I told you I would be the last face you saw. I always keep my promises."

Without a second thought, she sunk her dagger into the king's head. His body pulsed, blood spilling from his mouth onto the floor. Falling to Oslind's feet, he lay limp.

Dead. At last.

"The hostile king is dead! Surrender," Afissa ordered, her armor shimmering in the light of nearby orbs.

It didn't take long before the King's guards kneeled before her. She turned toward her son, a sad smile on her face before reaching down to take the crown off her husband's head.

"May I present the rightful King and Queen of Marvivia!"

A silent wave passed over the crowd as each person, regardless of what creature they were, took a knee. Afissa placed the crown atop her son's head before reaching behind the throne to pull out her own.

"From this day forth, Marvivia is united. Under the rule of King Oslind and Queen Brenna, we will no longer let our differences divide us." Pride beamed on the mother's face, watching her son take a seat on the throne alongside his bride.

The room erupted into cheer, Caspian and Cordelia rushing toward their mother and father in excitement. A moment of joy passed before all went silent again. Soft murmurs spread as Winnie turned, noticing who stood at the entrance.

Gali, in her corporeal form. A wave of cool air passed through the space as she towered over her creatures, striding toward the dais. Every creature bowed their heads, honoring the goddess as she joined the celebration.

"There is no need to kneel." Careful eyes watched, mermaids and selkies united in their curiosity. Her body swirled like restless waves, settling as she approached the two on the throne.

Kane shimmied his way over to Winnie, only to whisper, "Is that…"

"The one and only."

"You came," Brenna sighed, a tear rolling down her cheek.

"I promised, didn't I?" Reaching out her hand, Oslind and Brenna walked toward her. They placed their hands in hers, Gali's strong figure towering over the two sea creatures. "You have no idea the kind of power that lies within these waters now that your people are united. Though the battle is not won, and it will take some time before everyone agrees to follow you, you will ensure peace for generations to come. I can't imagine any two of my creatures more deserving than you."

Oslind glanced down at Brenna, pride and love glittering from his smile. Gali raised her hands, lifting them into the air with a gentle force. Twinkling blue light surrounded them, blinding those watching the spectacle.

When they lowered back onto the ground, Oslind looked down in shock as he rotated his fully restored foot. Brenna looked at her own body in confusion.

"I don't understand. I don't feel any different," she whispered, lowering her head as though she worried she'd offend her creator.

"Just because your skins are burned does not make you any less of a selkie. I have watched you stand up for your people through it all, and confront others when they were causing harm. You have also been fully restored, but now you will no longer need to rely on separate skins to change into your truest form."

Brenna blinked for a moment, processing the goddess's words. At last, she stifled a cry. "So after ten years... I'll swim again? Like I once did?"

Gali offered her a warm smile and careful nod.

Reaching for Kane, Winnie embraced him. His own grin beamed down at her as he mumbled, "You helped make this happen."

As the newly restored family shared a moment to themselves, Gali turned toward Winnie and Kane. It wasn't long before she stood in front of them. He straightened himself, letting go of Winnie as if caught by her own mother showing affection.

"It's an honor to meet you," he rushed, bowing his head.

"I imagine you'll be hearing from us very soon," she said, her vacant eyes staring at him intently.

"I...I'd like that very much." A look of pleasant surprise passed over his face, glancing down at Winnie hopefully.

Then, Gali turned to leave.

"Is it done? The first task?"

The goddess hesitated before adding, "I believe, for now. You'll hear from us soon regarding the next steps."

Winnie offered a quiet curtsy before the glow of azure light masked Gali's exit. A sigh escaped her, turning back toward the throne to see Oslind wrapping his arms around Brenna and their two children. *Gods, I'm tired,* she thought.

"Almost there," Kane mumbled, offering Winnie's cheek a quick kiss.

With a nod, they turned toward the exit. "Let's get back to Fox Manor, and start preparing the portal."

He followed close behind, though both turned back one last time to see the newly restored King and Queen of Marvivia.

49

WINIFRED
FOX MANOR - 1871

Aching arms pulled Winnie out of the water, landing along the rocks of Fox Manor's lake. Moonlight and twinkling stars glittered down as she removed the helmet and flippers. Placing them on the ground beside her, she rolled onto her back and looked up at the sky. Overcome by a wave of exhaustion, she couldn't contain a soft whimper.

"Ditto," Kane mumbled, flopping onto his back next to her.

"I didn't think it was possible to be this tired," she admitted, scooting closer to lay her head on his chest.

He leaned down, offering her forehead a quick kiss. "Gods, I've missed you. Holding you back in my arms like this… I honestly didn't think I'd get the chance again."

A quiet tear rolled down her cheek, nuzzling into his chest for warmth and comfort as if she couldn't get close enough. "There were a few times where I wasn't sure I'd make it back alive. And then I'd hear your voice, and I knew I'd be okay."

The corner of his mouth turned to a smirk. "You could hear me?"

"The whole time. Honestly, how much time did you spend singing rather than helping the others?" she teased.

A huff of amusement passed through his dreamy lips. "An embarrassing amount of time. How did you manage to resist the siren song? I pulled out some of my strongest tricks to make you come home."

"I haven't a clue," she admitted. "Guess it wasn't time to go home yet. I'm still learning how my new powers work."

There was a slight pause to their conversation before he finally asked, "Do you have to leave again?"

"Eventually, yes." Wiping away another quiet tear, he suddenly realized she'd been crying.

Pulling her into a tighter embrace, his presence felt like an all-over, soul-soothing hug. He said nothing, only held her close as though he never intended to let go.

"We need to get back to Chicago. Where the hell are they?" Winnie glanced at the water, thinking back to the plans she'd made with the new King and Queen of Marvivia.

Carefully, he leaned down toward her and planted his lips across her own. When he pulled away, he said at last, "You taste salty."

Winnie couldn't help but chuckle, her stress displaced for only a moment. "Seriously? Of all times? You think humor is appropriate right now?"

"It made you laugh, didn't it?"

Offering another kiss, she couldn't fight it anymore. The burning ember in Winnie's heart sank to her core, insides set ablaze with need. Weeks of pent up longing finally released as she moved in closer toward him, taking a seat in his lap. Tears continued to stream down her face, a mix of fear and confusion clouding her decisions. All she could do was try to detach herself from her emotions. Desperate to feel anything other than worry or sorrow, remorse or guilt, she instead ran wild fingers through his hair as their mouths intertwined.

"They'll be here any moment," he reminded, a teasing hand moving her wet hair aside. The other moved over her torso and down her back before gripping her waist.

"So kiss me until they get here," she insisted, silencing him with another peck.

Mimicking the teasing kisses he'd given her the last time they were together, she trailed her lips down the side of his neck. Soft moans escaped him as she continued to tease before he flipped her over onto her back. Landing firmly above her, a ferocious gaze eyed her every movement.

"Fuck, you drive me crazy. This skin-tight outfit certainly doesn't help," he mumbled, his teeth grazing her collarbone before plump lips skimmed her chest. When he pulled his attention up again, his hands moved along her wetsuit, diving further and further down.

"I drive *you* crazy? You're on top of me," she countered, fighting the urge to mimic his movements, restless hands aching to feel every inch of his body.

A deep chuckle escaped him, heating her insides even more as he bit his lower lip playfully. Kane's hands moved lower and lower, never ceasing their exploration. Lost in their own little world, the sound of someone clearing their throat startled them both.

"I'm so glad it's dark out here..." Oslind rubbed his head, covering his eyes with blushing cheeks.

"We were, um, waiting for you guys," she stuttered, leaping to her feet.

"That kind of waiting is how we ended up with twins," the mermaid taunted, walking past them toward the mirror portal to examine the damage.

Kane stood, straightening himself out. His voice lowered so only she could hear as he purred, "One day, perhaps we won't be interrupted. Then I can show you all the other wonderful things my siren song can do."

Offering her blushing cheeks one last kiss, he turned back toward the lake where Afissa and Brenna joined.

"Let's recreate this portal! And fast! I have an official wedding and coronation ceremony to plan!" Brenna clapped with excitement, striding to her love's side. "I apologize that it took us a little longer to get here. I was enjoying myself."

Oslind offered her temple a delicate kiss, turning toward the others before adding, "The connection is still there. We'll just need to repair the vessel."

Winnie stood behind them, awaiting instructions.

"It should be easy to recreate, then. Use us as a power source. Set aside what you know of coven magic, and just focus on making the portal on your own."

"Got it," Winnie mumbled, closing her eyes.

The group formed a semi-circle behind Winnie, each placing their hands on her shoulders. She put her own on the mirror, drawing on the intoxicating power of the creatures that fueled her. Envisioning the Chicago Orphan Asylum, an outline of the establishment formed in her mind and her skin buzzed with energy. It remained unlike anything she'd ever felt. But it still didn't seem to be enough.

"It's not working. I need all four elements."

With a sigh, Brenna added, "No you don't. I promise! Try again."

Fighting a wave of defeat, Winnie closed her eyes once more. On the tips of her fingers, she felt an unfamiliar power. In her mind's eye, she could see swirling vines waiting to be joined by the other elements.

"Kane, call on Caelus," she said, jutting her chin toward the mirror.

He didn't ask questions, creating a ball of swirling storm winds and offered them to the portal. Envisioning Aelius and Gali, she called on her deities next.

"I feel Ina on the other side. Will you help us?" Winnie waited for a response. A few moments passed before she offered a glowing ball of fire and water to the gateway.

At last, the mirror began to creak. Glass shards floated from the ground, squeezing into the openings. The connection sharpened, a clear outline of the inside of the orphanage forming as the Elements whispered soft praises in her mind.

"It worked! I don't know how, but it did."

In fascination, Kane touched the new portal. "I didn't know that was possible without a full coven."

"I told you it could be done," Brenna said with a confident shrug.

"It helps that the connection wasn't entirely severed," Oslind added, pulling his love in close.

Saying their final goodbyes, Winnie and Kane thanked Afissa, Oslind, and Brenna once again for their help. Winnie watched for a moment as they headed back toward the water, happily jumping into the lake and returning to Marvivia to await her order that their army was needed.

50

The moon and clouds clung to one another, hiding the stars away for the night. A shiver ran down Winnie's spine as the chilled December air reminded her that she was still sopping wet. *I need to get out of this wetsuit once and for all,* she thought.

"Ready to see everyone?" Kane asked, grabbing her hand and guiding her toward the mirror.

She nodded, hesitantly. "Will they be upset with me for being gone so long?"

"I doubt it," he shrugged. "I think they'll be thankful you're alive. Ezra's been worried sick about you."

"And your brother could probably care less," she mumbled half-heartedly.

"He shows his worry in mysterious ways." With his back to the portal, he guided her through. When they landed on the other side, he bumped into someone waiting.

"Winnie?"

"Ez!" She leapt past Kane, embracing her friend. He squirmed under her hold, noting the cold wet arms wrapped around him. "It's so good to see you!"

"Have you been waiting by the portal since I left?" the siren asked, offering Ezra a quick hug as well.

"No, not the whole time. A little voice told me I needed to be here. That you'd need me. Why are you both wet?" A grimace scowled down at her, peeling moist fabric from his arms.

"Long story," she sighed. "It's good to be back on land, though." Winnie took a deep breath in, thankful for the familiar smell of wood and leather. With her attention fixed on Kane, she added, "We should probably change before we try to find the camp."

He nodded, pulling her upstairs toward their shared living quarters. When the door opened, several sets of eyes landed on them.

"Look who I found," he announced, pulling her in behind him.

Thoren approached them both, retracting an intended hug. Instead, he pushed them both away with a pointer finger. "You smell like a fish market."

"We had to take a small detour to Marvivia," Winnie began. "On the bright side, we have an army now! In case the queen's hellhounds become a problem again."

"That would've helped us back in October," Melinda grumbled, stepping to the side of them but not accepting the wet hug Winnie offered. With arms crossed over her chest, she only glared. "We needed you here."

"I know, I'm so sorry I disappeared. I was ensuring we had enough soldiers in case we have to repeat Samhain."

"Well, they already attacked. Your friends have all been hurt since you've been gone."

Kane stepped between both young women in defense. "Easy, Mel. She's back now. There's more to the story than we have time to explain."

"And you're suddenly a rational human being? You lovesick fool," she hissed, taking a seat at the table.

"It seems I've missed a lot." Though she'd intended to mumble it to herself, the entire room nodded in agreement.

Melinda's voice carried from across the room. "Who's going to tell her about Tara?"

Winnie waited in nervous anticipation.

Kane seemed to note her worry, rushing to add, "She's alive."

"But not for long, because I'm going to kill her," Thoren countered, almost playfully as though they weren't speaking about one of her closest friends.

Winnie tried to speak, but nothing seemed to come out. At last, she asked, "What are you talking about?"

"She's sided with the hellhounds. I caught her together with Alaric." Melinda's words were short and clipped as she sipped on a cup of tea.

"There has to be some kind of misunderstanding. She wouldn't do that," she argued, taking a seat, and grabbing a cup for herself.

"Well, you're wrong. Your friend is a traitorous bitch, and I've had enough of her. We all have," Thoren spat.

He sounds almost as bad as Aalto, she shuddered.

"There's only so much betrayal my followers can handle before they eventually snap. Everyone gives into temptation eventually," Aelius purred in her mind.

With a shudder, she didn't have time to consider his implications.

"Things have been tense here lately," Kane tried to explain.

"We don't have time to waste. My parents are in danger. Where is the hellhound camp?" Winnie urged, trying to ignore their comments.

Melinda's cynical laugh echoed through the room. "We have no clue! The hellhounds packed up and left in the time it took you two to go swimming. Hope it was worth it."

Behind them, Cricket poked his head into the room. A few loud barks turned everyone's attention toward him.

"He's the only one who can get through the portal to their new camp," Ezra added, patting the shuck on the head.

"Take me there. Maybe I can get through," she insisted, glancing down at the swirling blue lines on her forearm.

After a quick change into winter clothes, the group headed

toward the old camp of the hellhounds. Walking through the streets of Chicago, she clutched the coat around her. Bits and pieces of what she'd seen while astral projecting two months before came back to her, recalling the dense tree line and fallen leaves they'd soon encounter. As they walked, the group remained mostly silent. Only Cricket's panting breaths were audible as they continued their trek.

At last, Melinda turned back toward her. "I can't believe you would just leave, and then try to waltz back in here as if nothing happened."

Winnie scoffed at first, her internal defenses setting off. She took a deep breath before responding. "I know you're upset, but…"

"Upset is an understatement. My friends and family, my city, have been in danger because of the mess you got us into. None of this would be happening if you hadn't held that seance!" Her umber cheeks flushed with anger, shoulders tensing.

"You think I don't realize that? I've been practically killing myself trying to right my wrongs! I am fully aware that all of this is my fault. I don't need you to remind me."

Melinda said nothing, kicking at the rubble beneath her feet. The group walked in silence for another twenty minutes or so, never saying a word. Eventually Ezra turned toward Winnie, his eyes widening as tension clung to the air like an incoming storm.

"So," he began, drawing out the vowel. He held his hands, pointing at buildings as they continued their long trudge. "What shall we do now that you're back? Once we've rescued your parents, of course."

Winnie opened her mouth to answer, though Melinda cut her off. "You will stay put! I swear to every God that exists, if you disappear again, you won't live long enough to say you're sorry."

Kane glanced down at her, a mental check in. Winnie could only shake her head, thinking: *She has the right to be angry. And so much more…*

"Well," Ezra sighed. "Probably for the best. The city seems more crowded than usual. Probably couldn't find an open seat anywhere to begin with."

Winnie scanned the area in concern. Though a few patrons wandered about, it was well past midnight. Pretty soon only beggars and working girls would be on the streets.

Thoren turned to his love, placing a hand on his back before noting, "There's hardly anyone out here."

"Very funny," he began with a nervous huff of laughter. When the group once again shook their heads, he added, "You're telling me you can't see all of these people standing and staring at us?"

Winnie scanned the area before gently saying, "Ez... Show me exactly who it is you're referring to."

With an eye roll, he pointed at the lines of somewhat transparent faces that glared at them as they passed. "You're messing with me, right? You can't see them?"

"They can't see spirits like I – we apparently – can."

Winnie's words seemed to spear him unintentionally. His eyes twitched, wrapping his arms around him like he needed a hug. One hand braced over his mouth, as though it might stifle a scream.

"Sp–spirits? I don't understand what you mean." He stopped walking entirely, glancing at those that still lurked in the shadows. He approached a man nearby, whose image faded in and out. "Bloody hell... how did I not realize you could see through them?"

Winnie stood at his side, placing her hand on his back in reassurance. Softly, she asked, "How long have you been seeing them?"

"I don't know, actually. I wouldn't know how to answer that question. Do you think...the man I've been seeing. The one I, you know," he paused with a gulp. "Has he been haunting me this whole time?"

"It's very possible. It sounds like you and I have some work to do after we get my parents back. You're a medium, Ezra. Oh, I can't wait to teach you how everything works!" Gently, she pulled his arm toward the group again with a wide grin. Only he didn't seem to return to sentiment. He could only nod, eyes glued to the lurking shadows as Cricket ran ahead of them.

They continued to walk for what felt like an eternity, eventually coming to a line of trees with a path that looked heavily traveled. Winnie cast a glowing orb of light out ahead of them, floating like a lantern to guide them through the dark. The snow along the ground was packed and muddied, several sets of footprints and pawprints back and forth between the city and the previously inhabited campsite.

"I recognize this path from my astral projection trip back in October. We're going the right way!" Winnie said hopefully, walking ahead.

"Yes, we already figured that out. While you were in Marvivia," Melinda sneered, a firm shoulder bumping into Winnie's as she passed.

Not too much farther into the woods, Cricket waited for them. He barked before darting to two marked trees and taking a seat between them.

"There," Melinda pointed. "This is where the Broderick trio saw the hounds leave."

Winnie squinted, trying to sharpen her mind. The tattoo on her arm flared in welcome, sensing the queen's ancestors not far off. A dim outline of tents and campfires shimmered through the veil. "I see their camp on the other side."

"How? We only see trees," Thoren asked, arms braced over his chest.

She glanced toward Kane, unsure how to explain. After a moment, he mumbled, "Just tell them the basics. We can explain everything else later."

"Boudicca and I are still connected. Perhaps that's why I'm

able to see past their wards." Avoiding their panic-stricken faces, she focused on the portal instead. Reaching for it, a glow warmed her hand as the queen's oddly quiet spirits slithered around inside. Her tattooed arm continued to smolder, awaiting the reunion with Alaric and his hellhounds.

"Don't be stupid," Ezra rushed, swatting her hand away from the portal. "You can't go through there! If you can see it but no one else can, that means she wants you to find them."

The shrill voice of the queen laced with alarm boomed through her mind. *"Step through. Your parents need you!"*

"Boudicca wants me to go through the portal. Why do I feel like that's not a good thing?" she asked, eyes peering at each member of the group.

"You should not be going by yourself. And before you start, because I know you, I'm not saying you can't protect yourself. But their camp is probably massive. And dangerous!" Ezra continued pulling her away from the portal.

"Let me try something." Kane grabbed a hold of Winnie's hand, his eyes widened. "I was right!"

"About?" Thoren asked impatiently.

"If I'm touching you, I can see the camp too."

His brother's eyebrows raised in surprise. "Maybe your spell worked after all."

"Spell?" Winnie waited, though he didn't seem ready to share.

"Later, I promise." At once, a beaming smile broke out across his face.

"You try," she said, reaching for Ezra.

He grasped her hand, only to shake his head. "I can't see anything."

"I have a feeling it'll only work for you two. For some reason, the hounds want you alone. You'll need to be prepared for anything," Thoren added, rubbing his head nervously.

"So this is obviously a trap, right?" Kane mumbled, his eyes

441

still glued to the portal before them.

"It always is, but we don't have a choice. My parents need us. Are you ready?" she asked, linking her arm with his.

With a cautious nod, both of them stepped toward the two trees as a glowing swirl of apricot light guided them through to the other side.

51

WINIFRED
HELLHOUND CAMP - 1871

Careful eyes scanned the hellhound camp, peeled and ready for anyone that may attack. Rows of tents filled with sleeping hounds waited quietly in the dark, a few scattered fires throughout, mostly burned down to embers and coals. The rich moon above lit their path, too afraid to create an orb that may attract attention.

"We don't know how long we have until they're alerted that we're here," she whispered to Kane. Behind them, Cricket came running through the portal.

"Cricket!" Kane hissed as loud as he possibly could before being heard. "Damn shuck. He's going to get himself killed. Or worse: us!"

"I'm sure he'll be fine. He can get back through without us."

Jutting his chin forward, he ushered her through the camp. Passing more makeshift homes, soft snores and the occasional low conversation sounded from inside the tents. A few campfires still had some remnants of the evening's dinner, pots of leftover stew and a few sides sitting around. Winnie snatched a piece of bread from a nearby table, munching on it as they walked.

"Seriously?"

"Don't you dare judge me. I'm starving!" She shushed him, pressing on ahead as muffled cries caught her attention. Grabbing Kane's arm, she motioned toward the sound.

Around the corner, massive cages large enough for circus

animals sat with huddling figures inside. Their chattering teeth were loud enough to hear several feet away as they approached in a hurry.

"Mum? Dad? Are you in there?" she whispered, searching the area for guards on watch. When she didn't see any hounds, she created a small glowing ball of light to help see who was inside.

"After this, you'll need to teach me that trick," Kane mumbled, his back to the cage and attention plastered to any sign of approaching movement.

At first, she didn't recognize the two huddled figures inside. Dirt and grime smeared across the faces of a man and woman, both pressed together for warmth. They certainly weren't clothed for winter, shuddering right out of their skin. As the light of the glowing orb met them, they flinched away in fear. The only thing Winnie saw were their hair colors: her tangled golden-blonde locks and the man's dusty brown hair. Both disheveled and unkempt.

"We're here to help you," she whispered. "Who are you?"

At once, the shoulders of the woman tensed. Emerald green eyes peeked toward her in fear, though she still hid her face. Tears welled in the center before she straightened herself up.

"Winnie?"

The familiar voice caught her attention, despite being raspy from dehydration. A pulse of electricity ran through her spine, realizing who was trapped inside the cage.

"Bea?" Moving the orb closer toward the woman, Winnie tried desperately to verify her suspicions.

"Bea as in 'tried to kill you' Beatrix?" His gaze flared in anger before once again peering behind them to ensure no one came to investigate the glowing white lights.

"Winnie, get me out of here. Please! I'm so cold," she whimpered, finally moving toward the edge of the cage. Blistered hands grasped the bars, quivering lips pleading with both of them.

"Bloody hell, Bea! How long have you been here?" Winnie's

attention turned toward the locks, trying to figure out a way to break them without making too much noise.

"A few months. They caught me leaving a seance one day back in October." Her voice continued to rasp, shaking the iron bars like it could help save her life. A sharp squeal of metal echoed through the camp.

Kane rushed to shush her. "Quiet, you! Or I'd be inclined to leave you here."

"Who's in there with you?" Winnie asked, still trying to see the face of the man huddled beside her.

"Not a clue. All he speaks is gibberish. He was already unstable when they brought him here. His madness has only gotten worse since joining me," Beatrix explained.

"When did he get here?"

"Right after I did." She tapped on the bars, rushing them once more. "Please hurry, Win. I can't take it anymore! They hardly feed us. I don't remember the last time I had a warm drink."

At last, Winnie opted for magical intervention. Calling on Gali, she focused her full strength on the lock. With the help of the surrounding chill, she cooled the metal to an almost shattering temperature. After a swift hit, the metal lock clattered to the ground with a soft thud. The little bit of noise sent her and Kane into a nervous frenzy, desperate to escape the area before being detected.

"Oh, thank you!" Bea cried, leaping from the cage and into Winnie's arms.

Kane's face turned to a tight frown, glancing at her former lover in disdain.

"Get him," she hurried, motioning for the man still huddled. He didn't seem to notice that his escape was imminent.

Kane ducked inside, pulling the incoherent man by the shoulder. One look at the grimey face and suddenly he backed away in a hurry. "Let's go."

"We can't leave him!"

The man turned toward the light at last, realizing there were others nearby. Cloudy eyes landed on the siren, backing away as his face contorted in manic fear. "You! I remember you! The angel of death!"

Winnie's blood ran cold, recognizing yet another voice. "Is that…"

"He said his name was Samuel," Beatrix whispered. "Do you know him?"

"He courted me long ago. How does Sam know *you*, Kane?" she asked, guiding Beatrix onto the siren's arm. Entering the cage herself, she examined the man carefully. "Samuel, can you hear me?"

"The angel of death… he's back," he cried, a ragged hand pointing at Kane as bloodshot eyes wept.

"Kane," she hissed, eying him with suspicion. "Why does he keep calling you that?"

The siren said nothing, only backing away and leaving Beatrix behind. "I'll go look for your parents."

"Wait!" Winnie helped Samuel out of the cage, his body worn to mere skin and bone.

"He speaks of the angel of death all the time. Of the vicious things that he endured at the hands of," Beatrix began, trying to help hold the man up despite her own body being frail.

"Let's focus on getting you two out of here," she mumbled, shushing Bea once more. "How are you in better shape than him?"

"He was already like that when those monsters brought him to the camp."

Winnie wracked her brain, trying to understand what the hell had happened to him since they'd ended their courtship.

"Sounds like loverboy is in big trouble." Boudicca cackled like a nagging itch that couldn't be scratched.

Beside them, a prowling figure waited. Before Winnie could

react, she recognized the tawny yellow eyes that stared back at her. Cricket ran toward them, grasping her coat and tugging her toward a different area than where they'd entered.

Hesitantly, she obliged the shuck and followed him through the camp. Tapping paws danced along the ground before a new set of trees. It took her a moment to realize a different portal stood before them.

With careful steps, she guided Beatrix and Samuel through the gateway toward an unknown location. Cricket waited on the other side, barking and attempting to usher them through. The trees and saplings looked familiar, a body of water lying just past the woodline. *This is the estate,* she realized. *This is how they keep getting through! Where they came in the night of Samhain.*

"Follow Cricket. He'll get you to safety! I have to go back, and find my parents."

Beatrix nodded, Samuel's arm slung across her shoulder as they limped after the shuck. Winnie turned back, ducking through the portal and entering the hellhound camp once more. Ahead, she heard the sounds of a few restless voices. Just as she was ready to round the corner, she noticed two hounds looking inside the now empty cage, rubbing their heads.

"Do we alert the others?"

"Let's see if we can find them first. Alaric will have our heads for dropping our guard," the other replied as they stalked off.

Winnie searched for Kane, trying to spot him nearby. Continuing her trudge forward, she noticed him up ahead, crouched behind a tent. Carefully she snuck up, attempting to be as quiet as possible. When she placed a delicate hand on his back, he jumped back in surprise.

"It's me!"

Through gritted teeth, he cursed her name. "You scared the shit out of me."

"And? Do you see them?" Winnie's breath clouded before her

as she whispered.

"I think so, but there's two hounds on guard. We'll have to take care of them quickly and quietly if we want to be sure. Unless of course you have any other exes they might be hiding here."

Winnie rolled her eyes before calling on Gali, imagining the two hellhounds surrounded by blue light. Just as she did, two pockets of water formed around their heads, blocking out any sounds they made as they grasped feverishly for their throats. It took a few minutes before their bodies fell to the ground, Kane guiding them down gently with a soft gust of air that muffled the fall.

"It's so creepy when you do that," he mumbled, inching his way toward the cage.

Inside, two hooded people waited with their arms bound behind them. One lay across the bed of the cage, the other sitting upright. Neither seemed to notice their approach.

"It's them," he whispered, pointing at the glowing purple bindings around their wrists. "I saw those cuffs on your parents at the manor."

Winnie recognized her mother right away, noticing the casual dress she often wore. Her father's familiar blue waistcoat lay along the cage, bloodied. Freezing the lock just as before, it fell to the ground with a swift hit.

Running into the cage, Winnie removed her mother's hood. Without hesitation, she rushed to her father's side next, checking to see if he was still alive. Two fingers rested along his neck, a slow steady pulse moving beneath his skin. Quickly shushing Milicent, Kane removed the gag around her mouth.

"He's alive?" Her voice was breathless, dark circles under her eyes from stress.

With a heavy sigh of relief, Winnie whispered, "He's alive!"

Kane pulled one of Ernest's arms over his shoulder as Winnie helped on the other side. Milicent trailed after them, following close behind. Attempting to head back toward the original portal, Winnie managed to stop him.

"Cricket showed me a way to the manor! Follow me!"

Without question, they both nodded and followed suit. Stepping through the portal, Beatrix and Samuel were not far off moving slowly toward the burned estate.

"Mum, can you handle this from here?" Winnie asked, pointing toward their home.

Milicent nodded reluctantly before asking, "You're not going back there, are you?"

"I have to look for Tara."

"Leave her," Kane urged. "I promise you, she's not in danger. She's with Alaric!"

"I'm not so sure," her mother mumbled. "I think he sees her as nothing more than a toy now that he got what he wanted from her. She's in just as much danger as we were."

Kane grumbled before conceding. "Fine, we'll go look for her. Together. We don't do this alone."

"Cricket, can you come with us and sniff her out?" Winnie asked, the shuck's head turned side to side as if he were processing her request. He barked, moving back toward the portal. "When we find her, I need you back here. You'll need to get the others from Chicago."

The shuck barked in protest.

"Please? We need them. I promise, I'll get Tara back!" Winnie leaned down to offer his ears a quick scratch before his attention turned toward the campsite.

They stepped through the portal for what would hopefully be the last time that night. Winnie couldn't help but notice that the camp still seemed quiet. Almost too quiet, it seemed, considering four of their prisoners had escaped. Nonetheless, she had a best friend to find.

Cricket's nose sniffed high in the air, searching for his beloved owner. At last, he darted for a nearby tent where he sat, waiting for Winnie and Kane to join him.

"She's in there?"

Cricket nodded before running for the portal again to fulfill the other half of his duty.

"Who knew shucks understood so much English," Kane noted with a slight chuckle.

Winnie ignored him, pressing her ear up to the tent. On the other side, she could barely make out any sound at all. Not a single rustling of fabric or snore was heard. Only more silence.

"I'm going in," she whispered. Kane grabbed ahold of her arm, though she yanked it from his grasp. "I don't care what you say. She's my best friend! I'm getting her out of here!"

Kane groaned, motioning for her to go ahead.

Winnie snuck toward the entrance. Peeking through the tent flap, she still heard nothing. Tossing a glowing orb of light inside, just dim enough to see, she carefully shuffled her way in. Kane waited outside, ready for anything.

"Tara?" Winnie whispered.

With such poor lighting, it took her a moment to realize a body lay sleeping on a small cot toward the back. Inside, a fire pit sat at the center, the embers barely lit. Winnie reached for the sleeping woman, recognizing the red hair immediately.

As Tara rolled over, her eyes widened in surprise. "What are you doing here?"

Shushing her swiftly, Winnie covered her friend's mouth and ushered her toward the exit. "We have to be quiet!"

"I'm chained!" she added, moving her blanket aside.

With a groan, Winnie called out to Gali again. *"One last favor?"* she asked, her head aching from overexertion.

Just like the first two locks, Winnie broke the center that bound Tara's feet. "Pick them up and carry them. We can get the rest off when we get back to the manor!"

Exiting the tent, Kane joined them. He sighed in relief before pushing them toward the estate's portal.

"He has my necklace! He can cross over into Fox Manor any time he wants!" Tara rushed, her voice a little too loud for comfort.

"We'll figure that part out later. Right now, we need to get out of here," Kane hissed, stopping by a tent to peer around the corner. On the other side, a group of four hellhounds exited their dwellings. "Shit, I think they've realized we're here."

"Where was Alaric when you found me?" Tara whispered, leaning in toward the other two.

Winnie glanced behind them, ready for anything. "We haven't seen him."

"That was his tent I was in! He has to be around here somewhere!"

Glancing at her friend in worry, Winnie groaned. "This is most definitely a trap." *I doubt I have enough left in me to conjure more bubbles to drown them,* she thought, devising a plan. It didn't take long before the hairs on the back of her neck stood. Burning eyes seemed to sear her skin, looking around in worry.

"Where are you taking my little fawn?" Alaric sang from behind them as a mass of hounds appeared from every nearby tent.

"Shit," Kane cursed, realizing they were completely surrounded.

"You're in a bit of trouble now, aren't you?" he mocked, seeming to revel in their panic.

"You know as well as I do that we can end this very quickly," Winnie spat with false confidence. *He doesn't need to know my mind and body are just about ready to give up,* she thought.

"I can promise you, he already knows," Boudicca whispered, her voice mocking as ever.

"You planned this, didn't you?" she asked, awaiting a response. Only silence moved through her mind.

"Why fight? I'm glad you're here, actually! You did exactly as we wanted." Alaric stretched his hands out around him, more and more hellhounds prowling and ready. "We've been waiting for you. You have something we need. Or rather, someone."

Winnie let out a grumbling moan before thinking: *There's no way we're walking away from this.* Glancing at her side, she watched Kane expand his wings. Before he could even suggest they fly up into the sky, a gun was already cocked and pointing at them.

"Put them away. There will be no flying off this time, pigeon."

The siren's eyes remained fixed to Alaric, tucking away his wings as instructed with a defeated sigh. He glanced toward Winnie before mumbling, "Now what?"

"We don't need you at all. You're just collateral at this point," the hellhound leader said with a wicked grin as a nearby beast punched Kane in the gut. The pistol moved to Winnie as she helped him regain his composure.

"Do what you want with me. Just let them go!"

"Are we so sure your friend here wants to go with you?" Alaric asked, a teasing lilt to his voice as he stretched his hand out to Tara. "You said so yourself, little fawn. There's nothing left for you back there. You're one of us now."

Tara stood for a moment in contemplation.

"Don't," Winnie pleaded. *What the hell is she thinking?*

"I'm sorry," she mumbled, her head lowering in shame. "I wish I could make you understand. I'm so feckin' sorry, Win." A tear rolled down her cheek as she moved behind the hellhound leader, whose wicked grin only widened at her betrayal.

"Let Kane go, and I'll do whatever you want!"

"I'm not leaving you!" he bellowed, hands still grasped firmly around hers. Another hit to the stomach forced them to part.

"You assume I have even an ounce of mercy left in me," Alaric countered. His eyes darkened with intent, whistling as though they were mere dogs. "Come on now, Winnie. Come with me. Leave the siren behind, or we'll go back to Fox Manor and kill every last one of the people there that you consider blood or friend."

"If I come with you, do you promise he'll be safe? And you'll leave the others alone?" Her heart broke speaking those words. *Anything to keep them alive,* she thought.

"Don't you dare go with him!" Kane shouted as the surrounding hellhounds pulled them apart.

"I make no promises," he taunted, glancing toward Tara in victory.

Mere seconds passed, though they felt like a lifetime as Winnie tried to make up her mind. When their fingers barely touched one another, she decided. Shooting a ring of fire at the beasts nearby, she opted for a fight. Her hands grasped Kane's firmly as he too sent a ring of air behind him to shove their attackers away.

Alaric sighed, releasing a shot that narrowly missed the two of them as they darted toward the portal. Behind them, the gun cocked once more. Winnie could feel it. Before her, Death appeared. The familiar figure of the entity she was beginning to despise, here to take another soul.

She glanced behind them as they ran, knocking into hellhounds and barreling through them with the use of their elements. But there were too many. At some point, she knew they'd make a mistake. Run out of energy. Nonetheless, they continued to flee with their hands intertwined.

Deep in her gut, she felt a familiar tingling. The pull of the Elements; the start of a jump. *"This is not the right time!"* she screamed internally, hoping they could hear her.

"Don't..." she heard, the sound of Gali's panicked voice swiftly interrupted.

Another gunshot broke her focus. A weightlessness surrounded Winnie, her vision going dark while lost in the void. Only the feeling of Kane's hand holding onto hers was a reminder that she was still alive. *Or am I?* she wondered as the darkness lived on.

Her ears rang, a sharp all-over zap electrifying her skin as she waited for her vision to clear. When Winnie opened her eyes, she didn't know where she was. All she could do was thank the Gods that Kane was at least beside her in one piece.

He retched, covering his mouth before gasping, "What the hell just happened? I've never felt anything like that before."

They no longer stood surrounded by hellhounds and their tents. Instead, they looked out over a small town, filled with wooden cottages and burning lamp posts. A group of onlookers stood off in the distance, young men outside of what looked to be an aged tavern. Nothing was quite familiar; older and different than anything she was used to.

"Where the hell are we?" she mumbled, trying to clear her head. "Did I take you with me on a jump? I didn't know I could do that."

"You're asking me?" Kane continued to rub his stomach when his attention snapped to the hoard of townspeople approaching fast.

"Where did they come from?" one of them yelled. Anger slithered in his voice, outsiders clearly unwelcome.

"I saw them! They appeared out of thin air!" a female voice cried, an accusing finger pointing at them.

"Thin air? Like…"

"Look at her arm! The mark of the devil!"

In an instant, they were surrounded by pitchforks, guns, and torches. The sounds of the villagers and their mania echoed in Winnie's ears.

Before she could say anything in defense, a reverend stepped from the tavern. "I know a witch when I see one. Arrest them!"

THE STORY CONTINUES IN...

BOOK 3
of The LONDINIUM SAGA

COVEN
OF THE
HUNTED

JM LEE

Acknowledgements

As always, I want to say thank you to the wonderful people in my life who encourage me everyday to keep going. Writing can be a long, lonely journey if you don't have people cheering you on. A special thank you also goes to my beta readers. Without you, this book wouldn't be possible.

Thank you to my friends and family who share and like every post, tell others about my books, and let me talk their ears off about fictional characters! You all mean the world to me.

And thank you to YOU, the reader. Without your support, this book wouldn't be possible. Whether we've met at a convention or through social media, I appreciate you as well!

If you want to support me as an indie author, please visit my website: www.jmlee.info

There is a ton of information on how to find my online, support my books, and where you can find me at upcoming events.

Instagram / TikTok : @jmleebooks

ABOUT THE AUTHOR

·······•))) ● (((•·······

JM Lee is an indie fantasy author for both YA and new adult audiences. Her first book, When October Ends, was published when she was 13. In later years, she published the second and third book of the "Novus Proprius Chronicles" and a variety of short stories. The series is currently getting a makeover as a sapphic dystopian fantasy.

Currently, JM Lee lives in Virginia with her three dogs and a growing family. After finishing high school, she attended Western Governors University and majored in Education. She hopes to inspire her students the way her teachers inspired her. As a proud member of the LGBTQ+ community, she hopes to help others with her stories!

To learn more about her, visit www.jmlee.info or visit her instagram profile: @jmleebooks

www.jmlee.info